Sharon
KENDRICK

Hot-Blooded Italians

MILLS &
BOON

Sharon
KENDRICK

COLLECTION

KINONE.

Revenge is Sweet

May 2015

London's
Eligible Bachelors

June 2015

The Millionaires' Cinderellas

July 2015

Hot-Blooded Italians

August 2015

Society Secrets

September 2015

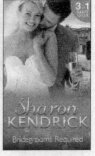

Bridegrooms Required

October 2015

Dear Reader,

I've known for a long time that I have the best job in the world—writing stories about powerful, complicated men and the women who love them—what's not to like? Some of these stories have stayed especially close to my heart and I'm delighted to announce that you can now read them for yourself if they're new to you—or maybe rediscover them if you loved them as much as I do.

I love them for different reasons. Sometimes because there's a heroine I can particularly identify with—like Rose in *Surrender to the Sheikh* or Sabrina in *The Unlikely Mistress*. Sometimes because I am unable to forget the hero—and I confess that they all have an unforgettable hero. I think about Dominic Dashwood in *Settling the Score* and all the fuss that book caused at the time. I think of the proud Russian, Nikolai, in *Too Proud to be Bought* and Ross in *One Husband Required*, who was a very different kind of hero. I can feel as if they're all in the room with me, urging you to read their stories, and I hope you will.

The collection runs from May through to October 2015, so please write or tweet me @Sharon_Kendrick and tell me which are *your* favourites.

Happy reading,

Love,

Sharon

Published in Great Britain 2015
by Mills & Boon, an imprint of Harlequin (UK) Limited,
Eton House, 18-24 Paradise Road, Richmond, Surrey, TW9 1SR

HOT-BLOODED ITALIANS © 2015 Harlequin Books S.A.

Sicilian Husband, Unexpected Baby © 2008 Sharon Kendrick
A Tainted Beauty © 2012 Sharon Kendrick
Marriage Scandal, Showbiz Baby! © 2005 Sharon Kendrick

ISBN: 978-0-263-25382-5

009-0815

Harlequin (UK) Limited's policy is to use papers that are natural, renewable and recyclable products and made from wood grown in sustainable forests. The logging and manufacturing processes conform to the legal environmental regulations of the country of origin.

Printed and bound in Spain
by CPI, Barcelona

Sicilian Husband,
Unexpected Baby

Sharon Kendrick once won a national writing competition by describing her ideal date: being flown to an exotic island by a gorgeous and powerful man. Little did she realise that she'd just wandered into her dream job! Today she writes for Mills & Boon, featuring often stubborn but always to-die-for heroes and the women who bring them to their knees. She believes that the best books are those you never want to end. Just like life…

CHAPTER ONE

EMMA felt the frisson of very real fear sliding over her skin. She looked at the lanky blond man standing in front of her and composed her face carefully—because the last thing she could afford to do was panic.

'But I can't afford any more rent, Andrew,' she said quietly. 'You know that.'

The man shrugged apologetically but his expression didn't change. 'And I'm not running a charity. I'm sorry, Emma—but I could get four times the amount I'm charging you if I put it back on the market.'

Like a robot, Emma nodded. Of course he could. Pretty little cottages in pretty little English towns were snapped up like hot cakes. Everyone, it seemed, was into rural living these days.

The man hesitated. 'Isn't there anyone you could ask? Anyone who could help? What about your husband?'

Quickly, Emma stood up, fixing a crumpled attempt at a smile to her lips and wondering if it fooled anyone. Just the very mention of the man she had married had the power to make her feel weak, but weakness had no place in her life, not any more. She simply couldn't afford to let it. 'It's very kind of you to be concerned, but it's my problem,' she said.

'Emma—'

'Please, Andrew,' she said, trying to keep her voice calm—because she never spoke of Vincenzo, not to anyone. 'Either I come up with the increased rent or I move somewhere cheaper—those are the only two solutions open to me.'

She knew there was also an unacknowledged third—Andrew had made that very clear in that sweet and polite English way of his. But she wasn't going to start dating him just to keep her rent at a below-market-rate level, and, anyway, she didn't want a boyfriend. She didn't want anyone in her life—she had no room, no time or inclination for a man. And desire had died in her the day she had left Vincenzo.

Andrew said goodbye, disappearing into the dank November air just as a whimper came from the small bedroom and Emma crept in to stare at her sleeping son.

Already ten months old—how was that possible? He was growing in leaps and bounds with every day that passed—developing his own sturdy little frame to go along with his very definite personality.

He had kicked his duvet away and was clutching his little woollen rabbit as if his life depended on it and Emma's heart turned over with love and worry. If there had been just her to think about, then there wouldn't have been a problem. There were plenty of jobs available which came with a room and she would gladly have taken any one of them.

But it wasn't just her. There was her son to think about—and she owed him the very best that the world could provide. It wasn't his fault that his birth had placed her in an impossible situation.

Emma bit her lip. She knew what Andrew had suggested made sense, but it wasn't as easy as that—and Andrew didn't know the details. Nobody did. Could she really swallow her pride and her beliefs and go to her estranged husband, asking him for financial assistance?

Was she perhaps due some, by law? Vincenzo was a fabulously wealthy man and—even though he now despised her and had told her he never wanted to see her again—wouldn't he play fair by providing her with some kind of modest settlement if she asked him for a divorce?

Tiredly, she rubbed at her eyes. What other solution did she have? She wasn't qualified for anything high-earning and the last time she'd gone out to work had ended up paying most of her meagre wages to the child-minder. And little Gino had hated it.

So she'd taken up child-minding herself. It had seemed the perfect compromise—she loved children and it was a way of earning money to pay the bills without having to farm out her beloved son to anyone else while she did so. But lately even that avenue of employment had caved in.

Several of the mothers had complained that her cottage was too cold for their children and demanded that she increase the temperature significantly. Two even removed their children straight away and her suspicions that there was going to be a domino effect and that the rest would follow suit were soon proved true. Now there were no more children to look after and no money coming in.

How on earth was she going to feed herself and Gino? Put a roof over their heads if Andrew increased the rent? Emma wanted to cry but she knew that she could not afford the luxury of tears—and tears would solve precisely nothing. There was nobody to dry them except for her and tears were for babies—except that she was determined her little boy was going to cry as little as possible. She had to be the grown-up now.

Opening the drawer of the small telephone table, she extracted the well-worn business card—her hand beginning to shake as she stared down at the name which leapt out at her like a dark crow from the sky.

Vincenzo Cardini.

Beneath it were the contact details of his offices in Rome, New York and Palermo—which she could never afford to ring in a month of Sundays—but also the number of his London offices, which she assumed he still operated out of regularly.

And yet it hurt to think that he might still own a luxurious tower block in the capital. To realise that he might have spent long and regular amounts of time in the same country as her and not once—*not once*—bothered to come and look her up, not even for old times' sake.

Well, of course he wouldn't, she scolded herself. *He doesn't love you any more, he doesn't even like you— he made that quite plain. Remember his last words for you—delivered in that deadly cold, Sicilian drawl of his.*

'Get out of here, Emma and do not come back—for you are no wife of mine.'

But hadn't she tried to ring him before, not once, but twice—and both times hadn't he humiliatingly refused to speak to her? What was to say that this time would be any different?

Yet she knew she owed it to her son to keep trying. She owed him the right to know something of the basic comfort which should be every child's entitlement and which his father's money could guarantee. Wasn't that more important than anything else? She needed to do this for Gino's sake.

Emma shivered, pulling her sweater closer to her slim frame. These days her clothes seemed to swallow her up. She generally wore layers and kept on the move in this chilly autumn weather to keep herself warm. But soon her son would be awake and then she would have to put the heating on and more of her precious pennies would be eaten up by the ever-hungry gas fire.

There was, she realised heavily, no choice other than to ring Vincenzo. Running her tongue around her suddenly parched lips, she lifted up the phone and punched out the number with a shaky finger, her accelerated heart rate making her feel dizzy with expectation.

'Hello?' The voice of the woman who answered was smooth and with only a trace of an accent, probably bilingual.

But Vincenzo only employed people who could speak Italian, as well as English, Emma remembered. He even preferred it if his employees also spoke the very particular Sicilian dialect—which was a mystery to so many. Because Sicilians looked out for one another, he had once told her. They were members of a unique club of which they were fiercely proud. In fact, the more Emma thought about it, the more surprising she found it that he had ever chosen to marry her at all—she who spoke nothing more than a smattering of anything other than her native tongue.

He married you because he felt obliged to, she reminded herself. *And didn't he tell you that enough times? Just as the marriage broke down because you were unable to keep your part of the bargain.*

'Hello?' said the woman's voice again.

'Would it be…?' Emma cleared her throat. 'Er, could you tell me how I could get hold of Signor Cardini, please?'

There was a short silence—as if the telephonist was shocked that a faltering unknown should dare to ask to be put through to the great man himself.

'May I ask who is calling?'

Emma took a deep breath. *Here we go.* 'My name is…Emma Cardini.'

There was another pause. 'And your call is in connection with…?'

So there was no recognition of her name and no knowledge of her status. No respect, either—and something deep inside Emma bristled with hurt and rejection.

'I'm his wife,' she said baldly.

The woman had clearly been wrong-footed and

Emma could almost hear her thinking—*What the hell do I tell her?*

'Please hold the line,' she said crisply.

Emma was forced to wait for what seemed like an eternity, while pinpricks of sweat beaded her forehead despite the chilly atmosphere in the cottage. She was just silently practising saying *Hello, Vincenzo* over and over in her head to make it sound as emotionless as possible, when the telephonist's voice broke into her thoughts.

'Signor Cardini says to tell you that he is in a meeting and cannot be disturbed.'

The humiliation hit her like a blow to the solar plexus and Emma found herself gripping on to the receiver as if she wanted to crush it in her clammy palm. She was just about to drop it back down onto the cradle when she realised the woman was still speaking to her.

'But he says if you would care to leave a number where you can be contacted, he will endeavour to ring you when he has a moment.'

Pride made Emma want to pass on the message that he could go to hell if he couldn't even be bothered to speak to the woman he had married.

But she could not afford the luxury of pride. 'Yes, here's my number,' she said quietly. 'Do you have a pen?'

'Of course,' said the woman in an amused voice.

After she had put the phone down, Emma went to make a cup of tea, cupping the steaming mug around her cold fingers as she looked out of the kitchen window at the little garden she had grown to love.

Shiny brown conkers from a large tree on Andrew's huge adjoining estate had fallen over the flint wall and all over her tiny lawn and path. She had planned to put one of those mini sandpits in an unused corner of the plot and to grow a fragrant white jasmine to scent the long summer evenings—but all those dreams seemed to be fast evaporating.

Because that was another downside she hadn't even considered until now. If she was forced to move from this rural idyll—where would her little boy play when he eventually started to toddle and then to walk? Very few cheap lets came with their own garden.

The ringing of the telephone shattered her troubled thoughts and Emma snapped it up before it could wake the baby.

'Hello?'

'*Ciao*, Emma.'

The words hit her like a bucket of ice-water. He said her name like no one else—but then, nothing that Vincenzo did or said was remotely like anyone else. He was unique—like a rare black glittering gem with dark danger at its very core.

Remember the way you've been practising saying his name in that bland and neutral way? Well, now is the time to put it into practice. 'Vincenzo.' She swallowed. 'It was good of you to call back.'

At the other end of the phone, Vincenzo's hard lips twisted into a cruel parody of a smile. She spoke as if she were about to purchase a computer from him! In that soft English voice which used to drive him crazy—

both in and out of bed. And despite the still-raw hostility of his feelings for her—even now he could feel the slow coil of awareness beginning to unfurl in his groin.

'I found a brief window in my schedule,' he said carelessly, flicking his dark gaze in the direction of the crammed diary which lay open on his desk. 'What do you want?'

In spite of having told herself that she didn't care what he thought of her any more, Emma was woman enough to know a painful pang of regret. He spoke to her with less regard than he might use to someone who was removing the garbage from his house. How quickly the fires of passion could become cold grey embers which just left a dirty trace behind.

So answer him in the same matter-of-fact way—keep this brisk and formal and it might not hurt so much. 'I want a divorce.'

There was a pause. A long pause. Eyes narrowing, Vincenzo leaned back in his chair, stretching his long legs out in front of him as he considered her statement. 'Why? Have you met someone else?' he questioned coolly. 'Perhaps planning on remarrying?'

His indifference pierced her—wounded her far more than it should have done. Could this possibly be the same Vincenzo who had once threatened to tear the limbs from a man who had asked her to dance, until she had calmed him down and told him that she had no desire to dance with any other man than him. No, of course it wasn't. That Vincenzo had loved her—or, at least, had claimed to have loved her.

'Even if I had met someone—I can assure you that I wouldn't be taking a trip down the aisle. You've put me off marriage for a lifetime, Vincenzo,' she said, wanting to try to hurt him back—but it was clearly a waste of time because his responding laugh was laced with cynicism.

'Which doesn't answer my question, Emma,' he persisted silkily.

Emma's heart missed a beat. 'And...I don't have to answer it.'

'You think not?' Vincenzo swung round in his chair and gazed out at the London skyline—at the spectacular sparkling skyscrapers which dominated it, two of which he owned. 'Well, in that case, this conversation isn't going to get very far, is it?'

'We don't need to have a *conversation*, Vincenzo, we need—'

'We need to establish facts.' His words iced into hers. 'Do you have your diary?'

'My diary?'

'Let's fix up a date to meet and talk about it.'

In the little cottage, Emma's knees sagged and she clutched onto the table for support. 'No!'

'No?' Now there was amusement in his voice as he heard the sudden panic in her voice. 'You really think that I intend to have this discussion about the end of my marriage on the *phone*?'

'There's no need for face-to-face contact—we can do it all through lawyers,' Emma ventured.

'Then go ahead and do it,' he retaliated.

Was he calling her bluff because somehow he suspected she was in a weak position? But he *couldn't* know that.

'If you want my co-operation then I suggest you meet me halfway, Emma,' Vincenzo continued softly. 'Otherwise you could have a very long and very expensive fight on your hands.'

Emma closed her eyes, willing herself not to cry—because he would seize on any outward sign of weakness like a vulture picking over a carcass. How could she have forgotten about that iron-hard resolve of his, that stubborn determination to get exactly what it was he wanted?

'Why would you fight me, Vincenzo?' she questioned wearily. 'When both of us know this marriage is dead and neither one of us wants it to continue?'

Perhaps if she had shed a tear, perhaps if her voice had wavered with just one tiny shiver of emotion—then Vincenzo might have spared her. But her cool, down-to-earth manner sparked in him a fury which had lain dormant since their marriage had broken down—and now he felt it spring into powerful and ugly life within him. At that moment, Vincenzo didn't really know or care what it was that *he* wanted—all he knew was that he wanted to thwart Emma's desires.

'Can you do Monday?' he queried, as if she hadn't spoken.

Blinking back the slight saltiness at the backs of her eyes, Emma didn't need to look in her diary—she didn't even have one. Why would she? Her social life was non-existent these days and that was the way she liked it.

'Monday seems to be…okay,' said Emma, as if she, too, had a rare *window* in her schedule. 'What time?'

'Where are you living? Can you do dinner?'

She thought about it—the last train back to Boisdale from London left just after eleven, but what if she missed it? Her friend Joanna would be happy to have Gino during the day, but taking him overnight would involve a little more juggling. Besides, she had never been apart from her baby boy for a night and she didn't intend to start now.

Ignoring the first part of his question, Emma forced herself to sound casual. 'Not dinner, no.'

'Why? Are you busy in the evening?' he mocked.

'I don't live in London. It's…easier if we do lunch-time.'

Vincenzo stretched as a glossy brunette in a close-fitting pencil skirt wiggled in to place a cup of espresso on the desk in front of him and he smiled, pausing while he watched the pert thrust of her buttocks as she sashayed out of the office. The smile left his lips. '*Sì*, then we will make it lunch,' he said softly. 'I'll have someone fix us something here. Come to my office—can you remember how to get here?'

But Emma baulked at the thought of going to his London headquarters—with its gleaming magnificence taunting her about the crazy inequality of their two life-styles. And his office wasn't neutral territory, was it? Vincenzo would have the upper hand—and there was nothing he liked more.

'Wouldn't you prefer it if we went out to a… restaurant?'

Once again Vincenzo thought he detected the waver of hope in her voice and he was surprised at the dark pleasure which washed over him as he swamped it. 'No, I don't want to go to a restaurant,' he negated silkily. And be constrained by the table between them, the hovering of waiters and the formality of the atmosphere? No way. 'Be here at one.'

And then to Emma's disbelief he terminated the connection and she was left listening to an empty dialling tone. Slowly, she replaced the receiver and as she glanced up caught a glimpse of herself in the small mirror which hung over the phone. Her hair looked lank, her face as white as chalk and there were dark circles beneath her eyes. And Vincenzo had always been so particular how he wanted her to look—she had been his little doll.

Although he was Sicilian, he had happily adopted the Italian ideal of *la bella figura*—the importance of image—of making the best of yourself. Biting her lip, she imagined the contempt in those mocking black eyes if he could see her now. And any contempt would surely put her at even more of a disadvantage.

Between now and Monday, she was going to have to do something drastic about her appearance.

CHAPTER TWO

HEART slamming against her ribcage, Emma stared up at the Cardini building, willing herself to have the courage to walk in. It was a beautiful structure—sleek and curved and fashioned almost entirely from glass. Its design had won awards and it screamed wealth from every polished pane, throwing her reflection back at her a hundred times over and seeming to emphasise her impoverished state in this wealthy area of London.

She'd had a nightmare time trying to find something suitable to wear—all her clothes were practical, not smart—and none of them was of the delicious costly quality which had become second nature to her as Vincenzo's wife.

In the end she'd chosen a plain dress, which she had jazzed up with a bright, clumpy necklace, and had polished her boots until she could see her face in them. Only her coat was good and you could tell—soft dark cashmere lined with violet silk which felt so delicious against her spare frame. Tiny, embroidered violet flowers were scattered along the hem of the expensive material, as if someone had flung a handful of flowers there, and they had stuck. Vincenzo had bought her that coat from one of Milan's costliest shops, slipping out from their hotel one afternoon, leaving her asleep and tousled in bed, to return with a large, ribbon-wrapped box.

She hadn't wanted to wear it today—it was too full of memories, too much a slice of the past. But it was warm and, more importantly, it was smart enough to take her anywhere. And what was the alternative? To waltz into the Cardini headquarters wearing her bargain faux-fur trimmed coat—the kind of which was usually snapped up by hard-up students?

Turning dizzily in the revolving doors, Emma entered the vast, airy foyer and walked up to the reception desk—a journey which seemed to take for ever.

The Madonna behind the desk gave her a bland smile. 'May I help you?'

'I have…I have an appointment with Signor Cardini.'

The woman glanced down at a list. 'Emma Cardini?'

'That's me,' agreed Emma, thinking that the Madonna couldn't quite hide her look of surprise.

A perfectly polished pink fingernail was pointed to the far end of the foyer. 'Take the elevator to the very top of the building and someone will be waiting there to meet you.'

'Thanks.'

As the lift shot silently upwards Emma thought how long it had been since she'd visited London—and how long it had been since she'd been out without her son. And never for a whole day, like this. Would he be okay? she wondered for the hundredth time since buying her ticket at Boisdale station. Or would he kick up when he realised that his mother was gone for more than an hour or two?

Pulling the pay-as-you-go cell phone from her handbag, she stared at the blank screen. No messages. She'd told Joanna to call her if she was worried about anything—*anything*—which meant that all must be well.

So do what you have to do, she thought, drawing a deep breath as the lift pinged to a halt and the doors slid open to reveal a glamorous brunette in a close-fitting pencil skirt and a blouse which was obviously pure silk. Her hair was piled artfully on top of her head, there were two starry diamonds sparkling at her ears, and suddenly Emma felt like a poor country cousin who had come visiting. Just how many beautiful women did Vincenzo need working for him?

'Signora Cardini?' asked the woman. 'Will you please follow me? Vincenzo's expecting you.'

Well, of course he's expecting me! Emma wanted to shout as she watched the woman wiggling her way towards a set of double doors. *And who gave you the right to call my husband by his Christian name in that gurgling and rather pathetic way?*

But he's not going to be your husband for very much longer, is he? And in fact, he hasn't been your husband for a long time—so better lose the unreasonable jealousy right now, Emma.

The doors were being opened with the kind of flourish which seemed to indicate that she was being summoned into the presence of someone terribly important and

Emma braced herself for the sight of Vincenzo, just as she had been doing during the journey here. But nothing could prepare her for the heart-stopping reality of seeing her husband again in the living and breathing flesh.

He was standing in front of the wall of glass which ran along one side of his arena-sized office—and so at first sight he was in silhouette. But the darkened outline only served to emphasise a physique which was utterly magnificent—all lean, honed muscle—the kind of perfection which sculptors had been using as the masculine ideal since the beginning of time.

His hands were splayed rather arrogantly over narrow hips, which tapered down to long, lean legs—but then arrogance had always been Vincenzo's middle name. He saw what he wanted and he took what he wanted—and he usually got it by a mixture of power and persuasion and sheer charisma.

Emma swallowed—the reminder pushing her into protective mode—because she had one most precious thing which Vincenzo could not be allowed to take and she needed all her wits about her.

'Hello, Vincenzo,' she said.

'Emma,' he responded, in a tone she had never heard him use before. Firing off a command in rapid Italian, which caused the brunette to quickly leave the office, closing the doors behind her, he stepped from the shadow and into the light and, in spite of everything, Emma felt her stomach turn quite weak as she looked up into his face.

For he was even more devastatingly gorgeous than she remembered when she had agreed to marry him.

Back then she had been carried along by the wild and dizzy excitement of being in love—so enraptured that she had not stopped to think that he was a truly remark-able-looking man. And then, when the marriage had begun to crumble, he had seemed cold, icy, uncaring—and she had shrunk from him and he from her.

But since then Emma had been through a lot—and a lot of it had been difficult. These days she was under no illusion that she had briefly dallied with a dream—and today Vincenzo looked like every woman's dream man.

He was dressed for business, in one of those amazingly cut suits which managed to be both formal and yet not in the least bit stuffy and could only have been made in Italy. He'd removed his jacket, revealing a white silk shirt which gave a tantalising hint of the rock-hard body which lay beneath. And he'd loosened his tie, too, and undone the top couple of buttons on his shirt, so that she could just discern the dark whorls of hair which grew there.

But it was his face which mesmerised most, and Emma allowed her gaze to reach it almost reluctantly—as if dreading the impact it was going to have on her. And it hit her with a painful shock as she realised she was looking into a hardened and cynical version of Gino's soft little features.

Had Vincenzo ever looked that soft and approach-able? Emma wondered as her eyes drank him in with a greed she couldn't quite suppress.

He would have been almost classically beautiful were it not for the fact that a tiny scar made a pale

V-shape in the dark texture of his shadowed jaw. And his face was hard, too, with black eyes glittering like jet and a smile which was edged with a kind of cruelty. Even when he had been in hot pursuit of her, he had always had that hard edge to him. A quality which had always made her slightly wary of him.

For he had always treated her with a kind of autocratic authority. She had just been another possession to acquire along the way—the virgin bride who had never managed to follow through with what his expectations of her were.

'It has been a long time,' Vincenzo said, and his voice sounded as bitter as unripe lemons. 'Here, let me take your coat.'

She wanted to tell him that she wouldn't be staying long enough to need to take it off, but he might prove to be difficult if she did that. What was more, she had agreed to have lunch with him and the central heating in the office meant that the coat was impractical. But the last thing she wanted was Vincenzo slipping the garment from her shoulders, his hands brushing against her vulnerable skin, the very gesture reminding her of so many undressings in the past....

'I can manage,' she said, wriggling out of the coat and hanging it awkwardly over the back of a chair.

Vincenzo was studying her with an air of fascination. He had recognised the coat immediately but the dress was new—and what a horrible little dress it was. His lips curved. 'What in *Dio*'s name have you been doing to yourself?'

'What do you mean?' With an effort she kept her

voice steady, trying to quell the fear that he might somehow have found out about Gino. But he couldn't have done or he wouldn't have been staring at her with that oddly distasteful look on his face. Not even he was that good an actor.

'You've been on one of those crash diets?' he demanded.

'No.'

'But you are too thin. Much too thin.'

That was what long-term breast-feeding did—she'd only stopped a couple of months ago—and if you threw in child-minding, gardening, cleaning, cooking, shopping and generally juggling her busy life without anyone else to help her, it was no wonder she'd lost serious amounts of weight.

'All skin and bone,' he continued, still in that same critical drawl.

Maybe she should have been insulted at his bald words for this was the man who used to tell her that she was a pocket Venus, that she had the most perfect body he'd ever seen on a woman. At least this way, his undisguised censure reassured Emma that the relationship really *was* dead—that, not only did he not like her, but it seemed that he did not desire her any more, either.

And yet that hurt. More than hurt. It made her feel less than a woman in all ways. A poor, desperate woman with her cheap clothes hanging off her—who had come crawling to her overbearing husband, clutching on to her begging bowl.

Well, you're not. *You're simply seeking something which is rightfully yours. So don't let him wear you down.*

'How I choose to look is my business, but I see you've lost nothing of your charm and diplomacy, Vincenzo,' she said tightly.

Reluctantly, Vincenzo gave a short laugh. Had he forgotten that she could give as good as she got? Hadn't that been one of the things which had first drawn him to her? Her strange kind of shyness coupled with the occasional ability to hit the nail bang on the head. Along with her ethereal blonde looks, which had completely blown him away. Well, if he met her *now*, he certainly wouldn't be blown away.

'You just look very…different,' he observed. Her hair was longer than he remembered—she used to always keep it cut to just below her shoulders and he had approved of that because it meant that it never tumbled over her beautiful breasts when she was naked. But now it fell almost to her tiny waist and looked in good need of a trim.

And her blue eyes appeared almost hollow, the sharpness of her cheekbones shadowing her face. But it was her body which shocked him most of all. She had tiny bones, but these had always been covered with firm flesh so that she was lusciously curved, like a small, ripe peach. Yet now there was a leanness about her which might be currently fashionable, but was not attractive. Not at all.

His damning assessment made Emma desperately want to draw his attention away from her. 'Whereas you look exactly the same, Vincenzo.'

'Do I?' He watched her, as a cat might watch a tiny mouse before it struck out with its lethal claws.

She flicked her gaze to his temples. 'Well, perhaps there are a couple more grey hairs.'

'Doesn't that make me look distinguished?' he mocked. 'Tell me, exactly how long *has* it been since we last saw one another, *cara*?'

She suspected he knew exactly how long it was, but instinct and experience told her to play along with him. *Don't anger or rile him. Keep him on side. Keep bland and impartial and thin and unattractive and hopefully he'll be glad to see the back of you.* 'Eighteen months. Time…flies, doesn't it?'

'Tempus volat,' he echoed softly in Italian—and indicated one of a pair of chic, leather sofas which sat at right angles to each other at the far end of the large office. 'Indeed it does. Have a seat.'

Sitting down also implied staying longer than she might wish, but Emma's knees by now were so weak with the swirl of conflicting emotions that she felt they might buckle if she didn't. She sank into the soft comfort of the seat and watched warily as he sat down next to her.

His presence unnerved and unsettled her as it had always done—but wouldn't she look weak and pathetic if she primly asked him to sit elsewhere? As if she couldn't cope with the reality of his proximity. And wasn't that another reason for coming here today—to demonstrate to him *and to herself* that what little they'd had between them was now dead?

Is it? she asked herself. Is *it*? *Of course it is, you little fool—don't even go there.*

'I'll ring for food, shall I?' he questioned.

'I'm not hungry.'

He stared at her. Neither was he—even though he had risen at six that morning and eaten only a little bread with his coffee. He thought how pale her skin looked—so translucent that he could see the fine blue tracery of veins around her temple. She wore no jewellery, he observed. Not those little pearl studs she used to favour and not her wedding ring, either. Of course. His mouth twisted. 'So let's get down to business, Emma—and, since you instigated this meeting, you must tell me what it is you want.'

'Exactly what I told you over the phone—or tried to. I want a divorce.'

His black eyes flicked over her, noticing the way that she crossed and uncrossed her legs, as if she was nervous. What was she nervous about? Seeing him again? Still wanting him? Or something else. 'And your reasons?'

Distractedly, Emma raked her hand back through her hair—then turned to him with appeal in her eyes, steeling herself against the impact of his hard, beautiful face. 'Isn't the fact that we've been separated all this time reason enough?'

'Not really, no. There is usually,' Vincenzo observed softly, 'a reason why a woman should wish to disturb the status quo for they are notoriously sentimental about marriage—even if it was a bad marriage, as in our case.'

Emma flinched. It was one thing knowing it, but quite

another hearing him saying it again so cold-bloodedly. And she had seriously underestimated what an intelligent man he was. Clever enough to realise that she wouldn't just turn up out of the blue, asking for a divorce, unless there was a reason behind it. *So give him the kind of reason* he *can believe in.* 'I should have thought that you'd be glad enough to have your freedom back?'

'Freedom for what, precisely, *cara*?' he drawled.

Say it, she told herself. *Say it even if it chokes you up inside to have to say it. Confront your demons and they will disturb you no more. You've both moved on. You've had to. And the future will obviously involve different partners—especially for Vincenzo.* 'The freedom to see other women, perhaps.'

A lazy and faintly incredulous look made his ebony eyes gleam and he gave a soft laugh. 'You think I need an official termination of our marriage to do that?' he mocked. 'You think that I have been living like a monk since you left me?'

Despite the lack of logic in her response, Emma's lips fell open in dismay as disturbing visual images lanced through her mind like a sharp knife. 'You've been sleep-ing with other women?' she questioned painfully.

'What do you think?' he taunted. 'Although you flatter me by presuming numbers—'

'And you flatter yourself with your false modesty, Vincenzo!' Emma said in a low voice. 'Since we both know you can get any woman to come running with a click of your fingers.'

'Like I got you, you mean?'

Emma bit her lip. *Don't destroy my memories*, she pleaded silently. 'Don't rewrite history. You came after me. You wooed me,' she protested in a low voice. 'You know you did.'

'On the contrary, you played a game,' he demurred. 'You were far cleverer than I gave you credit for, Emma. You played the innocent quite perfectly—'

'Because I *was* innocent!' she declared.

'And that, of course, was your trump card,' he murmured. Vincenzo leaned back against the sofa, arrogantly letting his gaze drift up her legs and over her thighs, which the cheap fabric of her dress was clinging to like cream. 'You played your virginity like a champion, didn't you? You saw me, you wanted me and you teased me so alluringly that I was unable to resist you. You saw me as a man who had everything—a Sicilian who would value your purity above all else and be bound by it!'

'I…*didn't*…' she breathed.

'So why didn't you tell me you were a virgin before it was too late?' he snapped. 'I would never have touched you if I'd known!'

She wanted to tell him that she had been so in awe of him and so in love with him and that was why the subject hadn't come up. That things had rocketed out of control. She had been at an utterly vulnerable time in her life and had thought him way out of her league—hadn't for a moment thought that the affair would progress through to marriage. Hadn't he told her—

fiercely and ardently—that he would one day marry a woman from his homeland, who would inculcate their children with the same values they had grown up with?

And yet on some far deeper level she *had* known that he would have run a mile if he'd been aware that she was a virgin—but, of course, by then she had been in too deep to be able to withstand the hungry demands of her body and her heart to risk telling him.

'I wanted you to be my first lover,' she told him truthfully. Because she had suspected that no other man who came into her life would ever come close to Vincenzo.

Vincenzo's lips curled in derision. 'You wanted a rich husband!' he stated disparagingly. 'You were all alone in the world with no qualifications, no money and no property—and you saw your wealthy Sicilian as a ticket to ride your sweet little body out of poverty.'

'That's not true!' said Emma, stung.

'Isn't it?' he challenged.

Colour flared into her cheeks. 'I'd have married you if you'd had nothing.'

'But fortunately for you it never came to that, did it, *cara*?' he retorted sarcastically. 'Since you already knew what I was worth.'

Emma flinched as if he had hit her—but in a way his words were more wounding than physical blows could ever be. *At least you know now what he thinks of you*, she thought to herself. But she was damned if he would see her break down in front of him. She would get what she came for and she would walk out of here with her head held high.

'Well, in view of what you've just said—at least neither of us can be in any doubt that seeking a divorce is the only sensible solution,' she said calmly.

Vincenzo stilled and something inside him rankled. He didn't like it when she used logic—it made her seem untouchable again and he was used to women always being passionate around him. So was Emma really immune to him—as unbothered by the idea of legally ending their marriage as she seemed—or was it all an act? Would she still turn on for him? he wondered idly.

Completely without warning, he leaned over her, almost negligently brushing his lips over hers, and smiled with triumph as he felt their automatic tremble at that briefest of touches.

Emma froze, even as she felt the blood beginning to heat her skin and the sudden mad thunder of her heart. 'Vincenzo,' she whispered. 'What the hell do you think you're doing?'

CHAPTER THREE

'JUST testing,' Vincenzo murmured, and returned his mouth to Emma's, feeling her rapid breath warming his lips, and he found he wanted to lick his way into her—every part of her—as he had done so many times before.

'Don't—'

But she wasn't pushing him away, was she? He could sense, almost smell Emma's desire for him—but then he had always been able to read her like some long and erotic book. At least until the relationship had withered away to such an extent that they could hardly bear to look one another in the eye, let alone touch one another....

Until that very last time. Just before she had walked out of the door into the blazing Roman heat—he had caught her to him and had begun to kiss her and she had kissed him back, angrily and with more passion than she'd shown for months.

He remembered rucking up her little skirt and pushing aside her panties and pushing into her: doing it to her upright against the wall, where she stood. Remembered her gasping her orgasm in his ear. And then, ignoring her protests that she would miss her flight, he had carried her up to their bedroom. To the bed they had not shared for weeks—and had spent that one long, last sleepless night imprinting himself on her body and her mind. Pulling out every sensual skill he had ever learnt and using them on her almost ruthlessly as she had moaned with pleasure and regret.

Dio, he was getting hard now just thinking about it. Too hard.

'Emma,' he ground out, and this time his lips didn't brush hers. They crushed them beneath his as ruthlessly as if they had been fragile rose petals beneath a hammer and as she gasped her fingers came up to wind themselves in the tousled thickness of his hair, just the way they used to do.

'V-Vincenzo,' she stumbled out, but the word was blotted out by his kiss—*their* kiss, because her moaned response surely made her a willing participant as she found herself blown away by the power of his touch.

Was it that she was so starved of any kind of adult comfort or pleasure that she found herself submitting to the sweet pleasure of his lips, like a woman drowning in honey? How long since she had been kissed? Not since last time this man had kissed her, and no man had ever kissed her like Vincenzo. No man could. He used his lips to cajole and tease, to tantalise. He made her feel like a woman. A real woman.

Emma moaned as he deepened the kiss in a way designed to have her melting like candle-wax. He knew exactly which buttons to press—he had once told her

that he knew her body better than he knew his own—
and no one could deny that. But with him it had always
been more than technique. It had been helped along
with love. At least for a while.

Love.

Mockingly, the word flew into her mind—for where
did anything even resembling love feature in this slick
seduction of his?

She twisted in his arms. 'Vincenzo…'

Reluctantly, he raised his face from hers, looking
down into the dazed dilatation of her eyes—the blue of
their rims barely visible, so dark were the pupils which
glittered back at him. Her lips were parted, begging to
be kissed, and even as he watched the tip of her tiny
little pink tongue—which he had tutored to bring him
so much pleasure—circled around the parted provoca-
tion of her dry lips. She wanted him, he thought with
grim satisfaction. She had never stopped wanting him.
He moved his hand to rest it with proprietorial careless-
ness on one knee and felt it tremble. Should he slide it
up slowly beneath her dress, to touch her searing heat
and make her moan again?

'What is it, Emma?' he asked softly.

'I…I…'

'Do you want me to touch your breast? Your beautiful breast?'

His other hand grazed negligently over an aroused
nipple and it felt as if it were scorching her skin—even
though she was covered by her dress—and Emma only
just managed to bite back a startled yelp of pleasure.

She felt as if she were standing on sensual quicksand—one false step and she would be submerged.

And then she stiffened. Had she imagined the faint buzz of her phone which was buried at the bottom of her handbag? She'd switched it to silent but left it on vibrate—so was she imagining that she could hear it? That her friend was trying desperately to get through to her to tell her that Gino was sick, or crying or just wanted his mummy.

Gino.

She had come here today—spending money she could ill afford on an expensive train ticket—in order to ask her estranged husband for a divorce. So what the hell was she doing in his arms, letting him kiss her, letting her body begin to flower beneath his practised touch? This was a man who *despised* her—he had made that quite plain.

Despite the screaming protest of her senses, she jumped up from the sofa and immediately felt dizzy, but at least she was away from his dangerous intoxication. Hiding her despairing expression, she walked over to the vast window—scarcely noticing the amazing view outside as she leaned back against the glass for support and forced herself to look him in the eye once more.

'Don't do that again, Vincenzo,' she said huskily. 'Don't *ever* do that again!'

'Oh, come *on*, *cara*,' he taunted silkily. 'Never is a long, long time—and you enjoyed that just as much as I did.'

'You…you *forced* yourself on me!' Emma accused, but to her fury he simply laughed.

'If that was force, then I'd love to see you capitulating,' he mocked. 'And please don't play the little innocent with me, because it won't work, not any more,' he warned. 'I know women well enough to know when they are longing to be kissed—and I know you better than most.'

This was *his* territory, she reminded herself—and he was looking dark and predatory and dangerously aroused. He had the upper hand in so many ways—mentally, physically, emotionally and financially—so what was the point in pursuing an argument she wasn't going to win? And did it really matter in the grand scheme of things whether she had surrendered or whether he had manipulated her? In the end it all came down to pride—and she had already decided that pride was a luxury she couldn't afford. So she should forget what had just happened and get down to the important bit.

Yet Emma knew that she was blocking out the most important bit of all. *What about Gino? Now that you can see for yourself that he is the living image of his father—aren't you going to tell Vincenzo that he has a son*? But she was scared—too scared to even want to try. If she told him—who knew what would come of it? Couldn't she just get what she had come for and think about the rest later?

'Are you going to give me a divorce?' she questioned unsteadily.

Silently, he rose to his feet and Emma eyed him as warily as she might have eyed a deadly snake which had just been set loose in the luxurious office. But to her surprise and fury he didn't come anywhere near her, instead went back behind his desk and appeared to check the screen of his computer! As if she had been a brief interlude—already forgotten—and he was now concentrating on far more important things!

'Are you?' she repeated.

'I haven't decided, because, you see, I'm still not sure about your motives for wanting one. And you know me, Emma—I like to have all the available information at my fingertips.' He looked up, his black eyes narrowing thoughtfully. 'You've told me that it isn't because you want to marry another man,' he mused. 'And I believe you.'

'You do?' she questioned, taken aback.

'Sure. Unless you're planning on marrying a eunuch,' he observed sardonically. 'Because you kissed me like a woman who hasn't had sex in a very long time.'

Emma blushed. 'You're disgusting.'

He laughed. 'Since when was sex disgusting? I'm being honest, that's all. So if it isn't a man, then it must be money.' He saw the automatic jerk of her body and knew he'd hit the spot. 'Ah, yes. Of course it is. My guess is that you're broke,' he continued softly. 'You dress like a woman who's broke and you have the general appearance of somebody who hasn't been taking care of herself. So what happened, Emma? Did you forget that you were no longer married to a billionaire but forgot to curb your spending?'

How laughably far from the truth he was—if this was anything to laugh about. And yet he *was* on the right track, wasn't he? He'd accurately judged her to be hard-up—and in Vincenzo's world, money mattered more than anything else. He could *understand* money. He could deal with money in a way he could never deal with emotion.

So why not let him think of her as just some gold-digger who missed the good times? Surely that would throw him off the scent of why she *really* wanted the money. And she knew enough about Vincenzo to realise that he would despise her even more if he thought she was simply inspired by greed. Why, she wouldn't see him again for dust!

'Something like that,' she agreed.

Vincenzo's mouth twisted. So much for all her pretty little denials that she had married him for his money. She had been seduced by his wealth, as he had suspected all along. But in a way, it made dealing with her far simpler.

'Some people might say that you weren't entitled to anything,' he observed.

An arrow of fear ripped through her. 'What are you talking about?'

Vincenzo shrugged. 'We were only married for a couple of years and there were no children. You're still young, fit, healthy—why should I bankroll the rest of your life simply because I made an error of judgement?'

She flinched. She'd thought that she had reached an emotional-pain threshold, but it seemed she had been wrong. 'I think that a lawyer might see things differently given the disparity in our circumstances,' she said in a low voice. 'As well as the fact that you wouldn't allow me to go out to work, so I'm not exactly number-one choice in the job market.'

'No.' He studied her, at the sudden shaft of harsh winter sunlight which turned her hair into pure, spun gold. 'And just how far are you prepared to go to get a quick divorce?' he questioned softly.

Emma stared at him. *'How far?'* she repeated blankly. 'I don't…I don't quite understand.'

'You don't? Then let me explain it to you so that there can be no possible misunderstanding,' said Vincenzo. 'You want a divorce, while I do not.'

'You—*don't?*' In spite of everything, her foolish heart gave a wild leap and she could barely breathe her next words out. 'May I ask why?'

'Think about it, Emma,' he murmured. 'My marital status makes me unobtainable—and it keeps women off my back.' His eyes glittered. 'Well, in a manner of speaking, you understand.'

Emma froze as his insulting words continued to unfold.

'The moment it becomes known that I'm back on the open market—then I'm going to have to contend with ambitious women, women a little like you once were, who might decide they'd like to be the next Signora Cardini. Who'd like a sexy Sicilian with a big…' his black eyes mocked her; he was enjoying see her wriggle uncomfortably '…bank account,' he finished provocatively as he stretched his arms lazily above his head. 'So you see, in order to grant you a divorce—well, you'd have to make it worth my while, wouldn't you?'

She could feel all the blood drain from her face. But surely he didn't... He couldn't possibly mean what she thought he was hinting at. 'I'm not quite sure what it is you're talking about.'

'Oh, I think you are,' he said softly. 'You want a divorce, and I want you. One last time.'

Emma's fingers crept up to her throat as if that would ease the terrible tension there—for she could barely suck air into her empty lungs. She shook her head, as if she'd misheard him. 'You can't mean that, Vincenzo—'

'But I do. One night with you, Emma. One night of pure and unequivocal sex. To kick over the traces of something which still feels faintly unfinished. One night, that's all.' His black gaze spotlighted her, a smile of unknown origin playing around the corners of his mouth. 'And then I'll give you your divorce.'

There was a long, disbelieving silence as they stared at one another across the vast expanse of the office.

'You...you...you're nothing but a *monster*!' Emma choked out, still not quite believing that this was happening. That the man she had married should be asking her to behave like a...like a woman who would sell her body to the highest bidder!

Vincenzo smiled, feeling the heady rush of pleasure adding to his aching sense of desire as he watched her eyes widen, her face blanch. For this was the woman who had hurt him—who had taken him for a ride, who had hidden the truth from him and ultimately turned her back on him. And he must never forget that, even if she did have the bluest eyes he had ever seen and lips which still begged to be kissed. 'You married me,' he observed caustically. 'You must have known that I had a some-what...*ruthless* streak. So how about it, Emma? You can't deny that you still want me.'

She shook her head in denial. 'No, I don't.'

His black eyes hardened and so did his groin. 'You little liar,' he drawled. 'But then, lying was always one of your talents.'

She stared at him, flinching from the accusation which was blistering from his black eyes. 'This isn't getting us anywhere. The answer is no. You can go to hell,' she said, grabbing her coat from the back of the chair where she'd left it. 'On second thoughts, hell would be too good a destination for you—they'd probably refuse to let you in!'

He was laughing softly as she headed for the door, watching as she hoisted her handbag over her shoulder, her blonde hair flying wildly behind her, like a pale banner. '*Arrivederci, bella,*' he murmured. 'I'll wait to hear from you.'

Ignoring the startled looks of the glamorous brunette outside his office and the Madonna still sitting at the reception, Emma didn't stop running until she was well away from the building and was certain that nobody was following her. She panted her way to the first bus stop she could find and swallowed down the hot tears which burned at her eyes.

Of all the humiliating propositions he could have put

to her—that topped the list. The man was a monster—
a *monster*! Stepping onto the lumbering double-decker
bus, she pulled out her cell phone, but thankfully the
screen remained blank. At least there had been no emergency calls from Joanna, which meant that Gino must
be all right. And they weren't expecting her back until
much later.

The large red bus moved slowly along in the bus lane
and normally Emma might have admired the glittering
circle of the London Eye, which looked so futuristic
compared to the ancient Houses of Westminster—but
she could see nothing. Feel nothing. Her mind and her
body felt numb—as if what had just happened had been
like a horrible dream.

An outsider might have urged her to play her biggest
card of all—and to tell the proud Sicilian that he was
now a father. But some bone-deep fear stopped her—
the very real fear that he would step in to take over or,
even worse, try to take Gino away from her. And given
his power and his wealth—when measured up against
her lack of skills and poverty—wouldn't he stand a
chance of being able to do just that?

Emma shook her head as she put her travel card back
inside her purse. She couldn't tell him—how *could* she?
And even if she did, he wouldn't believe her—for
hadn't it been her supposed infertility which had driven
the last terrible wedge between them and finally ended
their unhappy marriage?

She clamped her eyes closed and bit her lip to try to
keep the memories at bay, but that didn't seem to work.

Her mind had ideas of its own and it took her back—right back—to a time before all the acrimony and bitterness. A time when Vincenzo had loved her.

CHAPTER FOUR

EMMA had met Vincenzo when she was coming out of a vulnerable period of her life—not long after the death of her mother, Edie. Edie's illness had been sudden and Emma had dropped out of catering college to care for the woman who had given birth to her. She'd done it out of love and, yes, out of a certain sense of duty—but also because there was no one else to do it.

But Edie had fought her prognosis every bit of the way. The disease had dragged on and on and those final months had been spent in pursuit of an impossible cure. The slightest hint of any new treatment would be enough for the instant signing of cheques. Edie had gone to faith-healers and psychics. She had eaten nothing but apricots and drunk nothing but warm water for a week. She had undergone ice-therapy in an exclusive Swiss spa but nothing had made any difference; nothing could have done.

It had been a miserable time culminating in an angry death, and afterwards Emma had been left feeling empty, unwilling to go back to life at catering college, which she had seemed to have grown out of. Almost as an antidote to grief, she had taken a job in a shop while Edie's affairs were sorted out and the lawyers worked out how much money remained.

And that was when Emma had discovered that there was virtually nothing left. Huge debts had been run up to support all the alternative treatment—the family house had needed to be sold and after all the bills had been paid there had been nothing more than a few hundred pounds in the kitty.

Uncharacteristically, Emma had decided to blow the money. She'd seen too much sadness to want to plan for a future which no one could guarantee—and such a small amount could give her nothing in the way of security anyway. Life had suddenly seemed too short to measure out a cup of sultanas. She'd wanted sun and history and beauty of the harsh and uncompromising kind, so she had gone to Sicily.

And met Vincenzo.

It was one of those days which would for ever be etched on her mind in rich and vibrant colours. A rare break from her cultural tour of the island, and it found her on a stunning beach with her hat and her book, letting the warmth of the sun soak into her pale skin.

She was very aware that her blonde, English looks excited attention wherever she went and took care to cover her head and shoulders when she visited churches and cathedrals, as local custom demanded. Her dresses were always knee-length and her make-up kept so light as to be almost non-existent.

But on the day she discovered a deserted little cove not far from where she was staying, she gave in to what she had been longing to do. She peeled off her dress to reveal a sleek one-piece swimsuit and began splashing in the water as the dark cares of the last months were gradually washed away.

Afterwards she must have fallen asleep, because she awoke to see a shadow falling over her and a man standing looking down at her. He was dark and lean and muscular, his black hair ruffled by the faint breeze which blew in off the sea. But she had noticed him before—who wouldn't? She remembered seeing him while drinking her morning coffee in the square and he had zipped past on one of the little scooters which all the Sicilian men seemed to ride.

Up close, he was even more amazing—and he was looking at her now with a lazy and yet blatant sexual scrutiny. Maybe she should have been frightened, and on one level perhaps she was—but on another...

Something in his black eyes and faintly cruel lips cried out to some deep, elemental core which she hadn't believed existed—certainly not in her. Because Emma was a dreamer, a reader—and she had never met anyone who could match the romantic and physical impact of the characters she read about in novels.

Until now.

He was wearing a pair of faded jeans and an equally faded T-shirt and his bare toes dug into the soft, silvery sand.

'Come si chiama?' he questioned softly.

It seemed crazy—rude—not to give him an answer, and impossible, too, when those ebony eyes were searing into her and demanding one. 'Emma. Emma Shreve.'

'Ah, you understand Italian?'

She shook her head, telling herself that she shouldn't be striking up a conversation with a total stranger, but feeling carefree for the first time in ages. 'Not really, but I try—I'm not one of those people who go somewhere expecting that everyone should speak *my* language. And Italian's not too bad.' She sighed. 'It's Sicilian which is the killer.'

She hadn't known it at the time but it was exactly the right thing to say to a fiercely proud Sicilian. 'And what is *your* name?' she questioned politely.

'It's Vincenzo. Vincenzo Cardini,' he replied, watching her carefully.

It was to be a while before Emma was to learn about the far-reaching influence and power of the Cardini family. That day she assumed he was just a regular guy—though one with extraordinary charisma which seemed to sizzle off him in a searing dark heat. He sat down beside her and shared her water. He made her laugh. And when the sun was too hot, he took her for lunch in a luscious restaurant and bought her *sarde a beccafico*—the most delicious meal she'd ever eaten, and a dish whose complexity she would later learn displayed great wealth.

He spoke of the island of his birth with a passion and a knowledge which made all her guidebooks seem sorely lacking. He sighed when he told her that he came here only on vacation these days, and that his business was based mainly in Rome. She asked him lots of intelligent questions about his work, mainly to try to focus on something other than the rugged beauty of his face.

But when he tried to kiss her before they parted, she stopped him with a shake of her blonde hair.

'Sorry, I don't kiss strangers.'

He smiled a lazy smile. 'And I don't take no for an answer.'

'This time you do,' said Emma, but she wouldn't have been human if she hadn't been regretful as he put her fingertips to his lips instead and captured her eyes in a stare which made her feel weak.

Uninvited, he called at the small hotel where she was staying and naturally she agreed to see him again. How could she not, when already she was halfway in love with him, and he with her? A *colpo di fulmine*, he called it—but with the air of a man who had been visited by something unwelcome. A thunderbolt, he said darkly.

By day he showed her his island home—though he kept her away from any of his family. His own parents were dead, he had been reared by his grandmother and had hundreds of Cardini cousins who 'would not approve of us seeing one another, *cara*,' he told her lazily.

But what did she care about that when each night he took her a little further towards a pleasure she could not have dreamed existed? She had wondered if he might think her a clumsy innocent, but Vincenzo seemed to enjoy tutoring her as much as he enjoyed her instinctive restraint. He told her that it proved she was not easy, as so many of her compatriots were. The girls who came to Sicily looking for a dark and proficient lover and gave their bodies as casually as they gave their orders at the bars.

Everything seemed perfect until the night she at last allowed him to share her bed and the see-sawing of terrible emotions which followed their lovemaking. Pain, disbelief, joy—and then, finally, a red-hot kind of anger as he sat up in bed and stared at her as if he had been visited by a spectre.

'Why didn't you tell me?' he roared.

Emma shrank back against the rumpled sheets. 'I didn't know how to!'

'You didn't know how to?' he repeated. His voice was bitter. 'And so you have allowed *this* to happen.' He shook his dark head. 'I have robbed you of your virginity—the most precious thing that a woman possesses.'

But by next morning his rage had abated and in those next last few days he taught her how to love her body—and his. So that when he came to the airport to say goodbye, Emma wept for all that she had found and now would lose for ever.

She didn't expect to hear from him again, but unexpectedly he turned up in England—telling her furiously that he couldn't get her out of his mind, as if she had committed some kind of crime for being the cause of his obsession. When he discovered that she had no ties nor permanent job, he took her back with him to

Rome—where she realised that she was actually dating a fabulously wealthy man.

Installing her in his luxury apartment as his mistress, he bought her a brand-new wardrobe, dressing her up as if she were a doll and transforming her into a woman who turned heads. Emma blossomed beneath his attentions, though she was slightly shocked to discover that her transformation had unleashed a terrible kind of jealousy. He suspected even his friends of coveting her.

'You know that they want you?' he demanded.

'I can assure you that the feeling isn't reciprocated.'

'I cannot bear the thought of another man having you!' he raged. 'Not now—and not ever!'

Was it to possess her utterly and completely that he married her—or was it simply because he felt that he had compromised himself by robbing her of her innocence? But marriage also meant acceptability from his family in Sicily, and provided the respectable arena for something else Vincenzo wanted more than all the wealth in the universe.

'A son,' he breathed on their wedding night as he stroked her flat, bare belly and moved over her with dark intent. 'I will put my son inside your body, Emma.'

Who wouldn't have thrilled at that avowal? Certainly not a woman swept up in the dizzy whirl of love. But the tenor of their lovemaking seemed to change from that very moment. There seemed to be a *purpose* to it which had not been there before. And the inevitable disappointment each month when his longed-for son failed to materialise made Emma begin to get twitchy.

On one of their periodic visits to Sicily, even his favourite cousin Salvatore, who clearly still disapproved of her—marriage or no marriage—was heard to allude to babies. Or, rather, the lack of them. Emma felt both insulted, and hurt.

Soon the subject began to dominate their thoughts, if not their conversation—for Vincenzo flatly refused to discuss it—and, driven to despair, Emma went secretly to see an English doctor on the Via Martinotti in Rome.

The news was devastating enough, but Emma was frightened into stuffing the letter into a drawer, supposedly to disclose to Vincenzo when she found the 'right' time—though quite when she imagined that time might be always perplexed her afterwards. For how did you find the words to tell a man that his greatest wish was destined never to be fulfilled?

Vincenzo found the letter. Was waiting for her one afternoon with it crumpled in his hand, his face dark, an expression in his eyes she had never seen there before and which sent shivers of foreboding icing over her skin.

'When were you going to tell me?' he questioned, in a voice which sounded flat and unfamiliar. 'Or perhaps you weren't going to bother?'

'Of course I was!'

'When?'

'When the time seemed right,' Emma answered miserably.

'And when would that be? Is there an optimum time for announcing to your husband that you are unable to have his child?'

Emma bit her lip. 'We can investigate fertility treatment…*adopt*,' she ventured, but there was no answering light of hope in the stony black eyes. 'Or I can see another specialist for a second opinion.'

'If you say so.'

She had never seen Vincenzo like this before, like a tyre which had been lanced by a shard of glass—all the air and the life seemed to have left him.

Her infertility drove a further wedge between them—that was as clear as the stars in the night sky—but Vincenzo preferred to focus instead on her deceit. The fact that she had gone to the doctor *in secret*. That she had kept the fact *hidden* from him. Until one day Emma realised that, no matter how much she tried to explain or justify her reasons, he *needed* someone to blame, and who better than her? He had swum against the tide by marrying an English girl instead of a Sicilian one—but he had made a bad choice and chosen one who was barren, too.

It became one of those simple if heartbreaking decisions. Was she going to allow their marriage to wither away completely in front of her eyes, destroying even the few good memories left—or was she strong and brave enough to give Vincenzo his freedom by walking away?

He didn't fight her when she told him she was leaving—though his face became as hard and as forbidding as some dark stone. He probably wouldn't even notice when she was gone, she thought bitterly—for wasn't he just spending longer and longer days at the office, sometimes not even bothering to come home in time for dinner?

The icy chill which greeted her decision lasted until she reached the door, and then she turned to say goodbye for the last time, something in his eyes stopped her.

'Vincenzo?' she said, hesitantly.

And then he started to kiss her—and all the sadness and bitterness and lost love bubbled up and spilled over as he drove into her up against the wall by the front door. He made her miss her plane and then carried her upstairs one last time for one long night of exquisitely heartbreaking sex.

She opened her eyes as he was getting dressed and that was when his face grew hard and cold and he said it: 'Get out of here, Emma, and do not come back—for you are no wife of mine.' And then he turned away, and walked out of the room.

Later that morning her plane had taken off and she had been blinded by tears.

And about a month later had discovered she was pregnant....

'Next stop Waterloo!' The bus driver's voice broke into Emma's reverie and with a start she realised that the bus was slowing down outside the railway station. And that nothing had been resolved.

Like a woman walking in her sleep, she got off the bus and went into the station concourse to find a coffee shop, barely noticing the crowds of people milling around. It felt strange to be out on her own without a little baby in her care. How peculiar to just be able to walk up to a table and sit down without having to negotiate a buggy, or worry that he wouldn't want to sit still.

She stared at the creamy mounds of foam on her cappuccino as the dull feeling of disquiet refused to leave her—and it went much deeper than just the worry of how she was going to survive. No, her uneasiness had been provoked by seeing Vincenzo again—and no longer being able to deny the glaring truth.

That Gino was his living image!

Pulling her little photo wallet out of her bag, she stared down at the most recent snap of him and the sight of his gorgeous little face made her heart clench with pain and guilt. Had she been deliberately blocking out just how like his father he was? As a safety mechanism to protect her own broken heart, without thinking of *their* needs?

At that moment, the phone began to ring and she grabbed it. An unknown number. Yet Emma knew exactly who it was.

Heart pounding, she clicked the connection with a trembling finger. 'Hello?'

'Have you thought any more about my offer, *cara*?'

And suddenly Emma knew that she couldn't keep running away—because she had reached a dead end and there was nowhere left to run. And neither could she keep the truth from her estranged husband any longer. He needed to know about Gino and she needed to tell him.

'Yes,' she said slowly. 'I've thought about nothing else. I need to see you.' And why not get it over with?

What would be the point of having to arrange another day of babysitting when she was already here in the capital? 'I can meet you later, after all.'

So she had changed her mind, as he had known she would. In one lustful rush, Vincenzo experienced triumph, anticipation, and yet it was accompanied by a bitter kind of disappointment, too. For hadn't he admired the feisty way she'd thrown his admittedly insulting offer back in his face? Hadn't there been echoes in that of the woman he'd fallen in love with—the one who had shown restraint, who had refused to tumble into bed with him just because he had wanted her to?

But no. It seemed that he had been right all along, and that everyone had their price—even Emma. His mouth hardened. *Especially* Emma.

'I'm tied up with meetings all afternoon. Do you know the Vinoly Hotel?' he questioned coolly.

'I've heard of it.'

'Meet me there at six—in the Bay Room bar.'

Emma closed her eyes with relief. A public place. She could tell him there and that was the best possible option—for surely even Vincenzo wouldn't lose his rag in the middle of some fancy hotel. 'I'll be there.'

'*Ciao,*' said Vincenzo in a silky voice as he replaced the phone.

Emma dug her fingernails into the palms of her hands. She was going to have to ring Joanna and tell her she'd be later than planned and then she was going to have to find some way of occupying herself for the afternoon. To work out the best way to tell him that he had a child. She dreaded to think what Vincenzo's reaction would be—but, no matter what he threw at her, she must face it. She must be strong and take it. For her own sake—but, more especially, for Gino's.

CHAPTER FIVE

EMMA spent the afternoon walking aimlessly around the city and ended up window-shopping in the glitziest department store she could find, taking advantage of one of the rest rooms to wash her hands and fringe and apply a lick of make-up.

Vincenzo's comments of earlier had made her feel scrawny and unattractive—and that was the last thing she needed as she was about to walk into one of the capital's smartest hotels and drop this particular bombshell.

Her heart was thundering as she walked into the Bay Room bar and she could see Vincenzo standing talking to a member of staff—looking tall and eye-catching in his dark suit, and totally at home in this upmarket venue.

Nervously, she glanced around. Seated at the trademark triangular tables with their distinctive turquoise velvet seats were the movers and shakers of the city. Women wearing amazing sleek and expensive clothes and gravity-defying high-heeled shoes.

And, despite her newly washed fringe and the liberal amount of scent and hand lotion with which she'd doused herself in the rest room, Emma had never felt quite so out of place in her life. She felt like one of those characters from a Victorian novel—a scruffy little urchin who'd taken a break from selling matches on a street corner outside—and if there had been a choice, she would have turned around and walked straight out. But she didn't have a choice, not any more.

Vincenzo watched her walk in, his black eyes giving nothing away as they flicked over her in brief assessment. So she hadn't spent the afternoon buying herself something new to wear, he noted—as most women who were planning to sleep with a man again would do. Which must mean that she really *was* broke—or that she was still very confident about her sexual allure over him. His mouth twisted. Or both.

'*Ciao*, Emma,' he murmured as she approached.

'Hello,' she said, feeling ridiculously self-conscious, aware of the bizarreness of the situation and the fact that the member of staff was looking at her as if some alien had just dropped in through the ceiling.

'The *maître d'* has just been telling me that, unfortunately, all the tables are taken,' Vincenzo was saying smoothly. 'But that he has arranged drinks for us on the rooftop terrace.'

'You will find the view from the terrace infinitely superior sir,' said the *maître d'* with the affable smile of a man who had just been handed a large wad of money. 'I will have someone accompany you to the penthouse.' He snapped his fingers and a man in uniform who looked about twelve began to lead the way towards one of the lifts.

Emma's eyes told Vincenzo that she didn't believe a word of it and the mockery in his black eyes told her that he didn't care. But how could she possibly object with a third party present—and had he been banking on that? Or was it just that he was aware of his bargaining power and that she must play to his rules if she wanted her divorce settlement?

The silence was suffocating as the lift rode upwards and it seemed to grow more and more oppressive as the bell-boy showed them into what was clearly a very large suite of rooms dominated by a vast sitting room studded with dramatic arrangements of flowers. It was true that the view was magnificent—a floor-to-ceiling firework display of glittering stars and skyscrapers against the indigo backdrop of the sky. But more glaringly obvious was a set of double doors which led through to a room dominated by the biggest bed she had ever seen. Emma bit her lip. It was an insult—a blatant and glaring insult.

'Will there be anything else, sir?'

'No, that will be all, thanks.'

She waited until the boy had shut the doors behind him before turning on Vincenzo, who was taking his jacket off. 'You said a drink. This is a suite!' she accused.

Vincenzo smiled as he loosened his tie. So she wanted to play games, did she? 'The two aren't mutually incompatible, surely?' With a careless hand, he indicated the ice-bucket containing champagne. 'Drink all you like, *cara*.'

'Are you saying that a table wouldn't magically have

become available if you'd asked for one?' Emma asked, wishing she could rid herself of the terrible nerves which were criss-crossing through her stomach and beginning to tie it up in knots.

'I could have asked for one,' he conceded. 'But you cannot deny that up here it is so much more comfortable—and so much more private, of course.' He poured out champagne, which fizzed up like pale gold into two tall flutes, his eyes glittering with insolent challenge—wondering how long she was going to carry on playing the innocent. 'Take off your coat and lets have a drink. You said you had something you wanted to tell me.'

Nerves had suddenly clutched at her throat as if someone had placed their hands there and were squeezing all the breath from her body. Emma nodded, slipped her coat off, perched on the edge of the sofa and took the drink from him, although she noticed that he didn't pick up a glass himself.

It had been a long time since she'd drunk champagne and its sudden heady rush reminded her that she hadn't eaten anything since breakfast. She felt dizzy. Weakened by his proximity and the way that he was looking at her. *So tell him.*

'Vincenzo…this is very difficult.'

He sat down beside her. He could see her trembling and his lips curved into an arrogant smile. Had an earlier taste of his kisses reminded her just what she'd been missing? She really *did* want him. 'Is it?' he questioned, with soft arrogance.

Taking the half-drunk glass from her unprotesting fingers and putting it down on a table, he ran a thoughtful finger along the too-severe jut of her collar-bone, feeling her shiver beneath his touch. 'It's only difficult if we make it so. If you try and dress it up to be something it isn't. Why not just admit that we're still physically attracted to one another and that we both want this?'

Emma stared at him in rapidly escalating horror. He thought…he really *did* think she'd come back to strike the deal—a quick divorce in exchange for a night of sex. 'That wasn't what I meant.'

But Vincenzo wasn't listening. He was hungry for her, transfixed by the way her rapid breathing was making her breasts rise and fall—and he was feeling more fired up than he could remember feeling since that last time he'd made love to her. His mouth hardened. Or, rather, had *sex* with her. There had been no love involved in that last frantic coming together that day in Rome. Maybe there never had been. Maybe thunderbolts were merely the indiscriminate strikings of lust.

'I don't care,' he said deliberately. 'In fact, I don't care about anything—only this.'

His mouth came down on hers—a slow, drugging kiss with all the passion he'd displayed earlier in his offices, but this time there was a difference. This time they were not on *his* territory with the possibility that his assistant might wiggle her way in at any moment. And this time Emma knew that she was beaten—in every way. In a few minutes' time she was going to tell

Vincenzo something which would change his life irrevocably.

She was going to have to learn to live with his anger and the contempt she knew deep down that he was keeping on ice because at this moment he wanted her. And didn't she want him, too? If she was being honest, then she had never really stopped wanting him. So why couldn't she have this one last time before all the recriminations started? One last taste of bliss before the dark clouds descended.

'Vincenzo,' she groaned as she reached up to cling onto his broad shoulders and felt their muscular power. 'Oh, *Vincenzo*.'

He closed his mind to the memories stirred up by her breathless words, instead pulling her closer into his arms, feeling her petite frame trembling beneath his touch and the soft, silken spill of her hair as it brushed against his cheek. The fierce throbbing at his groin was setting him on fire, and he kissed her more thoroughly than he could ever remember kissing anyone before— his lips exploring hers as if he couldn't bear to tear his mouth away. What *was* it that she did to him?

'Touch me!' he urged huskily. 'Touch me the way you used to.'

The faint sense of vulnerability in his deep voice was almost too much to bear—as intoxicating as his shuddered entreaty—or was Emma just imagining that? Hearing what she wanted to hear. But either way, she was in too deep to want to do anything other than what he wanted—and she ran her hands luxuriously down over his chest, feeling the roughness of hair beneath the fine silk of his shirt.

'Like that?' she whispered.

'*Piu!*'

'More?'

'*Sì*! More. Much more.'

Her fingers whispered down to his groin, where he was unashamedly aroused, and he bit out a remark which sounded like some Sicilian curse, and she thought that it probably was. As if he despised being in thrall to his senses like this, even while his body revelled in it. 'Like this?'

'*Sì*, exactly like that. Ah, Emma,' he groaned. Pale witch of a woman! Experimentally, he ran his hands over her body—this body he knew so well—as if he were feeling it for the first time. And maybe he was. He frowned. It felt different. Not only a diminishment of flesh, but her breasts seemed to be a different shape, too—or at least as much as he could tell while she was still covered up. He cupped one and let his thumb graze across it.

'Take this damned dress off,' he instructed.

But even in the midst of her body's heated clamour, Emma was assailed by nerves. Surely he wasn't expecting her to leap up and start stripping off for him—the way she might once have done when they were newly married? In view of their situation wouldn't that be impossible? Why, she would feel as if he was buying her. *And isn't he?* jeered the mocking voice of her conscience. *Isn't he?*

But Emma closed her ears and her mind to the uncomfortable taunt and licked her dry lips. 'You…you take it off.'

'If you insist,' he murmured.

He was good at that, of course. He must have removed a million dresses in his time. And how many other women had he undressed since the last time she'd been in his arms? wondered Emma painfully as he peeled the cheap little garment from her body, letting it fall disdainfully to the floor.

As he moved away from her his black eyes scorched over her like a diabolical laser beam. 'Let me look at you.'

She wanted to shrink her arms over her chest and bunch her knees up to hide from the inevitable critical assessment of her scrawny body and her plain underwear, and her…

'Tights!' he bit out derisively. 'Since when did you start wearing tights?'

Since she stopped being a billionaire's possession, that was when. Maybe her estranged husband didn't realise that sliding into silk stockings and suspender belt wasn't exactly compatible with getting up at the crack of dawn to feed a baby.

The thought of the baby and what she was going to have to tell Vincenzo was enough to make Emma freeze momentarily—to want to call a halt to it and tell him that this was a fruitless exercise. But by now he was tugging the tights down over her ankles and off her toes and burying his head into the apex of her thighs—kissing her there, over her plain cotton panties, until she was wriggling impatiently, wanting him with a fierce desire which was almost unbearable.

'Vincenzo,' she gasped.

'You want to go to bed?' he demanded hotly.

And break the mood? Giving her time for second thoughts? Allowing reason to creep in and ruin something that was making her feel more alive than she had done in so long? Her head said this was probably one of the craziest things she had ever done but her body had other ideas. And he was still her husband, Emma thought achingly—surely this was her *right* as much as her pleasure.

'No,' she whispered, tangling her fingers in the ebony waves of his hair, the way she'd done innumerable times before. 'Let's do it here.'

Vincenzo groaned at her easy capitulation—at her effortless transformation from ice queen to siren. But he had always loved the fiery passion which lay beneath the cool blonde exterior. That streak of sensual unconventionality he had coaxed from her—at least until those last glacial months of the marriage. He had taught her everything she knew—why should he not taste the fruits of his labour one more time, to see if she had improved during his absence from her bed? 'Take off my shirt,' he gritted out.

Her trembling fingers struggled to slide the delicate fabric over the infinitely silkier surface of his skin, her fingers gently clawing in little circles at the whorls of hair which grew there, but he stilled them with the flat of his hand. 'Later,' he said unsteadily. 'There will be time for that later—but for now…'

He was pulling at the buckle of his belt and Emma was thinking that *there would be no later*—a certain knowledge told her that even while her nagging conscience urged her to tell him. Tell him *now*. But she did not heed it—she could not—for a broken little sound was torn from her throat as she touched her lips greedily to his shoulders and his neck. Her lips brushed against the rough rasp of his jaw, grazing softly along its proud, curved line, and she heard his ragged sigh of pleasure.

How cruel sex could be, she thought, with a shiver. And not just cruel, but clever, too—because it could make you feel things which weren't real. It could make you believe that you still loved someone…and she didn't love Vincenzo—of course she didn't. How could she possibly love him after everything that had happened?

She watched as he moved away to remove the last of his clothing and then pushed her back against the sofa as he came to her—with a dark, sexual power she had almost forgotten. For a moment time was frozen as he towered over her like some dark and golden colossus before he slid down onto her waiting skin.

'Vincenzo!' she gasped as he entered her with one long and delicious thrust, filling her completely. For a moment he stilled and looked down at her, his black eyes opaque with lust and a fleeting glimpse of something else, too—something which looked like anger. But surely not anger at a time like this? 'Vincenzo?' she said again, only this time on a question.

He shook his head slightly as he began to move within her, despising her sexual power over him even as he felt it rip his senses apart with such an overload of sensual delight. He stared down at the vision she made beneath him—her eyes tightly closed and her cheeks growing pink as she lifted those perfect legs and wrapped them tightly around his back.

And hadn't doing this to her haunted his dreams for too long? Surely this would rid him of her pervasive spell once and for all. His mouth hardened. 'Look at me,' he ordered softly. 'Look at me, Emma.'

Reluctantly, she allowed her eyelids to flutter open. When your eyes were closed you could imagine. Invent. Pretend that this was happening for no other reason than that two people loved one another. How far from the truth that was—how complex the motives which had brought both of them here, to this place. She stared up into the taut tension of his face. 'Oh, Vincenzo,' she whispered.

'Oh, Vincenzo!' he mocked as he curled the palms of his hands underneath her bare buttocks. 'Am I the best lover you've ever had, Emma?'

'You…you know you are!' she gasped out, aware that he wanted to hurt her—but suddenly she was past caring, for he had brought her to that point where it was all going to happen, and far sooner than she had thought. As if he were catapulting her up to the stars and then bringing her down again in slow and delicious motion. 'Vincenzo…oh, *oh!* Oh…*yes*…yes… *ye-e-s-s*!'

He felt her body clenching around him and forced himself to hold back for just long enough to watch her wild abandon as her head fell back and her nails dug into his shoulders. And then he let go and took his own pleasure and he could never remember it washing over him with such strength—making him completely powerless in its wake. It seemed to go on and on as if it were never going to stop—and even after it was over and had subsided he stayed inside her for a moment while the final spasms ebbed away.

He looked down at her flushed face, at the strand of hair which clung to one damp cheek. In the past he might have pushed that strand away and curled it around his finger, but not now—for such a gesture would imply some kind of tenderness, and tenderness was the last thing he was feeling.

He pulled out of her and moved away, getting up from the sofa and walking over to pour himself a glass of water, lifting it to his lips and drinking from it, his black eyes capturing her gaze over its rim. 'Do you realise that we were so *up for it*—as you might say—that we failed to consider contraception?' he mocked. 'But, as we both know, that is not a subject which needs trouble us.'

Disbelievingly, Emma stared across the room at him, trembling now. How unimaginably *cruel*. Had he saved the most wounding barb of all for last—to say something as confrontational as that, after they had just shared the greatest intimacy of all? To try to cold-bloodedly hurt her as nothing else could? Well, he was wrong—as he was about to discover—but wasn't his brutality at such a moment a timely reminder not to weave any foolish fantasies about Vincenzo Cardini?

'That remark was completely unnecessary,' she said stiffly.

'Was it?' he mocked. 'But it's the truth.'

Surely he was never going to believe her when she told him how very wrong he was? Emma reached for her bra and pants. She was going to have to tell him, but she was damned if she was going to be naked when she did so.

He watched her getting dressed but was disinclined to stop her. If he wanted her again then he would simply undress her quickly—but right now all he felt was distaste. How quickly the urges of the body could mask the reality of a situation, he thought—and once passion had been spent all you were left with were the cold, hard facts.

Emma was nothing to him now other than a duplicitous wife who had just submitted to sex in order to secure a speedy divorce deal! He began to pull his own clothes on, eager now to be away from her.

'Vincenzo.' Emma finished pulling her dress down over her head and pushing her disarrayed hair back from her flushed face before turning to face him. 'You remember I said that I had something to tell you.'

He barely flicked her a glance as he finished buttoning his shirt and slipped his shoes on. 'I can hardly wait,' he said sarcastically.

She drew a deep breath. How many ways were there to say it? Only one—because the words were so powerful that nothing, *nothing* was ever going to be able to lessen their irrevocable impact. But how could she tell him—how *could* she?

'Vincenzo. You've got…I mean…we've got…' Emma cleared her throat, aware of the furious, frightened hammering of her heart. 'The thing is, you see—we have a son. A son. You have a son.'

CHAPTER SIX

FOR a moment Vincenzo thought that he must have misheard her, though something in the strangled quality of Emma's tone alerted his senses to something far more complicated than a mere misunderstanding. Narrowing his eyes into disbelieving shards, he stared at her. '*What* did you say?' he questioned menacingly.

Emma swallowed. 'You've…you've got a son, Vincenzo. Or, rather, *we've* got a son. His name is—'

'Shut up—just shut up!' he bit out in disgust, his words silencing her and his hands clenching into fists by the powerful shafts of his thighs, caught up in the grip of a rage fiercer than anything he could remember. For a moment he wanted to storm across the room and shake her, but he didn't trust himself. His mouth twisted into a cruel curve of contempt. 'You can have your damned divorce, Emma—after all, you've just earned it. The sex was laughably brief, but as a cathartic measure it was probably worth it—just please don't spin me any more of your damned lies.'

Emma shook her head, blocking out his insults and

trying to focus solely on the truth. 'But it isn't a lie—I swear, it isn't.'

'You *swear* it?' His eyes were blazing black fire. 'How do you dare claim such a thing to me in view of our history?' he demanded, his mind spinning as he tried to pluck facts from her unbelievable statement. And one fact leapt out from all the others. He frowned. 'You say you have a child?'

'Yes.'

'But that is not possible.' He took an unwise step closer, his voice tight with gritted fury. 'You are infertile, Emma. You can't have children. The doctor told you so in one of your private consultations. He sent you a letter stating just that, which I still have in my possession. Surely you haven't forgotten that?'

'Of course I haven't forgotten—'

'Then how in hell's name can you have a baby, and how can I possibly be the father?' he roared.

Emma swallowed. 'Can we please talk about this calmly?'

'*Calmly?*' Vincenzo's voice was like black ice. 'Are you out of your mind? You drop a lie—'

'It's not a lie!' she repeated desperately. 'Why the hell would I lie to you about something like that?'

'I can think of a pretty good reason,' he retorted sourly. 'Missing my wealth and deciding you want a sizeable chunk of it might be enough to make you go ahead with some kind of scam—'

'*Scam?*' she echoed in horror. 'You think I'm some kind of...some kind of...cheap *con-merchant*?'

He shrugged, his heart pounding furiously in his chest. 'You've already proved that, Emma. You fooled me into believing that we were still trying for a baby, when all the time you knew that it was impossible. If that isn't conning someone, then I'd be interested to hear your definition of the word, *cara*.'

Never had a term of supposed affection carried with it such a wealth of withering scorn, and Emma almost recoiled from the look of disdain which sparked from his black eyes. Her tongue snaked around lips which suddenly felt like crumpled parchment. 'I never meant to deceive you,' she whispered.

'No?'

'I was frightened to let you know what the results were,' she said.

'So you treated me like a fool!' he accused. 'You just thought you'd keep me in the dark about something as important as that?'

'No. Of course not. It wasn't meant to be like that. I *was* going to tell you—'

'And what precisely *were* you going to tell me, Emma?' he questioned in a suddenly silken voice.

Emma relaxed a little. 'That I couldn't...couldn't have a baby.'

'Yet now you are telling me that the doctor was wrong? That all those months of trying vainly to conceive were an illusion—and that you *could* conceive after all?'

'Yes! My obstetrician said that these things do happen occasionally—'

'Miraculous,' he commented sarcastically. 'And when did this marvel occur? How old is the child?'

A part of her wanted to tell him to forget it—that she wasn't going to *beg* him to acknowledge his son, and that she had more than enough love to go round.

But Emma recognised that she must do this for Gino's sake. Because what if one day he turned round and demanded to know where his father was? She must be able to look him in the eye and tell him truthfully that she had told Vincenzo everything—every single fact— even if she'd told them to him rather late in the day. How Vincenzo chose to interpret and then act on those facts was up to him, but her conscience would be clear.

'He's ten months old,' she said—knowing that this was the big one and watching while Vincenzo's eyes narrowed in silent calculation. He was clearly doing some kind of rapid mathematical assessment about whether or not it was possible for him to be the father. And, yes, it was insulting, but her feelings were not the issue here.

'And when are you claiming that this conception took place?'

'It must have been that…that last time we were together. Do you remember?'

Now he gave a grim kind of smile. 'Do I remember? I am hardly likely to forget,' he said bitterly. It had been the first time they'd been together for weeks. Their relationship had gradually been eroding, but in the light of the news that she could not bear his child and all the accompanying deceit they had become strangers to one another. The letter she had hidden had become the symbol of all that was wrong between them. He began to doubt whether *anything* about her had been genuine.

'So were you really a virgin when I met you, Emma?' he had demanded icily one day, over breakfast. 'Or was that, too, a fabrication?'

He remembered the way that the light had gone out of her eyes and, yes, he had taken pleasure in that, too.

'Oh, what is the point, Vincenzo?' had been her dull response. 'If you can think so poorly of me, then there is no point in going on, is there?'

He remembered the feeling of relief which had washed over him, telling himself that he would be glad to see the back of her lying little face. True, he would have to live with the mockery of his cousins, who had always cautioned him against the marriage—but he could deal with that.

Yet the reality of their separation had proved harsher than he had anticipated. He had missed her bright blonde hair and her sunny smile and the way that her delicate frame used to complement his own powerful body so perfectly. Until he reminded himself that those were external things which were easily replaceable and that, in truth, he didn't really recognise the Emma he had married. His trust in her had been destroyed—and to a proud Sicilian man trust was everything.

He was aware of the bizarre situation in which he now found himself—aware of Emma standing wide-eyed on the opposite side of the luxury hotel suite, her cheeks still flushed from their lovemaking and her hair in disarray. So what was he going to do about her extraordinary revelation that he had fathered her child?

Giving himself time to sift through his options with a chilly detachment, which his business rivals would have recognised with sinking hearts, Vincenzo poured himself another glass of mineral water and drank from it. For once, he could have done with the slightly numbing effect of alcohol, but he needed his wits to be as razor sharp as they had ever been.

His black gaze bored into her like the twin barrels of a shotgun. 'The question is—whether or not I believe you,' he pondered. 'Or whether you're just spinning me a line to try to get your hands on as much of my money as possible.'

Emma choked back her instinctive gasp of distress. 'You think that I'd choose this particular method as a means of extorting money from a man like you? That I'd put myself through all this grief?' she demanded. 'Why, I'd rather scrub floors to earn a crust than do that!'

'So why don't you?' he challenged icily.

His words were the final straw—pushing her and pushing her until all her determination to stay calm flew out of the window and something inside Emma snapped. All the worry and the struggle of the preceding months, the huge decision to tell Vincenzo and then her own weakness in having just had sex with him—all these factors now ignited to explode into a debilitating cocktail of anger and indignation and sheer anxiety.

'Because I have a baby to look after and it's actually very difficult, if you must know! I'd pay more in childcare than I'd earn! But how would you know—when you've been cushioned by wealth all your life? Everything you've wanted has always been there for the taking. Money may have made your life easier, Vincenzo, but it has tarnished it, too, because you are unable to see anything except through its dark and corrupting influence. Every time you meet a new person the barriers go up and you're thinking, *Does this person want to know me, or do they want to get their hands on my millions?*'

'That's *enough!*' he snapped. 'I don't really think that you are in a position to give me a lecture on the morality of money, when your own morals are in radical need of an overhaul.' Deliberately, he let his gaze rake over her crumpled dress, at the sting of colour which still flushed her face. 'Tell me, did you have sex with me because you thought it would put you in a *better* bargaining position—because if I were you, I would really rethink your strategy in future, *cara*. Your worth would be greatly enhanced if you withheld the sex until *after* you had agreed the price.'

That did it. Her rage so blinding, her fury and her frustration and sense of self-recrimination were all so overwhelming that Emma just flew across the suite, launching herself at him, raining a battery of blows at the unforgiving wall of his chest.

But Vincenzo merely laughed, capturing her drumming little fists easily within the restraining grasp of his hands and stilling her with a contemptuous curve of his lips as he brought his mouth up close to her ear.

'Did you imagine that such a spirited display would have me eating out of your hand?' he whispered. 'Or eating you?'

'Vincenzo!'

'Vincenzo!' he mocked. And *wasn't* the fiercely hot kick of desire hitting him hard in the groin—and didn't he just want to press it against her warm, soft mound, to seek a quick and urgent release from this infernal desire? But sex without strings was one thing—having sex with her after what she had just told him was something entirely different.

Dropping his hands from her as if she were contaminated, he walked over to the other side of the room, his back facing her. People always said that Vincenzo's face was cold and shuttered—that working out what was going on in his head from the look on his face was like trying to read a stone. But Emma was better at it than most because inevitably she knew him better than most. And so he needed to be careful.

Staring out of the window, he studied the dark gleam of the river and the dazzling light from the buildings which were reflected on its rippling surface. Logic told him that she was lying—and it also told him that if she persisted with her crazy contention, then he should simply refer it to his lawyers. It wasn't exactly unheard of for fabulously wealthy men to be hit on by women with spurious paternity claims—but these days, fortunately, there were the means to establish the truth in such a claim.

He should tell her to get out, to leave the suite now—and he should put someone onto it in the morning. Why, he need not even meet with her again—it could all be put into the hands of his legal experts.

But some instinct made Vincenzo loath to follow the voice of logic, and he wasn't sure why. Was it because the sex between them had been utter dynamite—just as it always had been with her—and because it had awoken in him a hunger which she could feed better than any other woman he'd ever known?

Wouldn't it make more sense to play along with her—so that he could enjoy her body for a little longer before they parted for good? And wouldn't renewed evidence of her duplicity finally help dull the magic enchantment which she could still wield over his senses?

Turning back, he surprised her chewing on her bottom lip like a nervous exam candidate. So was she? Nervous? Of course she was.

'Where do you live?' he questioned.

'In a little place called Boisdale—it's about an hour's drive from here.'

'Did you drive here today?'

Still smarting from all the hurt and the pain—some of it admittedly self-inflicted—Emma wondered which planet he lived on, until she remembered. He lived on Planet Wealth. Vincenzo had guessed that she was short of money, but someone in his position would have no idea of what that would mean in real terms. To him, being broke might mean having a pretty standard car— the idea that she would simply be unable to pay for road tax and petrol, let alone the cost of learning to drive would be completely outside his experience.

'No, I still haven't got my licence,' she said, just wanting to get away now and as soon as possible. Away from that disdainful face and the memory of what she had just allowed to happen. All she wanted was to wash away every trace of him… She would blow the expense, put the immersion heater on and submerge herself in a hot, deep bath the minute she got home. 'No, I came by train.'

Emma glanced at her watch, but the blur of numbers danced in front of her eyes. At least she had told him, and he hadn't believed her. Gino would be unable to blame her and maybe this was all for the best. She need never see him again and she would manage. Somehow. 'And, in fact, I ought to be getting back.'

'Yes. I will order a car,' said Vincenzo, sliding his mobile phone from his pocket.

'That won't be necessary, thank you. I'll be fine.'

'You think perhaps I am playing the gentleman, *cara*?' he taunted silkily, with a shake of his dark head. 'Alas, you are mistaken. You may be content to take public transport, but I can assure you that I am not.'

Emma stared at him, putting her confusion and interpretation of mixed messages down to the fact that she was tired and aching. 'I don't quite understand what you mean.'

'Don't you?' questioned Vincenzo softly. 'Haven't you realised that I shall be coming with you?'

Emma stared at him in alarm. 'What, you mean—to Boisdale? But I thought…'

'What did you think?' he put in as her strained whisper faded into an open-mouthed look of disbelief.

'That you didn't believe me.'

'I don't.' His mouth hardened as he punched out a number on his phone, and said something swiftly in his Sicilian dialect, before meeting her gaze with cold, hard eyes. 'But the easiest way to rule out a whole load of unnecessary paperwork and time is to see the baby for myself.'

'You think you'll be able to establish his paternity just by looking at him?'

'Of course I do. The Cardini genes are unmistakable,' he said, his voice harsh as he called her bluff. 'You know that as well as I do.'

Emma swallowed. 'He'll be asleep.'

So now she had backed herself into a corner. 'So much the better—for I have no wish to unsettle the child.' A low beeping sound emitting from his phone alerted his attention and he shot Emma a disparaging glance. 'Now put your shoes back on, *cara*—and let's get this over with. The car's here.'

CHAPTER SEVEN

IT WAS the journey from hell.

Despite the quietly opulent luxury of Vincenzo's chauffeur-driven car, Emma sat bolt upright on the soft leather seat as if she were facing a firing squad. Yet that was exactly how it felt—only she happened to be facing the lethal weapons of his words rather than the cold metal of a gun.

But if she stopped to think about it—what had she really expected to happen? She knew what kind of man Vincenzo was—had she really imagined that he would just calmly accept such a momentous piece of information from her? Perhaps that he would just nod sagely and give her a divorce and then politely ask when it might be convenient for him to visit his son? As if.

What a fool she had been not to have anticipated this.

But at least this way it would soon be all over and there would be no awful delay to endure. No feeling threatened while she waited anxiously to see just what he would do next. Vincenzo would soon set eyes on Gino and would know instantly that the baby had

SHARON KENDRICK 85

sprung from *his* loins. Emma knotted her fingers together. And of course *that* would bring up problems all of its own—but at least she would have done the right thing, and after the initial anger had subsided, surely they were mature enough to work out some kind of effective compromise.

'So who has been looking after him today?'

The question shot at her from out of the gloom and somehow her estranged husband had managed to turn it into an accusation. 'My friend Joanna.'

'I see.' In the dim light Vincenzo's mouth twisted, but Emma noticed, as no doubt he had intended her to do. 'She is experienced in the care of children?'

'She's got a little boy about the same age,' Emma put in hastily, hating the fact that she felt the need to defend herself and yet wanting to impress on him that she *was* a good mother. 'And she's brilliant with him. This evening she's left her son with her husband so that she could put mine to bed in his own home.'

A long finger drummed a slightly menacing little beat on the taut surface of one tensile thigh. 'So tell me, Emma—how often do you leave your child with someone else while you go off to London to have casual sex?'

It was a bitter and damning allegation and Emma felt her body begin to shake with the injustice of it. She shook her head and stared up into his face, unable to help the indignant tremble of her lips. 'How *dare* you say something like that?'

'You mean, that the way you behaved today with me isn't the way you usually behave with men?'

'You know damned well it isn't!

Yes, deep down he knew that. It had been evident in the hungry way she had responded to him today—and in the general and conflicting air of untouchability which she had always possessed. Hadn't it been that very quality which had first so ensnared him and which had made him lose control more times than he cared to remember?

But Vincenzo was a Sicilian man—and that carried with it a whole lot of complex issues about how women should and shouldn't behave when it came to sex. Back there in the Vinoly suite, Emma had behaved with the wild abandon of a mistress—not a young mother who had left her baby for the day with someone who wasn't family! And although he had revelled in the experience they had just shared, there was a part of him which also despised it.

Vincenzo turned his head to stare at the darkened English countryside which was rushing past the window, watching as the car slowed and then passed through a surprisingly impressive entrance gate, before making its way up a wide, tree-lined drive. On the far horizon, he could see an imposing-looking house which stood in an elevated position, all lit up and glowing golden.

'You live *here*?' he demanded.

For one moment, Emma was so tempted to tell him that, yes, she did. That really she was simply *pretending* to be hard-up as some kind of diversion in order to amuse herself!

'Hardly,' she said drily. 'I rent a cottage in the

grounds. It's over there. Can you tell the chauffeur to turn to the right and then travel straight on past the lake?'

Vincenzo clicked on the intercom and spoke to the driver in rapid Italian as the limousine changed direction. It purred its way to a smooth halt in front of March Cottage and he found his eyes narrowing in surprise, for this was not what he had been expecting, either.

It was tiny; one of those cute little houses which always seemed to feature on the front of postcards—with its stone walls and some sort of leafy thing scrambling around the front door, over which hung an old-fashioned lantern.

Although a gust of cold wind whirled round them as they stepped from the car, Emma's palms were clammy with sweat as she turned to him, wondering what was going on behind that forbidding profile as he stared up at the front of the cottage. 'I'd better go in first and warn—'

'No.' The word silenced her just as much as the hand placed lightly on her forearm, his fingers curling briefly around her tiny wrist. He saw her blue eyes darken, and widen. His voice dipped to a silky threat. 'You do not need to warn anyone, *cara mia*. Come, I will accompany you.'

Emma felt trapped—but presumably that was what he had intended—and yet why on earth *should* she feel trapped? This was *her* territory now, not his. He was only here because he wanted to convince himself that the baby was not his. *Well, you are in for the shock of a lifetime, Signor Cardini*, she thought fiercely.

'Hello!' she called, pushing open the door, and saw a light coming from the sitting room.

Joanna was lying on the sofa, wrapped up in a blanket and watching TV—a banana skin and an empty coffee cup on the floor beside her. 'It's bloody freezing,' she complained as Emma walked in and then her face froze into a look of utter disbelief when she registered the rugged olive face of the man who was following her.

Pushing the blanket off, she sat up immediately. 'Ooh! Good grief! You must be—'

'This is Vincenzo Cardini,' said Emma without any further explanation, giving Joanna an I'll-tell-you-everything-later look. 'How's he been?'

Joanna appeared to judge the look correctly, though Emma saw her shooting curious glances at the tall, dark man who stood dominating the small space with a moody look. 'Oh, no trouble really,' she said. 'Though he didn't really want to settle—missing his mum, I guess. But he ate an enormous tea and afterwards I gave him a bath—though you really ought to see about getting Andrew to install a heater in the bathroom, Emma.'

'Andrew?' questioned Vincenzo dangerously. 'And just who is Andrew?'

'Andrew is my landlord,' said Emma quickly.

Black eyes bored into her. 'Oh, is he?'

She wanted to say that Andrew's identity was none of his business, but she had *made* it his business, in a way—first by allowing herself to be intimate with him, and then by announcing that he was the father of her child. Given Vincenzo's track record with jealousy and possession, was it any wonder that he looked like a volcano just about to erupt?

Joanna jumped up. 'Look, I'd better get off home.'

Emma nodded and flashed her friend a grateful smile. 'Thanks, Jo—I really appreciate it and I'll see you tomorrow.'

There was an uncomfortable kind of silence while Joanna picked up her coat and bag and went to reach for the discarded banana skin.

'Oh, don't worry about that,' said Emma quickly.

'I'll let myself out, then,' said Joanna.

But Emma barely heard her go. She felt rooted to the spot—not knowing what the hell she should do next—but it seemed that Vincenzo had no such problems with indecision.

'Where is he?' he demanded.

'In…in there.' She pointed at the bedroom door, which was slightly ajar, noticing almost dispassionately that her finger was shaking. 'Please don't wake him.'

Vincenzo's mouth twisted into a mocking parody of a smile. 'I have no desire to wake him. Believe me when I tell you that this is simply to put my mind at rest. One look and I'm out of here. Just show me the child.'

It was the most bizarre of all situations, creeping into Gino's bedroom, her heart frozen with fear and love, trying to see him as Vincenzo would be seeing him— as if for the first time in the soft glow of the night-light. And, no matter what lay ahead, Emma felt the sharp rush of maternal pride as she gazed down on her son.

He was lying on his back, little fisted arms bunched up alongside his head—as if he were spoiling for a fight. As usual, he had managed to kick off his covers and automatically Emma moved forward to pull it back over him.

'No.' Vincenzo's word stopped her. 'Leave it.'

'But—'

'I said, *leave it.*'

Her breath caught in her throat, Emma watched as Vincenzo walked slowly to the side of the cot, ducking his dark head and only narrowly avoiding missing the animal mobile which was swirling madly around above it.

For a moment Vincenzo just stood there, staring down—as motionless and as formidable as a statue constructed from some cold, dark ebony.

Emma felt her fingernails digging into her palms, wanting to break the spell of this terrible and uneasy situation, but somehow not daring to. This was his right, she realised—to take as long as he liked.

With a fast-beating heart, Vincenzo committed the scene to memory. The riot of dark curls and the rather petulant curl of the sleeping mouth, which was so like the one which stared back at him from the mirror each morning when he was shaving. Though the light was dim, nothing could disguise the unmistakably golden-olive glow of the child's perfect skin—nor the hint of height and strength lying dormant in his baby frame.

Vincenzo expelled a long breath of air—the harsh sound penetrating the stillness in the room like an over-pumped tyre which had just been punctured. And then, without any kind of warning, he turned and walked from the room.

Emma fussed around, straightening the covers and feathering her fingertips through the silken mop of Gino's hair—almost as if she were willing him to wake up. But he was deeply asleep—worn out, no doubt—and she could not continue to hide here like some kind of fugitive, just to escape Vincenzo's wrath.

And you haven't done anything wrong, she told herself.

She walked back into the sitting room, where Vincenzo was standing waiting for her with the grim body language of an executioner, his black eyes filled with a cold look of rage.

His mouth twisted as the word was wrenched from him like bitter and deadly poison. *'Puttanesca!'*

As an insult it happened to be grossly inaccurate—but Emma knew that it was the macho insult of choice whenever a woman was considered to have wronged.

'I am not a whore,' she answered quietly. 'You know that. That's a cheap slur to make.'

His voice was equally quiet. 'Maybe I knew it was the only one you would understand.'

Their eyes met in the most honest moment of communication they'd had all day and Emma could have wept at the way he was trying to hurt her. This whole scenario had been intended as a *solution*—and yet it seemed to have spawned a rash of unsightly problems of its own along the way, and she couldn't for the life of her work out how they were going to come to some sort of compromise.

Vincenzo had dragged his gaze from her white face and was looking around him now, as if barely able to believe the surroundings in which he found himself. The faded sofa with a faint white frill where some of the stuffing was spilling out. The tired paintwork and the pale rectangles on the wall where pictures must once have hung and then been removed. The overriding sense that this was simply somewhere temporary—a place for life's losers.

'You…dare to bring my son up in a place like this?' he questioned unsteadily. 'To condemn him to a life of poverty.'

So he had not disputed the paternity claim! Relief washed over her but was quickly replaced with fear. And curiosity.

'So you accept that he's yours?'

Vincenzo chose his words carefully. He had expected to walk into the nursery and to see a baby—and to feel nothing more than he would feel for any baby. And perhaps there would have been a flare of jealousy, too— at being forced to confront the physical evidence that the woman he had married had been intimate with another man.

But it had not been like that. In fact, it had been like nothing he could ever have imagined. Because he had known immediately. On some subliminal level it had been instant—as if he had been programmed to recognise this little boy. He had seen photos of himself as a baby—and the similarity between himself and this infant was undeniable. But it was more than that. Something unknown had whipped at his heart as he'd looked down at that sleeping infant. Some primeval recognition. Some bond stretching back through the ages, as well as a blood line to take him into the unknown future.

'What is his name?' he demanded as he realised he *didn't even know* his son's name.

'Gino.'

'Gino,' he repeated softly. 'Gino.'

He said it quite differently from the way she did—pronounced it as it was probably intended to be pronounced—but the expression on his face belied the slight sense of wonder in his tone. There was something so forbiddingly unfamiliar about the way he was look-ing at her—something so icy cold and critical as his gaze swept over her. And Emma knew that she had to be strong—hadn't she told herself that first thing this morning, at the beginning of a day which seemed to have stretched on for an eternity? She must not let him intimidate her.

'So where do we go from here?' she asked.

His eyes narrowed. She was still wearing her coat. So was he—but only a fool would remove it in these sub-zero temperatures. Was his son warm enough? Gino. This time he tried the word out in his mind and a dark swirl of unknown emotion began to weave dis-torting patterns around his heart.

Suddenly he stepped forward, his hand snaking out to bring her up close and hard into the heat of his body, her fragility sending his senses into overdrive. His free hand roved over her bottom, feeling its faint curve beneath the soft wool, splaying his fingers there as his heart began to pound, his arousal soaring as he ground its hard heat against her. 'Feel how much I want you?' he grated.

'Vincenzo!'

There was a bleak and glittering look of finality in the black eyes before he drove his mouth down on hers and this time his kiss was punishing; angry. If kisses were supposed to be demonstrations of love, then this was their very antithesis. But that didn't stop her responding to it—Emma couldn't seem to prevent herself, no matter how much the voice of reason screamed in her ears to try.

And wasn't there some primeval sense that the man who held her was the acknowledged father of her child? Now that he had seen Gino, seen him and accepted him—hadn't that somehow forged some kind of unbreakable bond between the three of them? Some ancient, golden trinity which had been completed by Gino's birth. *Oh, you fool, Emma*, she told herself. *Inventing fantasies because they'll make you feel better about doing...this...*

'Vincenzo!' she moaned, opening her mouth beneath his—feeling his masculine heat and sensing the urgent tang of his desire. He had started to unbutton her coat now, and she was letting him. Just letting him push the fabric aside and skim his palms down over her hips. And now he was rucking her dress up, brushing his way negligently up to the apex of her thighs, and Emma felt herself wriggle impatiently, scraping her own hands across the broad reach of his shoulders, wanting to rip the coat away from him. Wishing that all their clothes could disappear, as if by magic. 'Vincenzo,' she said, again—more urgently this time.

He felt the plunder of his mouth on hers, the fierce thunder of his heart—his body so hard that he felt he might die if he didn't plunge deep inside her molten softness. For a second he responded to her. Circled his hips against hers in a provocative and primitive entice-ment as old as time, and she swayed against him, as if he were sucking her towards him with some magnetic and irresistible force. He could rip her panties off as she liked them to be ripped, could straddle her until she screamed and bucked beneath him.

And then, as abruptly as he had caught her close to him, Vincenzo dropped his hands and let her go—not reacting when he saw her knees buckle, her hand reach out to grasp the arm of the sofa, to steady herself.

'What am I thinking of?' he questioned, as if speak-ing to himself, his voice distorted by the sound of self-disgust. Hadn't he been tempted just then to do it to her one more time—despite the fact that she had kept his son hidden from him? To maybe dismiss the driver and take her to bed for the night and wake up in the morning to the sound of his son?

But wouldn't that weaken his bargaining position if she sapped his appetite with her sweet sexuality tonight? And if he left her now, he would leave her aching, and wondering… For Vincenzo knew that surprise was the most effective element of all when you were bargaining hard for something.

'Ah, Emma,' he said in a voice of molten steel. 'Too many times I have listened to my body where you are concerned, *mia bella*. Too many times have you used your pale sorcery to ensnare my body and to make me so hungry with need that I cannot think straight, but not now. For this is too important. Now I need to think with my head, instead of with my…'

His mouth twisted as a quick, downward glance indicated the source of his discomfort and he saw the flush of colour which flared along her cheekbones. How could she still blush like an innocent virgin, even while she had just been writhing in his arms like a red-hot alley cat? He stepped back from her, further away from her temptation, his face growing shuttered. 'I shall return here tomorrow morning, at nine.'

Something in his voice alerted her to trouble. Real trouble. 'Return for *what*, exactly?' questioned Emma, trying to keep her own voice calm.

He raked his hand back through his tousled black hair. Wouldn't she just love to know what was going on in his mind? 'You'll just have to wait and see,' he declared softly.

CHAPTER EIGHT

EMMA spent a long, sleepless night—wondering how she could have been so stupid as to let herself be seduced by Vincenzo and lay herself open to all kinds of misinterpretation. She *knew* what his whole crazy, Sicilian attitude towards women was like. He would have considered her to have behaved wantonly—hadn't that much been obvious in the icy way he had looked at her? From the way he had dropped his hands from her body as if he had been holding something dirty and contaminated?

He clearly felt nothing but contempt for her, and if she continued to behave in a way which would only increase that view, then she was just weakening her own position.

Because she should never for a moment forget who she was up against; a man who represented the full might of one of the richest and most powerful families in Sicily. She had seen the light of battle flare in his black eyes—and Emma wasn't stupid. She had something which Vincenzo had yearned for all his adult life—his son and heir—and if they were no longer together as man and wife, then wouldn't he go all out to try to win custody?

As the pale light of dawn crept through the curtains she pulled the duvet close round her shivering body wondering how she could ever have been so naïve not to have anticipated this. Had she thought when she first went to him that Vincenzo might behave like a civilised human being—when he had never behaved with a shred of civility in his life? Because everything was black and white in Vincenzo's world. Women were sluts or they were virgins. Mistresses or wives. And she was never going to be able to change that.

So what would he do next?

As she climbed wearily from her bed, she tried to put herself in the mindset of her estranged husband. Would he try to prove her as an unfit mother? Would he attempt to use against her the very thing that she had gone to him for help with?

Pulling on a pair of old jeans and the thickest sweater she could find, Emma washed her face and hands and then went into the kitchen to make herself a cup of coffee before Gino awoke.

He slept later than usual. Which was absolutely typical, she thought. The one time she could have had a bit of a lie-in and here she was—prowling around the cottage, her nerves stretched tight as an elastic band, unable to settle to anything until at last Gino woke and she was able to hug his warm little body close to her.

She was mashing up some banana for his breakfast when the doorbell rang and she suddenly realised that she hadn't even brushed her hair properly. Still, at least Vincenzo wouldn't think that she was going on an all-out effort to…to… Emma frowned. How had he put it? To use her *pale sorcery*. But that was the trouble with Vincenzo—even when he was insulting you, he put it in such a way that it made you want to melt when you thought about it afterwards.

So don't *think about it*, she told herself fiercely as she pulled open the door, her defensive expression dying when she saw it was Andrew standing there, a bowl of eggs in his hand and a rather rueful expression on his face.

'Morning, Emma,' he said gruffly, holding the bowl out. 'I've brought you these. One of the farmers sent them over and I thought you might like them.'

Emma blinked. 'Oh. Well, thanks, Andrew—how lovely. We'll have them for tea.'

He was looking rather pink about the ears. 'Er, is it all right if I come in for a minute?'

Surreptitiously, Emma glanced at her watch. It was still before nine—Vincenzo was unlikely to turn up this early. And even if he did, she was separated from him, wasn't she? She happened to have a *life*—and that life didn't include him or his old-fashioned view on how she should live it.

'Of course,' she said brightly. 'I'm just about to feed Gino—do you want to put the kettle on and we can have a cuppa?'

He filled the kettle up and then turned to her, shifting from one foot to the other as if he were standing on something hot. 'It's just that I feel bad about announcing a rent increase when I know you can't really afford it. So why don't we forget we ever had that conversation?'

Emma blinked. 'Forget it?'

'Sure. After all,' he continued, with a shrug, 'you're a good tenant—and the place is pretty ropey, really. You can carry on as you were, Emma—I shan't mind.'

Emma turned her grimace into a smile as she poured out two steaming mugs full of tea and handed him one and then sat down to start feeding Gino. If only he had told her this before—then she needn't have ever gone to Vincenzo, cap in hand and asking for some kind of divorce settlement.

But that wasn't really true, was it? She had needed to speak to Vincenzo some time and maybe the rent increase had just brought matters to a head. She couldn't keep running away from him all her life, burying her head in the sand and avoiding the inevitable—because it had been inevitable that Gino would one day meet his father.

But at least Andrew's words had taken the sting and the urgency out of her situation. Removed that terrible, tearing feeling of panic.

'That's very sweet of you, Andrew—and I appreciate it.'

'No. Don't mention it,' he said gruffly, stirring his tea for a moment before looking up, his eyes curious. 'One of the groundsmen said there was a big car here last night.'

Emma's paused, the banana midway to Gino's mouth, before he grabbed for the spoon himself. 'Is there something written into my tenancy agreement which forbids that?' she questioned lightly as she helped him spoon it in.

'Of course not. It's just that you don't often have visitors, and I—' His head jerked up.

Gino's squawk from the high chair meant that Emma hadn't heard the knock at the door until it was repeated loudly—and so she barely noticed that Gino was shoving a fistful of pureed banana into her hair.

'There's someone at the door,' said Andrew unnecessarily.

She wanted to tell him to leave—to spirit him away, or smuggle him out of the back door, until she realised that she was thinking like a madwoman. Hadn't she vowed to be strong? *So stop acting as if you're doing something wrong.* Andrew was her landlord and he had a perfect right to be here.

She pulled the door open to find Vincenzo standing there and her heart leapt in her chest. For this was a casual Vincenzo—a different creature entirely from the office billionaire who had seduced her so effectively yesterday. Today he was dressed in dark jeans and a dark jacket. An outwardly relaxed Vincenzo—and somehow all the more dangerous for that. Like a snake asleep in the sun who, when disturbed, would lift its head and stare at you with its deadly and unblinking eyes.

'Good morning,' she said, thinking that the very greeting was a complete fabrication—because what was good about this particular morning?

He didn't acknowledge the welcome—his gaze instead flicking over her shoulder to survey the scene behind her. The baby sitting in a high chair, surrounded by mess—his attention caught by the noise at the door—and he was staring directly at Vincenzo, his dark brown eyes huge in his face.

Vincenzo felt a hot, almost painful curve around his heart as he stared back at the little boy with the same fascinated interest. But he was inhibited from doing what he really wanted, which was to walk straight over there and to pluck him out of the high chair, because there was a man—yes, a *man*—sitting in Emma's kitchen with his feet underneath her table and drinking a cup of tea. What was more, he had not risen to his feet as one of Vincenzo's employees would have done.

'And who the hell are you?' he demanded icily.

'I *beg* your pardon?' said Andrew.

'You heard me. Who are you and what are you doing here, in my wife's kitchen?'

'Your *wife*?' Andrew jumped to his feet and turned to Emma—his expression one of dismay and accusation. 'But you told me your husband wasn't on the scene any more!'

'Oh, did she?' came the dark, silky question from the other side of the room.

This was like a bad dream, thought Emma. She swallowed. 'I think perhaps it's best if you go now, Andrew.'

Andrew frowned. 'You're sure you'll be okay?'

It was sweet of him to have asked—but, with a slight

feeling of hysteria, Emma wondered what solution her landlord was about to offer to help get her out of this situation. Throw the simmering Sicilian off the premises perhaps—when he looked like some dark and immovable force? She managed a smile. 'I'll be fine,' she said reassuringly.

An awkward kind of silence descended while Andrew let himself out of the front door and the moment it had closed behind him Vincenzo turned to her, his face a study in repressed fury.

'You have been sleeping with him?' he demanded in a low voice, aware that there was a child in the room.

Angrily, she flushed. 'What do you think?'

'I think that he does not look man enough to cope with your voracious sexual appetite, *cara*—although it might explain why you were so unbelievably hot for me.' His black eyes scorched into her. 'But you haven't answered my question.'

'Of course I haven't been sleeping with him,' she breathed, hurt and indignant and shaking. But he had now turned away—as if he couldn't care less what the answer was. As if asking it had been nothing but careless sport designed to embarrass and humiliate her. And he had managed, hadn't he? Achieved just that with flying colours.

Instead, he was walking towards the high chair, where Gino was still staring up at him with the engrossed attention which an eager member of the audience might give to a stage hypnotist.

He stood looking down at him for one long, immeasurable moment while his heart struck out a hard and heavy beat. *'Mio figlio,'* he said eventually in a voice which was distorted with pain and joy. 'My son.'

Inwardly, Emma flinched at the raw possession in his voice even as she marvelled that Gino—*her* son—was not backing away from Vincenzo, the way he usually did with strangers.

But Vincenzo is not a stranger, is he? He is as close a blood relative as you are. And maybe Gino recognises that on some subliminal level.

'Vene,' Vincenzo was saying softly, holding out his hands. 'Come.'

To Emma's astonishment, the baby blinked and played coy a couple of times—leaning back against the plastic chair and turning his head from this way to that as he fixed Vincenzo with a sideways glance. But Vincenzo didn't push him, just continued to murmur to him in the soft, distinctive Sicilian accent until at last Gino wriggled a little and allowed Vincenzo to scoop him out of the high chair and into his arms.

Gino was letting someone he'd only just met pick him up and cuddle him! Emma's world swayed. She felt sick, faint and, yes...*jealous*. That Vincenzo should so effortlessly win the affection of everyone he wanted. 'He...he needs a wash,' she said shakily, blinking her eyes furiously against the sudden prick of tears, barely able to believe what she was witnessing.

There was a pause as Vincenzo flicked his gaze over her. At her matted hair and pale face—broken only by two spots of colour at the centre of her cheeks. At the faded jeans and bare feet—worn with a bulky sweater, which so cleverly concealed the petite curves which lay beneath.

He did not know of another woman who would dare to appear before him in such a careless state, and when he looked at her objectively, it was hard to believe that she was his wife. And yet those big blue eyes still had the power to kick savagely at his groin. To twist him up inside. 'And so do you, by the look of it,' he bit out.

Knowing that she was about to cry, Emma fled into the bathroom—locking the door behind her—and turning on the shower to drown the muffled sound of her shuddered breathing. She let the water cascade down onto her face to mingle with her tears as her troubled thoughts spun round like a washing machine. What had she done? What had she *done*? Opened the floodgates to Vincenzo's involvement—not just in her life, but in the life of Gino, too. And he had come rushing in with a great dark swamp of power and possession.

At least there was enough water in the antiquated tank for it to be piping hot—and as she washed the banana out of her hair it struck her that for once she was not running against the clock. She normally showered while Gino was sleeping, and often the water was tepid.

Of course, in her distress she hadn't brought a change of clothes in with her. So she wrapped herself in the biggest bath towel and wound a smaller one around her damp hair and self-consciously walked back through to reach her bedroom, steeling herself to see Vincenzo in her sitting room. But he hadn't even noticed her come in. He had other, far more important things on his mind.

Still carrying Gino, he was walking around the small room, stopping to peer at small objects—a photo of her mother here, a little clock she'd inherited there. And all the while he was speaking softly to Gino in Sicilian, and, directly afterwards, in English. And Gino was listening, fascinated—occasionally lifting his chubby little finger to touch the dark, rasping shadow of his father's jaw.

He's teaching him Sicilian, Emma realised, acknowledging the sudden bolt of fear which shot through her. But standing wrapped in a towel was no way to remonstrate with him, even if remonstration was an option—which she guessed it wasn't, not really.

Black eyes looked up over the silky tangle of Gino's head and met hers and he found anger vying with desire. But there was a child in his arms, a child who would be confused and frightened by any display of anger, and so Vincenzo forced himself to ask her a cool question. 'Good shower?'

'Lovely, thank you.'

He held her gaze as he let desire in. 'I can imagine,' he said softly, eyes now drifting to the soft swell of her breasts visibly curving beneath the thin material of cheap towel.

Now she was shivering with more than cold and Emma turned her back on him, hating the mixed messages he was sending out to her and the way they were making her feel. It was as if he wanted to weaken her in every way he could—first, by being proprietorial with Gino and then by that unspoken, sensual scrutiny. She felt in a complete muddle—as if the Emma of yesterday had disappeared and now a stranger had taken her place.

She dressed quickly, choosing a pair of clean jeans and a different sweater; her normal, daily, practical and presentable uniform, which never in a million years could be described as flattering. But Emma was glad. She was unwilling to 'dress up'—to look as if she might be trying to make an impression on him. Or have him accuse her of playing the temptress again.

Only when she'd brushed her hair and given it a quick blast of the dryer did she take in a deep breath and go back into the sitting room, where Vincenzo was now standing with his back to her, holding Gino and looking out down the garden at the spreading chestnut tree, as she herself had done a million times before.

Gino heard her first, for he turned in his father's arms and then gave a little squawk and began to wriggle towards her and Emma held out her arms and took her son, burying her face in his curls to hide the great rush of unknown emotion which was threatening to swamp her.

His arms empty without the baby's warm weight, Vincenzo walked back towards the window, his heart beating very loud and very strong, more shaken than he had anticipated. And when he turned to look at Emma, to look at her cradling the child in what he considered to be a completely over-the-top way, his mouth hardened.

She glanced up, trying to read his expression but failing as she encountered a stony black gaze which gave absolutely nothing away. But why should that surprise her? Apart from those first few, heady months—

when they had been rocked by the power of sexual attraction masquerading as love—she never *had* been able to tell what was going on in that head of his. He didn't ever tell her. He didn't *do* confidences, he'd once told her. As if talking about feelings made a man look weak.

'Do you have any coffee?' he questioned unexpectedly.

She felt wrong-footed. 'Probably not the kind you're used to. I keep it in the fridge,' she said, and then pointed at one of the kitchen cupboards. 'There's a cafetiere in there.'

'So you have not adopted the foul, instant-coffee habit of your countrymen,' observed Vincenzo caustically as he began to set about making a pot with the air of a man to whom the kitchen was unfamiliar territory.

Emma watched him, wondering how he did it. She knew that he had always had women waiting on him hand and foot all his life. Quite frankly, she was surprised he hadn't demanded that *she* make his coffee for him, except that even Vincenzo probably didn't dare try *that*. But how quickly he adapted, she thought reluctantly. To see him now, you would imagine that he had been making morning coffee since he was first permitted to put a flame beneath a pot.

So why couldn't he have adapted to married life so easily instead of embracing such an old-fashioned and autocratic relationship? It was as if by slipping that gold band onto her finger he had stepped back by a few decades.

Emma put Gino down onto the patchwork mat she'd

finished off in those last, tiring days of her pregnancy and put down his large cardboard box for him to play with. She had covered it with wrapping paper and filled it with washed and empty plastic containers of different sizes—some of them filled with beans and rice, which made varying sounds.

Vincenzo paused in the act of pouring out two cups of coffee, his lips curving in derision. 'Why is he playing with rubbish?' he demanded.

'It's a home-made toy,' defended Emma, standing her ground. 'He watched me make it—so it was educational. He even turns it into a drum kit by banging a wooden spoon against it! And children often appreciate a simple plaything more than an expensive one.'

'Which presumably you can't afford anyway?' he challenged.

Emma shrugged. 'Well, no.'

Vincenzo glanced around him, not bothering to hide his distaste as he sank onto one of the hard chairs around the dining table. 'Can't afford very much at all by the look of things,' he observed, and then put his cup down and his eyes lanced through her with a look of pure black ice. 'Which presumably is what brought you back to me.'

She didn't feel that now was the right time to correct him. To tell him that nothing had brought her *back to him*. That this was about the legal ending of their ill-fated marriage, and nothing to do with feelings. 'I wanted the best for Gino,' she said in a low voice.

'Did you really, Emma?' he queried silkily. 'Or did you just think you'd try to screw me for as much money as possible?' His eyes glittered. 'As well as screw me in other ways.'

Colour flared in her cheeks. 'Don't be so coarse!' she whispered, as if Gino might be able to understand his crude allusion and judge his mother to be morally corrupt. *And aren't you?* prompted the voice of her conscience. *Was it really appropriate behaviour to do what you did with your estranged husband in the Vinoly suite yesterday?*

Vincenzo shrugged and carried on as if she hadn't spoken. His tone was soft—presumably not to alarm Gino—but that did nothing to detract from the venom which underpinned it. 'If you'd really wanted the best for him, then you would have contacted me a long time ago.'

'But I tried,' she protested. 'I tried to ring you and you refused to take my call! Twice!'

'Then you didn't try hard enough, did you?' he snapped. 'Just enough to go through the motions, but with no real determination. But that probably suited you very well, didn't it, Emma, since everything seems to have been satisfying *your* needs, *cara*—and your desires?'

She stared at him, shocked by the bitterness in his voice.

'And it's *still* about your desires, isn't it?' he continued remorselessly. 'You came to me because you wanted money and wanted sex—and so far you've scored on one count.'

'I did *not* come to you for sex!'

'No?' he queried witheringly. 'Someone forced you to end up naked on the sofa with me, did they?' His eyes blazed. 'But nowhere in your schemes do you seem to have considered what the *child's* needs might be—'

'But I *did*!' Emma flared.

'Liar.' He leaned forward. 'You didn't think that it might have been a good idea to tell me about it when you discovered you were pregnant?'

'It isn't—'

'Or maybe when you went into labour, that I might like to have known?' His words ruthlessly cut through her stumbled explanation. 'Or when you'd given birth—that as the father I had an inalienable and un-questionable *right* to know about it. Didn't that occur to you, Emma?'

'We've been through all this,' she said dully. 'Even if you *had* shown me the courtesy of taking my calls, you wouldn't have believed me.'

'Not at first, perhaps,' he agreed through gritted teeth. 'But just as I'm doing now, I would eventually have come around to realising that we *had* conceived a child—even if it did happen to be in the most unfortunate circumstances possible.'

Emma flinched, feeling for Gino. 'Please don't talk about it in that way.'

'But it is true, *cara*.' His eyes mocked her. 'For surely even you would not deny that the circumstances surrounding his conception were regrettable?'

Regrettable. What a cruel yet emotionless word to use. What if she told him that her heart had been in bits that last day in Rome? That she had been aching and empty and longing for that sweet time to return, when all they had wanted or needed was love. That when he had pulled her into his arms as she'd been about to walk out of his life for good, she had been blown away by a passion which had seemed to mimic that time.

No, if she told him any of that, he would simply accuse her of lying again. Because, from the shuttered look of anger on his autocratic face, Emma could see that he had already made his mind up about her.

She couldn't help shivering as she put her coffee cup down on the table and stared at him, wondering what he was intending to do with his newly acquired knowledge.

'So...so what is going to happen now?' she questioned faintly. 'I'm assuming that you're going to want regular...access?'

He gave a short, disbelieving laugh. 'What do you think?'

She bit her lip. 'I don't know,' she whispered, but, knowing Vincenzo as she did, he was going to want to take it right to the limit. Would he want holidays in Sicily for Gino? she wondered painfully. An entrée into that harsh and beautiful world which would gradually exclude his pale English mother? She was going to have to be mature about this. To deal with it in a calm and reflective way and then maybe Vincenzo would respond in the same way.

'How best...how best do you think we should we go about it?' she asked as politely as if she were asking a stranger the time of day.

Vincenzo had spent the last twelve hours thinking of nothing else. There was only one solution and it was one that he had felt with a powerful and bone-deep certainty.

'You will return with me to Sicily,' he said flatly, his voice as dark as his face.

'You must be out of your mind,' she breathed, 'if you really think I'd go anywhere near Sicily again.'

Vincenzo's lips curved into a cruel smile. Oh, but she was playing right into his hands! 'Then do not come,' he said softly. 'But in that case I shall take Gino myself.'

'T-take Gino?' Emma's heart was beating so fast and so loudly that she could barely hear her own reply. 'You seriously think I'd let you take my son out of the country without me?'

'*Our* son. Who has a history which will not be denied him. I intend on taking him to Sicily, Emma—and trying to stop me will seriously backfire against you in the long run.' He rose to his feet, moving as silently as a jungle cat to stand directly in front of her. 'I already have a team of lawyers working on the case, and let me tell you that they were singularly unimpressed by your efforts to conceal my son from me.'

He steeled his heart against the sudden blanching of her cheeks. Damn her—and her penchant for acting vulnerable whenever she thought it might help her case. His eyes gleamed. 'The more reasonable your behaviour now, then the more sympathetic I am likely to be towards you in the future.'

Emma swallowed. 'Are you…*threatening* me, Vincenzo?'

'Not at all. I'm simply advising you to be amenable—'

'You *are* threatening me—I knew you would! You haven't changed a bit! No wonder I—'

But her words were halted by the soft dig of Vincenzo's fingers into her arms as he hauled her to her feet, and his face swam in and out of her line of vision. 'The past is just that. Past,' he said flatly. 'It is the present which concerns me now and my son *is* the present, as well as the future. I am taking him with me and if you intend to accompany us, then you will play the part of my wife.'

She stared up at him. It was as if she had slipped and were falling deeper and deeper into a dark hole of Vincenzo's making. 'Your *wife*?'

Ebony eyes burned into her. 'Why not? It makes perfect sense.' He saw the look of confusion darkening her blue eyes and felt the flicker of a pulse at his temple. 'Let's just say that it will ease the tension of an already difficult situation,' he continued. 'We might as well enjoy what pleasures we can while we have the opportunity to do so.'

Emma felt weak. He sounded so cold-blooded—as if pleasure were nothing more than the by-product of a bodily function. 'You can't mean that.'

'Oh, but I can,' he promised, with grim satisfaction. 'And I think you could usefully lose the outraged attitude, don't you? In view of your response to me, you're in danger of looking a little like a hypocrite.'

'Vincenzo—'

'No. No more arguments, not any more. You've

played according to your rules for long enough, Emma, and now it is time to play to some of mine.' His voice hardened. 'So pack the essentials and do it now, for we are going to London.'

Emma could tell from the obdurate look on his face and the flat tone of his voice that resistance would be futile. How could she possibly resist the powerhouse which was Vincenzo Cardini? But she had to try. 'Can't Gino and I wait here until we're ready to go?'

'And have you trying to run away from me?' His mouth curved into a sardonic representation of a smile as he ran a questing fingertip lightly over the sudden tremble of her lips. 'I think not. Do you have a passport?'

Dumbly, she nodded.

'Does Gino?'

'No.'

'Then I shall need to arrange that. And, besides, you both need a new wardrobe. If I am taking you back to Sicily, then my son will look like a Cardini and not some little pauper. While you…' his eyes glittered with a look which simultaneously appalled and yet thrilled her '…you will dress to please me. As a wife should dress.'

CHAPTER NINE

EMMA stared round the vast salon of the Vinoly suite in disbelief.

There were clothes everywhere.

Clothes which looked exactly her size and precisely the colours that suited her. Beautiful clothes. Dresses and skirts. Spindly-heeled shoes. Bras and panties. All in the finest and most costly materials—silks and linens and pure, soft cashmere.

'Where on earth did these come from?' she asked in a low voice, wondering where he proposed she wear those outrageous shoes in a country like Sicily.

Vincenzo's black eyes hardened. 'I chose them—or, rather, I briefed someone with my specifications of what you would require for your trip to Sicily. I told you, Emma—you cannot and will not appear before my family dressed as a tramp.'

'But I've lost weight,' she whispered. 'A lot of weight. How on earth could you know what size I'd be?'

His slow smile belied his slightly incredulous expression that she should have asked such a guileless question. 'I guessed—or, rather, I assessed. Don't forget you were naked in my arms not so long ago.' Carelessly, he plucked a blue silk dress from the hanger and held it towards her. 'Here. Go and put this one on. I think you should dress for dinner, don't you?'

Emma found her fingers curling around the soft material, fighting the temptation to dress up, as he wanted her to. Part of her loved the clothes—what woman wouldn't, when she had worn cheap and second-hand stuff for so long? But his manner was alienating her and she had to accept that maybe his attitude was intentional. Determined that she should accept his generosity while drumming into her that she should never forget it was charity—and that everything in life always came at a price.

But did she really have a sensible alternative when Vincenzo's words had the harsh ring of truth about them? If she turned up in Sicily looking like a tramp as Vincenzo himself had so sweetly put it, she would win the sympathy of no one in a country where appearance was everything. Could she really face his family's critical gaze if she stubbornly insisted on wearing the few clothes she had flung into a suitcase before their hurried exit from the cottage earlier?

Especially as Gino had already been kitted out as befitted the son of a billionaire.

On the drive back from the cottage they had stopped off at one of London's biggest department stores and Vincenzo had gone through it like a minesweeper. The finest clothes? Bought. The toughest yet most luxurious buggy? It was theirs. Cashmere blankets for the baby? Done.

She stared through into the bedroom at the beautiful cot which had been awaiting them on their return and where her beloved little boy now slept as soundly as a pampered prince and her heart turned over with guilt.

The Vinoly staff had been summoned to provide tea for the baby and afterwards he had squealed with delight as Vincenzo produced toy after expensive toy from a box, the like of which Gino had never seen. And although back at the cottage she had protested that babies were just as happy with a wooden spoon banging on the side of an old saucepan, now she could see that this was not quite true.

Even bath-time had been upmarket—his battered yellow duck forgotten in the face of the sleek little boat which bobbed over the fragrant surface of the water. Afterwards, Gino had been so exhausted that he had fallen asleep in Vincenzo's arms and a lump had risen in Emma's throat as she had watched him tenderly lay the child down in his cot.

On the one hand it was wonderful to see her baby enjoying the kind of comfort which every mother wanted for her child. To stare at Gino dressed in a cute and cosy sleep suit instead of layered up in the cheap vests and thin towelling which were his normal garb.

But even as she revelled in his obvious comfort, disturbing thoughts kept hitting her like a hammer-blow, wondering how she could possibly have denied him what was rightfully his for so long.

Her fingertips tightened around the soft blue silk dress. Wouldn't a refusal to wear it leave her looking like the hired help? 'Okay. I'll go and get changed,' she said.

'And dump those jeans while you're at it,' he suggested caustically. 'I don't ever want to see them again.'

His words stinging in her ears, Emma went into the bathroom and began to slither into her new clothes, feeling slightly awkward as the delicate lingerie came into contact with her skin and all her newly awoken senses.

She stared at herself in the mirror and it was like looking at a stranger. How long had it been since she'd treated herself to brand-new underwear and worn a decent bra which actually supported her? Or had matching lace-trimmed panties which made her feel both shy and yet decadent all at the same time?

The jeans which Vincenzo so despised lay in a crumpled heap on the bathroom floor and a last lingering flare of rebellion made Emma want to snatch them up and put them back on, along with her tatty old sweater. Behind their comforting bulk she felt safe from Vincenzo's sensual scrutiny—and you could hide behind such nondescript garments. But what was the point of adding fuel to the formidable fire of a man already angry enough?

Instead, she pulled the sleeved dress over her head and afterwards brushed her long hair so that it fell down in two shining blonde wings over her shoulders. The silk felt butter soft and hung in rich folds over her thighs and the colour brought out the blue of her eyes. This was how the wife of a rich man should dress, she realised.

The way she always *used* to dress in those final empty days of their marriage—when she would be shown off like some pretty accessory in public, while at home the tensions between them grew and grew.

At least this time she was under no illusions that Vincenzo loved her—and surely that should enable her to adopt some kind of strategy for how to deal with him, and, more importantly, how to keep her emotions in check. Because there would be nothing but danger and trouble ahead for her and Gino if she allowed herself to fall under Vincenzo's charismatic spell once more.

She would play the part required of her while they negotiated some kind of settlement. But they would be doing it on *his* territory and a place where she had always felt like an outsider. Where she had *been* an outsider. She needed him on her side, she recognised with a sinking heart—but she needed to keep her *emotional* distance from him. At least these fancy clothes might act as a kind of armour—allowing her to fit into his wealthy world, externally if nothing else.

Stepping from the bathroom, she saw that Vincenzo had gone into the bedroom to look at Gino and he was standing beside the cot, and, despite everything, Emma found her heart turning over with longing. Sometimes the past could play terrible tricks with your mind and your heart. Sometimes you could feel as if you were still in love with the man you'd married.

Had he slept with many women since they'd split up? she found herself wondering painfully. Plunged deep into their bodies as he had done to her in this very suite?

Her fingers curled into tight little fists. Well, even if he had—that was really none of her concern. His life was not her life, not any more.

Black eyes glanced up to meet hers with a mocking glance, but Emma could detect the darker emotions which lay behind it. Because she wasn't stupid. Or blind. She knew that beneath that ruggedly urbane exterior beat the heart of a primitive Sicilian man, with all the passion and possession which seemed to go along with that.

And because of that, she must tread very carefully. She needed to show him that she was a good mother. She needed to convince him that never again would she attempt to keep Gino from him. She would even eat humble pie if that was what it took to make things better between them. She wasn't going to have unrealistic expectations which could never be met—but surely they could work something out.

His eyes flicked over her from head to toe as he walked back from the bedroom looking all dark and predatory male, and Emma felt suddenly shy. Had she really lived with this man? Shared his bed every night? Now it seemed so long ago that it was like looking at another lifetime—she could barely remember it.

She attempted a smile. 'How do I look?' she said, taking the first tentative step towards a civilised relationship.

How did she look? A pulse beat at Vincenzo's temple. When she smiled like that you could almost forget that she was a lying and deceitful witch. Could almost imagine that she was that same shining blonde angel who had once captivated him. 'Come a little closer so that I can see you properly.'

Feeling a little like a slave who was being brought to stand in front of her master, Emma moved forward a little and gave another smile, more forced this time. 'How's that?'

'Mmm.' He studied her with the objective assessment of a man buying a new car. 'Well, you look a hundred times better than you did ten minutes ago,' he conceded softly. 'I would of course prefer it if you were wearing nothing at all, but it might throw up something of a distraction during dinner. Never mind, there will be plenty of time for that once we've eaten.'

Emma flushed. What a *hateful* way of putting it. As if she were to be served up to him like an after-dinner mint! 'I agreed to accompany you to Sicily,' she said, her voice shaking. 'I don't remember agreeing to anything else.'

'Oh, come on, Emma,' he taunted. 'Let's not pretend any more—what's the point? We've already had a taste of the forbidden and all it has done is awaken our appetite for more. You want me just as much as I want you. I can see it in your eyes, in the way your breasts peak when I look at them, in the way your body reacts to mine even though you're trying your best not to let it show. So why not capitalise on that?'

His words mocked her but that didn't seem to diminish the effect they were having on her. He was right, damn him. Emma suddenly felt as if she were on

fire as he pulled her into his arms. She wanted to tell
him that she was more than just a responsive body, that
she was a woman with feelings and a heart which had
been broken once and which she didn't think could bear
being broken again. 'But you said…'

'Mmm? What did I say?' he murmured as he pulled
her even closer and began to drift his lips along the
curve of her jaw.

'I…' His caress was too intoxicating. Emma couldn't
remember. Now his hands were on her breasts, playing
with them through the expensive silk of her dress, and
she felt their arousal pinpoint so exquisitely that it felt
almost like pain. 'Vincenzo,' she whispered.

'You like that, don't you?'

'Yes!' The word was torn from her lips as if she had
lost control of her speech. Again, it was as if he had cast
some powerful spell over her. All she could hear was
the thunder of her heart and all she could feel was the
soft, insistent aching of desire.

'Ah, Emma,' he said softly as his hand skimmed the
slippery surface of her silk-covered bottom. 'How
quickly you turn on.'

Only for you, she thought. *Only for you.* Emma
closed her eyes. One second more and it would be too
late and he would peel off the dress that she had only
just put on. Once more she would become a compliant
sex-object, further weakening her bargaining power
with a man who used women as puppets and playthings.
And Gino had only just gone to sleep! With an effort,
Emma pulled away from him, realising with a sudden

pang that he hadn't even kissed her. 'Don't,' she whispered.

His eyes narrowed. 'I thought we'd agreed to skip the game-playing.'

'This isn't a game, Vincenzo. Gino's next door, in case you'd forgotten.'

'I am hardly like to forget, am I?' he questioned bitterly.

Abruptly he dropped his hands and moved away from her as he fought the primitive urge to just push her to the ground and take her there and then. And yet, unexpectedly, he found himself surveying her with an element of approval. For wouldn't he have despised her if her cries of pleasure had woken up their baby son? If she had sought her own gratification at the expense of her son then wouldn't she have diminished her worth as a woman, as well as a mother?

'You ought to eat something,' he said suddenly. 'No wonder you're so damned thin—you've barely touched a thing all day. Let's go down for dinner. The hotel is happy to provide us with a trained nanny to babysit while we eat.'

She shook her head. 'I'd rather not leave him, if you don't mind. He might wake up and get scared and it's a brand-new environment and I'd hate him to cry for me and me not be here and I…' Her words ran out along with her breath and she stared up into his impassive face, giving a small shrug of her shoulders. 'I expect you think that sounds ridiculous?'

His eyes narrowed as he hardened his heart to the wide appeal in her blue eyes. 'Actually, I think it sounds admirable—and just the thing to impress the divorce lawyer. Top marks for diligence, Emma.'

'You honestly think…' Emma stared at him '…that's the reason I'm doing it—to earn some kind of Brownie points from a lawyer?'

Vincenzo tried to ignore the wounded look which had clouded those amazing eyes. How dared she look like some innocent young animal who had been unexpectedly felled by an arrow when she had been shallow enough to abandon her marriage at the first opportunity and then to keep his son hidden from him?

And yet Vincenzo had seen the evidence of his own eyes, which had forced him to contradict some of his earlier judgements. She might have brought the child up in relative poverty and she might dress like a pauper herself, but he could see for himself that Gino had been well cared for. He seemed to be a very contented baby and all the money in the world couldn't buy that.

'No,' he conceded heavily. 'I accept that you look after the child well.'

The compliment threw her. It was a capitulation she had not anticipated and Emma blinked, thinking that the unexpected consideration was almost more painful than the insults he had hurled her way. Because thoughtfulness was too close to kindness and it hinted at times past, when she had been at the centre of his universe. She wanted to grip his arms and to demand to know what had happened to that time and all those feelings, but she knew deep down that it would be a complete waste of time.

'In that case, why don't you order something from room service?' He flicked her a brief, hard smile before heading off towards the master bedroom. 'While I go and take a shower.'

Emma walked over to the giant desk, glad to have something to distract her from the thought of Vincenzo stripping off naked in the next room—though the menu slightly threw her, too.

How quickly she had forgotten what it was like to live the life of a rich woman. It seemed bizarre that a single dish on this fancy list cost more than her entire food budget for a week. On a normal day the idea that she could have carte blanche to select anything that took her fancy would have filled her with excitement, but this was not a normal day—not by any stretch of the imagination.

She ordered steak and chips, fresh fruit for pudding and half a bottle of red wine, and when the two waiters arrived with the trolley, Vincenzo was just emerging from the bedroom, dressed in dark trousers and a silk shirt. Tiny droplets of water, which glittered silver in the dark hair, gave off an air of intimacy. Why, to an outsider's eyes they must look like the perfect married couple, she thought wryly

They sat down in silence as silver domes were whipped from meals and the wine opened with flamboyant flourish.

Eventually, the waiters left and when the door had closed behind them Vincenzo frowned as she stared blankly at her plate. 'Just eat something, will you,

Emma?' he said impatiently. 'And stop sitting there looking so damned fragile.'

Quickly, she picked up a chip and ate it and the hot salty taste must have awakened her neglected taste buds because she began to eat with genuine hunger, finishing off half her steak before she noticed that Vincenzo was sitting staring at her with a mocking expression on his face, his own meal untouched.

'Better?' he queried sardonically.

'Much better,' she agreed lightly. But even though the food had restored some of her strength, the thoughts which swirled around in her head continued to make her feel uneasy. How strange and yet how familiar it felt to be sitting eating a meal with him like this again. And what on earth was it going to be like returning to Sicily, to the place where she'd first fallen in love with him?

But in a way it was easier to push the questions aside than to seek answers. To revel in this uneasy peace, however brief it might be. To pretend that they really *were* a happily married couple. With, of course, one notable exception. Because if she wanted to keep her heart safe, then she needed to keep her physical distance.

Ostentatiously, she yawned. At least there were lots of bedrooms in this luxurious suite and the beds were bound to be like welcoming havens where she could pull the duvet over her head and blot out the world for the night. 'I think I'll hit the sack,' she said. 'It's been a long day.'

Vincenzo smiled. At times she could be so utterly transparent. 'My very thoughts, *cara*,' he said softly. 'I can think of nothing better than an early night.'

'But…you've hardly eaten anything.'

'I'm not hungry. Well, at least…not for food. Only for you.' He took a slow swallow of red wine and put the glass down before rising to his feet and coming round the table towards her.

Emma's heart was beating fit to burst. 'I'm not going to go to bed with you.'

Softly, he laughed. 'Oh, yes, you damned well are.' He pulled her to her feet as if she were composed of nothing more than feathers and then tipped her face up towards him so that it was fully open to the blazing intensity of his gaze. 'We are going to share a bed as would any married couple if they were here tonight— and you'd better get used to it, Emma, because that's exactly what we shall be doing once we reach Sicily.'

'To save face?' she challenged, and as she saw his face darken she knew that she'd hit on a raw nerve.

'Perhaps there is something in that,' he conceded, in a rare moment of self-scrutiny, but then his mouth curved. 'But mainly because you always did give me the best sex I've ever had, and that much hasn't changed.'

Somehow he managed to make even *that* sound like an insult. 'And if I refuse?'

'You wouldn't dare refuse, even if you wanted to— or had the power to resist me,' he said softly. 'You have far too much to lose.'

Wildly, she shook her blonde head. 'That's sexual blackmail!' she protested.

'On the contrary, Emma,' he demurred as he brought her closer to his hard heat and saw her eyes widen in darkened disbelief and desire. 'I am simply allowing you the opportunity to act like this is nothing to do with you. That this…' and he felt her convulsive tremble as he trickled a fingertip across one very aroused nipple '…is not what you want me to do. I am happy to do that, *cara*, if it helps square it in what passes for your conscience. More than happy.'

And without further ado, he bent and lifted her into his arms, carrying her into the master bedroom, where he peeled from her body the brand-new blue silk dress which she had put on only a couple of hours before.

CHAPTER TEN

'LOOK, Gino, look! Imprint this moment upon your memory for ever, *mio figlio*—for this is the land of your father.'

Vincenzo's voice drifted on the clear air and Emma watched him carrying his son down the steps of the private aircraft, holding him carefully aloft as if he were in possession of a precious trophy. And despite powerful words which she suspected were intended to exclude her, she felt the tug of conflicting emotions at being back on the island she had always loved.

The first time she'd seen Sicily, she had thought it a paradise and one of which its people were passionately and rightly proud. But Vincenzo had been based at the Roman headquarters of the Cardini Corporation and that was where they had been based after their marriage. Yet they had always come here on high days and holidays and so she had seen the land in all its many guises. And the one thing Emma had learnt was that Sicily was a land with many different faces.

Along the coastline glittered lemon and orange orchards, which contrasted so beautifully with the dark green forests of the north-east. At the island's centre was land and rolling hills, with almond trees and olive groves and endless fields of wheat. And during the springtime the wild flowers made a bright rainbow of colours against the bright green of the fields.

The Cardini family had properties dotted everywhere—including a winter ski-lodge, where once she had squealed with excitement to see palm trees dusted with snow.

It was cold now, but the sky was bright blue and the sun was shining and Emma pulled her pashmina a little closer as she saw a car waiting for them on the airstrip.

'Is there a car seat for Gino?' she asked.

Black eyes met hers over the top of Gino's hooded little head. 'Of course there is. I have instructed that every preparation should be made for his arrival.'

He watched as she put the baby in the car seat and familiarised herself with the straps, his thoughts for once not focussed on her bottom or her duplicity, but on the dramatic change she and the baby had brought to his life. He had started to realise that with children around, you could operate on two completely different levels. There were all the mechanics of looking after a baby and the small talk which surrounded that—talk which usually bore no resemblance to the thoughts which were teeming around his head.

As he slid onto the back seat Gino made an affectionate lunge at him and Vincenzo's mouth automatically softened into a smile. It was impossible for your

heart not to lift in the presence of such an enchanting
baby, he thought—and it brought home to him how
much he had already bonded with his son.

He turned to the woman by his side, her blonde hair
tied back into a sleek pony-tail, her blue eyes huge in
her pale face. In a creamy cashmere coat, she looked expensive and pampered and scarcely recognisable as the
waif who had slunk into his office the other day.

'And how are you feeling this morning?' he questioned softly.

Emma was disorientated, that was how she was feeling. And still dazed by the speed at which things seemed
to have happened. Were still happening. Feeling dis-
placed in more ways than one, she found herself having
to fight against her own instincts. She wanted to reach
out to touch Vincenzo's lips, as if to reassure herself that
they were the same lips which had grazed over every
inch of her body last night at the hotel. Which had whispered to her in soft and sometimes harsh Sicilian words.
Which had bitten out a wild cry during his climax so that
just for a moment she had felt close to him once more.
But it seemed that once the sun had come up, they had
became formal strangers again, united only by the child.
Reminding her that this was nothing more than an arrangement with a very uncertain outcome.

*So stop burying your head in the sand, Emma. Start
confronting reality instead of lapsing into the temporary
magic of his lovemaking.* 'Vincenzo, we need to talk.'

'So talk.'

'We need to discuss what's going to happen once

Gino has met your family,' she said, and paused. 'About what we are going to do next.'

He turned to look at her, at the wary look which had clouded her blue eyes. What did she expect him to say in the circumstances? 'Now is not the time, Emma. I haven't decided yet.'

Emma shook her head in frustration. That was Vincenzo all over. That autocratic way he had of just closing off channels of communication and expecting her to go along with it. Well, maybe once she would have done, but not any more. 'But it isn't just *your* decision to make, is it?' she questioned softly. 'I have just as much say in the future as you do.'

Black eyes studied her. 'And how do you see that future?'

For a moment his voice sounded almost *reasonable*. Didn't she dare risk telling him the truth? Was there some corner of his hard heart which might listen to reason? 'I don't know,' she admitted in a strangled voice. 'I mean—I know you're going to want to see Gino and I'm not really in any position to try to stop you—'

'No, you aren't,' he interrupted softly. 'Even though you've done your level best to try.'

The look in his eyes was intimidating but hadn't she vowed that she wasn't going to let him do that any more? 'I just can't bear the thought that he'll spend time away from me. The thought that he'll grow up and I'll miss something. A word. A smile. A step. Or the fact that he might have a nightmare and call out for me.' Her mouth crumpled with pain. 'And I won't be there,' she said hoarsely.

He leaned forward then, his face savage, and it was as if the man who had brought her such sweet pleasure during the night had been vanquished by this suddenly threatening version of him.

'You don't think it's the same for me?' he ground out. 'You don't think that it might tear me apart to have to let him go now that I have found him at last?'

She wanted to say, *But I'm his mother!* Yet even in her turmoil she knew that this was the wrong thing to say, and not just because Vincenzo would shoot her down in verbal flames. But because she recognised with unwavering certainty that already he would lay down his life for his son.

Once he had declared his love for her with similar passion, but with a man and a woman it was completely different. You loved your child unconditionally but adult love could wither and die.

And suddenly a wave of regret washed over her and she found herself wishing for the impossible. That he still loved her and that they could make it work. 'Don't let's fight,' she whispered. 'Gino doesn't like it.'

Their eyes met for one long moment of silent battle before Vincenzo tore his eyes away from her lips and the urgent desire to kiss them. Instead, he turned his head to look outside the window, at the familiar landscape leading towards the lush countryside where the Cardini family had been making wines and manufacturing oils for over a century.

As always, the sight of his beloved island set his senses on fire, but today he felt as if they were ablaze and so hot that they were heating his blood to boiling point. It was fatherhood, it was coming home—it was both those things, but it was Emma, too, he realised bitterly. Despite the amazing discovery and distraction of fatherhood, she still intoxicated him like no other. Just as she always had.

And yet their affair should never have come to anything. Time and time again he had told himself that. She should have been just another English girl he'd had a fling with, which should never have lasted beyond the time of her holiday.

Her effect on him had perplexed and captivated him during their strange and fragmented courtship. For the first time in his life Vincenzo had found himself at the mercy of feelings he could not trust and, in the end, his judgement proved to have been flawed. For Emma had been a perfect mistress but a terrible wife. And now? Now she fell into the strange netherworld of being neither.

'At least tell me a little bit about where we're going to be staying?' Emma was asking, her soft voice breaking into his reverie. 'At the vineyard, I suppose?'

Vincenzo shook his head, forcing his mind back to practicalities. 'No, I don't stay there any more. Last year I bought a property a little distance away.'

She didn't realise she had been holding in her breath until it came out in a little hiss of relief. 'Oh.'

'You are pleased?'

Emma shrugged. The situation was difficult enough without an audience watching and analysing their every move. And what a critical audience it was. The Cardini vineyard was a massive, sprawling place with cousins dropping in and out as the fancy chose them. 'It is a bit of a relief,' she admitted. 'I've been dreading living in close proximity to all your relatives, if you must know. They never approved of me.'

'It was our marriage they may have had reservations about. It is strongly engrained in our culture that I should have married a Sicilian girl.'

'So they'll be delighted to have been proved right?'

'I don't think that anyone has ever considered the failure of a marriage any cause for celebration,' he said drily. 'Anyway, most of my cousins have been fixing up deals in North America. Even Salvatore isn't back until next week.'

Emma looked up. 'That long?'

'You sound anxious, Emma,' he murmured sardonically.

She wouldn't have cared if she'd never set eyes on any of his exacting cousins ever again—and Salvatore, the eldest, was the most exacting of all. 'I just wasn't sure…' she shrugged awkwardly '…how long we'd be staying on Sicily for.'

'Well, let me assure you that I wasn't planning on an overnight visit, *cara*,' he drawled.

Her fingers began to pluck at the pashmina around her neck, aware of Vincenzo showing his authority. 'What have you told everyone about Gino?'

'Just that I will be bringing my son to meet his family.'

She searched his face for clues. 'And how have they taken it? Didn't they ask questions?'

'They would not dare to,' he said softly. 'For that would be an intrusion. I am not seeking anyone's approval or judgement of what has happened, Emma. That is and remains private, just between the two of us.' He leaned forward and spoke rapidly to the driver as the car skirted a medieval headland, which Emma recognised as Trapani. 'Look over there, Emma,' he said. 'And you can see the Egadi Islands.'

Forgetting all the potential pitfalls which awaited her, Emma allowed her gaze to drink in a sea the colour of sapphire. 'It's gorgeous.'

'Do you remember the day we took the boat out?' he questioned, not meaning to.

'And drifted around for hours—' she began, suddenly realising where all this was leading her. Into dangerous waters, that was where.

Their eyes met. Was he recalling how he had taken her into one of the cabins and made love to her and when they'd returned to the deck the sun had been starting to go down in a blaze of fire? But then it had been about *more* than just amazing chemistry between them, a chemistry which undeniably still existed. Back then, they'd been floating along on a bubble of love and just because that bubble had burst it didn't stop it hurting when she let herself think about it.

'Tell me about your house,' she said instead, keeping the shakiness from her voice only with an effort.

An odd kind of smile edged at the corners of his lips. 'Why don't you take a look and see for yourself?' he said softly. 'It's up there.'

A house was obviously completely the wrong way to describe it because the building which swam into Emma's line of vision was in fact an old castle, complete with turrets, huge gates and a fabulous command over the surrounding countryside. The car drew nearer and she could see old stone walls and as they drove into an exquisite old courtyard dotted with palm trees and greenery, Emma swallowed. 'There's a tower,' she said, with a sense of disbelief.

'There are four of them, actually. And a chapel.'

'Mu-mu-mu-mum!' gurgled Gino.

The baby's voice stirred her into action and Emma got out of the car with knees which were curiously wobbly. Her senses shaken by the rush of beauty and the painful stir of emotion, she went round to the other door and began to lift Gino out. He made incomprehensible baby noises, his breath warm against her cheek, and her arms tightened around him. 'See where we are, darling?' she questioned shakily. 'Isn't it beautiful? It's a castle—a real, live castle!'

'Come and take a look at the view from over here,' said Vincenzo.

Trying to tell herself that she *wasn't* asleep, and that this wasn't some kind of amazing dream from which she would soon waken, Emma followed him across the worn stone and went to stare out over the view of soft green hills and the neat stripes of the vineyard. You could actually *see* the Egadi Islands on the horizon. Further along would be the amazing San Vito beach, where once she'd swum and walked in soft golden sands with Vincenzo all that time ago.

How many of the happy times she seemed to have overlooked, she realised. Had she buried them deep so that they would no longer have the power to hurt her, so deep that she had somehow forgotten that they ever existed? Maybe that was what they meant about memory being se-lective. But surely it was far safer that way than recalling the heights of happiness she had reached as a new bride. What would that do other than cause pain and regret?

Quickly, she walked to the other side of the court-yard where she could see down on a long rectangle of a swimming pool, set in an orange grove and sur-rounded by grey stone walls. And as her eyes took it all in, she heard the loud chiming of a bell in the tower.

It was, quite simply, breathtaking—and when she turned back, Emma's eyes were shining. 'Oh, Vincenzo, I'd forgotten just how beautiful it could be.'

Vincenzo surveyed her from between shuttered black lashes. And he had forgotten just how bright and blonde and beautiful *she* could be—with the same clear blue eyes and peachy skin making her look as young and as innocent as when he'd first met her.

'Come and see the inside,' he said, telling himself to ignore the softening of her features and the sparkle in her eyes. Her sudden enthusiasm had happened for a reason and he suspected he knew what that reason was. Had the contrast between the lifestyle she'd had in

England hit her hard now that she compared it with *his*? Was the enormity of what she had given up when she'd walked away only just hitting her? 'Follow me,' he clipped out.

Emma felt dazed as she followed Vincenzo through the castle. The interior was cool, with marble floors and dark beamed ceilings—and a series of rooms, each more elegant than the last. Eventually they reached the less formal of two lofty salons and standing there was a middle-aged woman dressed entirely in black, whose face seemed familiar.

'You remember Carmela?' queried Vincenzo.

The woman who had helped his grandmother rear him. Who had been kind to her when she'd returned from England as Vincenzo's bride. 'Yes, of course I do. *Buon giorno, Carmela. Come sta?*' It was worth pulling her very basic Italian out of the memory bank just to see Vincenzo's look of surprise, and the woman in black beamed with pleasure.

'Bene, bene, Signora Emma.' Speaking in a rapid stream of the Sicilian dialect, Carmela advanced towards Gino, who was eyeing her with extreme caution.

Each plump baby cheek was squeezed between Carmela's thumb and forefinger amid more exclaiming, to which Vincenzo made a murmured reply and Emma found herself smiling as she looked at him. 'What is she saying?'

'She is telling us that we have the most beautiful son in the world and I thanked her for confirming it. And she also said that her daughter, Rosalia, is coming over later. She has a boy a little older than Gino and she would be honoured to babysit for us any time.'

'I'm not leaving him with anyone he doesn't know,' said Emma quickly.

Vincenzo studied her for a moment. 'Then he will get to know them and soon,' he said, giving her an impenetrable look. 'For I intend that as many people as possible should make the acquaintance of my son and heir.'

His words were unashamedly proprietorial and a flicker of foreboding briefly unsettled her but Emma tried to banish it—telling herself that of course he made the declaration sound almost tribal, because that was the way it was here, in this fiercely proud family of his. And why *shouldn't* Vincenzo show his son off to the others? *Because it excludes me. Leaves me on the periphery, wondering where my place in all this is, and realising that I don't have one.*

But surely those were selfish thoughts, and not in her son's best interests?

'I need to change the baby,' she said.

Vincenzo nodded. She could be stubborn but at least nobody could accuse her of not being a hands-on mother. Because surely that would have been the worst-case scenario—to have an estranged wife who simply didn't care? Even some of his *married* friends in Rome had those kind of wives—ones who seemed happy to delegate all the childcare to some young slip of a thing, while the mothers were more interested in shopping and lunching and flying to Milan to attend the catwalk shows.

'Let me show you the bedrooms,' he said. 'Roberto

will have taken the luggage through by now. I thought that the suite at the far end of the castle would be best—then at least you won't have to carry Gino up and down those stairs.'

It was thoughtful of him; she couldn't deny that. The stairs *did* look precarious, all winding and steep like a mountain pass. 'And where are your sleeping quarters?' she questioned.

A smile played around the corners of his mouth. 'Please don't be naïve, Emma,' he murmured. 'As we discussed in London, we shall be sharing a bedroom, of course.'

Her heart missed a beat. 'So you can stay close to your son?'

'Yes, but also,' he whispered softly, 'to give me ample opportunity to enjoy your beautiful body.'

She felt torn between despair at his arrogance and a tearing elation at the thought of spending the night in his arms. As if she could hardly wait to claw at the oiled silk skin which sheathed his powerful and muscular physique. A time when hostilities could be forgotten, blotted out with bliss.

But sex isn't a cure-all, she reminded herself fiercely. *It's a danger and a distraction which can blind you from seeing the truth*. Yet she said nothing as she followed him through the seemingly endless maze of corridors to a sumptuous suite of rooms overlooking the lush and tropical gardens. What would be the point of raising another objection which he would simply shoot down in flames?

All their cases were already there and Emma set about unpacking Gino's, still unused to the range of luxurious new outfits and the sheer volume of choice. She changed his nappy and dressed him in a warm navy blue jump suit with the sweetest little sailor collar. And tiny sheepskin boots! Vincenzo was standing leaning against the window sill, just watching her, saying nothing.

Emma looked down at the floor doubtfully where ancient silken rugs were thrown over the stone flags. 'Will he be all right if I put him down there?' she questioned. 'Or would you like to hold him while I freshen up?'

He felt like saying sarcastically that he didn't actually need her permission to take his son, but was beginning to realise just how much she must have been tied by bringing up a baby, entirely on her own. He remembered his own childhood surrounded by Cardini cousins running in and out of his grandmother's home. There had always been a constant support mechanism for his uncles and aunts, he realised. But for Emma there had been none of that.

'What happens when he starts to crawl?' he questioned.

Emma walked into an exquisite, blue-tiled bathroom, aware that he was following her with Gino in his arms. She filled up a basin with warm water and began to wash her hands with soap which smelt of lime blossom, its suds soft and sensual as she washed away the inevitable grime of the journey.

She spoke to his reflection in the mirror. 'Crawling's when all the fun starts, apparently. He doesn't crawl yet, but the health visitor told me to get into practice so it won't come as a shock when he does.'

'You must never be able to let them out of your sight once they're mobile,' he said slowly.

'No.' Emma pulled the plug and turned round, her hands enveloped in the softest towel she had used in ages, thinking that they sounded like two rational people talking, instead of Emma and Vincenzo with their passion and their fury. 'Unless you put them in a playpen, of course.'

'You don't sound as if you approve of them.'

'Not really, no. They remind me of cages and babies aren't animals. They need the freedom to explore—but sometimes you need to keep them safe while you do something. Even if it's something like going to the bathroom.' Stupidly, she found herself blushing. Wasn't it funny that some things seemed even more intimate than sex? In the past she wouldn't have dared say such a thing to him. 'I'm sorry, I don't know why I told you that.'

But Vincenzo shook his head, filled suddenly with a strange rage—yet more against himself than at anyone else. 'Am I such a tyrant that you would not dare to speak of such things?'

Awkwardly, Emma shrugged.

'Tell me,' he demanded.

She looked into his black eyes. 'You didn't exactly encourage communication when we were married— but maybe that's best. It's the old-fashioned idea, isn't it—that a woman should be shrouded in mystique?'

He noted her use of the past tense. But she was right, wasn't she? The marriage *was* in the past.

'And I was too unsure of myself to know what to say to you,' she admitted. 'How much to confide and how much to keep inside.' She had become aware that she had somehow managed to marry one of Sicily's most eligible men and that discovery had blown some of her confidence away. She had felt too gauche and inexperienced to be able to live up to her new role. Instead of revelling in all the new pleasures and joys of married life, inside she had clammed up with fear. Maybe that was why she hadn't become pregnant.

'You were unhappy in Rome,' he said suddenly.

It sounded more an observation than a question, but he was looking at her as if he required an answer. 'Well, I was a bit lonely,' she admitted. 'Or, rather, I was isolated. I had my Italian lessons, but not a lot else. You were at work all day. And you refused to countenance the idea of me working.'

Vincenzo shook his head impatiently as she brought up the well-worn complaint. 'But you *had* no career, Emma,' he pointed out acidly. 'You had dropped out of catering school. So what would you have suggested? That I should have my wife—a *Cardini* wife—making *cupcakes*?'

His words were now edged with their familiar sarcasm and Emma looked at him with a steady gaze. Why should she think he'd suddenly become a reasonable man? Why, that would require a personality change so radical that he simply wouldn't be recognisable as Vincenzo at the end of it.

'Oh, forget it. It doesn't matter. And now if you'll excuse me—I need to feed Gino,' she said, in a flat voice.

CHAPTER ELEVEN

It was like being in limbo—that was if such a place could take you from one extreme emotion to the next, often in just a matter of hours. Emma was back in Vincenzo's arms and Vincenzo's bed and to the outside world she was once again Signora Cardini.

Except that she wasn't. Not really. Mostly, it was just an act they were putting on, where occasionally real feelings managed to struggle through the façade to make themselves known. Feelings which were mainly to do with their son and Emma clung on to that fact like a drowning woman scrabbling at a slippery rock. Their fierce love for Gino was the one genuine thing which sustained her, because the other stuff was pure, seductive danger.

How easy it would be to concentrate on the magic of her nights with Vincenzo, when she joined him in the huge bed which dominated the master bedroom of the castle. Where inhibitions had been banished. Where she slipped between crisp, cotton sheets to collide with the warm power of his naked body as he pulled her against his wild, seeking heat.

It was as if he was seeking to obliterate the memory of those last arid months in Rome, where their relationship had deteriorated to such an extent that they had become like icy strangers to each other. Now he seemed determined to take her to heights of passion which afterwards left her shaking and confused. Wondering how she could let herself be so carried away by such a proficient but ultimately emotionless demonstration of his sexual experience.

And wondering too how much she was going to miss him when she went back to England.

By day, Vincenzo showed a bemused and fascinated Gino his beloved island, while Emma reacquainted herself with a beauty she had forgotten—her pleasure tempered by the pain of remembering snapsnot moments which seemed to appear from odd corners of her mind when she was least expecting them.

A stunning view over the stunning coastline of the tiny island of Ustica, with its inky rocks and arid landscape, became merged with a memory of Vincenzo kissing her, telling her that her hair was like spun gold, only far more precious.

Why had it changed? Why did relationships change and then warp so badly that they became unrecognisable and you could never get the happiness back again? And why did you never realise the importance of tenderness, until it had gone?

But at least Gino was blossoming, settling into life

on Sicily as if he had been born to it. And maybe he
had—for that was certainly what Vincenzo seemed to
think. 'All Sicilians are tied by the heart to this island,'
he told her, in that drawlingly arrogant way of his which
broached no argument.

Some days, Carmela's daughter Rosalia brought her
own little son, Enrico, to play, and the two sturdy little
babies sat opposite each other on a large rug, alter-
nately glowering and giggling at each other.

'Think how it will be when they walk!' said Rosalia,
whose English was good.

Emma shot Vincenzo a quick glance. This wasn't a
permanent arrangement. He knew that and she knew
that—so surely he wasn't allowing everyone else to
think otherwise?

But she didn't get a chance to ask him—because
Salvatore and the rest of the Cardini cousins had unexpectedly flown in a day early and a large party was
being arranged at the vineyard so that they and the rest
of the family could meet Gino formally at last.

'What on earth am I going to wear?' questioned
Emma edgily, her nerves getting the better of her. Gino
had been sick on the white woollen baby suit she had
been saving ever since Rosalia had told her that Cardini
children always wore white for celebrations. It was the
most impractical thing she'd ever heard, thought Emma
crossly—pulling down another pristine little snow-
coloured top over his dark, silky curls.

'For a woman who looks best in nothing at all, it's a
bit of a dilemma,' Vincenzo murmured.

Emma shot him a glance, thinking how unusually satisfied he sounded. Like a lion in the jungle who had just eaten a large meal, its predatory nature quietened for a while so that you could almost be fooled into thinking it would be okay to stroke it. But, in effect, wasn't that exactly what had just happened?

Gino had spent the morning playing at Enrico's house and Vincenzo had rushed her straight back here to 'make the most of our free time, *cara*' as he had put it. This could have been translated into any language as him carrying her straight into their bedroom where he had proceeded to undress her and take her to bed. Which explained her high colour, which wouldn't seem to go away, or the fact that her heart was still pounding wildly with the memory of all the things he had done to her….

She looked up to realise that he was talking to her. 'What?'

'I said, do you want me to take over dressing Gino while you get changed?'

Emma nodded. 'Yes, please.'

She went into the dressing room and began to search through the hangers. What to wear in a situation like this was inevitably going to be a minefield, made worse by the critical presence of the chauvinistic Cardini men.

She ran her fingers along the row of clothes. Nothing too low, too short, too clingy or too revealing. And it was an afternoon/early evening party to accommodate all the young Cardini children who would be there, so it couldn't be too dressy, either.

In the end, she chose a simple cream cashmere dress,

buckled a soft leather belt around the waist and pulled on a pair of matching boots.

She walked out into the sitting room where they were waiting for her, and just for one moment Emma's heart missed a beat. Gino looked so *perfect* and he seemed so perfectly happy, too, as he nestled in the arms of his father, swiping little baby punches at his autocratic chin. Like the textbook father and son, they could have been used in an advertising campaign to represent masculine bonding.

And nothing is really as it seems, she reminded herself painfully. *Life, just like adverts, can be nothing but an illusion.*

'Are you teaching him how to fight?' she questioned reprovingly.

Black eyes were flicking over her. From the soft swell of her breasts to the indentation of her tiny waist and the slender curve of her hips, which was accentuated by the fine wool.

'Mmm?'

She wished he wouldn't look at her like that. It made her heart flutter. It made her body ache. And it made her heart yearn for what could never be. 'I *said*, are you teaching him how to fight?'

He smiled as he dodged another mock-punch from Gino's pudgy fist. *'Sì, cara mia,'* he murmured. 'All men need to know how to fight.'

She knew that it was pointless to protest that Gino wasn't yet a year old, just as she knew it was pointless to tell him to wipe that mocking look off his face. As if he was determined to taunt her with the slow smoulder of his eyes and his lazy scrutiny of her body.

Her fingertips fluttered anxiously to the buckle of her belt. 'Do I look okay?'

'You know you look utterly delectable. The mirror does not lie, Emma.'

She sighed and picked up her handbag. 'You don't get it, do you, Vincenzo? Women aren't seeking affirmation when they ask a question like that—they're seeking reassurance and it's usually because they're nervous. I just want to know if you think I am suitably dressed for a large Cardini gathering.'

He gave a slow smile. '*Indubbiamente,*' he murmured.

'What does that mean?'

'Undoubtedly.'

'Useful piece of vocabulary—I'll use it next time I'm in a shop,' she said.

'Or use it tonight in bed, when I ask if I have pleased you,' he murmured.

'As if you ever have to ask!'

'There *is* that,' he admitted, with unashamed arrogance and Emma had to turn away quickly.

This is getting too complicated, she thought as their words mimicked an easy intimacy. *It's starting to feel like something it can never be and you're going to get hurt if you're not careful*.

Vincenzo saw the sudden set of her shoulders as she turned away and his eyes hardened. Why had he allowed himself to forget that she was simply here on sufferance? Because her beauty had blinded him, that was why—just as it had always blinded him. He picked Gino up. 'Let's go,' he said roughly.

He drove them there himself and Emma's mouth was dry with nerves as the car bumped its way over the dusty track leading to the vineyard. It was a long time since she'd been here—to the beautiful estate which was centre of the Cardini industry. She had once asked Vincenzo why the road leading to the lavish home was so basic, and she had never forgotten his reply.

'Because we Sicilians do not flaunt our wealth,' he had said. 'We do not need to, for it is irrelevant. A man is still a man whether he owns a hut or a castle.'

It had gone some way towards explaining the complexity which lay at the heart of the Sicilian people and Emma had been intrigued by it. She had wanted to learn more. To begin to understand the people, and in so doing to maybe further understand the dark and complicated man she had married. But Vincenzo had thwarted all her efforts to delve beneath the surface. She had discovered that beneath his stony exterior lay yet more stone.

She glanced now at his hard, dark profile as he eased his foot off the accelerator and they drove into the huge courtyard, where cars were crowded in, side by side. 'Oh, heavens—it's *huge*!' exclaimed Emma. 'A full-blown family gathering!'

'But of course,' agreed Vincenzo. 'Everyone is here to meet Gino.'

Gino. Silently, Emma realised that what was on offer

here was so much more than he would ever have in England. And it wasn't just about wealth, she recognised. Here there were family. People who cared and who would love him with a fierce and unbreakable bond. If anything ever happened to her, Gino would be safe.

'Why didn't we start our married life here, in Sicily?' she questioned suddenly.

His eyes narrowed. 'Because my work was in Rome.'

'But—'

'Yes. I know. I could have worked anywhere.' Vincenzo put his hands on the steering wheel as if he were still driving, even though the engine was no longer running.

He did not find it easy to express his feelings; he never had. As a child there had been no mother to coax from him his anxieties and his fears and although his beloved grandmother had loved him fiercely, she had been a member of the old school. Where men were strong and never gave anything away and only women showed their emotions.

He wasn't finding it particularly easy now, but Emma was looking at him expectantly. 'I guess I thought that you would find the island too small and too claustrophobic,' he said slowly. 'That Rome might be a more compatible lifestyle for a young woman leaving England.'

But Rome had seemed too big. To buzzy. The rapid and sophisticated chatter of the Romans had dazzled and confused her, so that Emma had retreated inside herself, feeling isolated on all sides and growing further away from her husband.

Emma stared straight ahead. 'Anyway, none of that matters now, does it? Not really. It's the present we have to deal with.'

There was a fractured kind of pause.

'Let's go inside,' he said, his voice distorted with something like regret as he lifted Gino from the baby-seat and handed him to her.

But Emma lifted her face to his and for once she allowed her composure to slip. 'Vincenzo, I'm scared,' she whispered.

He looked down at her as she caught the baby close to her breast and the breath caught in the back of his throat. And at that moment he wanted…wanted…

The shutters came down again. 'There is no need to be,' he said unevenly. 'They're family.'

Yes, your family, she thought with a slight feeling of desperation. *And Gino's. But not mine. Certainly not mine.*

A murmur of excitement went up as they walked into the hallway and it seemed to Emma that about a hundred little girls of varying ages, all wearing pristine white frocks with different coloured sashes, came squealing out, closely followed by lots of dark, solemn-eyed little boys.

'Oh, my word,' murmured Emma as Gino clung to her neck like a little boa constrictor and screamed out his delight at all the attention he was getting.

There was a blur of introductions to Bellas and Rosas and Marias and Sergios, Tomassos and Pietros. After she'd said *ciao* to each and every one of them, Emma followed Vincenzo into the formal salon—aware that some of the women were looking at her with narrow-eyed suspicion. And if she was being entirely honest, could she really blame them? Wouldn't she have felt exactly the same if the positions had been reversed? They didn't know the whys and wherefores of the marriage breakdown or Gino's conception, because Vincenzo hadn't told them.

It would have been so easy to have blackened her name, her character and her morals, but he had not done so and Emma knew why. Because he was a proud man and pride would not let him. But in so doing, he had protected her, hadn't he?

She thought how ravishingly handsome he looked as he began to reacquaint her with faces from the past and introduce her to new ones.

'But here is someone who needs no introduction.'

Emma kept one hand firmly around Gino's back as she turned to greet the man who stood behind them.

Salvatore Cardini. One scant year older than Vincenzo. Two men who were closer than brothers and yet further apart than brothers could ever be. Theirs was a unique relationship. She remembered being told that Salvatore's mother had wanted to take Vincenzo in, to bring up the orphaned child as one of her own. But the boys' grandmother had been so heartbroken at the death of her daughter that caring for the infant son had been the only light on her inconsolable horizon.

So Vincenzo had been based with Nonna but had spent a lot of time at Salvatore's house. They had walked to school together. Learned to ride and shoot together. To swim and to fish, and then—when they had first reached a manhood which had captivated every female who came within their radar—to seduce any woman who had allowed herself to be seduced.

They looked startlingly similar, with their hard, proud features, haughty demeanour and amazing physiques—but Emma had never seen Salvatore's soft side. She'd always thought that maybe he didn't have one, but right now his face was more meditative than she remembered.

'*Ciao*, Emma,' he said slowly. 'You are looking well.'

She wondered how he might have phrased it if she'd turned up in her normal wardrobe instead of being kitted out by her estranged husband first. Whether he would have been quite so complimentary then! But she leaned forward to accept a kiss on each cheek, aware that Vincenzo had walked over to the other side of the room, leaving them alone together. Like throwing her to the lions, she thought.

'*Ciao*, Salvatore,' she echoed. 'You're looking well yourself.'

He allowed a rare smile, but he was looking at Gino now, fixing him with a piercing gaze as if he were stamping the image of the baby in his mind. And then he nodded. 'But he is the image of Vincenzo,' he breathed softly.

'Yes.' Had he doubted that Vincenzo was the father? she wondered. Of course he had—and who could blame him for doing that? 'Yes, he is.'

Salvatore now directed the gaze at her. 'So how have you been keeping?'

'Oh, you know. We've survived,' she said lightly.

'Yes, I can see that. But life should be about more than survival.' There was a pause. 'Vincenzo tells me that you are a good mother.'

To someone unused to the ways of Sicilian men this might have sounded patronizing, but Emma correctly read it as a huge compliment. She nodded, aware of a sudden deep pang of sadness. 'I hope so. It isn't difficult—he's such a wonderful little boy.'

'But he likes Sicily. He is at home here.'

There was an unmistakable undercurrent to his words. The dark, implicit threat which lay behind the social niceties. 'Who wouldn't like it?' she questioned evenly, but inside her heart was beating furiously with fear. Did he consider Gino to be like a pawn in a chess game—who could be moved around according to the game-plan of the Cardinis?

Vincenzo came back then and she was taken over to sit with some of the older women, where they were served coffee and some of the tiny cakes topped with *frutta martorana*—marzipan shaped and coloured to look like miniature pieces of fruit. But Salvatore's words kept echoing round and round in her head and Emma couldn't concentrate on food. She crumbled most of the sweet delicacy onto her plate—each morsel tasting like cardboard in a mouth grown as dry as parchment.

They didn't leave until gone seven, with all the Cardinis clustered on the doorstep waving them away, and Emma knew that the afternoon had been judged a success. But inside she felt unsettled—like a pack of cards which had been unshuffled. She no longer knew her place.

Yes, in a way this *was* a perfect kind of limbo, but none of it was real. She *knew* the reason she was here. The *only* reason she was here. Because of Gino. Take an unplanned and miraculous baby out of the equation and all you were left with was a man who was still enamoured of her body and a woman…

In the dim shadows of the car she shot him a glance. A woman who remained completely vulnerable to the love she'd once had for him. So what the hell was she going to do about it?

In the darkness, Vincenzo read the unmistakable tension in her body and his mouth tightened, knowing that he could put off the inevitable no longer.

He waited until Gino was asleep and they were sitting at the dining-room table with Emma's meal lying untouched before her, just as she had refused to eat at the party earlier.

A nerve flickered angrily at his temple. Was she hoping that he would read the signals she was sending out without having to say anything? Did she think he was blind? That he was impervious to her restlessness and desire to go home. And didn't she realise that such a scenario would never be allowed to happen?

'Emma. I believe there are matters we need to discuss, don't you?'

She lifted her head slowly, wanting to read something of his intentions in his face, but his features remained as closed as they had ever been. 'About?'

Against the crisp white linen tablecloth his olive fingers flexed and unflexed. So they were back to playing games, were they? Maybe they should talk about it when she was naked and pinned beneath him and begging him to do it to her some more. She was much more amenable *then*, wasn't she? 'About the future, of course.'

'Gino's future?'

'No, not just Gino's. Yours. And mine.'

If only his eyes were not as forbidding as his voice, it might almost have masqueraded as some kind of romantic proposition. But as it was, Emma's heart missed a beat. 'Go on,' she said tightly, her chest tight with fear at what might be coming next. 'I'm assuming you've got some ideas about how you wish to proceed.'

How cold she sounded! he thought. Less like a woman and more like a sulky robot or a trainee lawyer! Well, she had better learn that all the sulking in the world would not change his mind.

He fixed her in the fierce light of his eyes. 'I want Gino to live here in Sicily, Emma. You have to realise that under no circumstances will I allow him to go back to England with you, and what is more—I will not give you the divorce you crave.'

CHAPTER TWELVE

EMMA stared at Vincenzo, her lips trembling with horror, shaken to the core by his words—by their harsh tone as much as their content. And by the cold glint in his black eyes. 'But you said…or, rather, you intimated that this was just going to be a *short* trip to introduce Gino to Sicily and to your relatives!'

He gave a short laugh. 'And were you foolish enough to believe that?' he mocked. 'Did you really think that once I had given my son a taste of what is truly his—his heritage and his future—I would ever allow him to go back to the kind of life you had before?'

Emma shrank back as if he had hit her. 'So you…you *tricked* me,' she accused hoarsely. 'You…you made it sound like a temporary holiday and now you're effectively telling me that I'm a prisoner here on the island? Well, you may be rich and you may be powerful, Vincenzo—but this is the twenty-first century and life doesn't work like that. You can't keep me here against my will.'

'Just try me,' he challenged softly.

Some warning bell sounded loudly in her subconscious as she registered the simmering anger in his body, like some fierce and angry predator about to strike. With an effort, Emma sucked in a shuddering breath. She was going about this the wrong way. *Calm things down.* She tried a weak representation of a smile. 'Look, Vincenzo, let's be reasonable. You can't do this—'

'Oh, but I can and I will, Emma,' he interrupted implacably. 'Unless you are prepared to consider the alternative.'

'Alternative?' She stared at him suspiciously, like a drowning person who had just been thrown a life-raft, only to discover it full of holes. 'What alternative?'

Dispassionately, he studied the pale oval of her face. The bright blue beauty of her eyes. 'That we remain here. Together. As a married couple, bringing up Gino and any other children we may be blessed with.'

It sounded like a cruel joke, but she could see from the look of intent on his arrogant face that he was deadly serious. And yet his words sounded so utterly cold... 'Why would you want to do that?' she whispered.

'Isn't it obvious? You must know that I would never be content playing the role of part-time father. Just as you must know that I would never tolerate the idea of another man bringing up my son, or having any real or lasting influence in his life.' He saw her mouth crumple but he steeled himself against its soft appeal, reminding himself instead of the natural consequences of her beauty.

'And, yes, before you tell me that there *is* no other

man, maybe there isn't. At least, not at the moment,' he continued as little darts of jealousy began pricking at his skin. 'But one day there will be, and that much is as clear as night following day. A woman as beautiful as you is not destined to remain alone for long, Emma.'

Oddly enough, this hurt almost as much as anything else. She wanted to tell him that he was a stupid, dense man if he thought that she could ever even *look* at another man after him. But surely that would only pander to an ego which needed no bolstering? And Vincenzo was in no mood to believe her anyway.

'You're barbaric,' she husked, scraping the chair back against the floor as she stood up to face him.

'Am I?' He smiled as he rose to his feet and walked round the table towards her. 'But that seems to be what turns you on, isn't it, Emma?' he boasted softly. 'Maybe it's time you learned to embrace barbarism instead of pretending that it appals you.'

Her breath was coming in short, sharp bursts as she stared at him, shattered by the things he had said and his vision of the future. 'Stay away from me!'

'Say it like you mean it, and I might listen,' he taunted silkily as he pulled her into his arms. 'Though on second thoughts…'

Emma struggled, but only for a moment for his touch was like lighting a match to a piece of tinder. She seemed to have no control over her reaction to him, even though she gave a little moan of protest when he bent his head to graze his lips over hers.

His breath was warm against her mouth, his proximity

intoxicating. 'Why don't you think about my suggestion, Emma? Would it be so bad to live like this, mmm?'

This? But what was this, other than a wild and undeniable chemical attraction? Emma closed her eyes, not wanting him to read the hunger which must be written in them and yet still not strong enough to push him away, despite the fact that he was treating her like an object. A possession. Just the way he always had done.

Even if she did protest—what good would it do? For he would only use his sexual power to kiss her into a kind of melting and mindless submission. 'Vincenzo—'

'Think about it,' he urged huskily. 'We are good together. Many couples do not have what we have.'

'Other couples have compatibility!'

'Compatibility exists when we aren't trying to score points off one another.'

And other couples had love, of course. But she couldn't hope to expect that, not now.

'Do I have a choice?' she whispered, opening her eyes at last to look into the hard, shadowed face and the ebony gaze which lanced into her. 'No, of course I don't. You ride roughshod over everything, Vincenzo. You always did.'

'Yes, you have a choice about how you choose to live your life,' he argued. 'You can act as if you're here under duress, playing the victim-prisoner.' Reflectively, he lifted his hand to drift his fingertips in a soft, curving arc around her jaw. 'Or you can make the best of what we have. Gino. Health. Family. And enough money for life not to be a struggle.'

It was a disingenuous way to describe the vast Cardini fortune and the prospect of a loveless marriage—because when it boiled down to it she *didn't* have any options. How could she, broke and with no prospect of a career, possibly fight the might of Vincenzo Cardini?

Emma felt as if he had thought it all out and was presenting it as a *fait accompli*, while she had nothing to offer in the way of reasonable argument. And even if she had—even if by some remarkable fluke she succeeded in leaving—would Gino ever forgive her if she tried to take him away from all this? Would he one day look back and despise her for having put her own selfish wishes before his welfare?

She pulled away from him—away from the temptation of his touch which seemed capable of making her do things she had no wish to do. 'I can't think about it tonight,' she said, with a weariness which seemed to have penetrated her bones. 'It's been an exhausting day.'

'Then let's go to bed.'

'I don't want to go to bed with you.'

His lips curved into a mocking smile. 'Oh, but I think you do.'

In the circumstances she shouldn't have wanted him. Shouldn't have let him make love to her after issuing such a stark ultimatum. But she did. Heaven forgive her, but she did.

They had barely even shut the bedroom door behind them before he pushed her to the floor and took her with a hunger which she despised herself for matching, tugging urgently at the belt of his trousers as he peeled off her panties, choking out her pleasured shock as he entered her. Even her orgasm felt like a betrayal—her greedy body overriding something she felt instinctively was wrong. Because surely to settle for something as basic as this made a complete mockery of marriage?

Afterwards, they crawled into bed but Emma couldn't sleep. She lay awake until just before dawn, fretting as her heart banged painfully against her breast while the Sicilian slept beside her.

Deliberately, she rolled as far as she could from his body and the false comfort it offered. His proximity was dangerous—his warm heat lulled her into thinking that here she was safe, and she most definitely was not. Emotionally, she couldn't have been in a more perilous place than locked in this loveless marriage for the sake of their son.

In the quietness of the night she felt a tear begin to trickle from behind her tightly shut eyes and she rose before her husband was awake, dressing with a swift determination that he would not see her vulnerable. He might have tricked her into coming here and he might now be using all his power and his might in order to make her remain here as his wife, but she would protect herself. She would make sure that her heart did not get broken again, ruthlessly trampled on by a man who did not love her.

By the time Vincenzo emerged, yawning and stretching his arms like a well-fed cat, Emma was already in the salon, playing with Gino. The tall Sicilian paused by the door and she saw his black eyes narrow in question when he saw her sitting at the table, an empty coffee cup beside her.

'Buon giorno, bella,' he murmured.

'Hello.'

His gaze flickered over her face, so pale this morning and with dark circles shadowing her beautiful eyes. He saw the silken tumble of her blonde hair and felt the kick of lust at his groin. 'You are up early,' he observed softly.

She steeled herself against the rugged beauty of his face, but it was made easier by remembering his harsh ultimatum, his insistence that she stay here as his captive wife. 'Perhaps I should have run it past you first?' she questioned coolly. 'You'll have to tell me about that kind of thing—what is and what isn't expected of me—since I'm not exactly sure what your house rules are, Vincenzo.'

His mouth hardened. So this was to be the way forward, was it? Did she think she would break his resolve by adopting the look of an ice-maiden? By behaving as if she had frost in her veins? Well, she would soon discover that he would not be broken. 'You are not in prison!' he pointed out with icy chill.

'No, of course I'm not.' She gave him a serene smile. 'I'm here entirely under my own free will.'

'And now you are deliberately twisting everything I say!'

Emma shook her head and placed a silent finger over her lips, aware that Gino was watching them, his dark eyes switching from one parent to another as each spoke, like a tiny spectator at a tennis match.

'On the contrary, Vincenzo—I'm telling it exactly as it is. We both know why I'm here—because of our son—and so it's going to be pretty pointless if we then spoil it all by arguing in front of him. If you are determined that we're going to make him a family home here, then at least let's try and make it as non-confrontational as possible.' *If we can't have love, then surely we can learn to enjoy a type of harmony*.

'Emma—'

'Here, you take Gino.' Fixing a bright smile to her lips, she stood up and, depositing a quick kiss on Gino's chubby little neck, she handed him to Vincenzo. 'I'll go and get showered and changed. Did you have any particular plans for the day? No? Then I thought we could go into Trapani.' The words came tumbling out, as if she was using them to try to fill the aching space which lay between them. 'Take Gino in his buggy around the town and maybe have some lunch overlooking the sea. And then we can see about getting me some driving lessons.'

'*Driving* lessons?'

Emma adopted the look of a teacher who had just discovered that her prize pupil had failed the most elemental of spelling tests. 'Yes, of course. I'm going to need to learn how to drive, aren't I? To be able to get around the island when you aren't here.'

'But I will allocate to you a driver! Someone experienced who will be on hand whenever you wish. You know that.'

Emma shook her head. 'But I'm afraid that won't be good enough. I want *some* independence, Vincenzo,' she returned, and gave him a steady look. 'At least allow me that.'

Vincenzo frowned. He couldn't fault her logic and yet such logic unsettled him. He was used to passion when dealing with women—and with Emma more than most. She had been passionate last night when he had taken her—more than passionate; she had blown him away with her response to him. But this morning it was all so different. He felt as if he were dealing with a mannequin instead of a flesh and blood woman who had come to life so beautifully in his arms.

Yet how could he voice his displeasure at such an unsatisfactory state of affairs? He was restricted by the physical presence of his warm and vocal little son, and by his wife's rather stern directive that they should not argue in front of him. And she was right. Of course she was right. He had never felt quite so wrong-footed in his life.

Damn her!

'Very well,' he growled. 'I will speak to someone about teaching you to drive.'

She inclined her head in subordination. *'Grazie.'*

His mouth tightened. *'Prego.'*

But, in a way, Emma discovered that her determination not to let her defences down had became her saviour. Because it was almost easier to play the part of the precision wife than to simply be herself—that weak woman who still loved him. At least she now had a properly defined role with boundaries she could observe.

Somehow it was easier to keep her feelings for Vincenzo in check when she didn't allow them to surface at all. It was as if she had buried them all deep inside her, locked them away so they wouldn't trouble her and make her foolishly yearn to have them fulfilled. Wasn't it easier to retreat, to shut down and behave with the kind of politeness you might display towards a rather formidable flatmate, than to face up to the fact that you had nothing but a shadowy and meaningless marriage?

Only in bed did her façade slip. Only then could she give into what she most wanted to do—which was to cover every silken inch of Vincenzo's glowing olive skin with tiny butterfly kisses which made him moan. Somehow she managed to stifle her own cries of longing and love and to replace them with the shuddering sighs of pleasure which were never far from her lips.

And in the morning she always woke early, slipping silently from their bed before Vincenzo awoke, aware that it was harder to hide emotions in the stark morning light as she hurried in to check on Gino. Sometimes she would clutch her son so tightly, closing her eyes against the tousled dark silk of his curls as she wondered how this strange relationship was going to affect this beautiful child of theirs.

Then the new day would begin and the charade would start all over again. Outwardly perfect but inwardly disturbing. In a way, it was all too easy to step back and to view the two of them as others must see them. Two parents who loved their little boy, but who were poles apart.

But nobody knew the true dynamic of their relationship and, even if they had, no one would have tried to change it or to interfere. The local girls would not have dreamed of trying to snare away a married man and everyone else valued the Cardini connection far too much to ever want to rock the marital boat.

Invitations began to arrive—with people eager to meet Vincenzo's wife—and Emma knew that she was going to have to make herself learn the language if ever she was to integrate properly.

She spoke to Vincenzo about it one morning. They were breakfasting alone, since Gino had slept late—and when their son wasn't there, it sometimes made the tension between them much more tangible. He was their reason for being together…take Gino away and all you were left with was a vacuum.

Emma watched as Vincenzo sliced a pear in half and began to peel it. Those same fingers had slid so deliciously over her skin during the night, but in the cold light of day those intimacies seemed as if they had happened to someone else.

His dark face was shuttered and she thought that his proud mouth was curved into a faint look of disdain. Perhaps Vincenzo was tiring of this arrangement now that he'd had a chance to live it for a while and maybe he was having second thoughts about keeping his unloved wife here. But Emma had been thinking about how to make the situation more tolerable.

'I ought to learn the Sicilian dialect,' she said as the curl of fruit rind began to coil like a snake onto his plate.

His dark head jerked up. 'Ought?' he demanded, seizing on the lacklustre word as if it were an insult to his language.

Emma shrugged. Sometimes it felt as if she was just going through the mechanics of living and she suspected that today was going to be one of those days—when playing the part which had been assigned to her seemed like a hell of a lot of work. 'It will be a challenge,' she said. 'Both necessary and rewarding.'

Her dutiful words fell like dull blows to his head and suddenly Vincenzo felt like a man waking slowly from a dream—or some kind of drug-induced coma. He blinked as he stared at the woman who sat before him, her beautiful blue eyes dull, her wide mouth showing not the faintest tilt of a smile, and a thousand tiny darts of realisation pricked over his skin. He couldn't bear this; he couldn't bear the fact that he was responsible for what Emma had become.

The silver knife clattered to his plate; the fruit forgotten as he pushed it away. 'You don't have to learn to drive,' he said. 'Nor to speak the dialect, unless of course it's for Gino's sake—because naturally I intend that he should be fluent.'

Emma stared at him, stupidly aware that the flesh of his pear was quickly turning brown. 'I don't know what you're talking about.'

'Don't you?' He gave a mirthless smile. 'You can leave, Emma. Any time you like. You've won. You can go just as soon as you want.'

'G-go? You mean—'

'Leave Sicily.'

Her fist flew to her mouth. 'I'm not leaving Gino behind!'

Vincenzo's face hardened. 'I'm not asking you to,' he said, even though his heart felt as if it were going to split in two at the thought of having to say goodbye to his beloved little boy. 'You can take Gino with you,' he said raggedly. 'All I ask is that you allow me to see him as often as possible. That you let him come here to know, not just his father, but the Sicilian way of life.'

Emma's eyes narrowed. 'You're trying to trick me, aren't you?' she whispered.

'Trick you?'

She nodded, her heart beating wildly with fear. 'I know what'll happen. I'll let him come back for a holiday and you'll snatch him. You'll keep him here and I will be powerless to get him back—unable to fight the might of the Cardini family. That's what you're planning, isn't it, Vincenzo?'

There was a long, fractured pause and when Vincenzo spoke he felt as if every word were a stone. 'You really think I am capable of such a thing?' he questioned heavily.

Emma opened her mouth but something made her shut it again, knowing that the question was far too important for an instinctive, snapped response. She thought of how much Vincenzo adored his little boy with that fierce and yet tender paternal love which lay at the heart of the most macho Sicilian. And she thought of how much love Gino had to give—to both his parents. She imagined the little boy's tears and confusion and heartbreak if he was denied access to his mother, and deep down she knew that Vincenzo simply would not be capable of hurting his son in such a way.

She shook her head. 'No. No, I don't. It was a stupid, thoughtless thing to say and I said it in anger. I'm sorry.'

In a way, her sweet contrition in the face of all that he had thrown at her made it a million times worse—if that were possible—and Vincenzo felt as if someone were stabbing at his heart with a razor blade. 'Please don't apologise, Emma,' he said bitterly. 'Just tell me when you wish to leave and I will fix it.'

She stared at him. When she *wished* to leave? Did he think that she was like some little girl, with her own tame fairy godmother to grant her *wishes*? Remembering her vow not to show vulnerability, to be able to at least walk away with her pride intact, Emma rose from the table and went over to the window.

Through a wobbly blur of tears she stared out at the layered green beauty of the landscape and swallowed. 'I guess I'd better go as soon as possible.' Because surely that would minimise the terrible pain? A short, swift departure must be easier for them all, than a protracted farewell? 'If that's what you want,' she added woodenly.

For a moment Vincenzo felt the savage twist of dark and writhing emotions—feelings which he had spent a lifetime hiding from, the way he'd learnt to hide from the dark pain of his parents' deaths. And for a moment he thought of the easier, softer way which lay there for him to grasp. To tell her yes, *yes*—just go and go now. To get out of his life and leave him in peace—away from this searing pain and these terrible raw feelings.

But something in the resigned set of her narrow shoulders made him flinch. He could see the tremble that she was trying to supress and suddenly something much stronger than a desire to escape began to overwhelm him. It was like a slow bonfire which had been quietly smouldering away—as the feelings he had dampened down for so long, suddenly erupted into wild life.

'No, of course it isn't what I want!' he bit out. 'You really think I want you to go, Emma?'

'I know you don't want Gino to go.' She spoke the words very carefully, just so that there could be no possible misunderstanding.

'You,' he said urgently, and for the first time in his adult life his voice threatened to crack. '*Che Dio mi aiuti!* I don't want *you* to go!'

Emma turned and stared at him, clutching at the window sill, afraid that her knees would buckle and she would fall in some pathetic heap at his feet and all because she had got her wires crossed and misunderstood him. He was talking about Gino. About their son. 'I won't deny you access,' she breathed.

But Vincenzo was empowered by emotion now, overtaken by a hot heat and an urgent desire to tell her the things which had been staring him in the face for so long, only he had been too blind to see them. He crossed the room and took her in his arms, but she was like a lifeless puppet as she stared up at him, all the light gone from her eyes.

'This has nothing to do with Gino!' he declared. 'Not any more. It is to do with you. And with me. With my love for you, Emma—because I love you.'

She shook her head as salt tears began to well up in her eyes. He was mocking her. Taunting her with what might have been. 'No—'

'*Sì*! Heaven help me for taking so damned long to realise it—but I love you. The woman I married. Who captured my heart. Who bore my child and proved to be the finest mother in the world. The woman I never want to lose. The woman I will not lose!' he added fiercely. 'So long as there is air in my lungs and a heart which beats!' He stared at her. 'But can you love me, too? Or is it too late, Emma?'

The pause which followed his question seemed like a million years and yet it was over in the space of a heartbeat. She shook her head. 'No, of course it's not too late,' she whispered. 'I never stopped loving you, Vincenzo—God only knows I've tried often enough.'

The tears were streaming down her face now, threatening to choke her, and Emma reached out for him, touching her fingers to his face as if he were not quite real. As if Vincenzo could not be saying these things, or looking at her in a way she had almost forgotten.

But he was. Everything she had ever wanted was written there on the dark features of the man she loved, though it took a few seconds more before she dared allow herself to really believe it.

''Cenzo!' she sobbed.

'Shh.' He gathered her into his arms and cradled her close to his heart until her trembling and tears subsided. It was possibly the most innocent embrace that Vincenzo Cardini had ever had with a woman and yet without a doubt it was the most potent of all—as the intensity of his emotions rocked the very foundations of his world.

They stood there for a long time—until all the fraught fight had melted away—and Emma gave a soft, shuddering sigh against his neck. And as he tipped her face upwards Vincenzo wiped away the last tear which lingered on the soft rose flush of her cheeks and silently vowed that he would never make her cry again.

She bit her lip, knowing that there were still things she needed to say to him in order to put the past to rest. 'I should never have run away from Rome,' she whispered. 'When things started going wrong in our marriage, I should have stayed and tried to work it out. I should have talked to you about it. I've been a terrible wife.'

He touched his lips to her nose in the most tender of kisses. 'And maybe you wouldn't have been had I not stepped back by two centuries once I had married you,' he said softly. 'I was a bad husband, Emma. So you see, *cara mia*—we're equal.'

It was something Emma had never thought to hear from her macho, magnificent Sicilian. And even though she thrilled to his admission, there was another, elemental side to her which was contrary enough to fight against such a claim. 'Does that mean you won't ever again expect me to submit to your will?' she questioned innocently.

Vincenzo read the expression in her eyes perfectly and smiled, lacing his fingers with hers as he began to lead her towards the bedroom. 'Interesting question,' he mused softly, his thumb tracing a provocative circle over her palm. 'Why don't we go into the bedroom before our son wakes and discuss it properly, *bella*?'

EPILOGUE

As PARTIES went it was meant to be a simple occasion—
a large family lunch to say goodbye to Salvatore. But
for Emma it was important and significant—because it
was the first party that she and Vincenzo had ever
thrown as a married couple. She had fussed around in
the preceding week—making sure that the menu would
satisfy everyone and that there would be enough fresh
flowers to adorn the long trestle-tables which were laid
outside, beneath the trees.

Salvatore was leaving the vineyard and Vincenzo
was going to take over the running of it. Sicily was to
be their family home from now on. Where Gino would
thrive and God willing, they would fill their castle with
brothers and sisters for him.

'Why exactly is Salvatore going?' she asked him,
giving one final twirl in front of the mirror and hoping
that the green silk dress didn't look too dressy for a
lunchtime party.

Vincenzo shrugged and gave her a lazy smile as he
watched her slipping on a pair of soft suede shoes. 'He

is restless, *cara*. Now that he has seen us settled I think that he has seen the many advantages of married life, and I believe that he intends to sow his wild oats before taking a Sicilian bride.'

From what Emma had heard whispered among some of the women in the family, Salvatore had already sown quite a few! She raised her eyebrows as she lifted her hands to Vincenzo's shoulders and made an unnecessary adjustment to his jacket, but then she just loved touching him. Loved talking to him. Spending time with him. As he did with her. Love had liberated them both and left them free to show how much they cared, without boundary or restraint.

'We ought to go downstairs,' she said, reluctantly. 'The guests will be arriving in an hour or so and there's still loads to do and I want to rescue Carmela from Gino.'

'But everything is ready—you know that—and Carmela would happily take our son home with her given half a chance,' he demurred softly. 'And besides, there is something I want to show you.'

'Oh?' she questioned with a faint frown as he pulled her into his arms. 'And what might that be?'

'First I need to tell my wife how beautiful she is and how much I love her, and then…'

'Then what?' she questioned.

Vincenzo smiled, a smile edged with love and sensuality which Emma had grown to know so well. 'And then I give her…this.'

Emma looked down to see that he had taken a small leather box from his pocket, and in the box was a ring which he was sliding onto the finger of her right hand. Rapidly, she blinked, and not just because it was dazzlingly beautiful—a hoop of diamonds which sparkled like sunlight on the Tyrrhenian Sea—but because the faint glitter of tears in her eyes was threatening to put her waterproof mascara to the test.

'Oh, Vincenzo,' she whispered shakily.

'You like it?'

'I love it—how could I not? But why have you bought it? And why now?'

He smiled, his eyes soft and indulgent. 'Because I love you, in more ways than I can count. Because you are my wife and my soul mate and the mother of my child. Is that reason enough, *cara mia*, or shall I give you more? For I have a thousand reasons at my fingertips and then a thousand more.'

For a moment she felt too choked to say anything and then Emma flung her arms around his neck, holding him so tight, as if she could never bear to let him go—and she never would. Knowing that the love she shared with Vincenzo Cardini burned brighter than all the incandescent stars which hung every night like lanterns in the clear Sicilian sky.

* * * * *

A Tainted Beauty

CHAPTER ONE

SOMEONE was watching her.

The little hairs prickled on the back of Lily's neck and somehow she just *knew*. Lifting her head from her pastry-making, she narrowed her eyes against the brightness outside to see the powerful figure of a man standing at the far end of the garden.

He was as still as a statue. Only his thick black hair seemed to move—ruffled by the same faint breeze which was drifting in through the open kitchen door as she worked. Unconsciously framed by a tumbling bower of early summer roses, he looked like a dark and indelible blot on the golden landscape and Lily's heart gave a funny little kick as he began walking towards the house.

For a moment she wondered why she didn't feel more scared. Why she wasn't screaming the place down and grabbing the nearest phone to tell the police that some dark stranger was lurking in the grounds. Maybe because the sight of him was a distraction from the troubled thoughts which kept nagging away at the corners of her mind. Or maybe there was just something about this

particular stranger which overrode all normal consider-
ations. He looked as if he had every right to be there. As
if the soft summer day had been waiting just for him.

With a guilty kind of pleasure she watched the powerful thrust of his thighs against fine grey trousers as
he walked across the manicured perfection of the emerald lawn. The light breeze was rippling the white shirt
across his chest and defining the hard torso which lay
beneath. *Poetry in motion*, thought Lily longingly—and
could have watched him all day.

He grew closer and she could see the unashamed
sensuality of his face. Thick-lashed dark eyes, which
seemed to gleam with dangerous brilliance. A chiselled
jaw, shadowed with virile new growth. And a pair of
lips which she immediately began imagining imprinting
themselves on hers. The kick in her heart became a full-
scale football match as he stopped at the open doorway
and Lily felt almost *dizzy*. How long had it been since
she'd looked at a man and felt an overpowering sense
of desire? And how could she have forgotten just how
potent it could be?

'Can I…help you?' she questioned and then, realising how *passive* she sounded, she glared at him. 'You
scared the life out of me—creeping up on me like that!'

'I wasn't aware that I was *creeping*,' he answered. His
eyes met hers with a mocking look—as if he was perfectly aware that she had been drooling over him. 'But
you look pretty capable of holding your own against
any intruders.'

She realised that his gaze was now directed at her hand and that she was still holding her rolling pin, clutching onto it as if it were the latest thing in personal safety devices. Her tongue flicked out to moisten lips, which suddenly felt cracked and dry. 'I was just making pastry.'

'You don't say?' Ciro's amused glance took in the flour-covered table behind her: the fruit-filled pie-dish and sugar shaker. And suddenly his senses were alerted by more than her soft beauty. The rare smell of home-baking in the cluttered room made him think of a world he'd only ever glimpsed. A world of warmth and cosy domesticity—and he felt an unexpected twist of his heart. But with habitual ruthlessness, he batted away his uncomfortable thoughts and looked at the pastry-maker instead.

She was the most old-fashioned woman he'd ever seen. The kind of female he didn't think existed any more—at least, not outside reruns of old TV shows. A tantalising composition of curves and beguiling shadows, she was wearing an apron—and he couldn't remember the last time he'd seen a woman wearing one of those. Not unless you counted the French maid outfit which his last-but-one lover used to wear in the bedroom, when she suspected he was tiring of her—which he was. That had been chosen to highlight the wearer's nakedness, but this was a much more innocent variation. A deliberately retro version in frilly cotton, it was tied tightly enough to emphasise the tiniest waist he'd ever seen.

Some people thought it was rude to stare—but when a man was confronted by a beautiful woman, wasn't it an insult not to? His eyes drifted to her thick hair, which was the colour of ripened corn and piled high on her head with a haphazard collection of clips. Her skin was flushed and he was amazed that a neck that slender could possibly support the weight of all that hair. He wondered if she realised what a perfect picture of domesticity she made. And he wondered what it said about him that he should find such an image so unexpectedly *sexy*.

'So aren't you going to invite me in?' he drawled.

The egotistical certainty of his question made Lily spring into action. Why was she standing there like some sort of muppet while he ran those admittedly gorgeous eyes over her as if she'd been some sort of car he was considering buying? Wasn't that why men thought they could get away with arrogant behaviour, because women like her let them? Hadn't she learnt *anything* from her past? 'No, I am not. For all I know, you could be an axe-murderer.'

'I can assure you that murder is the last thing on my mind,' he said drily.

Their eyes met and Lily heard the sudden roar of blood in her ears.

'And you don't look in the least bit scared,' he added silkily.

She swallowed down the lump which seemed to have

taken up residence in her throat. It was true she wasn't exactly *frightened*. Well, not in the conventional sense. But there was something about him which was making her heart race in a way which wasn't a million miles away from fear. And the clamminess on the palms of her hands was going to play havoc with her pastry if she wasn't careful. 'It is normal to introduce yourself when you burst unannounced into someone's kitchen, you know,' she said primly.

He bit back a smile because even when women didn't know who he was, they were nearly always intimidated by him. But not this one, it seemed. Intrigued by the unfamiliar, he inclined his head as if they were being formally introduced at a social function. 'My name is Ciro D'Angelo.'

She stared into the dark gleam of his eyes. 'That's an unusual name.'

'I'm an unusual man.'

With difficulty, Lily decided to ignore the outrageous boast—mainly because she suspected it was true. 'And you're Italian?'

'Actually, I'm Neapolitan.' He gave a lazy shrug in answer to the question in her eyes. 'It's…different.'

'How?'

'That might take a long time to explain, *dolcezza*.'

The pounding in her heart increased especially when he said *dol-cezza* like that, though she didn't have a clue what it meant. She *wanted* to him to explain why Neapolitans were different but sensed that would be straying into even more dangerous waters. Instead, she deliberately glanced at the clock which hung next to the old-fashioned cooking range. 'Time which I don't have, I'm afraid,' she said crisply. 'And I'm still none the wiser. Just what are you doing here, Mr D'Angelo? This is private property, you know.'

Ciro gave an almost imperceptible nod of satisfaction because her question pleased him. It meant that news of his purchase hadn't been made public. Which was good. He hated publicity—but he particularly hated his deals getting into the public domain before the ink had dried on the paper. Despite his legendary prowess in the world of business, he was still superstitious enough to worry about jinxing things.

But her question also made him wonder who she was. The woman selling this house was middle-aged. He frowned as he racked his brains to remember the vendor's name. Scott, yes—that was it. Suzy Scott—all age-inappropriate clothes and too much make-up and a way of looking at a man which could only be described as hungry. He frowned. Was this domestic goddess old enough to be her daughter? he wondered, as he tried to work out just how old she actually was. Twenty-one? Twenty-two? With skin that clear and soft, it was hard to tell. And yet, if she *was* the daughter of the house— surely she would know it was about to pass into the ownership of someone else. *His* ownership, to be precise.

She was still looking at him questioningly and he noticed that a shiny tendril of corn-coloured hair was tickling the smooth surface of her cheek. Maybe he should just turn around and come back at a more legitimate time—but suddenly, Ciro didn't want to go anywhere. He felt as if he'd stumbled into a warm world which was so different from his own that he was curious to find out more. To discover its inevitable flaws so that he could walk away with his cynicism intact.

He gave a shrug of his powerful shoulders. 'I wasn't expecting to find anyone home.'

'You mean you have an expectation that all houses will be empty?' Aware that the pie would be ruined if she neglected it any longer, Lily curled the pastry around her rolling pin and then deftly flipped it over the top of the prepared pie-dish. 'What are you—some sort of cat burglar?'

'Do I look like a cat burglar?'

Glancing up from where her fingers were fluting the sides of the soft pastry, Lily thought not. She doubted that your average cat burglar would exhibit such a cool confidence if they'd been rumbled—though he certainly looked agile enough to accomplish the physical demands of the job. And it was frighteningly easy to imagine him clothed entirely in some sort of close-fitting black Lycra.

'You're not exactly dressed for it. I imagine that your expensive-looking suit might be ruined if you tried scaling the front of the house,' she said caustically. 'And in case you *were* thinking of scaling the front of this house—I can save you the time. You won't find any pr-precious jewels or baubles here.'

Viciously, she began to brush the pie crust with beaten egg, realising that she must be feeling especially vulnerable if she had just come out and told a complete stranger *that*. But Lily *had* been feeling vulnerable lately—and her stepmother's erratic behaviour hadn't helped. Never the easiest of women to get along with—Suzy had recently taken to moving the house's most valuable items up to her London home. Of course, she was perfectly within her rights to do so—Lily knew that. Suzy could do whatever she wanted since she had inherited every last bit of her late husband's estate. All the money he'd owned was now hers and so too was this beautiful house, the Grange.

Even now, the pain and injustice of it all could still hit Lily like a savage blow. Her father's death barely nine months after his second wedding had been sudden and unexpected and had left her with a numbing feeling of insecurity. Through her own grief and the heartbreaking task of comforting her younger brother, she had tried to tell herself that *of course* Dad must have been planning to amend his will. No father would want to see his two children left without any financial support, would he? But the fact was that he hadn't got around to doing it and it had all gone to his much younger wife, who seemed to have taken to widowhood alarmingly well.

Even the pearl necklace which Lily had been promised by her darling mother had been ferreted away to Suzy's metropolitan home and she had a sinking feeling she would never see it again. Was that why her stepmother had recently been shifting everything of value—afraid that Lily might pawn some of the precious artefacts when her back was turned? And the terrible thing was that an instant windfall *would* solve some of Lily's problems—because wouldn't it give her brother the security he deserved?

Ciro heard the tremble in her voice and wondered what had caused it. But his attention was distracted as she bent to place the pie in the oven, his eyes riveted to the seductive curve of her bottom. Her bare legs gave off a silky sheen and the little cotton dress she wore brushed close against her thighs.

'No, I'm not a cat burglar and I'm not after your jewels or your baubles,' he said unevenly.

Lily turned around to find his dark eyes fixed on her and, even though it was wrong, it felt good to have such a gorgeous man gazing at her with unashamed interest. Didn't it make her feel *desirable* for a change, instead of some invisible nobody who spent her whole time fighting off unspoken fears about the future?

'Then what are you doing here?'

'For some strange reason, it's gone clean out of my mind,' he said softly. 'I don't remember.'

Their gaze held and Lily didn't need the frantic bash of her heart against her ribcage to know they were flirting. It was a long time since she'd flirted with anyone and it felt…*dangerous*. Because the sensuality which was shimmering off his powerful body brought back too many memories and they weren't good ones. Memories of disbelief and heartbreak and a tear-soaked pillow.

'Well, *try*,' she said. 'Before I lose the little patience I have left.'

Ciro wondered what to tell her because it wasn't for *him* to enlighten her that he would soon be the owner of this house. But if she *worked* here...then wasn't it conceivable that he might keep her on once the sale went through? 'I've been looking for somewhere to buy,' he said.

Confused now, Lily stared at him. 'But this house isn't for sale.'

Ciro quashed a momentary feeling of guilt. 'I realise that,' he said truthfully. 'But you know how it is when you're scouting around an area—how you always notice the best things when you're not on a tight schedule? You see the sudden twist of a path, which makes you wonder where it leads. Yet the moment an agent starts detailing the square footage—you stop seeing a place for what it is, and it becomes simply real estate.'

'So you're saying you prowl around properties when you think they're empty—because they might appeal to you on an aesthetic level? No wonder I thought you were up to no good!'

But Ciro wasn't really listening. He found himself wanting to remove the pins from her hair so that he could see it tumble down over her shoulders. To splay his fingers over those fleshy hips and to dip his lips to the slender column of her neck and kiss it.

He told himself that he should leave right now and not return until the keys of the old house were in his hands. Yet the homeliness of the kitchen, combined with her old-fashioned body, was making him feel a sense of nostalgia which was sharpening his desire for her. Suddenly, it was all too easy to imagine what she might look like, naked—with all her curves and cushioned flesh. If he'd met her at a party, he would be well on the way towards making that fantasy a reality—but he'd never met a woman in a *kitchen* before.

'What can I smell?' he asked.

'You mean the cooking?'

'Well, you certainly haven't let me close enough to sample your perfume,' he drawled.

Lily swallowed, her skin prickling with nerves and excitement. 'There are several smells currently competing for your attention,' she said quickly. 'There is the soup bubbling away on the hob.'

'You mean home-made soup?'

'Well, it's certainly not out of a carton or a tin,' she said, with a shudder. 'It's spinach and lentil, lightly flavoured with coriander. Best served with a dollop of crème fraîche and a hunk of freshly baked bread.'

It sounded like an edible orgasm, Ciro thought irreverently and felt the heaving aching of his groin. 'Sounds delicious,' he said unevenly.

'I am reliably informed that it *is* delicious. While this—' she pointed towards a sticky-looking concoction which was sitting cooling on a rack '—is your common or garden lemon drizzle cake.'

'Wow,' he said softly.

She searched his face for signs of sarcasm but could find none and there was something about his almost *wistful* expression which made her throw caution to the wind. 'You could…try some, if you like. It tastes best when it's warm from the oven. Sit down and I'll cut you a slice. After all, if you've come all the way from Naples—the least I can do is show you a little English hospitality.'

Again, he heard the clamour of his conscience but Ciro blotted it out. Instead, he lowered himself into a solid-looking wooden chair and watched her as she moved around the kitchen. 'You still haven't told me your name.'

'You didn't ask.'

'I'm asking now.'

'It's Lily.'

His gaze travelled over her face and alighted on the soft curve of her lips. 'Pretty name.'

Hastily, she turned to take the milk-jug from the fridge, hating the fact that the meaningless compliment was making her blush. 'Thank you very much.'

'But I presume you have another name—or is that a state secret?'

'Very funny.' She met the glint of mischief in his eyes. 'It's Scott.'

'Scott?'

'As in great,' she explained automatically. 'You know, Great Scott—the explorer.'

'Yes, I know,' Ciro said, his mind spinning as he began to work out the implications. She *must* be related to the vendor. Yet how could that be when she didn't have a clue that the house had just been sold? When she didn't even realise that it had been on the market. He frowned, knowing that he had passed the point where he could decently tell her.

Except that wasn't quite true, was it? If she'd been middle-aged, or male and quite obviously a member of staff—he wouldn't have had any problem telling her that he was the new owner of this big house. It was her general gorgeousness which was making him hesitate about enlightening her. *And surely it wasn't his place to do so?*

He waited until she had poured tea and he'd accepted a slice of delicious-looking cake for which he now had no appetite, before broaching the subject again. 'So you live here?'

Lily was so busy gazing dreamily at the shadowed slant of his chiselled jaw that she didn't really stop to think about his question.

'Of course I live here! Where did you think I…' And then she saw something in his eyes which made her voice change and she put down the cup which she had been about to raise to her lips. 'Oh, I see,' she said slowly. 'You thought I worked here? That I'm an employee. The cook, perhaps? Or maybe even the housekeeper.'

'I didn't—'

'Please don't feel you have to deny it—or to apologise.' She saw the uncomfortable look which had
crossed his face and could have kicked herself. There
she'd been—drifting around in some crazy dream-world,
thinking that he actually fancied her when all the time
he was looking on her as the hired help! Well done, Lily,
she thought grimly. It seemed that her male radar was
as unreliable as ever. She shook her head. 'I mean, of
course someone like me wouldn't be living in a house
like this. It's much too grand and expensive!'

He winced. 'I didn't say that.'

He didn't have to, thought Lily. And anyway, why
deny something which was fundamentally true? She
did make cakes for a living and she *did* dress on a budget—because that was pretty much all she had to live
on these days. Didn't she squirrel away as much of her
meagre wages as possible to send to her brother Jonny
at boarding school—to stop him from standing out as
the poor, scholarship boy he really was?

Yet maybe Ciro D'Angelo had done her a favour.
Maybe it was time to recognise that nothing was the
same any more. She needed to accept that things had
moved on and she needed to move on with them. She
was no longer the much-loved daughter of the house—
because both her parents were dead. It was as simple as
that. Her stepmother wasn't the evil stereotype beloved
of fairy tales. She tolerated her, but she didn't love her.
And since her father had died, Lily had increasingly got
the feeling that she was nothing but an encumbrance.

She forced herself to say the words. To maintain her pride, even though she no longer had any legitimate position here. 'This is my stepmother's house,' she said. 'She isn't here at the moment, but she'll be back soon. In fact, very soon. So I think it's time you were leaving.'

Ciro rose to his feet, a hot sense of anger beginning to simmer inside him. Why the hell hadn't her stepmother told her that this house had been sold? That contracts had been exchanged and the deal would be completed within days. By the end of next week, the house would be his and he would begin the process of turning it from a rather neglected family home into a state-of-the-art boutique hotel. He frowned. And what was going to happen to this corn-haired beauty when that happened?

He made one last attempt to get her to stop glaring at him—to try to coax a smile from those beautiful lips or a brief crinkling of her bright blue eyes. He gave an exaggerated shrug of his shoulders, which women always found irresistible—particularly when it was accompanied by such a rueful expression. 'But I haven't eaten my cake yet.'

Lily steeled herself against the seductive gleam in his eyes—almost certain it was manipulative. What a poser he was—and how nearly she had been sucked in by his charm! 'Oh, I'm sure you'll get another opportunity to try some. There's a tea shop in the village which sells another just like it. You can buy some there any time you like,' she announced. 'And now, if you wouldn't mind excusing me—I've got a pie in the oven which needs my attention and I can't stand around chatting all day. Goodbye, Mr D'Angelo.'

She gestured towards the door, her smile nothing but a cool formality before she closed it firmly behind him— and Ciro found himself standing in the scented garden once more.

Frustratedly, he stared at the honeysuckle which was scrambling around the heavy oak door, because no woman had ever kicked him out before. Nor made him feel as if he would die if he didn't taste the petal softness of her lips. And no woman had ever looked at him as if she didn't care whether she never saw him again.

He swallowed as the powerful lust which engulfed him was replaced with a cocktail of feelings he didn't even want to begin to analyse.

Because he realised he hadn't thought of Eugenia.

Not once.

CHAPTER TWO

'I DON'T understand.' Feeling the blood drain from her face, Lily stared at her stepmother—as if waiting for her to turn round and tell her that was all some sort of sick joke.

'What's not to understand?' Suzy Scott stood beside the large, leaded windows of the drawing room—her expression registering no reaction to her stepdaughter's obvious distress. 'It's very simple, Lily. The house has been sold.'

Lily swallowed, shaking her head in denial. 'But you *can't* do that!' she whispered.

'Can't?' Suzy's perfectly plucked eyebrows were elevated into two symmetrical black curves. 'I'm afraid that I can. And I have. It's a fait accompli. The contracts have been signed, exchanged and completed. I'm sorry, Lily—but I really had no alternative.'

'But why? This house has been in my family for—'

'Yes, I know it has,' said Suzy tiredly. 'For hundreds of years. So your father always told me. But that doesn't really count for much in the cold, harsh light of day, does it? He didn't leave me with any form of pension, Lily—'

'He didn't know he was going to *die*!'

'And I really need the money,' Suzy continued, still without any change of expression. 'There's no regular income coming in and I need something to live off.'

Lily pursed her trembling lips together, willing herself not to burst into angry howls of rage. She wanted to suggest that her stepmother find some sort of job—but knew that would be as pointless as suggesting that she stop kitting herself out in top-to-toe designer clothes.

'But what about me?' she questioned. 'And more importantly—what about Jonny?'

Suzy's smile became tight. 'You're very welcome to stay over at my London house sometimes—you know you are. But you also know how cramped it is.'

Yes, Lily knew. But her thoughts and her fears were not for herself, but for her brother. Her darling brother who had already been through so much in his sixteen years. 'Jonny can't possibly live at the place in London,' she said, trying to imagine the gangling teenager let loose on all the ghastly spindly antiques which Suzy loved to keep in her metropolitan home.

Suzy fingered the diamond pendant which hung from a fine golden chain at her throat. 'There certainly isn't room for him and his enormous shoes littering up my sweet little mews house, that's for sure—which is why I've arranged for you to carry on living here.'

Lily blinked as a feeling of hope quelled her momentary terror. 'Here?' she echoed. 'You mean in the house?'

'No, not in the house,' said Suzy hastily. 'I can't see the new owner tolerating that! But I've had a word with Fiona Weston—'

'You've spoken to my boss?' asked Lily in confusion, because Fiona owned Crumpets!—the tearooms for which Lily had baked cakes and waitressed ever since she'd left school. Fiona was middle-aged and matronly and, to Lily's certain knowledge, she and her stepmother had never exchanged two words more meaningful than 'Happy Christmas'. 'To say what, exactly?'

Suzy shrugged. 'I explained the situation to her. I told her that I've been forced to sell the house and that it's left you with an accommodation problem—'

'That's one way of putting it, I suppose,' said Lily, trying to keep the bitterness from her voice.

'And she's perfectly willing to let you and Jonny have the flat above the tearoom—so you won't even have that far to go to work. It's been empty for ages—it's almost as if it's been waiting for you! So how's that for a solution?'

Lily stared at her stepmother, scarcely able to believe that she could come up with such an awful scenario and consider it a good idea. Yes, the flat had been empty for ages—but there was a good reason why. Nobody wanted to live right next door to the local pub—especially since it had undergone a refurbishment and acquired an all-day licence. The last royal wedding had inspired a feeling of 'community spirit'—which basi-

cally meant that there was now round-the-clock drinking by the locals—and a deafening din of noise, which
carried on late into the night.

Lily couldn't think of anything worse than finishing one of her shifts and then making her way up the
scruffy staircase to the two-roomed apartment above.
Yet what choice did she have? She was hardly in a position to flounce off and make some kind of life for herself somewhere else. She had Jonny to think of. Jonny
who relied on her to provide some kind of warm base.
To give him the security he so desperately wanted and
the home he really needed.

'So what do you think?' prompted Suzy.

Lily thought this was yet another example of how life
could kick you in the teeth. But what was the point of
saying words which would only fall on deaf ears? 'I'll
go and see Fiona later,' she said.

'Good.'

Her head still spinning from the bombshell which had
been dropped, Lily found herself wondering whether she
would see much of Suzy after this—or whether her stepmother would want to cut ties completely. And wouldn't
that be best, in the circumstances? Her father had been
the glue which had held the precarious relationship together and now that he wasn't here any more… 'Why
didn't you tell me, Suzy?' she questioned suddenly.

Suzy's manicured fingers nervously touched the diamond pendant once more. 'Tell you what?'

'That you'd decided to sell. If I'd known about it before, then maybe I could have mentally prepared myself. Worked out some different kind of fate for myself, rather than having it presented to me like this. Why spring it on me like this?'

Looking uncomfortable, Suzy wriggled her shoulders. 'That wasn't my doing. One of the conditions of sale was that I kept the identity of the buyer secret.'

'How bizarre. But presumably I'm allowed to know who it is now?'

'Well, not really.' Suzy's thumb moved rapidly over the glittering surface of the diamond. 'It's not for me to disclose anything.'

'Oh, for heaven's sake,' said Lily, her frayed nerves making her voice shake with unaccustomed anger. 'Is there really any reason…?' But her words tailed off as she heard the approaching throb of a powerful car and saw Suzy begin to swallow nervously. 'What is it?'

'He's here,' whispered her stepmother.

'Who's here?'

'The new *owner.*'

Lily heard a car stop and a door slam and then the crunch, crunch, crunch of heavy steps on the drive— and as the peal of the doorbell echoed through the large house some gut-deep instinct began to unsettle her. An instinct which was only compounded by the way that Suzy was touching her dark red hair—the unconscious gesture of a woman who knew that an attractive man was about to enter the room.

'Aren't you going to open it, Suzy?' she questioned,

her voice miraculously steady even though her heart was racing so fast that she was surprised she didn't keel over.

'Yes, yes. Of course.'

Clattering away on her high heels, Suzy went into the hallway and, through a kind of daze, Lily heard the opening of the front door and the sound of low voices. And one of them was a deep and accented voice… She wanted to scream. To put her hands over her eyes—to block out the now seemingly inevitable sight of Ciro D'Angelo walking into the room, her stepmother shadowing him like a bodyguard.

Lily wanted to feel anger—nothing but the pure, white heat of rage—but the worst thing was that her body seemed to have other ideas. Something he'd awoken in her the other day was clearly not going back to sleep. She felt the shimmering of awareness—as if every nerve-ending had become raw and exposed to his dark-eyed scrutiny. And far more dangerous was the urgent prickling of her breasts and the pooling of heat deep in her belly.

'Hello, Lily,' he said softly.

At this, Suzy stepped out of his shadow, her lips opening in bewilderment as she looked at each of them in turn. 'You mean you already know my step—, er—you've met Lily before?'

'Yes, we've met,' said Lily, forcing herself to speak. To wrest back some of the control she felt had been sucked from her by the dark and sexy Neapolitan. He might have purchased her home and her stepmother might have just announced that she was being offered a crummy flat above a tearoom as a poor consolation prize, but she was damned if she'd let Ciro D'Angelo see the distress which was chewing her up inside. *And wasn't some of the distress caused by more than fear of the future? Wasn't it motivated by the desire she felt for him—which served as yet another illustration of her shocking lack of judgement when it came to men?*

She pursed her lips together to stop them from trembling and it was a moment before she felt composed enough to speak. 'Mr D'Angelo was lurking in the grounds the other day—in fact, he crept up on me and gave me quite a scare. But instead of doing the sensible thing and phoning the police to say that we had an intruder—I was stupid enough to let him in and listen to his ridiculous story. Something about being entranced by a beautiful twist in a path and wondering where it would lead.'

'I'm flattered you remember my words so accurately,' Ciro observed softly.

'Well, please don't be flattered, Mr D'Angelo—because that wasn't my intention,' Lily said, even though at the time she'd loved the poetry of his words. What an impressionable fool she had been. 'You were sneaking around—'

'Like a cat burglar?' he interjected silkily.

Digging her nails into the palms of her hands, Lily met the gleam of his eyes, his words reminding her of that brief intimacy they'd shared. When she'd flirted with the idea of him wearing black Lycra and he had flirted right back. When she'd felt light-headed with the sensation of being with an attractive man and her body had felt like a flower in the full heat of the sun. 'Like a thief,' she said fervently.

'Lily!' Suzy had now taken up a central position, as if she were the referee in a boxing ring. 'You really mustn't be so rude to Mr D'Angelo. He has made me an extremely generous offer for the Grange…an offer I couldn't possibly refuse.'

'I can be anything I please!' said Lily. '*I* haven't been conducting secret deals with him!'

'I'm so sorry about this.' Suzy turned to Ciro, curving her shiny lips into an exasperated smile. 'But I'm afraid that because we're so close in age, I've always had difficulty disciplining her—even when my late husband was alive.'

'Cl-close in age?' Lily spluttered indignantly.

Ciro saw that Lily's face was ashen and, overcome by a mixture of protectiveness and fury, he turned to the older woman. 'Mrs Scott, I wonder if you'd mind providing some refreshment? I've flown straight from New York and—'

'Of course. You must be exhausted—jet lag always completely lays me out, too!' gushed Suzy. 'Would you like coffee?'

'Coffee would be perfect,' he said coolly.

Suzy looked across the room at Lily and for a split second she thought her stepmother was about to ask *her* to make it, as she normally would have done if she'd had friends round. But something in her expression must have made her change her mind because she merely gave her a quizzical smile. 'Lily?'

'No, thanks. I think I need a real drink,' said Lily, walking over to the drinks cabinet and yanking open the door, afraid that if she didn't occupy herself with something then she might just crumple to the carpet. She was aware of Ciro's eyes burning into her as she pulled out a crystal brandy glass the size of a small goldfish bowl and recklessly splashed in a large measure of the most expensive brandy she could find. Taking a large mouthful, she felt her eyes water and she almost choked as the fiery spirit burned her throat. But somehow she managed to swallow it down and quickly took another gulp to take the taste away.

'Easy,' warned Ciro.

She turned on him and the fear and insecurity she'd been suppressing now came bubbling out in a bitter stream. 'Don't you dare tell me to go "easy",' she breathed, because surely defiance and anger were preferable to the hot tears which were stinging at the backs of her eyes. 'I can't believe that you sat down in my kitchen—sorry, *your* kitchen—and gave me all that wistful stuff about soup, when all the time...' She drew in a shuddering breath and felt the brandy fumes scorching through her nostrils. 'All the time, you must have been laughing at me, knowing that you were now the owner of this house while I had no idea.'

'I was not laughing at you,' he ground out.

'No? Then why didn't you do the decent thing and tell me you were the new owner?'

'I thought about it.' He paused and he could feel the tension in his body. A tension which had been there every time he'd thought about her. 'But it wasn't really my place to do so.'

'Why not?' She met his eyes—the brandy now burning in her stomach, giving her the courage to level an accusation she might normally have bitten back. 'Because you were too busy flirting with me?'

He shrugged. 'There was an element of that,' he conceded.

'So, what? You thought you'd see how far you could get before you came out and told me?'

'Lily!' he protested, taken aback by her burning sense of outrage. *And wasn't her response turning him on? For a man unused to any kind of resistance from a woman, wasn't it turning him on like crazy?* 'I wasn't expecting to find anyone home—that much is true. And when I stumbled across you, well…'

His words tailed off because he was reluctant to explain himself. Admitting his feelings to women wasn't in his make-up—hadn't that been a complaint which was always being levelled against him? Eugenia had said it all the time, especially in those early days—when she had been trying to make herself into the kind of woman she thought he wanted.

Yet Ciro could never remember feeling quite so entranced by anyone as much as Lily Scott. She seemed to embody all the old-fashioned qualities he'd never found in a woman before—and hadn't her blue-eyed face and sexy body haunted him ever since?

'Well?' she demanded. 'You can't come up with a reasonable explanation, can you?'

Impatiently, he shook his head. 'If anyone should have told you, it was your stepmother.'

As if on cue, Suzy came back into the room carrying a tray with coffee and a plate of Lily's home-made ginger biscuits. Clearly she had overheard his last words because she put the tray down and gave him a reproachful look. 'That's not really fair, Ciro—since one of the conditions of your purchase was that I keep your identity secret.'

'My identity, yes,' he agreed, irritated by her overfamiliarity, because he certainly couldn't remember telling her to call him by his Christian name. Or to keep batting her damned eyelashes at him like that. 'But I certainly didn't ask you to keep quiet about the actual sale. No wonder Lily is hurt and upset if she's just been told that in a few weeks' time she has nowhere to live.'

Suzy pouted. 'Oh, for heaven's sake! This isn't some Charles Dickens novel! She's not some homeless urchin, you know. I offered her space at my London place, but she turned her nose up at it.'

Lily had had enough. Feeling slightly nauseous now, she put the half-drunk glass of brandy down on a table.

'I'm not some kind of *object* you can just move around!'
she declared.

'I don't like the thought of you being thrown out of
your home,' he said roughly, thinking that she was now
looking quite alarmingly *fragile*. 'And I'm willing to
help in any way I can.'

She met his eyes, hating the way her body prickled in
response to their dark and seeking gleam. 'Well, I neither want nor need your help, Mr D'Angelo,' she said,
with as much dignity as was possible when her head
was spinning from the hastily gulped brandy. With difficulty, she only just stopped herself from swaying, but
the movement was enough to make Ciro move.

He stepped towards her, his hand instinctively reaching out to catch her wrist and for a brief moment the rest
of the world seemed to fade away. Her skin seemed to
spark like a bonfire where he touched her and all she was
conscious of was him. *Him*. Staring into the fathomless
depths of his dark eyes, her mouth as dry as flour as she
imagined him kissing her. Imagined him pulling her into
the powerful and protective strength of his body and,
to her horror, her breasts began to tighten in response
to her fantasy. 'Get…*off* me,' she croaked, wondering
if he could feel the rapid thunder of her pulse and if he
realised what was causing it. 'Just let me go.'

Reluctantly, he let her hand fall—his brow furrowing
into a deep frown. 'Where are you going?' he demanded.

Lily glared at him. 'Not that it's any of your business,'
she said, 'but I'm going to work.'

'You can't—'

'Can't? Oh, yes, I can! I can do anything I please,' she said, cutting across his words with fierce determination. 'I believe your sale is completing on the third of the month, is that right? So I'll make sure all my belongings will be out of here by then. Goodbye, Mr D'Angelo—and it really *is* goodbye this time.'

She could feel his gaze burning into her as she walked out of the room and somehow she made it up to the bedroom she'd had for as long as she could remember. It was only then, surrounded by the comfort of the familiar which would soon be gone, that Lily allowed the hot tears to fall.

CHAPTER THREE

'SO WHAT do you think, Lily? I know it's a bit small.'

Fiona Weston's soft voice penetrated Lily's thoughts as she stared out of the dusty apartment window onto the street below. The village wasn't exactly in a throbbing metropolis, but it still seemed unbelievably noisy when compared to the peace and quiet she was used to. A cluster of men were standing outside The Duchess of Cambridge pub, all clutching pints and puffing away at cigarettes. A man shot past on a scooter and Lily winced as it emitted a series of ear-splitting popping sounds.

Well, she was just going to have to get used to it. No more fragrant roses scenting the air outside her window—and no more gazing out at the distant woods or gently rolling fields. Instead, she was going to have to learn to live with the sound of people and cars—because the village car park was only a short distance away.

'It's…it's *lovely*, Fiona,' said Lily, with as much enthusiasm as she could muster, though it wasn't easy. The brandy she'd knocked back earlier had left her with a splitting headache and she couldn't get Ciro D'Angelo's dark face out of her mind. Or the memory of the way she'd responded when he'd caught hold of her wrist.

It was bad enough that his purchase had caused this dramatic turnaround in her fortunes, but it was made much worse by her reaction to him. He had made her feel vulnerable and he'd made her feel frustrated, too. And while a part of her had hated the rush of pleasure she'd felt when he'd touched her—hadn't the other part revelled in the feeling of sexual desire? She forced a smile. 'Absolutely lovely,' she repeated.

'Well, if you're sure,' said Fiona doubtfully. 'You can move in any time you want.'

Lily nodded like one of those old-fashioned dogs her grandfather used to have in the back of his car and she remembered his positive outlook on life. Shouldn't she be more like that? To start counting her blessings? 'I can't wait! It's such a fantastically *compact* little apartment—and with a lick of paint and a few pot-plants, you won't recognise the place.'

'It could certainly do with a facelift,' said Fiona. 'Though I don't know where your brother's going to sleep when he's home from school.'

Lily had been wondering the same thing herself. 'Oh, he's very adaptable,' she said, wondering if sixteen-year-old boys *ever* stopped growing. 'And I'm going to splash out and buy a lovely new sofa-bed,' she added.

'Good for you.' Fiona smiled. 'Anyway, I've kept the rent nice and low.'

She mentioned a sum which seemed outrageously

modest. 'I can't possibly let you charge me something like that,' said Lily shakily.

'Oh, yes, you can,' said her boss, sounding quite fierce for once. 'You're a hard worker, Lily—and it's your cakes which keep the customers coming back for more.'

On an impulse, Lily reached out to hug the kindly woman who had given her flexible working hours since the village tearooms had opened. The undemanding job had provided refuge during the dark days of her mother's illness and her father's rapid remarriage. Hadn't it been a kind of release for Lily, to be able to lose herself in the simple routine of serving people cups of tea and slices of cake? And hadn't the reassuring routine helped numb the horrible reality of the district nurse arriving daily, to give Mum another pain-killing injection?

From working on Saturdays and during school holidays, Lily had gone full time at the age of eighteen and had never really looked back. She'd started as a waitress—and when Fiona had discovered that she had a gift for baking, she'd asked Lily to supply the cakes, which she'd done ever since. For a non-academic girl who needed to be there for her brother, the job had been a gift.

Turning away from the window, Lily smiled. 'Well, if that's all settled, I'd better get to work or we'll have some very discontented customers on our hands. And we can't have that.'

'No, we can't!' Fiona laughed as the two women went downstairs.

Pleased at having made a decision which seemed to be the only bright light on the horizon, Lily changed into her pink uniform and slipped on a pair of sensible shoes. But as she tidied her hair in front of the mirror she was horribly aware of the feverish glitter in her eyes and the two spots of colour which highlighted her pale cheeks.

She looked *different*.

Unsettled.

A little bit *wild*.

But it wasn't just shock at her changed circumstances which was responsible for her altered appearance. It was the reawakening of sexual desire, too, and she knew very well who was responsible for *that*.

The afternoon shift was hectic, but she was on duty with her friend Danielle, whom she'd known for ever. The tearoom's proximity to a church reputed to be the birthplace of a famous saint meant that there was always a steady stream of customers, but on a glorious sunny day like today the place was packed. The new ice-cream range was popular, they ran out of lemon drizzle cake— and Fiona had to drive to the cash-and-carry to stock up on strawberry jam. Yet Lily was grateful to be busy, because it stopped her from wondering just where her life was heading and what the future was going to be like now that the house had been sold.

Just before closing time, the last customer had wandered out and Danielle had disappeared to start the washing up, when the tinkling of a bell announced a new arrival. Stifling a sigh, which she quickly turned into a smile, Lily looked up from rearranging some cakes on a stand and looked straight into the dark eyes of Ciro D'Angelo.

Her smile froze to her lips as a shiver begin to skate over her skin. It didn't seem to matter that she was still angry with him—he seemed capable of creating a powerful reaction just by being in the same room. When he looked at her like that, she could feel the prickling of her skin in response.

'We close in ten minutes,' she said.

'I'll wait.'

Lily raised her eyebrows. 'Wait for what?'

'For you to finish.'

'Excuse me, but I think you might have mistaken me for somebody else.'

'I don't think you're easy to mistake for anyone else, Lily,' he said softly, making no attempt to hide the appreciative gaze which lingered on the luscious curve of her breasts. 'I've certainly never met anyone quite like you before.'

Angrily, Lily shook her head. There it was—another of those meaningless compliments which seemed to flow from his lips like honey. How many of those did he trot out on a daily basis, she wondered—and how many women ended up falling for them? She found herself lowering her voice, even though Danielle was well out of earshot and any sounds were drowned by the clatter of washing up. 'Didn't we just have a huge row?' she asked. 'And didn't I imply that I didn't want to see you again?'

Ciro shrugged. 'Things sometimes get said in the heat of the moment.'

'Things do—but I meant every word of them,' she insisted.

'Well, I'm here now—and the sign on the door says you're still open,' he said, pulling out a chair and lowering his powerful frame into it. 'So I'm afraid you're going to have to serve me.'

Lily shot an anxious glance at the door—longing for Fiona to return and yet dreading it at the same time. She wanted him to go and yet she wanted to feast her eyes on him. In a place filled with paper doilies and flower-sprigged cake stands, he made the tearoom look completely unsubstantial. It was as if a giant had walked into a model village and taken up residence there.

'I want you to leave,' she said breathlessly.

His eyes sent her a mocking challenge. 'No, you don't.'

His silken taunt had an alarming effect on her and so did the sensual message which underpinned it and Lily could feel the distracting tightening of her breasts. She sucked in a deep breath. 'Obviously, I can't physically eject you.'

He elevated his dark brows. 'I agree you might have a little difficulty,' he murmured.

She glanced at her watch. 'We have exactly seven

minutes until closing time—so I'd advise you to place your order quickly.'

'That's easy. I'd like some lemon cake—something like the one I missed out on last week.'

'I'm afraid we're right out of lemon cake.'

He gave a lazy smile. 'Is there anything else you recommend?'

'Well, since I make the cakes which are sold here, I'd recommend them all.'

Ciro's eyes narrowed. 'You do?'

'Yep.' She whipped out her order pad. 'And we've only got coffee or chocolate left—so which is it to be?'

'Scrub it.'

'Scrub what?'

'My order.'

He began to get up out of his chair and Lily felt her heart lurch with something which felt infuriatingly like disappointment. 'You've changed your mind?'

'*Sì, ho cambiato idea.* I have changed my mind.'

His sudden, seamless switch into Italian disorientated her, as did the fact that he had stepped up close to her—close enough to notice that dark rasp of new growth at his jaw which she had so wanted to touch before. And the stupid thing was that she still wanted to touch it. She wanted to touch *him*—to see whether he could possibly feel as good as he looked. 'What does that mean?' she questioned suspiciously.

'I'm agreeing with you. I don't want to sit here while

you wait on me with that tight and angry look on your face,' he said.

'I'm glad you've taken the hint to leave me alone.'

'But I haven't.' He smiled with the confidence of a man who knew exactly what her response was going to be. 'Not until you've said you'll have dinner with me.'

Lily felt the crashing of her heart as those dark eyes bored into her. She could feel her cheeks growing hotter by the minute. He was so…so…*sure* of himself. 'Are you out of your mind?'

'I think I am a little, *sì*,' he said, unexpectedly. 'Because I haven't been able to stop thinking about you. I keep remembering the way you stood in that kitchen, with flour all over your hands and an apron around your tiny waist, looking like some old-fashioned domestic goddess. And believe me, it is not usual for me to be so preoccupied with a woman.'

'I suppose it's usually the other way round, is it?' she observed sarcastically. 'Women completely obsessed by you from the moment they set eyes on you?'

'Can you blame them?' came his unapologetic response accompanied by the faintest suggestion of a smile. 'But my undoubted appeal to the opposite sex isn't why I'm here today. I want you to know that I feel bad about what's happened.'

'At least there's *some* justice left in the world.'

Ciro bit back a smile. 'It was wrong of me not to have told you I was buying the Grange. But you must agree that I found myself in a difficult position.'

In spite of her determination to resist him, Lily found herself hesitating because surely that was genuine contrition she could read in his eyes? And it wasn't really his place to keep her up to speed on what was happening with the house, was it? 'Suzy should have told me sooner,' she conceded.

'Yes, she should.' Sensing capitulation, Ciro smiled. 'So if there's no quarrel between us, then why not let me buy you dinner?'

She sucked in a deep breath. Maybe she should just be straight with him. Because Ciro D'Angelo was clearly a *player* and she didn't go in for casual sex with men—no matter how rich or how gorgeous they happened to be. 'I don't go out with men very often.'

'I find that very hard to believe.'

'Believe it, because it's true.'

'And I think you ought to make an exception in my case,' he murmured.

Lily stared into his dark eyes. His soft words were like fingertips whispering erotically over her skin. She should say no. Of course she should—because he was making her want to do things she didn't want to think about. Things she'd forgotten about. Or, rather, the person she'd forgotten about. The woman she'd been before her fiancé had dumped her. He made her want to wear silk stockings and tiny little scraps of barely there underwear. He made her want to feel his fingers tracking their way over her body and splaying against the cool flesh of her thigh. He made her feel things she'd forgotten she was capable of feeling—like pleasure and desire and a pure, raw yearning. And he might as well have had the word 'danger' stamped across his forehead in big red letters. 'I don't know,' she said.

Ciro smiled. He loved her hesitation. *Loved* it. 'Please.'

'And I'm just wondering,' she said slowly, 'why a cosmopolitan and obviously successful businessman like you is buying a big house in the middle of the English countryside.'

'You don't know?'

'How would I know, when it seems that I'm the last to know anything?'

There was a pause. 'I'm planning to turn it into a hotel.'

Lily's eyes widened. A *hotel*? 'You're going to turn the Grange into a hotel?' she breathed in horror.

'It will be a beautiful and tasteful hotel,' he defended. 'My hotels always are. Ask around if you don't believe me.'

But taste was subjective, wasn't it? Lily imagined the bedrooms turned from their faded familiarity into places with horrible swagged four-poster beds. She thought of corporate beige carpeting and those over-the-top hotel displays of flowers, which always made her think of funeral parlours. 'And that's supposed to reassure me?'

He felt like telling her that it was not her place to be reassured, yet he wanted her so much that he was prepared to overlook her impertinence. 'If it means that you'll have dinner with me, then, yes—be reassured. Come on, Lily. Just one evening. One dinner. What are you so frightened of?'

She wondered what he'd say if she answered 'everything'. If she told him that the whole world looked a terrifying place just now. That she was worrying about her brother's future. About how the two of them were going to adjust to living in that tiny apartment.

But hot on the trail of her fears came the realisation that she was becoming a bit of a hermit. She tried to remember the last time she'd been tempted to go out for dinner with a man. Her broken relationship with Tom had damaged her, yes—but wasn't she in danger of letting the damage deepen if she locked herself away, like some medieval woman in a tower? When had she last done something really reckless, just for the *hell* of it? Why *shouldn't* she spend the evening with Ciro D'Angelo—unless she really thought herself so spineless that she'd be unable to resist falling into bed with him?

'I don't want a late night,' she warned.

Ciro smiled as a feeling of triumph spread through his veins. 'What's your number?'

'407649,' she said, noticing that he didn't bother writing it down as he took a card from his pocket and handed it to her.

'I'll call you,' he said.

A figure appeared at the window—a middle-aged woman carrying jars of jam—and Ciro automatically got up to hold the door open for her, noticing her curious glance as she passed. Stepping outside into the sunlit day, his senses began to fizz with excitement. Because for a moment back then, he'd thought that Lily Scott was going to refuse to have dinner with him. A moment when he had tasted the unfamiliar flavour of uncertainty.

Yet wasn't this the way things were *supposed* to be, before emancipation had made women almost laughably easy? Before they'd mistakenly thought that behaving as predatorily as men was somehow a good thing. Men used to have to *work* at getting a woman into bed—this was just the first time in his life that it had ever happened to him.

He shot a last glance towards the tearoom, where he could see Lily's pink-covered curves in all their splendour and he could feel the powerful arrowing of lust. Was she aware that she had hooked him with a hunger which was tearing at his groin? His mouth flattened with a look which anyone who knew him would have recognised instantly. It was a look which preceded getting exactly what he wanted.

Because no matter how much she tried to resist him, Lily Scott would soon be in his bed.

She was, after all, only human.

CHAPTER FOUR

IT HAD been a *stupid* thing to agree to and Lily wondered what on earth had got into her. She should pick up the phone and tell Ciro D'Angelo she'd changed her mind. That she hadn't been thinking straight when she'd agreed to have dinner with him. But what could she possibly say to back that up, which wouldn't have her sounding like some kind of wimp?

I'm sorry, Ciro—but you make me feel all the things I've vowed never to feel again. You make me ache with longing when I look at you—and I don't do that stuff. Not any more.

But then it passed beyond the time when she could reasonably cancel—especially as her stepmother had come up to her room and started bombarding her with furious but unanswerable questions about why Ciro D'Angelo had asked her out in the first place.

After she'd managed to get rid of her, Lily grabbed a quick shower—only just emerging dripping into a towel, when her brother rang from boarding school. Jonny loved the Grange even more than she did but he spent the entire conversation reassuring her that the new flat was going to be absolutely *fine* and that she wasn't to worry about a thing. She realised that at sixteen he was in for something of a shock when he saw their new home for himself. Yet there had been something about his determined bravery which had made her mouth wobble and she'd had to try very hard not to cry. He'd had so much to cope with in his short life, she thought fiercely—and this was just one more thing.

By the time she put down the phone it was getting on for eight and there wasn't time for much more than a lick of lipstick, or to pile the damp strands of her hair on top of her head in a rapid up-do. She hesitated over what to wear but ended up wriggling into a dress which was always guaranteed to lift her mood, no matter what. She'd made it herself from a vintage pattern in the feminine design of the fifties—the only style which seemed to suit her curvy figure. It was deep-blue and fitted, the sweetheart neckline a little on the low side, but the ankle brushing hemline made the dress feel relatively demure. And that was important on this particular night. She had no intention of giving out the wrong kind of message to Ciro D'Angelo. Of making him think that she would just fall into his arms as she was certain that every other woman did.

Hearing the sound of his car roaring down the drive soon after eight, Lily picked up her handbag, aware of the simmering waves of anger emanating from her

stepmother who was standing by the front door like a
guard-dog.

'Do you know what kind of man he is?' Suzy demanded.

'I'm sure you're going to tell me,' said Lily flatly.

'A billionaire who's famous the world over for his
sophisticated conquests, that's who! A man who dates
supermodels and heiresses! Care to tell me where you
fit into that kind of world, Lily?' Running a speculative
palm over a short skirt which made the very best of her
undeniably good legs, Suzy adopted a look of sudden
coyness. 'Why, he's closer to *my* age than yours.'

Lily opened the front door. Was he? She guessed he
must be. What was he—mid-thirties? While Suzy was
only just forty herself. A faint shiver ran through her as
she looked at her beautiful stepmother and a disturb-
ingly graphic image came to mind. Of Suzy coming on
to Ciro and running those glossy red nails through the
ebony gleam of his hair. Suddenly, she felt sick. 'What
are you trying to say?'

'That he's out of your league!' With an effort, Suzy
forced a smile. 'I'm only telling you for your own protection, Lily. I just don't want to see you get hurt.'

'Of course you don't,' said Lily quietly, closing the
door behind her.

On suddenly shaky legs, she crunched her way over
the gravel to where Ciro was just getting out of the car.
And despite her reservations about her stepmother's motives, suddenly she could see exactly what Suzy had

meant. Out of her league? Why, in his expensive suit, with his skin burnished gold by the evening sun, he looked like someone who'd fallen to earth from a different planet.

Yet he didn't resemble the seasoned seducer Suzy had just described. In fact, he was looking at her with a heart-stopping smile curving the edges of his incredible mouth.

'*Dio, quanto sei incantevole,*' he murmured as he held open the car door for her.

Lily slid onto the low seat. 'You do realise that not speaking Italian means I'm at a disadvantage, and I don't have a clue what that means?'

He hesitated for only a moment. 'It means that you look very...*nice.*'

Lily suspected that the word 'nice' wasn't one which featured in Ciro D'Angelo's vocabulary. And the look he was slanting at her certainly didn't make her feel 'nice'. In fact, it was making her feel deliciously and dangerously sexy. Demurely, she smoothed her dress down over her knees as he closed the door. 'Thanks.'

He got in beside her. 'I've left the roof down—you don't mind? Women sometimes fuss about their hair.'

Quashing down her faint feeling of hysteria that already he was talking about other women, Lily shook her head. 'I've got so many pins in it that it would take a wind-tunnel to dislodge it.'

He shot her a curious glance. 'Do you never wear it down?'

'Not very often. It's so thick that it just gets in the way.'

'I'll bet it does.' Suddenly, he imagined what it might look like cascading over her bare breasts and an almost unbearable wave of desire washed over him. With an effort, he tried to think of something other than what kind of nipples she had. 'Have you decided where you're going to live?'

Lily gave a mirthless smile. He made it sound as if she had hundreds of choices at her fingertips. 'I'm going to be moving to the apartment above the teashop where I work.'

'And what's it like?'

She wondered how he would react if she answered 'like a shoebox'. 'Oh, it's very convenient for work,' she said stoically. 'It hasn't been lived in for a couple of years and it needs a little decorating. I want to make it look like home by the time Jonny arrives next week.'

Ciro's fingers tightened around the steering wheel as something unfamiliar exploded inside him. 'Jonny?'

'My brother.'

Her brother. If he'd suddenly heard that his share prices had just quadrupled in value, Ciro could not have felt more pleasure than he did at that moment. 'Your brother?'

'Yes. He's away at boarding school, but he'll be home next weekend. He hasn't seen the new place yet and I wanted to brighten it up for him.'

'How old is he?'

'Sixteen.'

'And you don't have any—'

'No, we don't have any parents.' Lily's words quickly cut through his as she anticipated the next question, because she'd heard it asked a million times before and always in that same slightly tentative tone which came pretty close to pity. 'They're both dead.'

'I'm sorry.'

'That's life.' She stared very hard at the road ahead. 'How about you?'

'My mother is still alive. She lives in Naples. My father…well, he died a long time ago.'

Lily heard the sudden bitterness which had entered his voice but the steeliness of his profile made her bite back the question which had been hovering on her lips. 'You see,' she said. 'Everybody has their own stuff which they carry around with them.'

'I guess they do,' said Ciro, finding himself in the unusual situation of having an intimate conversation with a woman he hadn't even had sex with. And the thought of having sex with her made him start to ache again.

'Why not just sit back and enjoy the ride?' he said unevenly.

Lily tried to do as he suggested, but it wasn't easy. She wanted to pretend that this was her life. She wanted to forget the cramped reality of her new home and the worry of how she could possibly make it feel big enough for Jonny, when he came home. And she wanted to stop feeling this powerful sexual attraction towards the dark and dangerous Neapolitan.

'Where are we going?' she asked.

'A place called The Meadow House—do you know it?'

'You mean the hotel?'

'That's the one,' he said, without missing a beat.

Lily gave her dress an unnecessary tug. 'You're staying there?'

'Mmm. I didn't want to drive back to London after dinner, and besides—' he glanced in his rear mirror '—I like to think of it as a bit of a fact-finding mission. Finding out what the local competition is like. They've just employed a Michelin-starred chef who's come from Paris to oversee the kitchen and I'm interested to know what's on the menu.'

Lily wasn't remotely interested in the food on offer, or the fortunes of some unknown chef, and she suspected that Ciro wasn't either. Because it didn't matter how he dressed it up. The bottom line was that he was taking her back to his hotel—and the message from that was loud and clear. He obviously expected her to sleep with him!

She glanced down at his powerful thighs. At the strong, olive-skinned hands which bit into the soft leather of the steering wheel as if it were a woman's flesh. *Of course he expected her to sleep with him!* He was a red-blooded Italian man and the atmosphere between them had been sizzling from the get-go. He was hardly bringing her to his hotel for an evening of sophisticated chit-chat!

But she was disappointed that he could be so...*obvi-*

ous. Despite all her reservations about this date, she'd expected him to at least have a *stab* at playing the gentleman. Did he really think she was going to fall into bed with him simply because she'd agreed to have dinner? She stared at the hedgerows which were whipping past them, their leaves gilded rose-gold by the light of the setting sun. Because if that was the case—then he was in for a shock.

Lost in thought, Lily barely noticed the rest of the journey until the car slid to a halt in the car park at the back of The Meadow House, alongside a fleet of other shiny and expensive vehicles. She followed Ciro into the main reception where everyone seemed to know him, and they were taken through to the garden at the back.

Here, the tables had been laid up as if the management had suddenly decided to hold an impromptu picnic. The place settings had a Bohemian look, with mismatched crockery and wine glasses which were coloured ruby, emerald and amber. Starry jasmine scented the air and tea-lights glimmered on every available surface, so that it felt like walking into an intimate arena of flickering light.

Despite her reservations about the evening ahead, or the fact that their arrival had attracted the interest of the upmarket diners, Lily was enchanted as she looked around. 'Oh, it's beautiful,' she said softly.

Ciro watched as the candlelight gilded her golden head. 'You've never been here before?'

'Never.'

He heard the trace of wistfulness in her voice as they sat down and once again he found himself wondering why she sometimes seemed so *lost*. As if she'd suddenly found herself alone in a great big world with most of the cares of it on her slender shoulders. *What had happened to make her like that?* He waited until they'd ordered and their champagne had been poured, before sitting back and studying her.

The candlelight was casting flickering shadows over the pale skin of her décolletage, deepening the shadows where her luscious breasts curved invitingly.

'Pretty dress,' he murmured.

'Really?'

'Really. Pretty colour, too. Did you buy it especially to match your eyes?'

Lily smiled. She'd bought the material because it had been in the end-of-line bin and an absolute bargain. 'Actually, I didn't buy it at all. I made it myself.'

'You make your own clothes?'

If she'd announced that she wing-walked on light aircraft, he couldn't have looked or sounded more shocked. 'You seem surprised.'

'That's because I am.' Ciro took a sip of water to ease the sudden dryness in his throat. 'I don't usually come across women who are quite so accomplished, or so hard-working.'

'No?' Lily couldn't stop herself. 'Then what kind of women *do* you usually come across?'

There was a pause as Ciro considered her question.

He thought of pencil skirts and killer stilettos. Of glossy lips and crotchless panties. Of women who were this soft, sweet creature's very antithesis. He thought of Eugenia, with her impeccable pedigree and beautiful, calculating expression. And he looked into Lily's blue eyes and nobody seemed to exist in that moment except for her. 'Nobody who matters,' he said softly. 'And here comes our food.'

The waiter brought plates of squash, fanned into artistic golden slivers and dotted with soft goat's cheese, and Lily stared at it, wondering if she would be able to do it justice. How ironic to be presented with such delicious food on the one time her normally robust appetite seemed to have deserted her. But maybe Ciro felt the same way, judging from the way he was picking uninterestedly at his starter.

Their barely touched plates were replaced with fish and vegetables and Lily forced herself to eat some more, looking up to find his dark eyes fixed intently on her as she finished a mouthful.

'I have spinach in my teeth?' she said.

He shook his head, envying any vegetable which had been given such intimate access. 'Your teeth are perfect. I'm just curious about you, that's all.'

She pushed her plate away and picked up her wine glass. 'In what way?'

'I want to know why you're leaving the Grange to share a flat above a tearoom with your brother.'

'Because my father didn't make a will.'

'Why not?'

Lily's fingers tightened around the stem of her wine glass, his words reminding her of all the upheaval which lay ahead. 'Because he remarried after my mother died—to a woman much younger than him. And presumably he was too…well, too preoccupied to remember to keep his affairs up to date. Not that there was much time for that.' She worried her teeth along the surface of her lip, almost glad of that brief moment of discomfort. 'They'd only been married ten months when he dropped dead from a heart attack.'

'I'm sorry,' he said simply.

The sympathy in his voice took Lily back to a memory she'd tried her best to erase—but some memories were too big and dramatic to ever forget. The image of her father clutching at his chest—his face waxy and beaded with sweat. The piercing sound of her stepmother's hysterical screams echoing around the dining room. After shouting at Suzy to call the ambulance, Lily had done what she could—but it had been in vain. A first-aid certificate was pretty useless when it came to singlehandedly trying to resuscitate a middle-aged man who was considerably overweight—and Tony Scott had been pronounced dead at the scene.

Quickly, Lily raised her champagne glass to her lips and took a deep mouthful, the sharp bubbles making her blink. 'Stuff happens,' she said, in a flat voice. 'You can't change it. Suzy got everything and I had to accept that.'

Ciro's eyes narrowed. She showed a remarkable lack

of resentment about her fate, he thought—especially as her stepmother seemed to have no qualms about sending her out penniless into the world.

'So you don't have an income?'

'Actually, I do,' she said defensively. 'It might not be quite in your league, but I make money from my cake-making and my waitressing, just in case you'd forgotten.'

Ciro bit back his instinctive response—that what she earned was little more than pocket money. 'It's admirable to find a woman who works so hard,' he said truthfully.

'Anyway,' she continued, brushing aside his unexpected compliment with the air of someone determined to change the subject, 'that's enough about me. You're the man of mystery—and so far I know very little about you.'

'I'm surprised you haven't looked me up.'

'And where would I do that?'

'On the Net.'

She stared at him curiously. 'Is that what people usually do?'

'It happens all the time.' He shrugged. 'Information is so easy to obtain these days—the only trouble is that not all of it is accurate.'

She heard the cynicism in his voice and thought that must be one of the drawbacks to being powerful—that people would always be interested in you. That they'd always know more about you than you did about them.

Always have an agenda, too, she guessed. 'Anyway, I don't even have a computer.'

'Now that,' he said, a smile curving the edges of his lips, 'I do not believe.'

'It's true! I've always been more of a doer, than a reader. And why would I want to waste my time looking at a screen and spending hours on all that social media stuff, when there are so many lovely things I could be looking at in the real world?'

He started laughing, the sound causing a silent couple at a nearby table to glance over at them with unconcealed envy. 'Are you for real, Lily Scott?' he questioned softly.

Lily felt disorientated. That soft, dark look he was giving her was making her feel weak. More than weak. It was making her feel *vulnerable*. And tense. Beneath the soft material of her blue dress she could feel the insistent tug of her nipples and the soft pooling of desire deep in her belly. *This is dangerous*, she thought.

'Yes, I'm real enough,' she said. 'But so far, you're not. What should I know about you before you bring in your fleet of bulldozers?'

'There seems to be a misconception about developers,' he countered. 'That they do nothing but destroy.'

'What, when really they're just sweet environmentalists who are planning to encourage swarms of butterflies into the area?'

'I'm not planning to raze the house to the ground, Lily.'

'Really?'

He looked straight into her eyes. 'Really,' he affirmed softly. 'I'm planning a conversion in keeping with the building, if you must know. I'll restore your beautiful house to its former splendour and turn it into a hotel. The kind of hotel where people will pay a premium for quiet and laid-back luxury.'

Lily stared at him. It didn't exactly fill her with joy to think of her old home being available for hire in the future. To imagine people renting out the room in which she'd been born. But maybe if it had to be sold to a hotelier, then Ciro D'Angelo might just be the best kind. Just imagine if he'd been planning to put an ugly housing development there, or had wanted to erect some horrible modern monstrosity in its place. 'I suppose that doesn't sound *too* bad,' she said cautiously.

'I'm glad that my scheme meets with your approval,' he said gravely.

'I wouldn't go quite that far—and you've still managed to avoid telling me anything about yourself.'

'What exactly do you want to know, *dolcezza*?'

She wanted to know what it would be like to feel his lips pressing down hard on hers. 'Do you have brothers?'

'No.'

Or how it would feel to be crushed against that hard and virile body. 'Sisters?'

He shook his head. 'No.'

With an effort, she pushed away her wayward thoughts. 'And was it a...*happy* childhood?'

His eyes narrowed. Should he come right out and tell

her the truth? That in its way, it had been a particular type of hell. He remembered lying in the silent darkness, listening for the first sound of his mother's high-heeled shoes hitting the marble steps. Holding his breath to discover whether or not she was alone or whether he would hear the murmur of male laughter and her own muffled response. He gave the hint of a shrug. 'It was okay.'

She wondered what had made his dark eyes grow so stony. 'Just okay?' she questioned.

A cool expression iced the dark angles of his face. 'Is this supposed to be a dinner date, or a therapy session?'

Through the flickering light of the candles she could see the tightening of his mouth and suddenly Lily didn't want to spoil the evening. 'I didn't mean to pry,' she said quietly.

But somehow Ciro knew that. Had he been unnecessarily harsh with her, when it had been concern and not curiosity which he could hear in her voice? 'You're talking about something which happened a long time ago,' he said. 'Something I prefer not to dwell on. At heart, all you need to know about me is that I'm just a simple boy from Naples.'

His expression was so irresistible, his assertion so completely outrageous that Lily started laughing. 'Of course you are.'

He leaned forward. 'Who badly wants to kiss the woman sitting opposite him.'

Lily put down her glass, afraid that the sudden trembling of her hand would cause it to topple. 'Stop it,' she whispered.

'Why? Is it so wrong to say what we've both been thinking all night?'

'You haven't got a clue what I'm thinking, Ciro.'

'Oh, I think I have a pretty good idea. I've been watching you very carefully and you cannot disguise the look in your eyes or the reaction of your body. I know you want me, Lily, just as I want you—and only a fool would deny that. I think I've wanted you ever since I saw you making pastry, wearing that cute, flowery little apron.'

Lily stared at him, her heart pounding. He was looking at her with an expression which was making her tingle with a delicious heat. Her skin felt as if it were too tight for her body—as if every pore of it were stretched like a drum—and suddenly she was scared. Her stepmother might have been motivated by self-interest, but everything she'd said about Ciro had been true, hadn't it? He dated models and actresses. He was wealthy and powerful. He came from a different world.

She smiled. The kind of smile she'd have given anyone if they'd just bought her a delicious supper. 'It's been a long day,' she said. 'And I'm pretty tired. I think I'd like to go home now.'

'Sure,' he answered, non-committally—not at all perturbed by her deliberate change of subject. He saw her relax as they both got to their feet but he didn't feel one pang of guilt as he uttered the words he didn't mean.

Because he wasn't planning to keep her here by *force*, was he? To take her upstairs to his suite and chain her to the huge bed. He was planning to kiss her, that was all. And after that, all her resistance would simply melt away—it was as inevitable as the rising of the moon which was gleaming silver in the sky above them.

This time, he didn't take her through the hotel reception on their way to the car, but pointed to a way which was heavy with the scent of newly mown grass.

'Where are we going?' asked Lily apprehensively as they stepped away from the lighted area around the tables.

'I thought that a woman who enjoys looking at the real world would enjoy a more scenic stroll to the car park, than walking through a busy reception area.'

Afterwards, of course, she berated herself for not having insisted on the more traditional route, but the illuminated trees he was gesturing towards looked too beautiful to resist. And the winding path was cleverly lit to make Lily feel as if she'd fallen into some magical woodland. Silvery light illuminated the smooth trunks of the beech trees and tall grasses waved their feathery golden fronds. If it had been any other time and with any other person, she might have taken more pleasure in the surreal beauty which surrounded her.

But as they walked along she found that she could scarcely breathe... She was so *aware* of him. Every single part of him. Her nerve-endings seemed to be screaming out to have him touch her. To follow up the

unashamedly erotic promise of his words with his hands
and his mouth.

She'd never been so glad—nor so sad—to see his
gleaming sports car and as he bent to put his key in the
lock of the passenger door he suddenly halted—as if
someone had just told him to freeze.

'Lily,' he said softly.

Just that. Maybe if he'd said something clever or flir-
tatious, then she would have been left feeling cold. As
it was, she just stared into his eyes, their darkness fath-
oms deep—and she was lost.

And Ciro D'Angelo must have instinctively known
that because he made a throaty little murmur as he pulled
her into his arms and began to kiss her.

CHAPTER FIVE

IT WAS a kiss like no other and it reeled Lily straight in. The first brush of Ciro's lips against hers set off a sizzling reaction, which instantly made her want more. At first he teased her with the lightest of kisses and then he deepened it, provocatively licking his tongue inside her mouth—and it felt such a wickedly intimate penetration that her knees sagged.

Maybe that was the signal he'd been waiting for. The one which made him catch her by the waist while his other hand reached up to cushion her head, still kissing her with a thoroughness which took her breath away. She could feel his fingers impatiently weaving their way into her hair as he pushed her back up against the car. Suddenly, she was trapped, with no place to go—but surely this was a trap that no woman would want to escape?

Against her back was the coolness of the car and at her front was one hot and very aroused man. Her palms were splayed out over the smooth metal, she could feel the weight of his body pressing hard against hers—but not as hard as she wanted him. There was the sense that he was on fire, but was somehow managing to hold it back. As if he was deliberately banking up the flames of desire so that they smouldered away intensely.

And Lily couldn't stop herself from responding. It had been a long time since she'd been kissed—and she realised that there was no feeling in the world like this. She'd forgotten that passion could swamp you with its powerful sweetness. Could make the rest of the world recede until it seemed completely inconsequential. His kiss made her troubles fade away until it was only her and him and a hunger which was building and building—making her body shake with longing.

She opened her mouth wider to give him better access and he moaned in response as if she had just done something very clever. *I shouldn't be doing this*, she found herself thinking as his hand moved away from her hair to cup one aching breast. *And I definitely shouldn't be doing it with him.* It took every bit of resolve she possessed, but somehow she tore her lips away from his and stared dazedly into his face.

Struggling to recover his breath, Ciro raked his gaze over her, taking in her darkened eyes and parted lips. The swollen thrust of her breasts strained towards him invitingly. He knew he should take her inside before things happened. Before they got so carried away that it would be as much as he could do to stop from unzipping himself and slipping aside her panties and just doing it to her there, right up against the side of the car.

He moved his hand inside the bodice of her dress where he could feel the peak of her hardened nipple against her bra and had to close his eyes briefly, seriously afraid that he might come there and then.

'Let us go up to my suite,' he said urgently as he drew his thumb over the sensitised nub and felt her shiver in response. 'Before someone comes out and finds us and we get arrested for public indecency.'

The breath had caught in Lily's throat and she felt as if someone were trying to tear her in two. On the one hand she had the sensation of Ciro playing with her swollen breast and the correspondingly acute shafts of pleasure which were shooting through her. While on the other...

She swallowed.

He was pressing his erection flagrantly against her belly! He was talking in a low and insistent voice about taking her up to his suite. And what would that involve? A dishevelled journey past the knowing eyes of the hotel staff, followed by a terrible walk of shame in the morning. What did she think she was *doing*?

With an effort she peeled her clammy palms away from the car and pushed them up against the solid wall of his chest.

'I think you forget yourself,' she said fiercely.

Ciro's eyes narrowed and for a moment he thought she was joking—because surely she wasn't pushing him away after the chemistry which had just combusted between them? But then he saw the mulish expression

which had tightened her lips and it dawned on him that
she might actually mean it.

'You don't want to make love with me?' he questioned, his accent sounding far more pronounced than
usual.

'Make *love*?' she snapped. 'Is that how you describe
doing it out of doors, up against a car?'

He thought her accusation a little unjust, considering
that she had been a very willing participant—but his indignation was quickly replaced by another wave of lust.
And suddenly he didn't want her angry, with those darkened eyes spitting indignation at him. He wanted her soft
and gentle again. He wanted to take her up to his suite
and undress her very slowly. To lay her down on the bed
and explore her body with his eyes and his hands and his
mouth. He wanted to spread wide her beautiful thighs
and slowly ease himself into her tight and waiting heat.

'It is true that we got a little carried away,' he said
unevenly.

Lily shook her head, unable to believe that she'd behaved so badly—and after everything she'd vowed, too.

'I th-think that's something of an understatement,'
she said shakily, repositioning the pins in her hair with
trembling fingers. 'Now will you take me home, Ciro?
Because if you won't, then I shall just walk inside and
order myself a cab.'

Ciro frowned with frustration tempered by a feeling
of awe. Didn't she realise that she was turning down a
man reputed to be one of the best lovers in Italy? He

thought about all the women who came onto him and shook his head in slight bemusement. It seemed that Lily Scott's behaviour really did match her prim appearance—and that she had a steely morality about her.

'Of course I will take you home,' he said, pulling open the car door and meeting the look of suspicion which had narrowed her eyes. 'Oh, please don't worry,' he added acidly. 'I am not so desperate for a woman that I will leap on her after she has said no.'

Lily nodded, grateful she wasn't going to have to hang around for a taxi—because what on earth would the hotel reception staff think?

'Thank you,' she said stiffly as she got into the car, wishing she didn't *care* what other people thought—but the truth was, she did. Maybe it was a consequence of having been jilted and those awful days when she'd been at rock-bottom and not sure who knew that Tom had gone and who didn't. When she'd thought that people were talking about her behind her back and judging her. Wondering what was so wrong with her that a man could just walk away and marry somebody else. That rejection had deeply affected her behaviour; it still did. Clipping shut her seat belt, she stared ahead.

Climbing into the driver's seat beside her, Ciro closed the roof of the car, his mind spinning. Suddenly he felt at a loss—he, who was never at a loss. There'd never been a situation with a woman which he didn't know how to handle—except maybe for the time he'd lost his virginity, aged fifteen. Actually, even on the night he had bade farewell to his innocence, he'd taken to sex like a duck to water. Hadn't his thirty-year-old lover lain satiated on the bed afterwards, stroking his balls and telling him that he was going to make a lot of women very happy?

The crude progression of his thoughts did little to sate his sexual hunger but it did have the effect of bringing him to his senses. Wasn't it a terrible reflection of the life he lived, that he was shocked when a woman actually behaved like a *lady* for once? And didn't part of him actually *admire* Lily's stern rejection of his sexual advances?

He glanced at her, seeing the stony set of her profile as she stared fixedly ahead of her. 'I have a feeling that you might be expecting some sort of apology for what just happened.'

'It was a regrettable mistake,' she said calmly. 'That's all.'

Ciro clutched the soft leather of the steering wheel, scarcely able to believe his ears, and if he hadn't been so frustrated he might almost have laughed aloud. A *regrettable mistake*? Was she *serious*? Judging by the look on her face, it seemed as if she was. And wasn't that a little hypocritical? Why, she'd hardly behaved like the Madonna herself, had she?

'And are you always such an enthusiastic participant when making "regrettable mistakes"?' he questioned coolly.

'Perhaps I was led astray by someone with considerably more experience than me.'

Doubtless, she had meant the remark to be a criticism, but Ciro found himself giving a nod of satisfaction as he realised its implications. Of *course* he was more experienced than she was! Only an innocent or a very experienced woman would have behaved with such heart-stopping passion and then acted outraged—and she certainly wasn't the latter.

His thoughts began to race—and in a previously unexplored direction. He had found the evening surprisingly enjoyable, apart from its frustrating conclusion. He had actually enjoyed talking to her. She wanted to take it slowly—well, what was wrong with that? Wasn't that the way that people always *used* to behave, before the women's movement and freely available contraception led to the expectation of instant gratification?

Imagine what it would be like to actually have to *wait* for a woman to go to bed with you. To have to quash the urgent tide of sexual desire which was swelling up inside you. Mightn't that produce the most sensational love-making of all?

His car swung into the long gravel drive which led to the Grange and he sensed her tension as she looked up towards the upstairs windows, where a light was still on. Was the greedy stepmother still up and waiting for her? he wondered. And if that was the case, then maybe it was best that he *had* brought her home. Not good for either of their reputations if he'd brought her back tomorrow morning, still wearing the same dress…

'Stop just here, will you?' said Lily quickly.

She had already unclipped her seat belt and was reaching for the door-handle. 'Don't worry, I'm not going to bite,' he said wryly.

Lily thought how ironic it was that he should have said that, when not so long ago she'd wanted him to graze his teeth all over her aching nipple. 'Thank you very much for the dinner,' she said formally. 'I enjoyed it very much.'

He gave a low laugh. She really *was* a one-off. She sounded so *uptight*. But despite his intense frustration, he felt an unfamiliar sense of exultance, too—because the novelty of this situation was exhilarating. How many times had a woman said 'no' to him and meant it—even though the chemistry between them had been sizzlingly hot? Never. It had never happened to him before. He saw a woman, he wanted her and then he bedded her—it was as simple as that. Except this time. This time it had been nothing like that. 'So when am I going to see you again?'

There was a split-second pause before Lily turned to face him, steeling herself against his dark beauty and knowing that she'd be crazy to put herself in a similar position again. To open herself up to a vulnerability which she knew to be dangerous and to run the risk of being rejected again. She'd managed to hold him off be-cause some shred of decency had arrived in time to stop her making a fool of herself, but she couldn't guarantee being strong enough to resist him next time. Especially not if he used that abundance of Neapolitan charm to whittle away at her already weakened defences. When even now she was having to fight the urge to throw herself into his arms and lose herself in the fleeting passion of his kiss. 'You're not,' she said quietly.

Ciro's dark brows rose in disbelief. 'Excuse me?'

She licked her dry lips. 'You're not going to see me again.'

'Why not?'

'Because I don't really think I'm your kind of woman.'

Night-dark eyes pierced her with their ebony gleam. 'And don't you think I ought to be the judge of that?'

'No,' she said fervently, telling herself that she mustn't let his persuasiveness influence what she knew to be the right decision. 'I don't. Because I don't think you're thinking straight—not at the moment, anyway. We…we live in different worlds, Ciro—you know we do. You're an international hotelier from Naples and I'm…well, I'm a small-town girl who bakes cakes and waitresses for a living. Perhaps we'll run into each other once you start work on making the house into an…' she gulped down a lungful of air '…hotel. But if we do, then it's probably best if we just smile politely at each other and go on our separate ways.'

Ciro shook his head. *Smile politely? Go their separate ways?* Did she have no idea about the kind of man he was? As if he would ever smile politely at a woman he was planning to take as his next lover. His masculinity had never been outraged—but, to his surprise, it was not anger he felt as a result, but a fierce sense of destiny. And of challenge, too. Did she really think he would take no for an answer, when he wanted her more than he had ever wanted any woman?

But Ciro knew the value of biding his time. Of waiting until the moment was right to strike—wasn't that one of the reasons why he was so successful in business? He got out of the car to open the door for her and held out his hand to assist her. After a moment of hesitation, she took it and her lips parted as their flesh made contact, as if an electric current had just passed between them. And didn't it feel exactly like that to him? It was so *physical*, this reaction between them, he thought. So uniquely *chemical*. He wanted to kiss her again, to sear his mouth against hers and remind her just what she was missing, before getting in the car and driving away.

But Lily was making him react in a way which was unfamiliar. He saw the small glance she sent towards the upstairs window and a fierce wave of something which felt like protectiveness washed over him.

'Lily,' he said softly.

She narrowed her eyes at him suspiciously. The last time he'd said her name like that she had just melted into his arms—and wasn't she tempted to do it again? 'What?'

'You know I'm happy to move your belongings into your new home? You only have to say the word and I will help in any way I can. I told you that before and nothing has changed.'

She nodded, too chewed up to speak as a terrible sadness rushed over her. What, and have him witness

her emotional crumbling as she said goodbye to her old
life? Watch as she embraced a future which at the moment looked bleak? Never. Never in a million years.
She forced a smile. 'It's very kind of you, Ciro—but I'd
rather do it on my own.'

Frustratedly, he balled his hands into two tight fists.
'Your stepmother is moving to London?'

She nodded. 'That's right.'

'So you won't have anyone round here you can rely
on?'

Now was not the time to tell him that she'd never been
able to rely on Suzy. That it had been a long time since
she'd been able to rely on anyone. Now was the time to
convince him she was going to be absolutely fine on her
own—even if at that precise moment she didn't really
believe it. 'I'll be okay.'

She turned to walk away but he reached out to catch
hold of her wrist—its slender paleness making his own
hand look so big and dark in comparison. He could feel
the urgent hammer of her pulse and the desire to hold her
close was almost overwhelming. But he fought it, just as
he seemed to have been fighting his feelings all evening.

'Promise me one thing,' he said.

She gave a brief laugh. 'I can't possibly promise anything until I know what it is.'

He smiled, because wouldn't he have said exactly the
same thing himself in the circumstances? For a small-
town girl, she certainly wasn't stupid. 'You've still got
my details?'

She nodded, thinking of his cream business card, which was tucked away inside her purse.

'*Bene.* Then I want you to promise me that if you get in any trouble—with the apartment or with your brother, or *anything*—that you will come to me and let me help you. Will you do that, Lily?'

Lily hesitated. At that moment he seemed to symbolise all the things in life which she didn't have—strength and power and safety. If it had been anyone else, then she might have accepted. But she knew that there was only one reason why Ciro was offering his assistance—and that was to get her into his bed.

Her fingers tightened around her clutch bag as she shook her head. 'I appreciate your offer, Ciro, but I've already told you that I can't accept—and I meant it. Thanks again for dinner, and goodnight.'

And with that, she walked away—aware that he must still be standing there watching her because there was no sound of the car door slamming. No sound other than the sudden eerie swoop of an owl as it hooted in a distant tree.

In fact, she didn't hear his car driving away down the gravel drive until she had slipped upstairs to her room, thankfully without Suzy hearing her. Until she had peeled off the blue dress and thrown it to the ground with an uncharacteristic lack of care.

Wearing just her underwear, she stood looking in the long mirror, her fingers creeping guiltily to her breast and cupping it, just as Ciro had cupped it earlier. And she closed her eyes with sweet, remembered pleasure.

It was only then that she heard the sound of his car driving away, spraying gravel in its powerful wake.

CHAPTER SIX

THE icy water hit her face with a welcome shock and Lily was just dabbing another handful over her puffy eyes, when the doorbell rang. She stilled, cold water dripping down her fingers, thinking that she might ignore it—until she realised that it was probably only Fiona. Her boss was the only person who'd called since she had moved into the tiny apartment. Nobody else had been here apart from her brother and he…he…

Sniffing back another stupid tear, she wiped her hands and went to open the door. No point in hiding away like some sort of cave-dweller and making her sense of isolation even more complete. She pulled open the door and the breath caught in her throat as she saw who was standing on her doorstep. His dark hair was ruffled and he was dressed down in a dark T-shirt and black jeans which hugged the taut length of his thighs.

'You,' she breathed, her heart racing as she remembered his kiss in that darkened car park. Remembered the way he'd cupped her straining breast and traced the rough pad of his thumb over its puckered nipple. During that brief passionate interlude, he had made her feel like a woman again and she had *wanted* him. Oh, God, yes. She had wanted him with a fierce hunger which still haunted her.

'Me,' said Ciro, his eyes narrowing with shock as he took in her appearance—her blotchy face and puffy red eyes.

'Who let you in?'

'The other waitress. Danielle, I think her name-badge said—but what does it matter? What the hell has happened?'

'Nothing.'

'Doesn't look like nothing to me,' he observed caustically. 'You've been crying, Lily.'

'So I've been crying. So what? Should I have asked your permission first?'

Ciro scowled as a primitive urge made him want to reach out and protect her. He wanted to haul her up against his chest and tell her not to cry. That he was going to dry her tears and make everything better. 'Can I come in?' he said.

Her lips about to frame the word 'no', Lily realised it was one of those questions which didn't really require an answer because he was walking inside and she was actually pulling the door open wider to let him pass. And that was a mistake, she realised. A big mistake. She'd thought that the apartment had looked tiny when her brother had been here at the weekend, but Ciro made it look like toy-town.

'This is *it*?' he queried incredulously.

His question voiced nothing more than her own thoughts about the size of her new home, but it hit a very raw nerve. Lily had spent three busy days decorating before Jonny's visit. She had slapped on two coats of white emulsion in an effort to make it look bigger. She had hung mirrors everywhere to reflect back the light. In the limited space available, she'd positioned pot-plants and some carefully chosen family photos and had scattered cushions over the brand-new sofa-bed. But none of her efforts had changed a thing. The flat had still looked exactly what it was—a cramped place which was much too small for a gangly teenager with sneakers the size of dustbin lids.

Not that Jonny had complained. She almost wished he had. The brave look he'd adopted had seemed too heartbreakingly old for his sixteen years. It had made her want to cry—to rail against a fate which had already robbed him of so much of his childhood. And after he'd gone back to school she had found the crumpled letter which had fallen from his rucksack—and that was when her own tears really *had* come.

'This is it,' she agreed, wishing that Ciro didn't look so infuriatingly strong and dependable as he stood in the centre of the minute sitting room. Because by some kind of weird osmosis his towering strength seemed to emphasise her own terrible sense of weakness. 'What do you want?' she croaked.

What did he want? Ciro took in the belligerent set of

her mouth, which wasn't quite managing to disguise the fact that it was trembling. Her question was a pretty difficult one to answer. What would she say if she'd known that he'd been waiting for her to call after that frustrating conclusion to their dinner date? That he'd found himself looking incredulously at his mobile phone for a message which had never arrived? He'd thought that she would be unable to resist coming back for a little more of his love-making. That once she'd realised she was uselessly depriving herself of pleasure she'd see sense and come round to his way of thinking. He'd thought she would be in his bed within days. But she hadn't. There had been nothing from Lily Scott but a resounding silence.

He'd waited. And waited. Until he couldn't wait any more—and had come here today thinking that he wanted to find the quickest way into her bed. But now he wasn't sure what he wanted any more because the sight of her puffy eyes was filling him with a feeling he wasn't used to. As if he wanted to ring-fence her from trouble and keep her safe from every bad thing the world could throw at her. He frowned. So what the hell was *that* about?

'Are you going to tell me why you've been crying?' he demanded.

Lily stared at the ground, swallowing down the infuriating tears which kept springing to her eyes. 'None of your business,' she muttered.

'Lily.' And when still she didn't respond, he said her name again. 'Lily. Will you please just look at me?'

Unwillingly, she lifted her head to meet his dark gaze. 'What?'

'Why have you been crying?' he repeated.

Why did he think? She could have given him a whole list of reasons. Because it was no fun living in a place which was next door to a noisy pub. Because she was still exhausted after having done the move herself—stubbornly hiring a van which had been bigger than anything she'd ever driven before. What a nightmare it had been trying to manoeuvre the cumbersome vehicle around the village green, while all the regulars had stood outside The Duchess of Cambridge, shaking with laughter. But all these irritations had been eclipsed by her discovery that Jonny was just about to have his hopes and dreams crushed by their new-found poverty.

She shook her head, terrified that the tears would return and that this time they wouldn't stop. That they would pour down her face in an unstoppable flow and she would turn into a blubbering mess in front of him. She wanted to keep her mouth clamped tightly shut and refuse to answer and yet there was something so unyielding about him. Something so strong and determined—as if he wasn't going anywhere unless she provided some sort of answer.

She gave a small shrug. 'It's just been more difficult than I thought—moving in here. It was hard saying goodbye to the Grange, and even harder knowing what furniture to bring here.' Her stepmother had taken anything of value, of course, and most of the stuff left over had been far too large and grand to ever contemplate putting in a tiny flat above a cake shop.

Lily had managed to hang onto her mother's old writing desk and the painting of a ship which had hung in her father's study and always fascinated her when she'd been a child. Other than that, she had taken very little. Her new sitting room now contained an old, overstuffed armchair, a table which was slightly too big—and the new sofa-bed which looked completely out of place. She remembered the pitiful sight of Jonny's six-foot frame barely able to be accommodated within its cheap frame and she stared defiantly at Ciro, as if he was to blame. And he *was* to blame, she told herself fiercely. If he hadn't bought the Grange then none of this would have ever happened.

'And my brother was here this weekend,' she continued.

'Jonny?'

She was surprised he'd remembered his name and, somehow, that small touch of thoughtfulness made it even worse. She could feel that scary helplessness welling up inside her again and the tears she'd been trying to suppress started to slide remorselessly down her cheeks again.

Ciro stared at her, his face tensing. 'Lily?'

'No!' she protested, wiping a clenched fist across her face. 'It…it's not such a big deal. We'll work it out.'

'Work *what* out?'

'It d-doesn't matter.'

'Oh, believe me—it does,' he said grimly, putting his hands on her shoulders and guiding her towards the sofa and gently pushing her down onto it, before heading out of the room towards the kitchen.

'What do you think you're doing?' she called after him.

'I am making you tea. Isn't that what you English always do in times of trouble?'

The remark—delivered in his deep, Neapolitan accent—might have made her smile if the circumstances had been different. As it was, she'd never felt less like smiling and she was just blowing her nose into a sodden tissue when Ciro came back into the room, carrying a loaded tray.

He put the tray down on the table and stared at her with a stern expression. 'So what's happened with your brother which has made you cry?'

Slumped with exhaustion against the sofa, Lily watched as he poured her a cup of horribly weak tea and a terrible urge to tell him washed over her again. Maybe it was because she had bottled things up for so long that it felt as if she was threatening to explode. Or maybe it was because he just looked so determined that she suspected he wouldn't leave until she'd given him the information he wanted.

'He's been offered a place at art school.'

'Well, that's good, isn't it?' His dark eyes narrowed as she blew her nose again. 'Not the most reliable job in the world in terms of future employment, but if he's talented…'

'Yes, he's talented!' Frustratedly, she shook her head. 'And no, it isn't good.'

'Why not?'

She stared at him. Was he really so dense that he couldn't see—so that she'd be forced to spell it out for him, syllable by humiliating syllable? Maybe it was vulgar to mention the precarious state of her finances—especially to a man who had clearly never known such a predicament himself. But she knew it was too late for restraint, that she'd gone too far to stop and she needed to tell *someone.* 'Because it costs money to go and study in London. Money we haven't got.'

'You haven't got any tucked away somewhere? No stocks? Shares? That kind of thing?'

'Do you think I wouldn't already have redeemed them if I had any? When I said that my stepmother had inherited everything, I meant it.'

There was a moment of silence during which Ciro despaired at his lack of insight. Why the hell hadn't her words sunk in properly? Maybe he'd been too distracted by the sight of her heaving breasts, or the tantalising strand of hair which had flopped down around her tear-stained cheek. Or maybe he just never bothered to look at the detail of other people's lives. He knew that if she hadn't sold the Grange to him, then her stepmother would have found another buyer. But he could also see that in her emotional state, Lily might see *him* as partially responsible for her brother's thwarted dreams.

So what was he going to do about it? Given the vast resources at his disposal, couldn't he reach out to help her, even though so far she had stubbornly resisted any attempt to do so? She'd even refused his offer to provide a removal lorry and he'd heard through the grapevine that she had driven a large van rather dangerously around the village green.

She was certainly stubborn—and proud. It seemed she would rather struggle on independently than accept the assistance which he could provide. He found himself comparing her to the women he'd known in the past. He thought about Eugenia in particular—and her never-ending hunger for all things material. Yet as he looked into a pair of shimmering, bloodshot eyes he realised that Lily Scott couldn't have been more different.

Her flowery dress revealed her bare knees and her shoulders were slumped dejectedly—and in that moment she looked so damned young and *vulnerable* that he felt an aching sense of destiny deep inside him. Walking over to the sofa, he sat down beside her, seeing the startled question in her blue eyes. Slipping his arm around her, he brought her up close. 'Come here,' he said.

'Don't,' she whispered, but it was a word which lacked conviction because the truth was that it felt wonderful to be close to him again—to feel the heat of his powerful body next to hers. Only this time it wasn't sex which had brought her here—but something nearly as

potent. It was safety. And solace. It was the feeling that
nothing could harm her as long as Ciro was near. She
felt *protected* by him—as if he could throw a charmed
and protective circle around her—and that was a dangerously heady feeling. She wanted to burrow her head
up against his chest, like a little animal who had found
itself a safe haven. But somehow she resisted and stayed
right where she was.

'Why didn't you come to me for help, Lily?' he demanded. 'When I told you that you only had to call me.'

She shook her head. 'You know why.'

He pulled her against him, so that her face was close
to his neck and he realised that he was holding his
breath—unsure whether she'd shy away. He felt the delicious warmth of her breath against his skin as a bitter
truth washed over him. Yes, he knew why she hadn't
asked him for help. Because she thought he would ask
for something in return. For *sex*. Briefly, he closed his
eyes. Was that true? Had he made his benevolent offer
out of the goodness of his heart, or because he wanted
something much more fundamental from her?

Suddenly, he was angry with himself. After years of
meeting women who just wanted to get into his trousers or his bank account, he had finally met one who
didn't. Who worked hard for a minimum wage and put
the needs of her younger brother above her own. She
hadn't fallen into bed with him, even though her hunger had easily matched his. She hadn't phoned him, or

stalked him. She hadn't engineered an 'accidental' meeting in order to save face.

She had behaved like a lady from the start, while he had responded by coming onto her with the finesse of a randy soldier who hadn't been near a woman for months. He could feel the whisper of her breath on his skin, soft and rhythmical, like a warm balm. He remembered that first moment of seeing her, all warm and flushed from her baking—when the thunderbolt had hit him. He found he could imagine a child at her breast. His child. He could imagine Lily making an exemplary mother. She represented an innocent yet seductive world he had never known and suddenly he saw that it could be his. *She* could be his.

For a moment he stilled as a powerful wave of certainty washed over him and he tilted her chin upwards so that her bright eyes were looking straight at him. 'I think I'm going to have to marry you,' he said.

Blinking away the last of her tears, Lily looked at him in disbelief. For a moment she thought she must have misheard him, but the expression on his face was deadly serious. 'Have you taken leave of your senses?' she breathed.

'Maybe I have.' He shrugged. 'I don't seem to have been thinking very straight lately—but maybe that's the way it's supposed to feel when you meet a woman who is like no other woman you've known.'

'What are you talking about, Ciro?'

'I'm talking about a solution to your problems. I think

you're going to have to marry me, Lily,' he said, the tip of his finger tracing a path over her suddenly trembling lips. 'Let me take care of you—and your brother. There's no need for him to turn down his place at art school—as my brother-in-law, he won't have to worry about a thing.'

Lily tried to tell herself this couldn't be real. She tried to fight against it, more as a defence mechanism than anything. But his words were unbearably tempting—and not just because she recognised that he could change Jonny's future by taking away all the doubts and uncertainty. It went deeper than that. Her thoughts were now taking her to a place which was dangerous as she acknowledged the impact this man could have on her emotions as well as her finances.

'Tell me you don't mean it,' she said, trying to inject a note of humour into her voice. 'Either you've had a knock on the head—or you've been drinking.'

He gave a low laugh. 'Neither. I *do* mean it and do you know why? Because you thrill me, Lily. You thrill me in a way I've never been thrilled by a woman before. I admire your prudence and your pride. And in a crazy kind of way, I like the fact that you refused to go to bed with me the other night.'

'Is that something which is unheard of, then?'

'Yes,' he answered simply. 'No woman has ever turned down the opportunity to have sex with me. Only you. And your old-fashioned values appeal to something fundamental in me—something which I've discovered is important. You see, I've never come across such qualities in a woman before and I may never do so again. And that's why I want you to marry me, Lily. Be my wife— and I will give you everything you need.'

Distractedly, she shook her head. 'You don't know what I need.'

'Ah, but I do, *dolcezza*. You need a man who will take care of you. Who will provide for you and let your brother fulfil his potential. While you...' He framed her face with his hands, seeing the wariness which had darkened her blue eyes. 'You can give me exactly what I want.'

She met the heated gleam of his gaze as a shiver of awareness whispered over her skin. 'And what might that be?'

He shrugged, as if he was silently acknowledging that his ideas were outmoded—that few men would have admitted to what he was about to say. 'I want a conventional wife in a conventional role. Someone who will create a home for me. Who is waiting for me at the end of the day—not a woman fighting her way into some damned job every morning, who's too tired for dinner when she gets home. I want someone who respects her body enough to cherish it, in the way that you do. I want *you*, Lily,' he said simply. 'I've wanted you since I saw you standing in the kitchen, making pastry. I remember walking towards you and thinking that any moment I would wake up and find that I'd been dreaming. But each step which took me towards you made me realise that I was wide awake. I saw some flour on your nose and wanted to reach out and brush it away. And then you looked into my eyes and I felt the thunderbolt. I'd heard other men speak of it before, but up until that moment I didn't believe it existed. At least, not for me.'

'What thunderbolt?' she echoed in confusion, because her own memory of the day was that it had been bathed in glorious sunlight.

'In Italy we say *un colpo di fulmine*. Literally, a bolt of lightning. It is what happens when you look at a woman and suddenly you are struck here. Here.' And he laid his hand over his chest. 'In the heart.'

Lily could feel the deep pounding beneath her palm, aware of the significance of what he was telling her— wanting to believe him and yet too scared to dare. Yet hadn't she felt it, too—a powerful connection when she'd seen the dark stranger in the garden and her heart had clenched tightly? Hadn't he seemed to symbolise everything she'd ever wanted in a man? He still did. But the main reason she had pushed him away was because she was frightened of the way he could make her feel.

She knew only too well that feelings made you vulnerable. They left you open to heartbreak, and pain. She remembered how devastated she'd been by her fiancé's sudden exit from her life and had vowed never to put herself in that position again. And Ciro's proposal was nothing but a whim, she told herself fiercely. How could he possibly be offering her marriage when they barely knew one another? It was about control and desire. About getting her into his bed, no matter what the price.

Reluctantly, she wriggled away from the warmth of his embrace and met the speculative look which gleamed from between his narrowed eyes.

'It's an amazing offer,' she said slowly. 'But it's also a crazy one—and I can't do it. I can't marry you, Ciro— and when you've had a chance to think about it, you'll thank me for it.'

CHAPTER SEVEN

BUT Ciro didn't thank Lily for turning down his proposal. On the contrary, her refusal to marry him fed a desire for her which was fast approaching fever-pitch, until he could think of nothing else. For the first time in his adult life, he had come up against something which eluded him. A woman who was strong enough to resist him. And it was driving him crazy.

He thought of Eugenia. Beautiful, high-born Eugenia, whom everyone had thought he would marry. He'd thought so himself, until he'd come to realise that her love of money and power eclipsed all the values he held so dear. He remembered the defining moment which had signalled the end, when a woman had been flirting outrageously with him at a dinner party. Eugenia had noticed, of course, but instead of showing indignation she'd hinted that she could be very 'grown up' about relationships, if he was prepared to be understanding. The implication being that he could always buy his way out of a difficult situation. That if he were ever to stray— then she would be prepared to turn a blind eye. She'd

delivered the killer blow with a speculative smile. Just
as long as he rewarded her with some expensive little
bauble or trinket.

Eugenia's vision of the future had resembled the sophisticated bed-hopping he had witnessed as a child and
it had sickened him. Ciro had ended the relationship
that same night and his desire for a decent and innocent
woman had been born. The cynic in him had never believed he'd find her—but now he had. Lily Scott embod-
ied everything he'd ever dreamed of in a woman. And
she had turned him down!

He began to set about changing her mind. To work
out what it would take to sway her. For a man who had
never had to really try—Ciro now found himself having
to make an exception. But then, rising to a challenge had
always been an integral part of his make-up.

He sent her flowers—a tumbling mass of blooms
which were scented and white. The bouquet was accompanied by a simple, hand-written note, which read:
*If I promise to behave myself, then will you have din-
ner with me?*

She told him afterwards that the note had made her
smile—but she said it in a way which suggested that her
week had been light on humour. Over dinner that night
he discovered that her brother had gone back to boarding
school and was about to turn down his offer of a place at
art school. He saw the way her face was working, as if
she was struggling to contain her emotions, and he felt
an overwhelming sense of frustration, knowing that he

could solve her brother's dilemma in a heartbeat. But he also knew he couldn't help her unless she was prepared to accept his help.

She told him more about her life at the Grange and he realised how difficult it must have been, living with the avaricious stepmother who had become the mistress of the house. She opened up enough to tell him that Suzy had taken stuff which had belonged to her father, which by right should have gone to Jonny. He heard her voice stumble and that was when he discovered the story of her mother's missing pearls. A beautiful and priceless necklace which had been in her family for generations.

'Let me get this straight, Lily,' he said slowly, staring into her bright blue eyes. 'You're telling me that your stepmother stole your pearls?'

Quickly, she shook her head. 'Oh, I'm sure she didn't think of it as theft. She just took them up to London and—'

'Are you expecting to ever see them again?'

She bit her lip. 'Well, no,' she admitted.

'Then that's theft,' said Ciro as a cold kind of rage filled him.

He spent the next two days in London and when he returned, he phoned Lily and asked if she'd like to go to a concert in the grounds of a nearby abbey. Her voice lifted as she accepted—almost as if she had missed him as much as he had her.

Ciro felt an immense glow of satisfaction as he got ready for the evening ahead and even the English weather seemed to be on his side. It was one of those magical summer nights, with a huge moon, and they could hear heartbreakingly beautiful strains of violin music drifting through the warm air as they walked towards the venue.

He fed her chocolate and sips of champagne and, during the interval, pulled a slim leather box from the depths of the picnic basket, where it had been nestling in a napkin.

'What's this?' she questioned as he handed it to her.

'If I were to tell you, then it would only spoil the surprise. Go on—open it.'

Lily fiddled with the clasp, the odd note in his voice making her feel suddenly nervous. She flipped up the lid, dazedly sitting back on her heels as she stared at the contents in disbelief. For there, reposing against folds of satin with a fat and creamy gleam, lay the familiar strand of pearls which had belonged to her darling mother. For a moment, her hands were shaking so much that she let the box slip from her hands and it was Ciro who retrieved it. Ciro who carefully removed the pearls and then looped them around her neck, his warm fingers brushing briefly against her skin.

'Oh, Ciro,' she whispered. Her hand reached up to touch them and for a moment she remembered her mother wearing them, looking so beautiful and elegant in those long-ago days before the cruel illness had ravaged her. Her eyes were brimming with tears as she met his compassionate look and it took a moment before she had composed herself enough to speak. 'Where did you get them?'

'Where do you think?'

'From Suzy?' And when he nodded, she blinked at him in surprise. 'She gave them to you?'

He resisted the temptation to tell her that he'd paid well over the odds for the necklace. That Suzy Scott had recognised how much he wanted them and an envious look had hardened her eyes as she'd realised why. She had asked for a sum which had been astronomical by anyone's standards but he had paid it instantly, because the thought of bartering with such a woman had filled him with distaste.

'Yes, she gave them to me.' His eyes narrowed. 'And I'm giving them back to their rightful owner.'

'Oh, *Ciro.*' She tried to find words to thank him but nothing would come—only a convulsive kind of swallowing as she realised the significance of what he'd done. What a wonderful and thoughtful gesture to have made.

'And I know it's shameless of me to strike at a moment of such high emotion, but I can be completely shameless at times.' He picked up her hand and began to brush her fingertips against his lips. 'Which is why I'm asking you again to marry me.'

'Ciro—'

'I could give you a hundred reasons why it makes sense—starting with the fact that I want to help your brother achieve his dreams by funding his place at art school.'

'That's another pretty shameless statement,' she said, shivering as she felt his tongue slide slowly against her middle finger.

He met the darkening of her eyes. 'But there are plenty of others. Top of the list is probably my insane desire to kiss you.'

She swallowed, gathering up the courage to tell him the truth. 'I think that might be near the top of my list, too.'

He moved her fingers away from his mouth and bent forward, his lips grazing hers and feeling her body shiver with desire as he pulled her close. Lacing his fingers in the thick chignon of her hair, he kissed her as he couldn't ever remember kissing a woman before—hard and deep and passionate. He heard the throaty moan she made as she wrapped her arms around his neck and felt the wild thunder of his heart. He stopped only when his lungs were so deprived of air that he felt almost light-headed and then he drew his head away and looked down at the hectic glitter of her eyes.

'But first I need you to marry me,' he said unevenly.

And Lily knew she was all out of excuses. That it would be madness to say no—even if she wanted to. She could feel the smoothness of the pearls against her skin and she could feel her heart lifting with gratitude for what he'd done. A man like Ciro would be easy to love, she thought. Oh, so easy.

'And I need you to marry me,' she said, her voice trembling with emotion.

CHAPTER EIGHT

'I'M SCARED,' said Lily.

Staring at her ghostly image, she looked up to meet Danielle's eyes, which were reflected back at her in the silvered opal mirror. 'I know it's stupid, but I am.'

'Because?' asked Danielle patiently.

Lily touched her fingers to the exquisite veil which flowed down over her shoulders and the woman in the mirror mimicked the movement. Would it sound crazy to admit to feeling lost in Il Baia—this vast Neapolitan hotel of Ciro's, where she and Danielle had been staying in the days leading up to today's ceremony? Or to try to explain that the beautiful city of Naples and strange language were a complete culture shock to someone who'd spent most of her life in and around Chadwick Green? It was as if the reality of Ciro's wealthy life and powerful influence had only just sunk in and she wondered whether she would be equipped to deal with it. In the passion of the moment, it had been all too easy to say yes to his proposal of marriage—but here in the sumptuous confines of his life, she wondered how she would cope with being his wife.

She shrugged and the delicate silk of the bodice whispered over her shoulders. 'I can't imagine living here in Naples.'

Danielle made a minor adjustment to the wreath of white roses which sat on top of Lily's piled up hair. 'Oh, Lily,' she said, her voice as briskly cheerful as it had been all morning. 'All that will change with time. You've got to give yourself a chance. It's just normal pre-marital nerves, that's all.'

Was it? Lily wondered. Her mother's pearls gleamed softly at her neck and her heart was beating out a strange new rhythm as she gazed at herself in all her wedding finery. Did all brides feel this way? As if they were poised on a very high diving board but not quite sure how deep the water beneath them was? Probably not. But then, most brides knew their husband far more intimately than she knew Ciro.

She had thought that once she'd agreed to marry him he would want to consummate their relationship, but that hadn't been the case. He wanted to hold off until their wedding night. He told her he loved the fact that she'd refused him. That it made her different from every woman he'd ever known. He told her that he found it a *challenge* to wait—that his desire for her was building and building with every day that passed.

The waiting game was almost over and tonight was the big night—when they would be joined together in the most fundamental way of all. But Lily wished this terrible sense of foreboding would leave her. The sense that something was slightly off kilter. Was it because she still hadn't plucked up the courage to tell him about her relationship with Tom—even though Tom no longer mattered? She'd kept putting it off and putting it off, unwilling to cast any shadows over the sunny days leading up to the wedding. And now she'd left it so long, it was too late. The bride wasn't even supposed to *see* her husband until she met him at the altar—so what was she supposed to do? Text him now and tell him she'd once been engaged to another man?

'I don't know if I can go through with it, Dani,' she said hoarsely.

'Of course you can.' Danielle brushed down the skirt of her blush-pink bridesmaid dress and smiled. 'Because in a church not far from here awaits the kind of man most women would kill to marry. Think about it this way. You're in a beautiful city, staying in an amazing five-star hotel overlooking the bay—a hotel which happens to be owned by the man who will soon be your husband. You're in *Naples*, for God's sake—and about to marry one of its most famous residents! It's normal for a bride to feel scared before she walks down the aisle—but you have more reason than most to do so.'

'I do?'

'Of course you do! You're a foreigner here—and it's going to take a while before you feel like you fit in. Just don't expect too much.'

Once more, Lily touched the pearls at her neck. 'I don't think his mother likes me.'

'Why not?'

Lily recalled Leonora D'Angelo's demeanour when Ciro had taken her round to be introduced. The way she had presented two cool cheeks to be kissed, before looking her up and down with narrow-eyed assessment. And Lily had felt like a galumphing giant in comparison to the perfectly groomed and elegant woman who sat dwarfed in an enormous chair.

Everything in the dimly lit Neapolitan apartment had seemed so *fragile* and it had made her move carefully, almost exaggeratedly—as if afraid that a sudden move might knock over one of the priceless-looking antiques which adorned the room. And hadn't there been a noticeable lack of affection between mother and son? Ciro's cool attitude towards his mother seemed to have been more *dutiful* than loving. For a moment that had scared the hell out of Lily and she wasn't sure why.

'She seemed to disapprove of me,' she said.

'Well, that's a relief!' Danielle grinned. 'No mother on the planet ever approves of her son's bride—that's a given! They're always as jealous as hell until the requisite replacement boy-child makes an appearance. What did she say?'

Lily stared down at her glittering sapphire and diamond engagement ring. She couldn't blame the awkward atmosphere on the language barrier since Ciro's mother spoke English as perfectly as her son. She had just felt *wrong*. As if her pale, English curves would never fit into the sleek and moneyed world which the D'Angelos inhabited.

But if she was being honest, it was more than Leonora D'Angelo's attitude which had given her cause for concern. His cousin Giuseppe, who was to be their best man, seemed to have reservations about her, too. Ciro had told her that the two men were very close—more like brothers than cousins. But over dinner, the handsome blue-eyed Giuseppe had seemed to be studying her intently—as if he was trying to work her out. Or had her pre-wedding nerves just imagined that?

'So are you saying you want me to go and talk to Ciro?' Danielle's voice broke into her worried thoughts and Lily watched as her friend walked over to the window and stared out at the blue sweep of the bay. 'In front of the two hundred assembled guests who will be filing into the church, even as we speak—and somehow explain to him that you've changed your mind about marrying him?'

For a few seconds, Lily allowed herself to play out the scene in her head—imagining the uproar and embarrassment as all the guests turned to one another in horrified question. And that was when she started laughing at the ridiculousness of it all. What was she *like*? Wasn't this what she'd secretly been dreaming about, almost from the first time she'd seen him? When her heart had tumbled into a place she hadn't been expecting—and she had connected with him in a way which had taken her completely by surprise? Wasn't this the end-product of weeks of frustration and years of yearning—that soon she would have someone to love? Someone who seemed to need all the love she could give him—because she thought she detected a great core of loneliness at the very heart of Ciro D'Angelo. The man who seemed to have everything except for the one thing that money couldn't buy.

'No, I haven't changed my mind, Dani. And you're right. It's just stupid nerves which made me forget just how lucky I am.' She stood up and the layers of white tulle fell to the ground in a soft whisper. 'Come on, let's go—because I'm not sure whether it's the done thing in Italy for the bride to be late and I have a very nervous brother next door, who has been railroaded into giving me away!'

Lily was much too nervous and excited to take much notice of the bustling streets during the short drive to the church and she listened to Jonny and Danielle's excited comments with only half an ear. But as the car drew up outside the small church she felt a strange sense of approaching destiny.

There was a sudden hush as she stood in the arched doorway of the small church, dimly aware of the overpowering scent of flowers and the sudden swell of organ music. For a moment she was aware of the enormity of the step she was about to take, before reassuring herself that was perfectly normal, too. Because it *was* important. One of the most important days of her life.

Smoothing down her veil, she looped her arm through Jonny's and began the slow walk down the aisle, aware of the collective turning of heads as she passed the people who were mostly strangers to her. But there was only one person in her line of vision. One person who dominated it all. Who had dominated her life from the minute he'd walked into it on a sunny English day.

Toweringly dark and impossibly gorgeous—there seemed almost an *edge* to him today. It was as if the impeccably formal clothes had distanced him and made him into someone different—someone she didn't really know. He was at home here, Lily thought suddenly. At home among all these sleek and sophisticated people, while she was the pale Englishwoman who knew nobody. Her heart missed a beat and for a moment she felt as if she couldn't go through with it, her step faltering slightly as her white shoe stepped into a pool of rainbow light which poured down from the stained glass window. She saw Jonny glance at her, his gaze concerned.

And then the man waiting at the altar slowly turned his head and Lily's heart fired into life again, crashing against her ribcage so hard that she wondered if the movement was visible beneath her delicate dress.

This is Ciro, she thought—and felt a soft, creeping pleasure as she walked towards him, looking up to meet the dark blaze of his eyes as she finally reached him. The man she had grown to admire and to respect. Who had somehow got back her mother's pearls and sternly told her that it would be a crime if her talented brother didn't achieve his potential. The man who had done so many loving things to get her here today. Her darling Ciro.

'Okay?' he mouthed at her, and she nodded, sliding her hand into the waiting warmth of his.

The service was conducted in both languages and Lily managed to repeat her vows without stumbling—though her finger was trembling as Ciro slid the golden ring onto it. And then the priest was pronouncing them man and wife and the congregation had started clapping and he put his face close to hers, a smile nudging at the edges of his lips.

'You look beautiful,' he murmured.

'Do I?'

'More than beautiful. Like a flower. Soft and pure and white—like the Lily you were named after.'

'Oh, Ciro,' she whispered.

He smiled. Her face was upturned, her lips trembling with eagerness, but the kiss he grazed over her lips was breathtakingly short and deliberately so. They still had a wedding breakfast and reception to get through before they could be alone as man and wife. And he had waited much too long for this to want to do anything but savour her at his leisure. 'Come on, let us go and meet our guests,' he said.

The reception and the first night of their honeymoon were being held at the Il Baia hotel which had the added pressure of everyone falling over themselves to please Ciro. Lily had wondered if he wouldn't rather spend his wedding night anonymously, rather than in a place where everyone knew him—but he had shaken his head.

'It means we can slip away from the reception without making a fuss,' he'd murmured. 'And it wouldn't be a very good advertisement for the hotel if the boss spent his wedding night in a rival establishment, now would it?'

Lily supposed it wouldn't, and by early evening, she couldn't have cared less where they were going—she just couldn't wait to get there. Her face ached from all the photo-taking, she'd shaken a million hands during the line-up and she'd barely managed to get close to a morsel of food, let alone eat any of it. She tried not to be overwhelmed by the vast amount of Ciro's friends, compared to the small clutch of people she'd flown out from Chadwick Green. And she tried not to feel insecure when she looked at all the beautiful women who chattered so vivaciously, expressively swirling their hands around as they talked.

At least Jonny seemed to be enjoying himself with a group of Ciro's younger cousins, while Danielle was certainly getting plenty of offers to dance. And Fiona Weston was eating some sort of dessert called *sfogliatella*, and trying very hard to find the recipe for it.

By nine o'clock, when Lily was in serious danger of flagging, Ciro put his arm around her waist.

'I think it's about time I took you to my bed at last,' he murmured. 'How does that idea appeal to you, Signora D'Angelo?'

She leaned her head against his broad shoulder, thrilling to the possessive note in his voice and to the sound of her brand-new title. She was Ciro's *wife*, she thought ecstatically and all her uncertainties melted away. For the first time in a long time she would have someone to lean on. Someone who would be watching out for her as she would be watching out for him. Someone whom she could love and support in turn. Her *partner*, in every sense of the term. 'Oh, yes, please,' she whispered.

'Then let's slip away—without any fuss.'

A glass elevator zoomed them up to the honeymoon suite, which was situated at the very top of the beautiful building. As they stepped inside Lily became aware of a large salon with elegant sofas, lavish displays of flowers and a bucket containing champagne which had been placed there for the newlyweds. Terracotta tiles led outside to a flower-filled terrace and beyond that was a breathtaking view of the bay, under the ever-watchful eye of Mount Vesuvius.

'It's exactly like looking at a picture from a travel brochure,' she exclaimed as she stared at the dramatic outline of the famous volcanic mountain.

But the views and the luxury were forgotten the moment her husband took her into his arms, his lips brushing lightly against hers, and Lily could feel his incredible restraint as he pulled her close to his aroused body.

'I feel I've waited for ever for this night,' he said unsteadily.

'Me, too.' She put her arms around his neck. 'And now it's here.'

'And now it's here,' he repeated. 'Are you nervous?'

She thought about his experience. About what he might expect of her. And once again she felt a brief pang of unease as she wondered whether she should have told him. But how *could* she come out and say it, especially now? 'A little,' she answered truthfully.

'Some nerves are perfectly natural, but I will show you that there is nothing to be scared of.' His smile was reassuring as he gestured towards the ice-bucket. 'Would you like a glass of champagne?'

Aware of an increasing feeling of trepidation, Lily shook her head, carefully removing the wreath of roses and the veil which was still pinned tightly to her head. She hung the veil over the back of a chair and looked at him. Was it madness to find herself thinking that she just wanted to get this bit over with? As if this was a necessary hurdle to clear—so that afterwards they could relax properly and just enjoy the rest of the honeymoon and their life together?

'Can we just go to bed, Ciro?' she blurted out. 'Please.'

His momentary surprise was eclipsed by an intense feeling of satisfaction. Shyness and eagerness—could there be a more perfect combination? 'Oh, Lily,' he murmured. 'My beautiful, innocent bride—for whom I have waited as I have waited for no other woman.' Ignoring her small squeal of protest, he picked her up and carried her into the bedroom, his arms sinking into the massed layers of her tulle skirt before setting her down on the cool, marble floor.

'I want you to do something for me,' he said as he slid the zip of her dress down in one fluid movement and it sank to the ground like a fresh fall of snow.

'Anything,' she whispered. She stepped out from the circle of the discarded gown so that she stood before him in just her white lacy bra, her thong panties, a pair of lace-topped stockings and matching suspender belt. The high white silk wedding shoes made her much taller than usual and they made her stand differently, too, so that the jut of her hips seemed to be on display, and she saw his eyes darken.

'Let down your hair,' he said suddenly.

'My hair?'

'You realise that I've never seen your hair loose before?' he questioned unevenly. 'And somehow it seems symbolic that it should be tonight when you set it free.'

His dark eyes were blazing with *wonder*...as if all this was very new for him and of course, it was. And Lily realised just what it was that made marriage so special and profound. He had never done this before and neither had she. Made love to her *spouse*—which happened to be a very old-fashioned word, but in that moment she *felt* old-fashioned. And that was how Ciro liked her to be, wasn't it?

Lifting her hand to the intricate topknot, she pulled out the first pin and dropped it onto an adjacent table as the first shiny strand tumbled down. Ciro sucked in a breath as the second pin was removed, and then a third—and as each one liberated another thick lock it was accompanied by the tinny whisper of each falling pin.

His throat was bone-dry by the time she'd finished and his groin was threatening to explode. She looked like a goddess, he thought. Like a creature who represented the fields and the harvest—with that glorious corn-coloured spill of hair.

'Promise me something?' he questioned.

Her eyes met his and she tilted him a smile. 'You know where I stand on promises, Ciro.'

'Ah, but this is one you can easily keep, *dolcezza mia*. Promise me that you'll never cut your hair.'

For a moment, she hesitated. He made it sound as if her long, cascading hair was what defined her—and something about that made her feel faintly uneasy. Yet the look of appraisal which was making his dark eyes gleam like jet quickly had her nodding her head in agreement. 'Okay, I promise,' she said softly.

'Mille grazie,' he murmured as he pulled her close, framing her face in his hands before lowering his mouth to hers.

He kissed her until she moaned. Until he felt her weaken in his arms and then he picked her up and carried her over to the bed, laying her down on its centre, before removing her shoes and dropping them to the floor. For a moment he thought of leaving her wearing her provocative underwear. If it had been anyone other than Lily, he would have done just that. But she was not one in a long line of lovers who always tried to outperform themselves in order to please him. He did not need the titillation of seeing her curvaceous body encased in scanty pieces of silk and lace—he wanted to see her naked. To feel her naked. As close as it was possible for a man and woman to be. Because this was his wife. His *wife*.

Wriggling his hand behind her back, he unclipped her bra, a shuddered sigh escaping from his lips as her lush breasts were freed of their lacy confinement. Dipping his head, he started to suckle her and a shaft of pleasure shot through him as he circled his tongue around each pert nipple. Hooking his fingers into her panties, he slid them down over her thighs—unable to resist the brief brush of his thumb against her clitoris, smiling at the squeal of pleasure she gave in response.

'Ciro,' she breathed, her fingers scrabbling wildly at his shoulders.

Her fervour pleased him almost as much as her body, but he realised that, although she was now naked, he was still fully dressed and so he backed away from the bed.

'Don't move,' he instructed as he saw her mouth begin to form a circle of objection. 'I need to get rid of these damned clothes.'

'I'm not going anywhere,' she whispered.

'Good,' he said, unbuttoning his shirt with fingers which were shaking like a drunk's.

Lily's heart pounded as she watched him undress,

carelessly tossing his jacket onto a nearby chair in a way she suspected was uncharacteristic. Because even in jeans, he somehow always managed to look immaculate. Maybe that was an Italian thing. 'Shouldn't you hang that up?' she questioned nervously as his white shirt fluttered to the ground.

Pausing midway through easing his trouser zip down over his aching hardness, Ciro registered the sudden shyness in her voice and he gave a low laugh as he pulled his trousers off and wriggled out of his boxers.

'If you think,' he said as he joined her on the bed and pulled her warm and compliant body into his arms, 'that I am capable of anything right now other than maybe this…'

This was a kiss. A kiss which seemed to go on for ever. Which made the world shift and blur, leaving Lily a helpless victim of her senses. He moved his lips away and began to touch her breasts, his fingers drifting in provocative circles over her aroused flesh. She felt his hand skate proprietorially over the flat of her stomach and her eyes flew open to find that he was watching her, his dark gaze fiercely intent. 'Oh, Ciro,' she breathed.

'What is it, *angelo mio*?' he murmured, moving his hand down and rubbing his fingers luxuriously against the soft bush of curls.

'Oh, Ciro, I…" His thumb flicked across the engorged button of flesh which was concealed beneath the damp tangle and she gave a moan of pleasure because this was just *bliss*. She felt all the worries of the past recede. She saw nothing ahead but a bright and gloriously golden future. And Ciro was responsible. He was the one who had taken her fortunes and turned them around. The man who had picked her up when she was at her lowest ebb. Who had seen something in her. Something good. Something he liked enough to make him want her as his wife. He had scooped her up and made her feel safe and, now that the nerves of the wedding ceremony had passed, she could concentrate on all the glorious possibilities of the present. An overwhelming sense of *gratitude* washed over her and so did something else. Something which was bubbling up inside her and which felt too big and too important to hold back. Something she could give to him, with all her heart, if she dared to open the floodgates. 'Ciro?'

'What is it, *dolcezza*?'

'I...I love you,' she whispered.

There was a pause. 'Of course you do,' he murmured. And even though countless women had said it to him in the past, even though he had always dismissed the pat little sentence as meaningless—her declaration pleased him. Because she was his wife and she *should* love him. Just as he would love her in every way he could.

Lily's lips were tracing heated little kisses across his throat and he realised that they hadn't even discussed contraception—but that, for once, it really didn't matter. She was his wife. If she got pregnant, so what? Wasn't that what marriage was all about? He moved over her, touching his mouth to hers, feeling his erection pushing against her belly—and it was bigger and harder than he could ever remember feeling before. *Dio*—but this was so close to pleasure that it almost felt like *pain*. And not just in his body—for wasn't there an unfamiliar ache deep in his heart as he looked at her?

'I don't want to wear protection,' he said, his voice shaking as he made this unusually candid admission. 'I want to feel you. Just *you*, Lily. My skin against your skin. My hardness against your softness. No barrier, *mio angelo*—no barrier at all.'

'Then don't,' she said shakily, her arms wrapping around his broad back, her lips kissing his neck—inhaling the raw, citrusy smell of him, scarcely able to believe this was happening. 'Don't wear anything. Just… make love to me, Ciro. Please. Or else I think I'm going to die with the wanting.'

For a split second, something inside him jarred. Was it the sudden urgency of her words which surprised him—or just the assertive way she had expressed them? Yet Ciro knew he should rejoice in the fact she was relaxed—because wasn't tension supposed to be the enemy of a virgin's enjoyment? He splayed one hand luxuriously over her peaking breast while the other positioned himself to where she was wet and waiting. He could feel the powerful roar of his blood as it pounded senselessly around his veins and her wide blue eyes looked straight up into his.

'Lily,' he said, and entered her, his body taut with restraint as her velvet heat enclosed him.

'Ciro,' she breathed.

He saw her eyes close, saw her body shudder as he began to move, slowly at first, but gradually thrusting deeper and deeper—deeper than he'd thought he could ever go. Never had any woman ever felt so sweet nor so delicious—but then, never had he felt this aroused. 'I'm not hurting you?' he gasped.

The sweet rhythm had been consuming her, but now Lily's eyes snapped open to see his eyes searching her face—as if wanting clues about how much pleasure he was giving her. Hurting her? Why, nothing could be further from the truth. She didn't think that anything had ever given her so much pleasure as this *intimacy* of being joined with her husband. Her beloved husband. Instinctively, she gave a great bubbling sound of laughter as her arms looped around his neck, her bent legs lifting to entwine themselves around his broad back.

'Hurting me?' she murmured as she jutted her hips against him with practised ease. 'God, no. It's…it's… oh, Ciro—it's *amazing*.'

A hint of darkness momentarily clouded his overwhelming pleasure—but the writhing thrust of Lily's hips against his swollen hardness was enough to suck him right back in there again. He groaned as he juggled pleasure with restraint. It was torture holding back like this but Ciro knew he must temper his hunger. Because didn't they say it took virgins longer to achieve orgasm? And there was no way his new wife was going to miss out on *that* on her wedding night.

But suddenly she was clinging to him, her thighs digging into his sweat-sheened back as if she were riding a horse. Suddenly, her lips were torn away from his as she tipped her head back with an exultant moan—and he watched the telltale arching of her back as she started to come.

He waited only for her shuddering orgasm to fade and then Ciro let go completely. He heard the disbelieving cry which seemed to come from somewhere deep inside him. Felt the exquisite contractions which forced all the seed pumping from his body, straight into her wet and pulsing warmth.

Perhaps he might still not have guessed—at least, not then. He was so silken-deep in pleasure that he might simply have closed his eyes and drifted off to sleep, had Lily not begun to wriggle her toes up and down the sides of his body with an erogenous agility which spoke volumes. The rapturous aftermath of his orgasm began to disintegrate, like the lick of the incoming tide against a sandcastle built on the edge of the sea. He spanned his hands over her hips and lifted her slightly away from him so that their eyes were on a collision course, but Ciro was careful not to accuse. Because he might simply be mistaken. Please God, may he be mistaken.

'You liked that?' he questioned softly.

'You know I did,' she whispered, wishing that he'd bring her back down on top of him so that she could carry on kissing him.

There was a heartbeat of a pause. 'You know, for a

minute back then I almost thought that you were…experienced.'

The word was used almost casually, but Lily wasn't a fool. She could hear the faint brittleness which underpinned it, even if she hadn't been able to see the sudden hard glitter of his eyes. She bit her lip, searching for the right words to say, but she couldn't seem to find them anywhere.

'*Are* you, Lily?' he questioned softly. 'Are you experienced?'

There was a pause. 'Not very,' she admitted.

'Not *very*?' He stared at her, disbelief welling up inside him like a bitter tide. For a moment he thought that he might be mistaken. That it was something which was lost in translation between two people who spoke different languages. But the shrinking look in her eyes told a different story. Naked, without the prim clothes which made you think of wholesomeness and innocence— Ciro realised he was seeing the real Lily for the very first time. The flesh which he'd only ever seen covered with retro clothes was as creamy and as delicious as he'd imagined. The hair which he'd found so alluring now spilled gloriously over the pillow, just like every fantasy he'd ever had. But now it seemed to mock him because the image she'd presented was nothing but an illusion and he felt the kick of pain in his heart as he registered just how *wanton* she looked.

Yet why should he be so surprised? Why had he ever thought she was different from all the others, when it turned out that she was exactly the same? He remembered his own mother—too wrapped up in her own desires to spare much time for the little boy who waited alone in the big, cold mansion. Remembered his nameless fears as he'd lain awake night after night and wondered if she would return home alone or not. He remembered Eugenia and the way she'd hinted that sexual straying was *negotiable*. Had he thought he'd found illusive innocence in the wholesome-looking Lily—only to discover that he had been duped all along?

He felt the violent slam of his heart against his ribcage but he asked the question anyway. Knowing that he was nothing but a crazy fool to cling onto a last shred of hope as he looked deep into her blue eyes. 'So were you a virgin, Lily?' he bit out painfully. 'Or was your bridal innocence nothing but a sham?'

CHAPTER NINE

LILY'S heart sank as she met the dark accusation which blazed from Ciro's eyes. His hands were digging into her hips; she wondered if he realised that—or whether her skin was just more sensitive than usual because of the amazing orgasm he'd just given her. It shouldn't *matter* whether or not she was a virgin, she told herself fiercely, and yet hot on the heels of that thought came another. *Stupid* Lily for not having told him sooner. Stupid, stupid, *stupid*. And how best to tell him now, in these awful circumstances? When they were both stark naked and he was staring at her with an expression she'd never seen on his face before and would be quite happy never to see again.

'No, I wasn't a virgin. But then...' she tried a smile which didn't quite come off '...neither were you.'

A fierce pain shafted through his heart and his throat felt as if it had been dusted with gravel. 'Ah, but I never pretended to be otherwise, did I? Unlike you.'

He pushed her away from him, positioning her against the rumpled bank of pillows before getting up off the bed—as if he wanted to put as much distance between them as possible.

'I didn't *pretend*!' she protested, the cool air rushing over her bare skin and making her acutely aware of his physical absence.

'Didn't you?' He flicked her a contemptuous look as he reached for his boxer shorts. 'You certainly didn't bother to correct my assumption that you were innocent, did you, Lily? Nor bother enlightening me that you'd had other lovers before me—other men who have been *intimate* with your body. You went along with it, didn't you?'

Lily bit her lip as his words hit a nerve, knowing that he was speaking the truth. She *had* let herself go along with it for all kinds of reasons. She'd known that he respected her *because* she'd kept him at a distance. That women who didn't fall into bed with him were something of a rarity in his life. And she hadn't seemed able to stop herself from buying into his fantasy. She'd liked the way he made her feel. She'd liked it too much. He had made her feel cherished—as if there *had* been no man before him. He still did. Tom was like a shadow in comparison. Couldn't she make him understand that?

'I know I should have told you,' she said carefully. 'I know that now. But it was so easy to go along with the amazing time we were having and I didn't want to spoil what we had.'

'So you thought you'd wait until our wedding night to spring your little surprise on me, did you? Until you'd

ridden me like a hooker? Forgive me if I don't commend
your sense of timing.' He saw her flinch at his crude
statement, but he didn't care because the dull, blunting
pain of betrayal was hurting his heart. 'How many was
it, Lily?' He held up his hand, where his golden wedding
ring seemed to catch the light and mock him. 'Less than
the fingers on one hand—or is that a conservative es-
timate? As many as fifty, maybe? No wonder you were
so damned good!'

'Not lovers in the *plural*!' she cried, cringing beneath
the contempt in his dark eyes as he started sliding the
silken boxer shorts over the taut length of his thighs.
'There's been only one before you!'

'And that's supposed to make me happy?'

Looking at him, she couldn't imagine that anything
would make him happy right then. Unless some last-
ditch attempt at logic might appeal to his wounded sense
of pride. 'You didn't tell me about your previous lovers.'

'Not in detail, no—but I certainly didn't twist the
truth to make myself into something I wasn't.'

She sucked in a deep breath, knowing that she needed
to confront what lay at the bottom of all this. 'Was my
supposed virginity so important to you, then, Ciro?' she
questioned quietly.

There was a moment's silence as he met her bright
blue gaze but he hardened his heart to it. 'You know it
was,' he said coldly as a pulse began to flicker at his
temple. He watched as her fingers grabbed at the rumpled sheet, bringing it up to cover the soft blur of curls

at her thighs. And he realised that she was no different from any other woman—willing to stoop to any deception if she thought she was in with a chance of hooking a wealthy man.

Eugenia had made it clear that she would overlook anything, just as long as she was adequately rewarded—but at least she had been *honest* about her motives. She hadn't pretended to be a sweet innocent, acting as if butter wouldn't melt in that delicious mouth of hers. Cleverly buying into his ultimate fantasy of marrying a woman who was a virgin.

'Ciro, come back to bed. Please.'

His mouth twisted. 'What a fool I've been,' he grated. 'A fool to have been sucked in by your soft curves and homespun talents. By your supposed innocent primness.' He picked up his discarded shirt and slid it on over his broad shoulders. 'The first and only woman who didn't allow me to seduce her. My ideal woman, or so I thought.'

Lily flinched, holding her hands out towards him in a gesture of supplication. 'I should have told you,' she said, watching as he pulled on his trousers. 'But I didn't, and you never actually asked me. And Tom wasn't—'

'Tom?' he bit out.

'He was the man I was going to marry.'

'You were actually going to *marry* him?'

'Yes,' she admitted. 'But he called the wedding off when he met someone else.'

'When?'

'Two days before it was supposed to happen.'

Some deeply buried shred of compassion implored Ciro to offer her sympathy for having been jilted. Some small inner voice called to him and asked whether her experience might have affected the way she had subsequently behaved with him. But his sense of being wronged was so great that he did not heed it. The pain in his heart was far too strong to contemplate any easy forgiveness towards her. He had been brought up to suspect the motives of women and Lily Scott had just reinforced his judgement. 'And did he thrill you?' he questioned, walking towards the bed and towering over her as he finished buckling his belt.

Lily stared up at him, her heart beating with a mixture of fear and excitement—wanting more than anything that he would just take his trousers off again and get back into bed with her and…and…

'Did he, Lily?' he demanded, his heated question breaking into her shockingly erotic thoughts. 'Did he thrill you? Did he make you come when he touched you?'

She knew that she should answer his outrageous question truthfully. That there could now be nothing but complete honesty between them, if there was to be any chance of salvaging this. Who was to say that something good couldn't rise from the ashes of this terrible showdown they'd had? But not at any cost. Because there was no way she could answer something like that with any degree of dignity. And besides, she wasn't able to give him the only answer he wanted to hear. 'I don't think you have any right to ask me something like that,' she said quietly.

He turned away, sick with disgust at himself—and sick with jealousy, too—her refusal to answer telling him everything he needed to know. Because he had wanted her to blurt out that she had never known pleasure before him. That no other man had made her cry out in helpless rapture. But they had, hadn't they? This man *Tom*. The man who had abandoned her. Who had taken the virginity which should have been *his* to take.

'I should have listened to Giuseppe,' he said bitterly.

Lily's ears pricked up at the mention of the cousin who had looked at her so assessingly, his blue eyes narrowed with suspicion. 'Why, what did he say?'

He shook his head. 'That you sounded too good to be true. But I blocked my ears to it all.' His laugh was bitter. 'And I fell for your pretty play-acting. Your outraged behaviour when I pushed you up against the car when the reality was that you were gagging for it.'

Her hand flew to her mouth. 'How dare you say that?'

'Because it's *true*!' All true, he thought grimly. His pure and prim Lily had been nothing but an illusion—a woman he'd conjured up from the depths of some bizarre fantasy. He felt the cold clamp of a nameless emotion as it closed round his heart, sealing up cracks which had started to appear when he'd met her. Slipping on his socks and shoes, he picked up his jacket from where he'd flung it over the chair, then hunted around until he had located his car keys.

The jangling of metal brought Lily to her senses. 'Where are you going?' she questioned.

'Out!'

'Ciro—'

'Before I say or do something I may later regret,' he said, turning away from her distress and from those blue eyes which were now brimming with unshed tears. Wrenching open the door, he slammed his way out of the suite.

Lily's heart was pounding so hard that she lay back weakly against the pillows, her eyes fixed on the closed door, praying for him to come back. To take her in his arms and to tell her that he was sorry he'd lost it. To tell her that he'd been unreasonable and could they please just forget it had ever happened and start over.

He didn't, of course. The minutes ticked by with excruciating slowness until an hour had passed, and then another. Through the open shutters she could hear the faint drift of music and laughter. And the irony didn't escape her that downstairs people were still celebrating their wedding, while upstairs the bride lay alone in the honeymoon bed.

She glanced at the ornate clock hanging on the far wall to see that it was well past midnight. Where *was* he? It dawned on her that he could be in any one of a hundred places she didn't know about. Because she knew so little of his life here. And in that moment, Lily realised how alone she was. Alone in a strange city, having married

one of its major players—and then been abandoned by
him in the most bitter of rows.

What the hell was she going to do?

For a moment her fingers twisted at the sheet, her
mind spinning with possibilities until she came to a sudden decision, motivated by something which had defined
her life so far. Something called survival.

Was she going to lie there feeling sorry for herself because Ciro D'Angelo had judged her so negatively? No
way. Just because she'd let all his harsh accusations wash
over her, didn't mean she had to continue being a mindless *victim*. She picked up her phone and punched out
his number, but wasn't surprised when it went straight
through to voicemail. She left a message in a surprisingly calm voice—saying that she didn't think it was a
good idea to go driving in the middle of the night when
he was clearly in such a volatile mood. And could he
please just let her know he was safe.

Half an hour later, a stark two-word text came wing-
ing back.

I'm safe.

And that was that. Lily was left in the vast suite without a clue where he was, or when he'd be coming back. It
promised to be a long night. She had nowhere to go, she
realised as she slithered into the warmth of an oversized
bathrobe—and no one she could talk to. All the people closest to her were here at the hotel—but she could
hardly go knocking on Danielle's door in the middle of
the night to tell her that she'd been deserted by her new

husband. Apart from the shame of admitting something like that, wasn't there still part of her which was hoping that once Ciro had calmed down they could talk about this like adults and maybe get round it?

Yes, she'd been wrong not to tell him about her past—but surely he could understand why she had allowed herself to be swept along by the romance and security he'd been offering her? He'd said he *wanted* to help her, and he had gone all out to get her to agree with him. Did that count for nothing—and was he now going to deny the existence of the lightning flash of attraction which had hit them both? Surely their future didn't have to be governed by something as unimportant as her virginity.

But it was important to him, she realised. It was important in a primitive way which most men wouldn't admit to. In the same way he'd admitted to all that stuff about wanting a wife who would always be waiting for him.

She must have fallen asleep because when she awoke, the suite was filled with the pale apricot light of dawn. Slowly she sat up in bed, her heart almost leaping out of her chest when she saw the dark figure who was seated at the other side of the room, silently watching her. He had removed his jacket and wore his white shirt and dark wedding trousers. But his feet were bare, his eyes were blank and his mouth was tight and unsmiling.

Suppressing a shiver, Lily ran her hand through the mussed tangle of her hair. 'Where have you been?'

'Out.'

She didn't react. So was this how it was going to be from now on? She wanted to hurl herself at him, to demand to know whether he had sought refuge in the arms of another woman. Someone who would soothe him and be indignant that he'd been short-changed by his bride. But Lily knew that misplaced emotion and unfounded fears weren't going to help her at a time like this. That if there was any hope of salvaging this whole mess, then she needed to be calm. To show him that she could still be strong. More importantly, that she cared about him.

'I was worried about you.'

'Why?'

'Because you drove off in such a rage—for all I knew, you could have had some kind of accident.'

'And wouldn't that have made it easier for you?' he asked, in a flat, deadly voice.

'E-easier for me? What are you talking about?'

'Billionaire groom's car plummets off coastal road,' he intoned, still in that same flat tone—like a radio commentator making a sombre announcement. 'Leaving his bride of less than twenty-four hours a widow.'

'Ciro! That's a terrible thing—'

'The operative word being *billionaire*, of course,' he mused. 'The widow takes it all—the money, the houses, the share portfolio. Wouldn't that be the perfect solution, Lily? After all, you were prepared to pretend to be something you weren't in order to secure a marriage to a rich man. Maybe you've been praying to get my money sooner rather than later?'

'Stop it,' she breathed.

He shook his head with an air of disbelief, like a man who had just emerged unscratched from the wreckage of a plane. 'But I guess I have nobody to blame but myself for what's happened. For once in my life, I was completely blinkered. So blinkered that I walked straight into your honeyed trap—though if I'd stopped to think about it, it was glaringly obvious what you were trying to do. You were so desperate to secure your house and your future—'

'And you were so desperate to be the first man to lay claim to my body,' she flared back, reeling at all the emotional ammunition he was firing at her.

'Yes. Yes, I was.' He stared at her, as if trying to make sense of it. 'I am an experienced man of the world and usually I can see right through any form of deception. But I have to say that you really got me, Lily. You were so...*wondering*. So unbelievably sweet. Like it was the first time for you.'

'Because that's what it felt like!' she protested, her voice trembling now. 'It really was like that.'

He leapt on her words, like a hungry dog on a bone. 'So you didn't feel anything for the other man you were engaged to?'

She bit her lip. It would have been so easy to say no. That she'd felt nothing at all for Tom—but that would have been a lie. And there weren't going to be any more lies. No matter how awful the consequences, she could no longer shy away from the truth. 'Yes, of course I did,' she whispered.

Ciro stood up as if he'd been struck—the pain nearly as bad as it had been last night when he'd discovered that another man had been the first to give her pleasure. He walked over to the double doors which were open to the spacious terrace, beyond which the dawn-washed bay glittered beneath the rising sun. This wasn't how it was supposed to be. They should have been making love now. And when the sun was a little higher they should have been taking breakfast out there on the terrace, against the backdrop of the most beautiful view in the world. Afterwards, he'd been planning to surprise his new bride with a boat-trip for two along the Amalfi coast, where a sleek yacht lay bobbing in the water—ready to take them to any number of paradise destinations.

And now?

Now it all felt so *empty*.

He turned back to face her, thinking how beautiful she looked, her sapphire eyes glittering wildly in her pale face. He should tell her to get the hell out of his life. To walk out and leave him alone and he would pay her off with a no-fuss divorce.

But the beat of his heart and the heat in his groin were clouding his judgement. Her body was sending out a siren call he'd denied for too long to be strong enough to resist, when it was sitting right there in front of him, on a plate. He began to walk towards the bed and saw her eyes darken as he stood over her, seeing the way that her fingers clutched at the all-enveloping bathrobe.

'What are you doing?' she whispered.

'Nothing, at the moment. Why, what do you want me to do?'

She wanted him to stop looking at her like that—as if she were a piece of *meat* and he were some hungry predator who was about to make a big meal of it. 'I want you to leave me alone.'

'No, you don't.'

'I do, I...*oh*!' Lily fell back against the pillows as he sank down on the bed, his mouth finding hers and prising her lips open with the expert play of his tongue. And she was letting him. Letting his fingers splay over her breast as the robe fell open—and the instinctive cry of pleasure she gave in response to his touch felt like a betrayal. There was still time to struggle. Still time to push him away, even as his hand was reaching for his belt. So why was she *helping* him? Why was she tugging at his trousers and then at the silken boxes which hugged the hard curve of his buttocks? Why the hell didn't she do something as he reached for a condom, which he was now sliding on with a daunting efficiency?

And then he was ripping the shirt from his shoulders and somehow the robe had been pulled from her body. He was prising open her thighs and she was letting him—*wanting him*—so on fire and so wet for him that she sucked in a gasped cry of pleasure as he entered her. For a moment he stilled and then he bent his head to whisper in her ear.

'So why don't you show me what you can do, baby?'

It was an unforgivingly contemptuous remark to make in the circumstances and Lily closed her eyes as she prayed for strength to tell him to stop, knowing that he would comply in an instant. Because hadn't he already demonstrated his steely self-control where sex was concerned? But the truth was that she didn't want him to stop. She couldn't bear him to stop. When he was deep inside her like this, wasn't there the sense that they were at one—only if it was in a purely physical sense?

She placed the flat of her hand on his chest and pushed, until he was lying on his back with her on top, still intimately joined. Her hair fell forward as she began to move, tentatively at first and then, as he gave a shuddered moan, with more confidence. Her soft thighs gripped the hard bone and sinew of his hips. She revelled in the erotic contrast of his taut masculinity against her pliant femininity. She felt the hardness of him deep inside her as she rode him with a hunger and an anger she'd never felt before. And when she saw control begin to slip away from him, she lowered her head and began to kiss him—even though at first he tried to turn his head away. But not for long. With a little moan of capitulation he let her deepen the kiss and he caught his hands to her waist as he came to a shuddering orgasm deep inside her.

She felt the ragged warmth of his breath against her

neck as the spasms died away into a soft stillness. For a while, they lay there in silence until he carefully withdrew from her and she felt a great pang of disappointment—hating herself for missing the intimate feel of his body so much.

He turned onto his side, propping himself up on one elbow and leaning over her—his lips very close to hers. 'That was a little one-sided,' he mused.

Lily swallowed. 'It doesn't matter.'

'Oh, but it does.' Slipping his hand down between her thighs, he began to move his fingers against her heated flesh. 'It matters a lot.'

'Ciro—'

'Shh.'

It was quick and it was perfunctory and Lily was much too turned on to be able to stop him from bringing her to another gasping orgasm, which he didn't even bother to silence with a kiss.

Afterwards she felt like turning her face into the pillow and weeping with shame, but she vowed that Ciro would see no tears from her. She had to face the truth—no matter how unpalatable that might be. She couldn't just shrug off all the responsibility and place all the burden on him. If this was a blame-game then there were two players, not one. *She* had helped to create this situation. She'd known the kind of man he was, with his old-fashioned ideals—and she had allowed herself to play along with it. Yes, it had *felt* real to her, but Ciro didn't care about that. He cared about her deception. About the smashing of what he'd believed in—and there was no going back. They needed to confront the future and they needed to do it with dignity.

'So where do we go from here?' she asked slowly.

Ciro looked down at her flushed face and saw the pulse which was beating frantically amid the dampened hair at her temple. Where indeed? He felt the bitter taste of regret, knowing he shouldn't have done that. He shouldn't have had sex with her again—nor brought her to such a cold-blooded orgasm afterwards. He despised himself for his actions—even while his body still shivered with remembered pleasure of how good she'd felt.

For a long moment he was silent as he weighed up all the possibilities which lay open to them. 'If we hadn't consummated the marriage, then we could have had it annulled,' he said. 'As it is, I think we should put an end to it as soon as possible, don't you?'

Lily thought about a pet dog she'd once had—her beloved Harley, who had lived to a ripe old age. When he had become sick the vet had talked about 'putting him out of his misery'. Well, that was exactly what this felt like. Only without the long and happy life in between.

Well, she was damned if she was going to ask him if they couldn't try to work it out—not when he'd clearly made up his mind that it was over.

'I can go back to England,' she said quietly.

Ciro shook his head, his mind working quickly, the way it always did when he saw a problem which needed a solution. 'No, Lily. That's where you're wrong. I don't want any more drama—and you flouncing out with a haunted face and accusing eyes is the last thing I need. My marriage ending within days will either make me look like a fool—or a bad judge of character. And I will countenance neither.'

'So this is all about *your* reputation, is it, Ciro?'

'What do you think?' he questioned roughly. 'I have worked hard to build it and I will not have it wrecked by you.' He paused, his heart beating heavily as he looked at her. 'If you agree to my plan, then you'll get what you wanted all along. The Grange will still be yours and I will ensure a generous settlement in return for your co-operation.'

Lily heard the steely note of negotiation which had entered his voice and stared at him. He looked like a *stranger*, she thought. A dark-faced and grim stranger. 'What do you mean by cooperation?'

He shrugged. 'It isn't complicated. You play the part of my beloved wife for six months—after which time we will tell the world that you are homesick. That you miss England too much to make the marriage work and that we are parting amicably.'

'And if I refuse?'

'I don't think you will.' His black eyes hardened and so did his lips. 'You see, you aren't really in any posi-tion to refuse, Lily.'

She opened her mouth to contradict him, to tell him that she could refuse anything she pleased. But the truth was that she was filled with a weariness which seemed to have seeped deep into her bones. And that, right now, she couldn't face going back to the tatters of the life she'd left behind in England.

CHAPTER TEN

'You were very quiet tonight.'

Ciro's words broke into the silence of Lily's thoughts and a whisper of awareness shivered over her skin as he joined her on the balcony. Suddenly the terrace of their apartment seemed the size of a matchbox as he dominated the space around him, just as he always did. The glitter of the starry sky, the dark lick of the waves in the bay—all these seemed to fade into nothingness as he came to stand beside her. She could sense the warmth of his body and smell the raw tang of his aftershave. And it didn't seem to matter how much she tried to fight her attraction towards him, or how often she told herself that it was dangerous to still feel this way about him—nothing ever changed. She continued to want her husband with a fierce hunger which had shown no signs of abating.

They had arrived home a short while ago and she'd gone outside into the warm night air to drink in the view she had grown to love. The magic of the southern city which had captured her heart these last few months—a heart for which her husband had no use.

'You didn't enjoy the evening?' he questioned.

Lily felt the faint whisper of the sea breeze on her bare shoulders and swallowed down a painful sigh. Did he really have no idea why she was so preoccupied? Didn't he realise that no matter how wonderful the opera or after-show party, or whatever other glitzy event they happened to be attending, it didn't make up for the tense reality of their married life. That every second spent beneath his unforgiving gaze was like having a knife twisted in her stomach.

It isn't complicated, Ciro had said on their wedding night—when he had proposed the idea of a six-month marriage for the sake of propriety.

Like hell it wasn't.

It was about as complicated as it could get.

She stared at the diamond sparkle of the sea and the brooding silhouette of Mount Vesuvius in the distance. Did he really find it *uncomplicated* to maintain the illusion that they were a pair of blissful newlyweds, when nothing could be further from the truth?

That was the trouble. Yes, he did. Ciro had a skill which seemed sadly lacking in her. It seemed that he could compartmentalise everything with an ease which would have been almost admirable if it hadn't been so breathtakingly cold. And he could do it so well that at times she'd almost been sucked into believing it herself. Like when he introduced her to people she hadn't met before and his hand would stray to rest protectively at the small of her back—as if he were finding it difficult to refrain from touching her. And Lily's heart would crash like crazy as his fingers massaged the knotted tension in her spine, wondering if he'd forgiven her. But then she would look up into his dark eyes and see nothing but coldness there.

Which either meant that her husband was a brilliant actor who could successfully hide his feelings from the world—or just that he didn't *have* any feelings for her any more. That the supposed 'lightning flash' he'd once felt had been extinguished by her deception.

The morning after their wedding, he had cancelled their honeymoon yacht trip along the Amalfi coastline and Lily had tried telling herself that was a good thing. Because could there be anything worse than being stuck on a boat with a man who was simmeringly angry with you? Yet inside she had been heartbroken—like a child whose birthday party had been called off at the last minute.

So they'd come back to Ciro's apartment and Lily had tried telling herself that surely it couldn't be *that* difficult to maintain their fiction of a relationship—especially as her husband had gone straight back to work instead of taking a planned sabbatical. She was here in Naples, surrounded by beauty and culture and—even if her marriage *was* a disaster—this was an opportunity she'd never have again. She was determined to put a brave face on it. To keep smiling, no matter what. To keep praying that maybe her husband's anger might fade away and that he might let her close enough to love him…

But her prayers went unanswered. The only time he let her close was when he was having sex with her—and she liked *that* far too much to tell him not to do it, no matter how much her battered pride urged her to push him away.

She turned to face him now as the silver moonlight cast indigo shadows on his sculpted features and the sight of him in his dark evening clothes still had the power to make her quiver with lust. 'Of course I enjoyed the evening,' she said. 'The opera was magnificent.'

'I know it was.' There was a pause as he drifted his gaze over her. 'Everyone was commenting on how beautiful you looked.'

She looked up into his dark eyes. 'And what did you say?'

Ciro reached out to frame her cheek with the palm of his hand, feeling the familiar thunder of his pulse. 'Oh, I agreed with them. Because nobody has ever denied your beauty, Lily,' he said softly. 'Least of all me.'

'Ciro—'

But he silenced her breathless whisper with his lips, acknowledging the sweet power of sex to blot out his misgivings, as he pulled her into his arms. Because sometimes when she looked at him with those big blue eyes she made him want to melt. She made him feel almost…*vulnerable*—just as he'd done when he'd made his wedding vows in that music-filled and fragrant church.

When he'd felt as if he was poised on the brink of something momentous—only to discover that he was marrying a woman he didn't really know. Who had taken his half-formed dreams and smashed them beneath her perfect little feet until they lay shattered and unrecognisable.

Ciro had been angry with Lily for her deception, yes, he had. But once his anger had died away, he had been almost *grateful* to her. Because it had felt wonderfully familiar to lose himself in the old, familiar coldness—to feel that iciness encase his heart once more. It had put him back in the emotional driving seat, where nothing or no one could touch him. Or hurt him.

In the darkness of the Neapolitan night, he slipped his hand inside the bodice of her dress and heard the rush of her breath as his fingers encountered the silken feel of her bare skin. 'Bed, I think,' he said unsteadily and led her unresisting inside, where he proceeded to strip off her clothes with ruthless efficiency.

His skin was hot against hers and by the time he entered her, she pulled him to her with a fierce hunger, as if she couldn't get enough of him. Her lips sought his and she moaned as he crushed his mouth onto hers, moving inside her body in a way which soon had her shuddering helplessly in his arms. Afterwards she clung to him, her hands clasped behind his neck—only loosening their grip when sleep crept over her and she lolled against the bank of pillows. Deliberately, Ciro rolled over to the other side of the bed—as far from the soft temptation of her body as it was possible to be. He had been doing this more often of late—rationing the time she spent in his arms and telling himself that he needed to get used to solitude again. Because soon his beautiful, duplicitous bride would be heading back to England and he would be left alone…

He slept restlessly, with dreams which left him feeling spooked, and when he awoke, it was to find Lily gone—just like in the dream. For a moment he lay there, staring up at the streaks of sunlight which were dancing across the ceiling—and a terrible sense of darkness invaded his soul.

He showered and dressed, then walked out onto the terrace to find her sitting drinking coffee—her eyes concealed behind her large sunglasses as she automatically bent to pour him a cup. She was wearing a pale, silken robe which had been part of her trousseau and it was easy to see that she was naked underneath.

'So what are you planning to do today?' he asked, a flicker of desire shimmering over him as he began knotting his tie.

From behind the concealment of her shades, Lily watched him. His black hair glittered with tiny drops of water and his skin was still glowing from the shower. He radiated energy and vitality from every pore and, even though he looked cool and businesslike in his lightweight suit, her instinctive feeling was one of pure lust.

Guilt, too. She mustn't forget her ever-present sense of guilt, must she? She remembered the way she'd been last night, in his arms. The way she'd moaned his name out loud as she climaxed—the way she always did. It was all too easy to close her mind to her nagging uncertainties when he was deep inside her like that. She'd just lain right back and enjoyed every second of his love-making and afterwards she had...had...

'Blushing, Lily?' he murmured as he gave his tie one final tug and reached down for his coffee. 'My, my—it's a long time since I've seen you blush.'

She heard the censure in his voice and bristled. 'Perhaps you think only women with intact hymens should be permitted to blush?'

'Isn't that a little crude?' he murmured.

'Which you never are, of course?'

His black eyes glittered. 'You didn't seem to be complaining about my crudity last night.'

'I doubt whether you've ever had any complaints in that particular department, Ciro.'

Feeling another jerk of desire, he walked over to the edge of the terrace, as if he just wanted to get a better look at the bay. It was a view he'd grown up with and yet which now seemed subtly altered—as everything familiar in his life had been altered.

Had he thought that this charade of a marriage would be easy? That he would pleasure himself with Lily for six, short months and that each time he did he would find himself growing a little more distant from her? Yes, he had. Of course he had. Because that was what he had *wanted* to happen and Ciro was a man who always made things happen.

He had expected his anger to remain constant, while his passion declined—the way it always did when a relationship with a woman was on the wane. The only trouble was that it hadn't worked out like that. A welcome immunity towards her simply hadn't happened and he was no closer to feeling indifferent towards her. In bed and out, he wanted her now as much as he'd always wanted her.

It perplexed him. It was driving him crazy. He told himself over and over that she was a liar who had been prepared to lie in order to secure her future. That she would never understand what made a traditionally Neapolitan man like himself tick. But none of his convictions seemed to last beyond a minute and that confused the hell out of him. What did she *have* that made him instantly want to lose himself in her—as if she alone possessed the balm which could soothe his troubled spirit? Had she cast some kind of spell on him, the moment she'd entered his life?

'Ciro?'

'What?' he growled, turning back to face her, letting his eyes drift over the spill of her hair, which was cascading all the way down her back and wondering whether he should postpone his first meeting and take her back to bed.

'You asked what I was planning to do today.'

'Did I?'

She gave a tight smile but secretly she was rather relieved by his air of distraction, knowing he wasn't going to like what she had to say. 'I thought I'd go and see your mother.'

This piece of information wiped all the confused thoughts from his head and had him frowning as he looked at her. 'Why would you want to do that?'

'Because she's your mother. And I'm your wife.'

'But you're not *really* my wife, are you, Lily? We both know that.'

'I may not be your wife in the true sense of the word—but your mother doesn't know that, does she? And if you want to maintain this fiction of a marriage, then visiting her seems the right thing to do. Anyway, I'd like to go and see her. I can't keep spending every day exploring churches and listening to Italian lessons on my headset while you go out and make yet another fortune.'

She saw his eyes narrow and knew he was still bemused by her insistence on learning a language which wasn't going to be of any use to her in the future. She'd argued with him over this—saying that no new language would ever be wasted. He seemed to think that now she had access to his bank account, she'd want to spend all her days spending it. But Lily hadn't done that—something which she knew perplexed him. She had fallen in love with Naples, and pride made her want to make herself understood while she was living there. For a few brief months, she wanted to feel part of this warm, southern paradise.

Ciro mulled over this latest surprising development. 'My mother isn't a great socialiser,' he said repressively. 'I doubt whether she'll agree to see you.'

'She already has.'

'Scusi?' He stared at her in disbelief.

'I rang her yesterday and said I'd like to go round and she's invited me for coffee.'

Ciro felt the slow build of anger though he couldn't quite pinpoint the cause of it. Because she hadn't checked with him first? Or because he felt uncomfortable about her seeing a woman with whom he'd always had a difficult relationship? 'You went behind my back and phoned my mother and arranged to meet her?'

'Yes, Ciro—if that's how you want to look at it, I did. I committed the heinous crime of trying to be polite—something which is obviously beyond your comprehension.'

'There's no need to be insolent.'

'Why, have you taken out a monopoly on insolence?' she challenged.

Their eyes met in a silent tussle of wills and for one brief moment Ciro almost smiled. But any humour was dissolved by what she'd just told him. *Why was she starting up a pointless relationship with his mother?*

'Is there nothing I can say which will change your mind?'

'Absolutely nothing. Short of you getting hold of some chains and imprisoning me in the apartment, I'm going round there for coffee this morning.'

'Then so be it.' He picked up his briefcase and his mouth hardened. 'But she can be a difficult woman. Don't say I didn't warn you.'

His words still ringing in her ears, she got ready for her meeting with her mother-in-law, changing her outfit three times and ending up feeling hot and flustered. A taxi took her to Leonora D'Angelo's large apartment and when she was shown into the dimly lit salon she felt big and clumsy compared to the bird-like frame of Ciro's mother.

Lily perched on the edge of a velvet chair and accepted a tiny cup of coffee and a wave of sadness washed over her. How long had it been since she'd sat and drunk coffee with her own mother like this? She wondered what advice she would have given her about Ciro, and realised how much she still missed her.

Despite her advanced years, Leonora D'Angelo remained a handsome woman, with dark eyes so reminiscent of her son and a bone structure which emphasised her angular jaw. She wore a plain grey dress and a twisted gold necklace and on her bony fingers glittered an impressive array of diamonds. She leaned back in her chair and gave Lily a cool smile.

'So. The younger Signora D'Angelo is looking a little pale. You are settling well into Naples, I hope?'

Lily managed to produce a smile, wondering what her mother-in-law would say if she came out and told it how it really was. *I'm just about managing to tolerate living with a man who despises me, even though the*

*feeling isn't exactly mutual. Because learning to unlove
someone isn't as easy as you might think.* 'It's a beautiful city,' she said politely.

Leonora nodded. 'I think so—though, to many,
Naples is an enigma. A place of light and dark. Where
sometimes you turn a corner and never quite know what
you'll find.' She gave a thin smile. 'Perhaps a little like
my son.'

Lily's heart began to pound as she wondered if
Leonora was going to talk about Ciro—because would
she be able to sustain the lie of their marriage to a
woman who knew him better than anyone? 'Really?'
she said, because she couldn't think what else to say.

'I am pleased that Ciro has decided to settle down at
last. It has certainly been a long time coming. Sometimes
I wonder why that should have been, but there again…'
There was a pause as Leonora's voice tailed off and
she narrowed her fading dark eyes. 'Does he talk much
about his childhood?'

Lily shook her head. 'Not really.'

'He hasn't told you that he was unhappy?'

At this, Lily felt a little helpless. It wasn't really her
place to disclose things he'd said to her in confidence.
Disclosures which could be potentially very hurtful to
his mother. The things Ciro had said were half-admis-
sions which didn't make up a complete picture—like
pieces of a jigsaw puzzle with the edges missing. She'd
managed to discover that he was often left to fend for
himself—and that, despite the army of servants, he'd

been a lonely little boy. And how could she possibly turn around to Leonora D'Angelo and tell her that he had also hinted about his mother's love-life and that he heartily disapproved of it?

'Ciro is a very private man,' Lily said, hoping that would be an end to it, but it seemed that was not to be the case because Signora D'Angelo put her untouched coffee down on a highly polished table.

'I was very depressed after I gave birth to him, you know.' Leonora's cultured voice gave an unexpected crack.

'No,' said Lily quietly. 'I didn't know.'

'There was no understanding of the condition back then, of course—and people certainly never spoke of it, because depression has always carried its own kind of stigma. It was expected that a woman should just carry on and it would all work out. And I tried to make that happen, I really did—but my mood was too dark to be lifted.' There was a pause. 'Did you know that his father left me?'

Uncomfortably, Lily nodded. 'He did mention that.'

Leonora shrugged as if it didn't matter and Lily thought that she almost carried it off—but not quite. And suddenly she got a frightening image of herself in some lonely future, shrugging her shoulders and explaining that her Neapolitan marriage hadn't worked out, with a voice like Leonora's—which wasn't quite steady.

'The marriage was not what he thought it would be. He had married a vivacious socialite,' said Leonora. 'Not a woman who could hardly be bothered to get out of bed in the morning. It was highly unusual for a man to leave his wife and child in those days and after he'd gone, I was...*afraid*. Yes, afraid. Frightened of being on my own. Of having sole charge of a boy as strong and as wilful as Ciro with no father figure to look up to. And ashamed of having been rejected. I wanted a man for my son—and, yes, I admit, I wanted a man for *me*.'

'Signora D'Angelo,' interrupted Lily quickly. 'You don't have to tell me all this.'

'Oh, but I do,' said the older woman, her voice a little bitter now. 'Because maybe you might be able to explain to Ciro why I did what I did. To make him listen in a way that he refuses to do with me.'

Lily bit her lip. If she told the truth—that Ciro wouldn't dream of listening to a word *she* said—then wouldn't that just worry her mother-in-law even more? She gave a weak smile. 'I can try.'

Leonora clasped her fingers together in her lap and her diamonds glittered. 'Things were different for women then—especially here. Naples has always been one of the most traditional and male-centred of cities. It was frowned on to be a deserted wife—especially as everyone else I knew had a husband at home. Maybe I was desperate and don't they always say that desperation shows?' She gave a wry kind of laugh. 'Maybe that was why I never married again, although I used to date men, of course. I used to bring them back here—'

'Signora D'Angelo—'

'Sometimes just for drinks, or for coffee. Sometimes—not always—just to talk. I was *lonely*, Lily. Very lonely.'

Lily nodded as she saw the stark pain in Leonora's eyes. 'Yes, I can imagine,' she said quietly.

'But Ciro was fierce, even then. He hated it. He hated the men. He wanted his mamma to live like a nun and I wanted to live like…well, like a woman.' Leonora swallowed. 'It made us grow apart. It drove a wedge between us and that is something I bitterly regret. And nothing I have said or done since has softened his stance towards me because he has refused ever to discuss it.'

Lily felt a terrible sadness overwhelm her because she could see the problem from Leonora's point of view, as well as from Ciro's. She could imagine the little boy wanting to protect his mother from the men he resented—too young to realise that she needed something other than the love of her child to sustain her. Leonora had wanted to find a man whom Ciro could look up to but had never managed it—and it must have seemed to him like a constant stream of strangers entering his home. Barriers had sprung up between mother and son and time had only made them more impenetrable.

Suddenly, it made it more understandable why Ciro had reacted so badly to the discovery that she wasn't a virgin. Had emotion overcome reason, to make him believe that his supposedly innocent wife would one day take up with other men, as his own mother had done? Or had he simply decided that her lack of innocence equalled a predatory nature? He was a man who saw things in black or white—even women. Especially women. Madonna or Whore. Lots of men thought that way, didn't they? And it wasn't difficult to see which category he had placed her in.

'Won't you talk to him, Lily?' said Leonora suddenly. 'Won't you try to explain to him what it was like for me?'

Lily heard the faint tremor in her mother-in-law's voice and saw what lay beneath the sophisticated veneer: a frightened woman who was afraid of growing old and dying without the forgiveness of her only child.

'I can try,' she said, knowing that she would give it her very best shot. Because what did she have to lose? Even if Ciro was angry with her for interfering, it wasn't going to change anything between *them*, was it? She was leaving him—and Naples—that had already been decided. Yet if she could leave knowing that she had helped reconcile mother and son—then wouldn't something good have come out of all this mess?

Leonora's disclosure had the effect of making Lily feel as if she'd woken up from an anaesthetic. Of making her want to rediscover something of herself. She realised she had stopped being the Lily who loved to create a cosy nest around her. She'd been so busy trying to *survive* in this hostile atmosphere that she'd completely forgotten who she really was. Yet hadn't Ciro fallen for the woman who had baked cakes and tried to create a warm home? Even if he was still angry about her lack of innocence, surely she could remind him of the woman she had once been and all that she had represented to him.

Suddenly, she could understand his refusal to look beyond the boundaries he had created for himself. She suspected that it was a defence mechanism—to stop himself from being hurt again, the way he'd been hurt as a child. He was a strong man who hated showing vulnerability, but couldn't she convince him that she would never willingly hurt him—not ever again? That if he could forgive her past mistake, then she would gladly open up her heart and love him with every fibre of her being? That she would be loyal and true to him in every way she could.

Filled with sudden hope, Lily found the nearest shop to their apartment. It was a small, dark place with an ancient fan which cut inefficiently through the warm, heavy air. Outside were boxes of oranges and tomatoes and inside were bottles of wine and rows of sweet biscuits. It took her a while to find what she was looking for, but eventually Lily managed to cobble together the ingredients for a cake, much to the surprise of the old woman who served her. Maybe she found it strange that the fair foreigner who spoke such faltering Italian should be baking a cake.

Back at the apartment, she set to work, finding a roasting tray which would serve as a cake tin while seriously wondering whether Ciro's state-of-the-art cooker had ever been used before now. But it felt good to lose herself in the familiar rhythms of baking. To hear the

slop of the eggs as they fell onto the flour with a little puff, like smoke. She listened to the beating of the
wooden spoon, which her cookery teacher had always
said sounded like horses clip-clopping over cobblestones.
She grated zest from the juiciest lemons she had ever
used and soon the incomparable smell of fresh cake was
filling Ciro's very masculine apartment.

She heard the front door slam soon after six. Heard
him dropping his suitcase onto the floor and the momentary silence before his footsteps headed towards
the kitchen. His face registered very little when he saw
her, save for a barely perceptible narrowing of his eyes.
Perhaps he was noticing the inevitable smears of cake-
mix on her cotton dress since, naturally, she had no
apron here.

'What are you doing?' he questioned slowly.

'You mean apart from making a cake?' she enquired,
determinedly cheerful as she opened the smoked glass
door of the oven to extract it.

Ciro watched the curve of her bottom as she bent forward and it mimicked the very first time he'd seen her
baking, when he'd been blown away by the sight of her
luscious young body. The memory should have filled
him with desire but instead all he felt was a crushing
sense of sadness. He stared at the cake as she put it down.
'What's all this in aid of?'

Would she sound crazy if she told him that she'd
needed to reclaim something familiar? Something which
would make her feel like herself again—instead of a

woman who was just playing a part. She lifted her eyes
to meet his, praying for his understanding.

'I've just realised how long it is since I've done any
baking. Would you like some? It always tastes best when
you eat it straight from the oven.'

He shook his head as her words seem to fly out of
the air to mock him. She'd said them once before, a long
time ago—and they reminded him of everything he'd
hoped for. All those simple pleasures which now seemed
a world away from the bittersweet reality of their life together. 'No, thanks,' he said, wondering why he should
care that her face had crumpled with disappointment
and that she was biting on her lip as if she was trying to
stop it from trembling. 'Did you go and see my mother?'

'I did.'

'And?'

Lily stared at him. Maybe if he'd been a little more
understanding—a little kinder—then she might have
trodden carefully. If he'd accepted a slice of warm cake
as a gesture of conciliation, then inevitably she would
have softened. But in that moment his cold face seemed
to confirm all the things his mother had said about him
and any thoughts of diplomacy rushed straight out of
her mind. 'She told me a few very interesting things.'

Ciro loosened his tie. He wanted to affect lack of interest, to tell her that he didn't really care, but the truth
of it was that his curiosity had been aroused. 'Oh?' he
questioned. 'Such as?'

She sucked in a deep breath. 'Such as you've never

forgiven her for having boyfriends when you were young.'

There was brief, disbelieving pause. 'She said *what*?' he questioned dangerously.

'Did you know that your mother suffered post-natal depression?' she asked quickly. 'And that was one of the reasons your father left her?'

'So it was all his fault?' he snapped.

'It's nobody's *fault*!' she retorted, but she could feel her heart pounding against her ribcage. 'It's just the way things were. Nobody was doing very much about post-natal depression back then. Your mother told me...well, she said she wanted you to have a father figure you could look up to.'

'That was very *good* of her,' he ground out. 'She certainly auditioned enough men for that particular role!'

'You're hateful,' Lily whispered as she saw the unforgiving hardness in his eyes. 'Can't you see that your mother's getting older and she's terrified she's going to die and that none of this *stuff* will be resolved?'

'That's enough!' he snapped.

'No, it's not,' she fired back. 'It's not nearly enough! I actually found myself feeling sorry for her, for having to put up with your coldness and your control-freakery ways all these years. Except that now I discover that I'm doing exactly the same. I'm behaving in a way I'm growing to despise.'

His voice was a hiss of deadly silk. 'What the hell are you talking about?'

'I'm talking about me accepting the unacceptable! About us maintaining this façade of a marriage for however many months you think we should—just for the sake of your damned *image*!'

There was a pause. 'But we agreed, Lily.'

'Yes, we did,' she said. But hadn't there been an ulterior motive behind her easy agreement, even if she hadn't acknowledged it at the time? Hadn't part of her hoped that time might dissolve some of his anger towards her? That they could get back some of what they'd once had— something which she had called love and which she'd hoped Ciro might one day come to feel for her, too. Except that they hadn't, had they? He had shown no sign of softening—not to the woman who had given birth to him, and not to the woman he'd married either. No matter what their supposed 'sins' were, there was no forgiveness in Ciro D'Angelo's heart for the women who had hurt him. And the longer she stayed, the more damaged her own heart would become. Especially as she just couldn't seem to stop loving him, no matter what he threw at her.

'But I've changed my mind,' she said slowly. 'I can't maintain this false life with you any longer. And I want to go back to England.'

'You can't do that,' he said repressively.

'Why, won't you allow me to?' Fearlessly now, she met his dark eyes. 'Will you go one step further in your very convincing role as tyrant husband and try to stop

me? Chain me to the sofa, perhaps—or keep me on a
very long leash?'

She didn't wait for him to answer, just ran to the
bathroom and locked the slammed door behind her. She
stared at her ashen face in the mirror and heard the loud
beat of her heart, knowing there was one certain way
guaranteed to give her back her freedom. But could she
do it? Could she go through with it?

She was in there for ten minutes before she heard him
calling her name and knew she had to face him—because wasn't that the whole point of what she'd done? But
the taste in her mouth was bitter as she slowly opened
the door to him and she saw the revulsion in his eyes
even before she heard the ragged breath of horror he
sucked in.

'Per l'amor del cielo!' he exclaimed harshly. 'Lily,
what have you done?'

She saw his disbelieving gaze travelling over her
shoulder, where thick strands of her hair were lying all
over the bathroom floor, like shiny heaps of harvested
corn. Together with an unfamiliar lightness of head, she
felt the jagged, shorn locks brushing against her jaw and
she raised it up towards him in a defiant gesture.

'What have I done? I've broken my promise,' she said,
unable to keep the emotional tremor from her voice, because that revulsion was still on his face. And for the
first time ever, she recoiled from the hand that reached
out and touched her. For once, the feel of his fingers on
her arms did not trigger off an unstoppable lust but a

sensation of disgust. How could she have let herself stay in such a terrible situation? Giving herself night after night to a man who clearly despised her. Did she have no pride; no self-respect?

She pulled away from him, her breath coming short and fast from her throat. 'I've cut my hair!' she declared. 'It's something I said I wouldn't do but now I have. I've broken my promise and it's symbolic and final. I'm freeing you from our marriage, Ciro—and I'm freeing myself, too. And I want…no, I *need* to go home.'

CHAPTER ELEVEN

HE DIDN'T try to stop her. That was the part which shattered Lily most of all. Ciro didn't say a word to try to change her mind about leaving. Yet when she stopped to think about it—had she really expected anything different? Had she imagined that her proud and unforgiving husband would turn round and beg her to stay? To maintain this farce of a marriage?

In fact she was taken aback by the speed of his reaction to her demand to go home. It was as if he'd suddenly realised that the kind of woman who hacked off her hair in a moment of high emotion would never have made a suitable wife for a high-born Neapolitan. His face looked as if it had been sculpted from a hard, dark marble as he looked at her.

'Perhaps this is all for the best,' he said, in an odd, flat voice. 'When do you want to leave?'

'As soon as possible!' she blurted out, knowing that to prolong this state of affairs would be an agony which would only add to her growing heartache. 'I'll fly out this afternoon, if I can.'

His horrified gaze returned to the piles of silken hair which were still lying on the bathroom floor and then he lifted reluctant eyes to the shorn strands which untidily framed her face. 'Wouldn't you rather go and see a hairdresser first?'

His question only added to her distress, even though she suspected he might have a point. Because didn't the hasty cut give her the appearance of some crazy woman, who would bring disrepute to the D'Angelo name?

She shook her head. 'I'll cover it up with a hat.' Her voice rose to a note of near-hysteria. 'Who knows? It might start a new trend of do-it-yourself hairdressing.'

Ciro felt the twisting of some nameless emotion as he looked at her, thinking that the short style made her face seem all eyes. Enormous sapphire eyes which were glittering up at him with the suspicion of tears.

'I'll have my lawyers draw up a contract—and the Grange will be signed over to you as part of the divorce settlement. I will also honour my commitment to pay your brother through his course at art school.' He gave a bitter laugh. 'You might as well leave the marriage with what you came into it for. Riches beyond your wildest dreams, wasn't it, Lily?'

The accusation hit her hard and Lily sucked in an unsteady breath, feeling slightly ill as she realised that he'd written her off as mercenary. 'I don't want anything from you, Ciro.'

'You want the Grange.'

Fighting back tears, she shook her head. 'I don't want

it that much.' Because wouldn't her old family home feel *tainted* if she accepted it under such dreadful circumstances? Wouldn't *she* feel tainted if she came over as greedy and grasping? And she was damned if she was going to give Ciro yet another reason to despise her.

'You want your brother to go to art school.'

'Not at any price. We'll work it out somehow. If Jonny is good enough, then he'll get a scholarship. And if he's not—well, something else will come his way, because that's how life works for most people.'

'Proud words, Lily—but I doubt whether you mean them.' His mouth gave a twist. 'You'll soon change your mind when you speak to my lawyers. I always find there's something very persuasive about seeing hard offers of cash written down in black and white.'

'But that's where you're wrong, Ciro,' she returned, the cynicism of his words sending an icy shiver down her spine. 'When will you get it into your head that this was never about the money?'

'Then what was it about?' Dark eyebrows arched with arrogant disbelief. 'The thunderbolt?'

She wanted to say yes. To tell him that what he'd felt about her had been mutual—but what would be the point when he'd never believe her? Ciro had fallen for someone who didn't really exist—a make-believe woman he'd put on some unachievable pedestal. And maybe she'd fallen for someone who didn't exist, too. Because no matter how powerful his passion for her, there was no way that he was ever going to make a good husband. What kind of future could ever be found with a man who was always so coldly judgemental about women?

'It doesn't matter any more,' she said, in a small voice. 'It's over.'

Ciro flinched as her words filled him with unexpected pain, but he told himself she was right. It *was* over. And maybe her abrupt departure would be best—for both of them.

He made a couple of telephone calls and two hours later he was carrying her bags downstairs, where a driver was waiting to take her to the airport. The last thing he remembered seeing was the glitter in her bright blue eyes, before she quickly put on a large pair of shades. Then she tugged at the floppy straw hat which concealed the unfamiliar hairstyle and, almost impulsively, stood on tiptoe to brush her lips over his cheek.

'Goodbye, Ciro,' she said, in a strange, gulping kind of voice. 'You…you take care of yourself.'

'You, too,' he said—but a sudden sense of something almost like *panic* unsettled him. As if he'd just jumped out of an aircraft and forgotten to put on his parachute. 'Lily—'

'Please. Let's not drag this out any more than we need to,' she said quickly as she moved away from him and climbed into the car.

He watched as she was driven away, waiting for her to turn back to look at him one more time—but she didn't. All he could see was the stiff set of her shoulders and the large hat which hid her shorn head from the world. For a moment he stood completely still, oblivious to the people who passed him by. And when eventually he went back inside, he was surprised to find that his heart was still heavy, though he reassured himself that such a reaction was only natural after such an unexpectedly emotional departure. And that within a few days the memory of his brief marriage would fade.

But it didn't happen that way. The reality was very different—and it took Ciro by surprise. He found that his life had changed in so many ways. It had changed by her coming here, as well as by her leaving. And it was the little things which seemed to mock him most and to remind him that she really had gone. Suddenly, the bed seemed too big. He would wake in the mornings, his hand groping towards the space beside him, to find nothing but emptiness and an unruffled sheet instead of Lily's soft and welcoming body.

He soon discovered that, once word got round that his wife had gone back to England, he was being seen as being 'back on the market', with a corresponding flurry of interest from the opposite sex. And he didn't like it. He didn't like it one bit. The women who came onto him repulsed him and he found their conversation dull. He realised that Lily had been excellent company on their many evenings out—as well as having many other obvious attractions once they'd returned home. Dinner suddenly seemed either a too-solitary meal, or a ritual to be endured amid company he had no wish to join.

He phoned the London office of his lawyers, wanting

to hear that she had grasped the very generous settlement he was offering her—as if hearing that would remind himself of her mercenary nature. But she had done no such thing. Slowly, Ciro registered what the bemused voice of his lawyer was telling him. That Lily D'Angelo was walking away from the marriage with nothing.

'Nothing?' Ciro echoed in disbelief.

'Niente,' came the answer in Italian, just so there could be no misunderstanding.

Ciro brooded. He asked someone he knew in London to investigate what she was doing and the answer which came back surprised him. She was still living in the apartment above the tearoom and had resumed her job as a waitress. She had gone back to Chadwick Green. It perplexed him to think she had settled for so little when she could have had so much—and it threw all his certainties into doubt. Until some news came to him from the same investigator, which he regarded with a grim kind of satisfaction.

She had put her mother's pearls up for auction!

Ciro felt a resigned satisfaction as he read that the beautiful necklace had exceeded its reserve price many times over. The necklace which had reminded her of her dead mother had been sold to a mystery buyer in America. So much for sentiment! He remembered the way her blue eyes had clouded over when she'd told him that her stepmother had taken them. And her touching gratitude as he'd recovered them and placed them around her neck. He'd imagined that she had been thinking of her mother at the time, when the truth was far more materialistic. She had realised, of course, the enormous value of the jewels—and known that they would always provide her with a sizeable little nest-egg until she found herself some other poor sucker to support her.

Ciro threw himself into work in an attempt to get her out of his mind, but that very same week brought a postcard from England. It was from Lily's brother—an odd composition of clashing colours which he'd clearly painted himself. The message on it was brief.

> *Hi, Ciro. Got thumbs-up from art school this a.m.*
> *due to exam results. Start September. Just wanted*
> *to thank you (or perhaps I should say* mille grazie!*)*
> *for making it all possible. See you soon, Jonny.*

Ciro stared at the card in confusion. The sentiment expressed seemed to suggest that Jonny had no idea his sister and her new husband had parted. More than that, he also seemed to be under the illusion that Ciro had financed his art-school funding. What the hell was going on?

He walked out onto the terrace, his heart beating very fast as he tried to piece it all together. Until he realised that there was only one possible source for the funding—and all the implications which came from that. He bunched his hands into two tight fists which hung by the sides of his tensed thighs. *Had Lily sold her mother's precious pearls to put her brother through school?* Had he misjudged her all along?

He stared out at the dark blue blur of the bay but he could see nothing except the glitter of his wife's eyes as she said goodbye to him. He felt a terrible regret wash over him. What had he *done*?

He stood there as the sun sank into the water, until the terrace was lit only by the silver light of the rising moon. Was it too late to go to her and ask for a forgiveness he did not deserve? One which his proud and defiant Lily would probably not give. His mouth hardened as he went back inside to get his passport. Maybe it was too late, but he knew he had to try.

But first there was something he needed to do.

CHAPTER TWELVE

THE windows weren't dirty by any stretch of the imagination, but Lily was still determined to give them a polish. Danielle had repeatedly teased her and said that these days she was nothing but a 'clean freak' and Lily hadn't bothered to deny what was essentially the truth. Because she *did* find housework oddly soothing. It didn't demand too much and it helped make her little apartment look as good as possible. She would listen to the radio, her thoughts easily distracted by the phone-in conversations. And listening to other people talking was much easier than having to talk herself. When people asked *her* questions these days, she didn't know how to answer. But there was no point worrying about it. It was still early days after the break-up of her marriage and she was still trying to settle back into her old life.

Her old life which had become her new life.

She'd been back in Chadwick Green for almost a month now and, in many ways, it was almost as if nothing had changed. The tearoom was still there and so was her little apartment. And her friends. A concerned Fiona had told her that of course she could have her old job back, and Danielle had been overjoyed to see her. But of course, they were worried about her—even though they did their best to hide it. The sight of her radical haircut had visibly shocked them—as had her unmistakable weight-loss.

Danielle had come right out and asked her what had happened in Naples and Lily had been tempted to offload some of her terrible heartache. But how could she possibly explain the convoluted chain of events which had led to her return? She thought about Ciro. She thought about him nearly all the time. About all the hopes he'd had for their future—hopes which she had shared. About each of them wanting to build something strong and permanent: a unit which would last. But look at how they had failed. She'd been so quick to condemn him for his old-fashioned immovability on the subject of her virginity. She had been so frustrated by his inability to adapt to what was, rather than what he wanted it to be. She could see that in a way it had been a *relief* for him to think that she was some kind of gold-digger and predator, like the other women he'd known.

Yet she had deliberately kept her sexual history a secret, hadn't she? She couldn't deny that. She'd done it because she'd wanted to hang onto the dream he'd been offering her. She had allowed herself to paint a false image of reality, to pretend it was the way she'd *wanted* it to be. It didn't matter what her motives had been—that had been wrong. So it followed that she had an equal part to play in the breakdown of their marriage. Their brief love and the subsequent fall-out was intensely private. She would not blacken her husband's name—not to anyone. How could she, when she still loved him?

Outside, the weather had been sunny and golden. It had been one of the best English summers on record and there had been times when Lily wished it had been otherwise. Wouldn't it have reflected her mood if they'd had the usual downpours of rain, or a spot of unseasonal cold which meant you were tempted to put the heating on? As it was, she had no desire to go out and get some sun on her pale skin—or to join Danielle on a train trip down to the coast. It was bad enough having to listen to the loud revelry of the drinkers who were currently cluttering up the front of the pub next door.

Determined to make the windows look diamond-bright, she filled a bowl with hot water and placed it on the window sill, aware of how bare her neck felt without the tickle of a long strand of hair which occasionally used to tumble down. Her shorn hairstyle still took some getting used to and it made her smile when people who knew her did a double take when they first saw it. She'd been to the nearest big town and put herself in the hands of a hairdresser recommended by Danielle, emerging with her corn-coloured hair shaped close to her head and feathered around her face. After the initial shock, she was beginning to like it. It made her look different, yes—but maybe that was a good thing. She *was* different and there was no denying that. She'd been through a big, painful experience and something like that always changed people.

She cleaned and polished the windows, then opened them wide to let in some fresh air. Cars slid past on the road outside and as she listened to the rising laughter of drinkers outside The Duchess of Cambridge she wondered if she would always feel this way. Would she ever feel like part of the real world again, instead of someone who didn't fit in? Or was she doomed to be one of those shadowy figures who always sat on the sidelines, for ever mourning their lost love?

She was just about to go and make some tea when her attention was caught by the sight of someone walking across the village green towards her. She blinked. An instantly recognisable man with jet-dark hair and a towering physique. He was wearing a snowy shirt and some fine grey trousers and the similarity to the first time she'd ever seen him was so marked that her heart clenched painfully in her chest.

Ciro!

Ciro?

She gripped the window sill for support, sucking in a ragged breath. Because it hurt to see him. It hurt because it reminded her of what she could have had. And because she still loved him.

His powerful stride quickly brought him beneath her window where he stopped and looked up to see her framed there and their eyes met in a long moment. She drank in the sight of him—the angled slant of his cheekbones and the thick lashes which made his dark eyes look so smoulderingly sexy. His hair gleamed like tar in the bright sunlight and his olive skin had a soft, golden glow. But his expression was grim as he nodded his head in greeting, like someone giving themselves a silent pep talk.

Lily was aware that the sound of the drinkers had died away and it seemed as if the whole world were silent and holding its breath, save for the birdsong which twittered through the air. She leaned forward, her heart pounding so loudly she was certain he must be able to hear it. She opened her mouth to speak, trying to keep the quaver from her voice—to make herself sound stronger than she actually felt. Because she hoped she'd got through the worst of the hurt and she didn't think she could bear to go through it all again. 'What are you doing here?'

'No ideas, Lily?'

'The tearoom's shut,' she said flippantly.

'I don't give a damn about the tearoom. I've come to see you.'

She sucked in another breath. Hadn't they said everything there was to say? Weren't his team of fancy lawyers drawing up the wretched divorce papers even now? 'Why?'

Ciro's eyes narrowed. Her stark question was completely at odds with her delicate appearance and he paused as he studied a face made elfin by her new feathered hairstyle—flinching to think it had been his cruelty which had made her chop off her glorious hair. He'd had a statement planned—whole reams of things he'd intended to say when he saw her. But now all words failed him—except perhaps for the only ones which mattered.

'I've come to say sorry.'

Lily felt dizzy, wondering if she'd imagined those words, but the unusually sombre expression on Ciro's face told her she hadn't. Dimly, she registered that there was still an unusual silence outside the The Duchess of Cambridge and how much the regulars would be loving this. She pulled herself together. 'We can't have this conversation here.'

'Then you'd better come downstairs and let me in.'

Lily's heart raced even though she felt a mild flare of irritation. So he'd lost none of his customary arrogance! But she felt weak as she went downstairs and weaker still when she opened the door and he looked at her with such longing and regret in his dark eyes that her heart turned over. Seeing him this close again made her realise how much she had missed him—in every way it was possible to miss a man. Her instinct was to hurl herself into those strong arms and let him hold her and tell her that everything was going to be okay, but she'd learnt by now that her instincts were often dangerous.

So she stepped aside to let him in, aware of his raw, tangy scent as he passed and realising that the small hallway was much too claustrophobic for any kind of conversation. That his compelling proximity might have her doing things she would later regret. And that she

needed to put some real space between them. 'You'd
better come upstairs.'

Ciro followed her up the narrow stairway, trying not
to be mesmerised by the sway of her bottom and the
swish of her cotton dress as she walked. The pulse at his
temple was hammering and the inside of his mouth felt
like sand. Had he thought that the apology he'd uttered
downstairs would be enough and that she would forgive
him instantly? Maybe he had. He was not a man known
for saying sorry and perhaps he had overestimated its
effect on people.

He walked into the sitting room and saw that she had
been working hard. New, flower-sprigged curtains hung
at the windows and she had made some sort of throw
which partially disguised the sofa bed. Over the fireplace
hung a large and brightly coloured painting whose style
he recognised instantly.

'Jonny's?' he asked.

It wasn't what she had been expecting him to say and
she turned to him with a slightly puzzled look on her
face. 'Yes. How did you know?'

'Because he sent me a postcard. He has a very recognisable technique.'

'Have you come up here to discuss Jonny's artistic
merits?'

'Actually, they do have some relevance on what I'm
about to say.'

Lily's eyes narrowed. 'Now I'm intrigued.'

'You sold your mother's pearls to pay him through art school, didn't you, Lily?'

Her eyes widened. 'And if I did?'

'Yet you turned down what was rightfully yours.' He lowered his voice as he studied her closely. 'A divorce settlement which meant you could have kept the necklace which meant so much to you.'

She shook her head and in that moment she could have pummelled her fists against him in frustration. 'You just don't get it, do you, Ciro? All your life you've seen things in terms of credit and debit. Everything for you is quantifiable. Everything has to have a *price*!'

'But that's where you're wrong, Lily,' he said, shaking his head. 'I *do* get it. I just wonder why it took me so long. You didn't accept the settlement because you didn't want to be beholden to me in any way.'

'Oh, bravo,' she applauded softly.

'But it's more than that. I suddenly realised that you don't care about *things* as much as you care about people. That the most precious piece of jewellery in the world—even if it did have immense sentimental value—would mean nothing to you if it meant that your brother's dreams were thwarted. So you sold the pearls to put Jonny through art school.'

Lily walked over to the window, but stood with her back to the view. 'How did you find out?'

'That postcard he sent was to thank me for funding his place. I realised then what you must have done.'

'Okay, so now you know. But none of what you've told me tells me why you're here, Ciro.'

Had he thought that might be enough? That his opening words of apology accompanied by an explanation might be sufficient for her to forgive him? Yes, he had. But he could see now that he had been wrong. That her blue gaze was very steady. He had hurt her badly, he realised—and she was scared he was going to hurt her again.

'Because I'm sorry for having judged you so wrongly,' he said savagely. 'That I was right about you all along— that you aren't like other women. And that there isn't a predatory or mercenary bone in your beautiful body.'

Lily sucked in an unsteady breath. 'Don't—'

'No, wait. I haven't finished.' He suddenly realised why he'd always damned the words 'I love you' as being too easy to say, because in a way—they were. But he also knew how important they were. That they meant so much—and especially to women. But right then, he discovered that they meant a lot to him, too.

'I love you, Lily,' he said simply. 'And my life has been empty without you. I thought I'd be able to go back to the man I'd been before, but I can't and, what's more, I don't want to. *Because I am no longer that man.* You have changed me, Lily. You've changed the way I think. The way I view the world—and other people in it.'

'Ciro—'

'Let me tell you this,' he said urgently. 'After you'd gone, the apartment seemed so...*empty* and I thought about everything you'd said about me and about my unforgiving nature. I sat there for a long time mulling it over and then I went to see my mother—'

She blinked in surprise. 'You did?'

'Yes, I did. For the first time in my life, I listened properly to what she had to say. I tried to see what had happened from an adult point of view, rather than a child's. She asked for my forgiveness and I gave it to her and then I asked for hers, and she reciprocated. And I wept,' he admitted, feeling the lump rise in his throat as he remembered the powerful emotion which had taken him by surprise. 'But I was weeping for my own lost love as much as anything else. Can you believe that, Lily? Ciro D'Angelo shedding tears?'

She nodded. 'Yes, I can—and so what? Tears don't make you less of a man,' she declared fiercely. 'They make you more of a man. Because a man who is afraid of showing his feelings is an emotional coward and you're no coward, Ciro!'

He walked over to the window to where she stood, her face working furiously as she tried to contain her own emotion. And he was staring at her as if it had been a lifetime since he'd seen her rather than a few short weeks. 'My mother told me something I already knew—that you were the best thing that had ever happened to me and I had been a fool to let you go. But how could I have stopped you from going, when I had judged you so harshly? I realised I had to ask for your forgiveness—and to ask whether you'd consider coming back to me.'

For a moment he didn't speak, but maybe that had something to do with the difficulty he was having framing these very important words. 'To be my wife again, only this time—my wife in every sense there is. No pretence, Lily. Only honesty. And love. Enduring love.'

Lily bit her trembling lip. Surely he must have read the answer in eyes which were suddenly having to blink back tears of her own? But through her haze of gratitude that he had come to her like this, she realised that she must take her part of the blame. That Ciro should not bear all the burden of what had gone wrong.

'I was wrong not to have told you I wasn't a virgin.'

'It doesn't matter,' he said, feeling like a man who had been walking around half-asleep. How could he have ever thought it important enough to risk losing her?

'I realise that it probably seemed like a deliberate deception, but that's not how I ever intended it to be, Ciro. You see, I loved you so much that it felt like the first time and the only time for me. You made the past fade into something so insignificant, it was almost as if it had never happened.'

'You *loved* me?' he repeated, his eyes narrowing. 'Past tense?'

'I love you—present tense,' she said softly. 'Now and always. My darling Ciro. The man without whom I feel only half a person.'

For a moment he was too choked to speak. Too full of emotion to do anything but pull her into his arms and to hold her very tightly. At last he lowered his head and kissed her, as he'd dreamed of doing since that bleak day when she'd walked out of his life. When he had pushed her so far that there had been nowhere left for her to go.

But there was no need for her to run any more. No need for him to have to go and find her. From now on they would always be together—either here, or in Naples. Wherever they were didn't matter, just as long as they were together. Because when they were together, any four walls became a place they could call home.

EPILOGUE

CIRO looked at the large canvas. 'What's it supposed to be?'

'Don't be so obtuse, darling,' whispered Lily. 'It's *you*, of course. Jonny's very proud of it—and all his tutors all love it. So you mustn't say anything negative about it over lunch. Promise me.'

Ciro screwed up his eyes to observe a crudely drawn circle containing two black spots and a large splodge of orange, shaped like a carrot. He failed to see any resemblance to himself, indeed to anything at all—except perhaps for a snowman. But if the connoisseurs in the art world applauded it, then who was he to question their judgement?

'I promise you I will give him nothing but the praise he so richly deserves. And since it's helped earn him a distinction and the opportunity to go and study in Paris, then it must be good,' he told Lily diplomatically.

Lily gave a little sigh of pleasure as she thought about Jonny's wonderful degree results, wondering if this much happiness could possibly be good for a person.

Sometimes she'd wake up and wonder if she might be dreaming—usually when she got out of bed in the morning and wandered out onto the terrace of their Neapolitan home to stare at the matchless view of the bay. But she was just as likely to wake up with disbelieving pleasure in her old home.

Ciro had decided against turning the Grange into a hotel. Instead, they had lovingly restored it into the beautiful home it was meant to be and which they visited whenever possible. She knew that he intended it should go to Jonny and, indeed, there was plenty of room to provide a huge artist's studio for her talented brother. In fact, there might end up being several studios. Jonny had been speaking to Ciro about the possibility of opening up the house for painters who were financially stretched—as artists so often were. And Ciro had warmly embraced the idea.

She looked up to find his dark eyes smiling at her and she smiled back. 'I'm just going to freshen up before lunch.'

'Then I will wait for you here, *dolcezza*,' he murmured indulgently.

Finding a restroom and running her wrists under the cold tap, Lily stared at herself in the mirror, thinking how much she had changed. And how women's lives were often reflected in their hairstyles. For the first few years of their marriage, she'd kept the style really short. Ciro had insisted he liked it—and she believed him. That declaration meant a lot to her, for all kinds of reasons—though she was no longer the insecure woman who believed he only fancied her when she had cascading hair! People often told her that with her elfin look she reminded them of the actress Mitzi Gaynor, who had also worn the distinctive nineteen fifties clothes which Lily favoured.

But lately, she'd made a few sartorial decisions. For a start, she was letting her hair grow—because it required too much in the way of maintenance. And soon, she wasn't going to have quite so much time for getting her hair cut…

The other thing she'd done was to start buying clothes in more contemporary styles. Money was no longer tight and it was foolish to pretend that it was. She didn't have to make them herself any more—and there were plenty of designs which suited her, since curves seemed to be back in fashion. And besides, what woman wanted to get stuck in a fashion rut? These days, she experimented with sharp, modern looks—and floaty creations in pure silk for more formal functions.

Her fingers drifted to the row of creamy pearls at her neck. Ciro had managed to buy them back—*again*. Though he'd told her with mock severity that this was getting to be a habit and that this time they were keeping them. He'd said that maybe one day they'd have a daughter of their own who would wear them. Lily smiled dreamily at her reflection. Maybe they would.

She went back to where Ciro and her brother were waiting for her. Jonny's hair had grown—it fell almost to his shoulders now and his soulful good looks attracted plenty of attention from the opposite sex. In fact, there was a gorgeous creature hanging onto his arm, wearing a sequinned mini-dress, improbably teamed with a pair of pink wellington boots.

'I thought I'd walk Fleur to the station before lunch,' he said. 'If that's okay, sis?'

'That's absolutely fine,' said Lily. 'Ciro and I will wait for you in the restaurant. It was lovely to have met you, Fleur—and hope you have a great summer.'

'Thanks,' said Fleur, with a smile. 'And you.'

Lily looped her hand through Ciro's arm as they watched the young couple walk away, thinking how curiously *grown-up* she felt today.

'You're very quiet,' he murmured. 'Which usually means trouble. Shall we go to the restaurant and I can buy us a very nice bottle of champagne while you bask in the glory of your clever brother and you can tell me what's on your mind?'

She turned her face up to his, her eyes shining. 'That sounds perfect. Though I don't think I'm going to be drinking any champagne.'

'But we're supposed to be celebrating.'

'And we are,' she whispered. 'But there's more than one cause for celebration. I've got something to tell you. I was going to wait until tonight, until we got home, but I don't think I can wait a minute longer.'

He stared at her with an expression she'd never seen

on his face before. 'You're going to have a baby?' he questioned unsteadily.

'Yes.' She nodded her head, her lips clamping together to try to keep back her tears of joy. *'Yes!'*

For one long moment he did nothing, as if the words were taking time to really sink in. And then Ciro put his arms round her and kissed her. He kissed her so thoroughly that she was giggling as they came up for air. And then he bent his head and kissed her some more.

But fortunately they were in an art gallery, where love was one of the things which kept painters in business. And nobody paid the slightest attention to the man and the woman who stood locked in passionate embrace beneath a brightly coloured canvas.

* * * * *

Marriage Scandal,
Showbiz Baby!

CHAPTER ONE

A THOUSAND FLASHGUNS lit the sky and the Mediterranean night was turned into garish day as the crowd surged forward.

'Jennifer!' they screamed. *'Jennifer!'*

Jennifer paused and smiled, the way the studio had taught her— "Don't show your teeth, honey—they're so English!"—but the irony of the situation didn't escape her. You could be adored from afar by so many— yet inside be as lonely as hell.

She placed one sparkle-shoed foot on the step of the red carpet—the famous red carpet which slithered down the steps of the Festival Theatre like a scarlet snake. Oh, yes. A snake. Lots of those around at the Cannes Film Festival.

At the back of the building lay the fabled promenade of La Croisette, where lines of palm trees waved gently in the soft breeze. Beyond foamed the sapphire-edged waters of the Mediterranean, into which the evening sun had just set in a firework display of pink and gold. But, despite the warmth of the May evening which caressed her bare shoulders, Jennifer couldn't stop the tiptoeing of regret which shivered over her skin.

Memories stayed stubbornly alive in your head, and you couldn't stop them flooding back—no matter how hard you tried. She'd been in Cannes with Matteo during that first, blissful summer of their ill-fated romance, and she associated the whole dazzling coastline with him. Matteo had introduced her to the South of France and the heady world of films—just as he had introduced her to white wine and orgasm. Everything in life she thought worth knowing he had taught her.

'You okay, Jen?' came the gruff voice of her publicist, Hal, who—along with an assistant, had been shadowing her like a bodyguard all day, as if afraid that she wouldn't actually turn up for the screening of her film tonight. And, yes, she'd been tempted to hide away in the luxury of her hotel room—but you couldn't hide from the world for ever. Sooner or later you had to come out—and it was better to come out fighting!

Weighted by her elaborate blonde hairstyle, Jennifer dipped her head so that her low words could be neither lip-read nor heard by the crowds who were pushing towards her from behind the barrier ropes.

'What do you think?' she questioned softly. 'I'm being forced to parade in front of the world's media and pretend I don't care that my husband has been flaunting his new lover.'

'Hey, Jennifer,' said Hal softly. 'That sounds awfully

like jealousy—and you were the one who walked out of the marriage, remember?'

And for good reasons. But she knew it was pointless trying to explain them. People like Hal thought she was mad. They had told her in not so many words that she couldn't *expect* a man like Matteo to be faithful. As if she should just be grateful that he had cared enough to put a shiny gold band on her finger. Well, maybe her expectations were higher than those of other people in the acting world, but she wasn't about to start lowering them now.

'It's just harder than I thought it would be,' she murmured.

They'd only split six months ago, and yet already the press had started describing her as 'lonely' and 'unlucky in love'—because, unlike Matteo, she had not fallen straight into the arms of a new lover. Maybe it was different for women. Didn't they say that men recovered more quickly from a break-up?

Her pride had been wounded and she wasn't sure she was ever going to be able to replace the man who had been her husband—though that was what the world seemed to want. She just wanted to get through this first public appearance at the world's most famous film festival—then surely anything else would be easy-peasy. Please God, it would.

'Jennifer!' screamed the crowd again.

'Don't even *attempt* to sign autographs,' warned Hal. 'Or there'll be a riot!'

'You mean there isn't already?' she joked.

'That's better,' Hal murmured approvingly. 'Just keep smiling.'

But as Jennifer began to slowly mount the staircase she heard different voices, which somehow managed to penetrate the clamour of her fans. The clipped, intrusive tones of professional broadcasters. Here we go, she thought.

'Hey, Jennifer—have you met your husband's new lover yet?'

'Jennifer! GMRV news! Any plans for a divorce?'

'Jen—are the rumours that Sophia is pregnant true?'

Pregnant? Surely that must be some kind of cruel joke? Jennifer gripped onto her sapphire silk clutch-bag so hard that her knuckles showed up white, but then she automatically relaxed them just in case a camera should pick up the tell-tale tension.

'Jennifer—how do you feel about seeing your husband here tonight?'

At first Jennifer thought that she must have misheard the last statement—her ears playing tricks with her and plucking a wrong note from out of the sea of sound. Matteo wasn't here tonight—he was miles away, in Italy, and she had agreed to attend the Festival because she had known that. They hadn't seen each other in months, and Jennifer was still emotionally wobbly. She wasn't naïve enough to think that their paths would never cross, but had just hoped that it would be without an audience. Especially so soon.

Like a child swimming in choppy waters and searching for a life-raft, she looked round at Hal—but the sudden frozen set of his shoulders made her tense with a terrible growing suspicion.

She tried to catch his eye, but he was steadfastly refusing to meet her gaze. And then the press pack were closing in again, and Jennifer's gaze was drawn upwards, as if compelled to do so by some irresistible force.

Until she saw him—and her ears began to roar as the world closed in on her.

It couldn't be. Please, God—it just couldn't be.

But it was. Oh, it was—for there was no mistaking the dynamic presence that was Matteo d' Arezzo.

Jennifer felt sick and faint—but somehow she sucked in a slow breath of oxygen and managed to keep the meaningless smile on her face as she gazed in disbelief at the man who was standing at the top of the red carpet, surrounded by a small bunch of sychophants—as if he were king of all he surveyed.

His Italian looks were dark and brooding, and his body was lean and honed and shown off to perfection in the coal-black dinner suit. Legs slightly parted, his hands deep in the pockets of his elegant trousers, his casual stance stretched the material over his thighs— emphasising their hard, muscular shafts…leaving nothing about his virile physique to the imagination. Long-lashed jet eyes glittered in the olive-gold of his face, and they flicked over her now in a way which was achingly familiar yet heartbreakingly alien.

Jennifer's heart contracted in her chest. It had been so long since she'd seen him. Too long, and yet not long enough.

And women were screaming his name.

Screaming it as once she had screamed it, in his arms and in his bed.

Matteo.

She felt like a mannequin in a shop window—with the look of a real person about her, but a complete inability to move.

But she *had* to move. She had to.

The cameras would be trained on both faces. Looking for a reaction—any reaction, but preferably one which would provide the meat for a juicy story.

She willed some warmth into her frozen smile and began to walk up towards him, thanking her impossibly tight silk dress for the slowness of her steps.

It was a walk which seemed to go on for ever. The roar of the crowd retreated and the blur of their faces merged, and as she grew closer she could see the dark shadowing of his jaw and the cruel curve of his lips. Men like Matteo did not grow on trees, and his outrageous beauty and sex-appeal often made the casual observer completely awestruck. Well, he would not intimidate her as he had spent his life intimidating the studio. He was her cheating ex-husband—nothing more and nothing less—and she needed to take control of the situation.

She lifted her head as she reached him. 'Hello, Matteo,' she said coolly.

To see her was like being struck by lightning, and Matteo could feel the hot rods of desire as he saw the creamy thrust of her breasts edged by silk as deeply blue as the ocean. He tensed, his mind racing with questions as he stared down at his estranged wife.

Che cosa il hell stava accendo?

But his face stayed unmoving, even though his groin had begun to tighten, and he cursed his erection and despised the unfathomable desire which made him so unbearably hard. For there were women more beautiful than Jennifer Warren—but none who had ever made him feel quite so...so...

He swallowed down thoughts of what he would like to do, and how much he despised himself for wanting to do it. Weak was not a word he would ever use to describe himself—but something about the physical spell his wife had always cast over him was as debilitating as when Delilah had shorn off Samson's hair...

What the *hell* was she doing here? And why the *hell* had he not been told?

He knew that the cameras were trained on him—and on her—waiting for their reactions. A flicker of emotion here. A tell-tale sign there. Something—anything—to indicate what either was thinking. And if they couldn't find out, then they'd make something up!

Training took over from instinct and he kept the tightening of his mouth at bay. Only the sudden steeliness of his eyes hinted at his inner disquiet, and that was far too subtle to be seen. He would give them nothing!

The glance he gave Jennifer was cursory, almost dismissive—but visually it was encyclopaedic to a man who had grown up appreciating women, who could assess them in the blinking of an eye. He felt the quickening of his pulse and the silken throb of his blood, for the bright blue silk of her dress clung indecently to every curve of her magnificent body.

For a moment he ran his eyes proprietorially over the soft swell of her breasts and the narrow indentation of her waist, and he did so without guilt. Why the hell should he feel guilt? She was still his wife—*maledicala*—even though her greedy lawyers were picking over the carcass of their marriage.

Two of the Festival staff moved towards him to usher him inside, but he waved them away with a dismissive gesture.

Should he turn his back on her? That was what he *wished* he could do. But he decided against it—for would that not just excite more comment from the babbling idiots who would fill their gossip columns with it tomorrow?

Instead, he gave a bland and meaningless smile as she reached him, and looked down into her sapphire eyes, which were huge in a china-white face and blinking at him now in that way which always made him…

Don't do vulnerable, Jenny, he thought. Don't turn those big blue eyes on me like that or I may just forget all the anger and the rifts and do something unforgivable, like taking you in my arms in full view of the world and kissing you in a way that no man will ever come close to for the rest of your life.

'What the hell are you doing here?' she said weakly.

'Wondering if you're wearing any knickers,' he murmured.

'I'm surprised you haven't worked that out for yourself—women's underwear *is* your specialist subject, isn't it?'

How crisp and English she sounded! Just like when they'd met—and then he'd been blown away by it. That cool wit and ice-hot sexuality. But—like a rare, hothouse flower—she had not survived the move to the tougher climes of Hollywood. Her career had flourished, but their relationship had withered.

'Oh, *cara*, don't you know that when you're angry you're irresistible?'

She wanted to tell him that she didn't care. But it wasn't true. Because if she didn't keep a tight rein on her feelings then she might just let it all blurt out and tell him things that he must never know.

That the pain of seeing him was almost too much to bear, and that in the wee, small hours of the morning she still reached for the warmth of her husband in the cold, empty space beside her.

Then remember, she told herself fiercely. Remember just *why* you've haven't seen him in so long.

'I had no idea you were going to be here,' she said, gritting her teeth behind her smile.

'Snap!'

'You didn't know either?'

His black brows knitted together. 'You think I would have come here if I *had*?' he demanded softly. '*Cara,* you flatter yourself!'

Oddly enough, this hurt more than it had any right to and almost as an antidote to meaningless pain, Jennifer forced herself to ask the question which twisted her gut in two. 'Is your girlfriend with you?'

His mouth hardened. 'No.'

Jennifer expelled a low breath of relief. At least she had been spared *that*. Fine actress she might be, and pragmatic enough to accept that her marriage to Matteo was over, but she didn't think that even she could have borne to see the smug and smiling face of her husband's new lover. 'I'm going inside,' she said, in a low voice.

He gave a cold smile as he walked up the red carpet beside her and into the glittering foyer. 'Looks like we've got each other for company,' he drawled. 'Pity we're both on the guest-list, isn't it, Jenny? I guess that's one of the drawbacks of a couple making a film together and then separating soon afterwards!'

'Matteo!' It was Hal's voice. He had obviously judged it safe to talk to them.

Jennifer and Matteo both turned and—for all their

differences—their expressions were united in a cold-eyed assessment of their publicist as he panted his way up the stairs and gave them both an uneasy smile.

Matteo spoke while barely moving his mouth. 'You're history—you know that, Hal,' he said easily. 'You tricked me to get me here, and you bring me face to face with my ex-wife in the most awkward of circumstances. I am appalled—*furious*—at my stupidity for not having realised that you would stoop to this level in order to publicise your damned film. But, believe me, I shall make you pay.'

'Now, let's not be hasty,' blustered Hal.

'Oh, let's,' vowed Jennifer, her bright smile defusing the bitter undertone in her voice. 'This is the most sneaky and underhand thing you've ever done.'

An official appeared by their side, a brief look of perplexity crossing his brow as he sensed the uncomfortable atmosphere. He made a slight bow. 'May I show you to your seats, *monsieur, madame*?'

Matteo raised his elegant dark brows. 'What do you want to do, Jenny? Go home?'

She wanted to tell him not to call her that, for only he had ever called her that. The soft-accented and caressing nickname no longer thrilled her or made her feel softly dizzy with desire. Now it mocked her—reminding her that everything between them had been an utter sham. And did he think she was going to hang her head and hide? Or run away? Was his ego so collossal that he thought she couldn't face sitting through a performance of a film she had poured everything into?

'Why should I want to do that?' she questioned with a half-smile. 'We might as well gain something from this meeting. And at least the publicity will benefit the box office.'

Matteo's mouth twisted. 'Ah, your career! Your precious career!'

Censure hardened his voice, and Jennifer thought how unfair it was that ambition should be applauded in a man but despised in a woman. When she'd met him he had been the famous one—so well-known that she had felt in danger of losing herself in the razzle-dazzle which surrounded him.

It had been pride which had made her want a piece of the action herself—to show the world that she was more than just Matteo's wife—but in the end it had backfired on her. For her own rise to superstardom had taken her away from him and spelt the beginning of the end of their marriage.

She didn't let her smile slip, but her blue eyes glinted with anger. 'We're separated, Matteo,' she murmured. 'Which no longer gives you the right to pass judgement on me. So let's skip the character assassination and just get this evening over with, shall we?'

'It will be my pleasure, *cara*,' he said softly. 'But you will forgive me if I don't offer you my arm?'

'I wouldn't take it even if you did.'

'Precisely.'

Jennifer had been dreading the première, but it was doubly excruciating to have to walk into the crowded cinema with her estranged husband by her side. All eyes turned towards them with a mixture of expectancy and curiosity as they took their seats in a box. For a few seconds conversation hushed, and then broke out again in an excited babble, and Jennifer wished herself anywhere other than there.

But there was no comfort even when the lights were dimmed, because for a start she was sitting right next to him—next to the still-distracting and sexy body. And the giant image which now flashed up onto the screen made it worse. For it was Matteo. And Jennifer. Playing roles which they must have been crazy to even consider when their marriage had been showing the first signs of strain.

They'd been cast as a couple whose marriage was being dissected in an erotically charged screenplay. There were other characters who impacted on the relationship—but the main one was the other woman. The irresistible other woman, who threatened and ultimately helped destroy the happiness of the couple who'd thought they had everything.

Art imitating life—or was it life imitating art?

It wasn't real, Jennifer told herself fiercely. If she and Matteo had been strong together, then no woman—no matter how beautiful—could have come between them.

But it was still painful to watch. And even if she closed her eyes she couldn't escape, for she could still

hear the sounds of their whispered lines, or—worse—
the sounds of their faked cries of pleasure. Hers and
Matteo's. His and the other woman's. How easy it was
to imagine the other woman in his arms as Sophia, and
how bitterly it hurt.

Jennifer watched as her own screen eyes fluttered
to a close, her lips parting to utter a long, low moan as
her back arched in a frozen moment of pure ecstasy.

'I'm *coming*!' she breathed.

All around her Jennifer could hear the massed intake
of breath as the people watched her orgasm—watched
her real-life husband follow her, his dark head sinking
at last to shudder against her bare shoulder.

She closed her eyes to block out the sight and the
sounds—but nothing could release her from the torment of wondering what the audience were thinking
and feeling. Perhaps some of them were even turned
on by the blatant sexuality of the act.

It was a ground-breaking film, but now Jennifer sup-
pressed a shudder. It no longer looked clever and avant-
garde, but slightly suspect. What kind of job had she
been sucked in to doing—to have stooped so low as to
replicate orgasm with her real-life husband while the
cameras rolled?

And then—at last—the final line. The amplified
sound of herself saying the words 'Now she's gone.
And now we can begin all over again.' The screen went
black, the credits began to roll and there was a moment

of stunned silence as the cinema audience erupted into applause.

The lights went up and Jennifer stared down at her hands to see that they were trembling violently.

'Ah! Did the emotion of the film get to you?' mocked the silken tones of Matteo, and she looked up to see that his eyes were on her fingers. 'You've taken your wedding band off, I see?'

She nodded. 'Yes. I threw it away, actually.'

His black eyes narrowed. 'You're kidding?'

'Of course I'm not.' Jennifer wouldn't have been human if she hadn't experienced a thrill of triumph at the look of shock on his handsome face. But any triumph was swiftly followed by anger. Did he think it a comparable shock to seeing those snatched long-range photos of him kissing Sophia in a New York park?

She turned her blue eyes on him. 'What on earth *does* a woman do with a redundant wedding ring?' she questioned in a low voice. 'I don't have a daughter to leave it to, and I'm too rich to need to pawn it. So what would you suggest, Matteo? That I melt it down and have it made into earrings—or else keep it in a box to remind me of what a sham your vows were?'

He bent his head towards her ear, presumably so that the movement of his lips could not be seen, but Jennifer felt dizzy as his particular scent washed over her senses.

'How poisonous you can be, Jenny,' he commented softly.

'I learnt it at the hands of a grand master!' she returned, as he straightened up and she met his cold smile with one of her own. 'Oh, God,' she breathed, their slanging match momentarily forgotten. 'Here they come.'

Matteo shook himself back to reality, irritated to realise that he had been caught up with watching the movement of her lips and the way that the great sweep of her eyelashes cast feathery shadows over the pure porcelain of her skin. Insanely, he felt himself grow hard.

But he wouldn't beat himself up about it. You didn't have to be in love with a woman to want to…to…

Dignitaries were bearing down on them. He could see a cluster of executives and all the other acolytes that the film world spawned. His eyes narrowed and he turned to Jennifer.

'You're not going to the after-show party, I presume?' he demanded.

'Why not?'

'Perhaps it bothers you that I will be there?'

'Don't be silly, Matteo,' she chided. 'You aren't part of my life any more—why on earth should it bother me?'

His eyes hardened. 'Then we might as well go there together. *Si?*'

That hadn't been what she'd meant at all. Jennifer opened her mouth to protest, and then shut it again. Maybe this way was better. She would have Matteo by her side as they walked down the endless red carpet and into the waiting car. And while he might not have been faithful at least he had always protected her, and she missed that. Badly.

'People will talk.'

'Oh, Jenny.' His laugh was tinged with bitterness. 'People will talk anyway. Whatever we do.'

She met his eyes in a moment of shared understanding which was more painful than anything else he had said to her, for it hinted at a former intimacy so powerful that it had blown her away.

And suddenly Jennifer wanted to break down and weep for what they had lost. Or maybe for what they had never had.

'Come on,' said Matteo impatiently. 'Let's just go and get it over with.'

CHAPTER TWO

SOMEHOW THE LONG scarlet flight of steps seemed safer this time around—and so did the legion of press waiting at the foot of them. As if Matteo had managed to throw the mantle of his steely strength over Jennifer's shoulders and was protecting her and propelling her along by the sheer force of his formidable will.

Even the questions which were hurled at them about their relationship had somehow lost their impact to wound her. As if Matteo was deflecting them and bouncing them back with one hard, glittering look and a contemptuous curl of his lip which made women go ga-ga and photographers quake.

The party was in one of the glitziest hotels along the Croisette itself, but Jennifer found herself wishing that it was being held in one of the restaurants which lined the narrow, winding backstreets where Matteo had once taken her. The *real* Cannes—where such luminaries as Elizabeth Taylor and Richard Burton had eaten. But it didn't really matter where the party was—she was going to stay only for as long as necessary and then she was leaving. That way she would save her face and save her pride.

They were in a room which was decorated entirely in gold—to echo the colour of the Festival's most prestigious award, the Palme d' Or. The walls were lined with heavy golden silk, like the inside of a Bedouin tent, and there were vases of gold-sprayed twigs laced with thousands of tiny glimmering lights. Beautiful young women dressed in belly-dancer outfits swayed around the room, carrying trayfuls of champagne.

But once she had accepted a drink Jennifer deliberately walked away from Matteo. She didn't need him, and she was here to show him *and* the rest of the world just that. She was an independent woman—why would she need anyone? That was what her mother had always told her, and it seemed that her words had been scarily prophetic.

The party might have had a budget to rival that of a small republic, but it was a crush—and less hospitable than some of the student get-togethers Jennifer had gone to in her youth.

An aging but legendary agent was holding court. A nubile starlet was not only falling out of her dress but also falling over from too much wine, by the look of her. A raddled-looking rock star was looking around the room with a stupid grin on his well-known face and suspiciously bright eyes. And from out of the corner of her eye she saw Matteo being surrounded by a gaggle of glamorous women.

Welcome to the world of showbiz, thought Jennifer wryly. But inside she was hurting more than she could have imagined it was possible to hurt.

She dodged passes, questions, and having her glass refilled—managing instead to find a very famous and very gay British actor who was standing in the corner surveying the goings-on with the bemused expression of a spectator at the zoo. Jennifer had played Regan to his King Lear, and she walked up to him with a sigh of relief.

'Thank heavens,' she breathed. 'A friendly face with no agenda!'

'Hiding from the vultures?' he questioned wryly.

'Sort of. Congratulations on your knighthood by the way. What are you doing *here*?'

'Same as you, I imagine. I may be an old queen—and a knight now, to boot—but I have to please my publicist like a good boy.'

'Don't we all?'

He surveyed her thoughtfully. 'I see you arrived with that adorable man you married—does that mean you're back together?'

In spite of the room's heat, Jennifer trembled—but she was a good enough actress to inject just the right amount of lightness into her voice. 'No. We're just playing games with the press. The marriage is over.'

'Sorry to hear that,' he said carelessly. 'Occupational hazard, I'm afraid. You'll get over it, duckie—you're young and you're beautiful.' He sighed, his eyes drifting to Matteo once more. 'Mind you—so is he!'

Jennifer grimaced a smile. 'Yes.'

'Go home and forget him,' he said gently. 'And stay away from actors—they're feckless and unfaithful and I should know! Marry a businessman next time.'

'I'm not even divorced yet,' she said solidly. 'And even if I were, this thing has scarred me for life—I'm through with marriage. Anyway—better run. Lovely to see you, Charles.'

They exchanged two butterfly air-kisses and then Jennifer resolutely made her way towards the door and slipped away—not noticing that she was being followed by a Hollywood icon who had just gone through divorce number four.

Not until she was in a quiet corridor and he moved right up close behind her.

Jennifer jumped and turned round. 'Oh, it's *you*, Jack!' she exclaimed nervously. 'You startled me!'

He flashed his trademark smile. 'Well, well, well,' he drawled softly. 'Maybe my luck has changed for the better. You look damned gorgeous.' He crinkled his blue eyes and directed his gaze at her chest. 'So, how's life, Jennifer?'

Jennifer knew that his fame meant he got away with stuff that other men would be prosecuted for, and she should have been used to the predatory way that such men feasted their eyes on her breasts, but the truth was that she didn't think she'd *ever* get used to it. 'I'm fine, thanks,' she said blandly.

'Well, since we're in the same boat, maritally speaking...' His voice dipped suggestively and his swimming pool eyes gleamed. 'It can get a little lonely in bed at night—what say we keep each other company?' And then his eyes narrowed as a shadow fell over him and he looked up into a pair of black, glittering eyes. 'Well, well, well,' he blustered. 'If it isn't the Italian Stallion!'

Matteo wasn't bothered by the star's slurred insult, but he felt a shimmering of intense irritation as he saw the fraught expression on his wife's face. That and the blunt hit of jealousy.

'Are you okay, Jenny?' he demanded.

She wanted to tell him that it was none of his business, but instead she looked straight into his eyes. And, in one of those silent looks between two people who have lived together which speak volumes, her eyes told him that, no, she wasn't okay. 'I was just leaving.'

'What a coincidence,' Matteo murmured. 'So was I.'

The sex symbol frowned in confusion, looking from Matteo to Jennifer like a spectator at a tennis match. 'But I thought—'

'Well, don't,' Matteo interjected silkily. 'You're not paid to think—you're paid to act...pretty badly, as it happens, which is why your career is on the way down.'

And he took Jennifer's hand in a proprietary way which made her momentarily long for the past and loathe herself for doing so as he led her down a corridor.

'What do you think you're doing?' she demanded, shaking him off once they were out of sight.

'You wanted to get away from that *strisciamento*?'

'Well, yes. But not with *you*!'

'Are you certain?' His eyes glittered. 'I've discovered a service lift which bypasses all the press—if you're interested?' He arched his dark eyebrows as they came to a discreet-looking steel door at the end of the corridor which was light-years away from the luxury of the guest lift they'd ridden up in.

'Aren't you the clever one?' she questioned sarcastically.

'But of course I am—we both know that. Coming?'

Jennifer hesitated.

'Unless you're secretly hot for the *bastardo*?' he suggested silkily. 'And want to stick around?'

Jennifer glanced back along the corridor and then stepped into the lift beside Matteo, pointedly moving as far away from him as possible as the doors slid shut on them.

'You're going to have to watch your step, Jenny,' Matteo said softly as the lift began to whirr into action. 'Men like that eat women for breakfast.'

Jennifer stared at him in disbelief. 'How dare you?' she questioned. 'In view of what's happened how *dare* you take a holier-than-thou opinion on another man's behaviour? Have you tried looking at your own lately?' She clenched her hands into two tight fists, her breath coming hot and fast as the words came spilling out of her mouth. 'How's your *girlfriend*, Matteo?'

Matteo's eyes narrowed. 'Jenny, don't—'

'Don't you *dare* tell me "Jenny, don't"! Remind me of her name again.' Jennifer faked a frown. 'Oh, yes— Sophia! Not exactly a household name at the moment, but I guess that'll soon change with the magic of the d' Arezzo influence.'

'You didn't knock it when you used it yourself,' he challenged softly.

'You *bastard*! At least I was known for being a good actress *before* I met you—and not for pouting and lounging around half-naked in some over-hyped perfume advertisement! So, was she worth it?'

Matteo's black eyes flared. Had he meant so little to her that she could enquire after another woman as if she were asking the time? For, while he accepted that their marriage was over, Matteo knew that if he bumped into any lover of *hers* he would want to tear him limb from limb.

'I don't think that's any of your business, do you?' he drawled. 'You wanted a divorce—and you're damned well getting one! Technically, that makes me a free man, Jenny—and at liberty to date whom I please.'

'But you weren't *technically* free in New York, when you started your affair with her, were you, Matteo? When the cameras caught you kissing her?' The words were out before she could stop them and he stared at her, an odd expression in his eyes which Jennifer had never seen before.

'I hadn't slept with her then,' he said slowly.

The use of the word *then* cut through her like a knife. 'But now you have?' She swallowed. 'Slept with her?'

It was both a statement and a question, and there was a long and uneasy pause. For, no matter what the circumstances leading up to the act had been, Matteo knew he had broken his marital vows. 'Yes.'

Jennifer clamped her clenched fist against her mouth as the cold rip of jealous rage tore through her heart. But what had she expected? For him to carry on denying a physical relationship? To pretend that his undeniable attraction towards the stunning Italian starlet had remained unconsummated?

Matteo was a devastatingly attractive and *virile* man. He needed sex like most men needed water. Well, she had asked the question, and she had only herself to blame if he had given her the answer she had dreaded.

She had thought that the pain of their break-up couldn't possibly get any worse, but in that she had been completely wrong. He had said it now. He had slept with Sophia. His body had lain naked against hers, warm skin against warm skin. He had entered another woman, had pushed inside her and moved and then thrown his head back and groaned out his pleasure in the way she knew so well—the way he had done with her.

And spilled his seed inside her? Made this other

woman pregnant, like the pressmen had suggested earlier?

Biting against her fingers, Jennifer fought hard to prevent herself from retching. The mind could be a wonderfully protective organ—allowing you to block things out because they were too painful to contemplate—but it could be capricious and cruel, too, and Matteo's words triggered an inner torment as images of his infidelity came rushing in, like some unwanted and explicit porn film.

Jennifer leaned against the steel wall of the lift, beads of sweat gathering above her upper lip as she pictured her husband naked with another woman.

Matteo frowned and made an instinctive move towards her. '*Cara*, you are faint?'

'Don't you *dare* call me that!' she spat, and shrank even farther against the metal, which felt cold against her bare back. She wiped the back of her hand over her clammy face. 'And don't you dare come *near* me!'

A wave of sadness washed over him and he wondered how something which had seemed so perfect could have deteriorated into a situation where Jennifer was staring at him as if he was her most dangerous and bitter enemy.

Maybe he was. Maybe that was what inevitably happened when a marriage broke down. Maybe the myth of an 'amicable' divorce was exactly that—a myth.

He stared at her as she moved a little restlessly, as if aware of how tiny the enclosed space was. Her proximity was distracting. Matteo's senses felt raw—as if

someone had been nicking at them with a razor. Yet
when he looked at her he felt nostalgic for times past,
and that was always painful—for it had never been real.
Because memory played tricks with your emotions. It
tampered with the past and rewrote it—so that everyone saw it differently. He knew that Jennifer's version
of it would be different from his own, and there was
nothing he could do about that.

But maybe that was only part of it. For the eyes didn't
lie, did they? He studied her and thought how much time
had changed her. Tonight she was all sleek Hollywood
film star—her heavy blonde hair caught up in an elaborate topknot with a few artistic tendrils tumbling down
around her face. Her gym-tight body was encased in
clinging sapphire silk, and she was bedecked in priceless diamond and sapphire jewellery.

How little she resembled the rosy-cheeked girl with
tousled hair and bohemian clothes he'd fallen in love
with. Was it the same for her? Did she look at him and
see a stranger in his face today?

And a floodgate was opened as the reflection triggered a reaction. Forbidden thoughts rushed into his
head with disturbing clarity, and Matteo remembered
the pure magic of meeting her. Of feeling something
which had been completely alien to him.

CHAPTER THREE

MATTEO HAD BEEN filming in England. The 'Italian Heart-Throb'—as the newspapers had insisted on calling him—had agreed to play Shakespeare. It had been a gamble, but one Matteo had been prepared to take. He had been bored with the stereotypical roles which had brought him fame and riches, and eager to show his mettle. To prove to the world—and himself—that an Italian-American *could* play Hamlet. And why not? All kinds of actors were switching accents in a bid to show versatility in the competitive international film market. Some had even won awards for doing just that.

Jennifer had been playing Ophelia—but not in his film. She'd been what they called a 'serious' actress—stage-trained, relatively poor, and rather aloof. He had gone along one evening to watch her perform and had been unable to tear his eyes away from her.

They'd been introduced backstage, and he'd been both intrigued and infuriated when she'd given a slightly smug smile which seemed to say *I know your type.*

'I loved your performance,' he said, with genuine

warmth, before realising that it made him sound like some kind of stage-door Johnny—*him*!

'Thank you. You're playing Hamlet yourself, I believe?' she questioned, in the tone of someone going through the motions of necessary conversation. Almost as if she was *bored*!

'You do not approve?' he challenged. 'Of someone like me playing one of your greatest roles?'

Jennifer blinked. 'What an extraordinary assumption to jump to! I hadn't given it a thought.'

And he knew that she spoke the truth. For a man who held the very real expectation that every actress in Stratford would be anticipating his visit as if it were the King of Denmark himself, Jennifer's uninterest inflamed him.

She was studying him, her head tilted slightly. 'But your reviews have been spectacular,' she conceded, in the interests of fairness. 'So well done.'

He knew that. Every theatre in the world wanted him, and Broadway was putting irresistible offers on his agent's table. But somehow Jenny's quiet compliment meant more to him than all those things. 'Have dinner with me tonight,' he said suddenly.

Jennifer put her head to one side, her tousled hair falling over her shoulders. 'Why should I do that?'

A stream of clever retorts could yield entirely the wrong result, Matteo realised. For the first time in his life he anticipated that she might do the unthinkable and *turn him down*!

'Because my life will be incomplete if you do not,' he said simply.

'You can't say things like that!' she protested, biting her lip with a mischievous kind of fascination.

'I just did,' he drawled unapologetically.

She stared at him for a long, considering moment. 'Okay,' she said, and smiled.

And there it had been—like all the old songs said—something about her smile.

Matteo had never really believed in love—considering it something which existed for the rest of the world, but which excluded him. He had seen glimpses of it, but never before had he felt the great rush of passion and protectiveness he experienced with Jennifer that day, which had been the beginning of their tempestuous and ultimately doomed union.

And now?

Now he believed that what had happened had been a cocktail of hormones which had combusted at a time in his life when he'd craved some kind of excitement. He had been right all along. Love was not real. It was a story they fed you which sold movies and books. That was all.

Jennifer rubbed distractedly at her forehead. 'This lift is taking for ever.'

He had been so lost in his thoughts that he hadn't noticed.

'Is it?' he questioned, as there was a sudden lurching kind of movement, followed by complete and deafening silence. Matteo looked from the disbelieving accusation in Jenny's eyes to the stationary arrow on the illuminated panel. 'Maybe you're right,' he mused. 'Seems like we've run into a little trouble.'

'Please tell me you're joking.'

'You think I'd joke about something like that? You think perhaps I've set this up?' he demanded. 'Lured you into this lift so that I can be alone with you?'

Jennifer turned glacial blue eyes on him. 'And have you?'

He gave a short laugh. 'Have I? Believe me when I tell you, *cara*, that I can think of a lot more agreeable companions to be stuck with than a woman who does not seem to know the reason of the word "trust"!'

'And I'd rather be with the devil himself than some arrogant and egotistical sex maniac who can't resist chasing anything in a skirt!'

His black eyes narrowed as he felt the bubble of rage begin to simmer up. 'You dishonour me with such a description!' he declared furiously.

'It's the truth!'

'Ah, but it is *not* the truth, and deep down you know that, Jenny! You saw the amount of women who threw themselves at me! It was never the other way round.'

Yes. Those women who would pass him their telephone numbers openly in restaurants, right in front of her face, as if she were just part of the furniture. Or those others, who would use more devious methods to get the attention of the devastatingly handsome actor.

The shop assistants and the flight attendants who would slyly slide him their details. The doctors and lawyers who would invent the need for a meeting with him. It seemed that none of them had any shame—any woman with a pulse wanted her husband.

'Did you ever stop to think what it was like for me, as your wife?' she demanded.

'Of course I did! You made it damned impossible for me to do otherwise!'

'Did you? I think you used to treat it as an amusing little game—batting those gorgeous eyes as if to say, *I'm not even doing anything, and still they bother me!*'

'Oh, Jenny—that was *your* insecurity talking, not mine. I'd gone beyond the stage where I needed fans to bolster my ego.' His eyes darkened. 'But, beyond refusing to leave the house, the only way to stop women coming on to me was to increase our security—and that brought its own claustrophobia.' There was a pause. 'And anyway, you know damned well that I pushed those women away.'

'But you stopped pushing eventually, didn't you, Matteo?' she questioned, and she felt that familiar pain stabbing at her heart. And although part of her wondered why she was putting herself through yet more pain, she couldn't seem to stop herself. 'When you looked at Sophia. And you wanted her. Are you denying that?'

There was another kind of silence now—fraught and terrible in the already silent lift. Yes, he had been guilty of the sin of desiring another woman, but it should have remained just one of those unacted-upon desires which made up a human life. People were not immune to desiring other people even if they *were* married. Only the truly naïve believed otherwise. And it was the naïve who fell victim to mistaking that forbidden desire for love. Matteo had seen it, and known it for exactly what it was. Unfortunately, Jenny had not.

He had been filming with Sophia, and their on-screen chemistry had been so hot it had sparked off the set. Everyone in the industry had been talking about it. And eventually Jennifer had got to hear about it.

But even if she hadn't developed such an obsession with it their marriage had already been at crisis point. Their work schedules had kept them apart so much that all she'd been getting were reports from the newspapers and photos of him with Sophia. She had picked away at the rumours—like a teenager worrying at a blemish on her face—until eventually her jealousy and suspicions had blown up. Trust between them had already been destroyed by the time he had kissed Sophia.

'You can't deny it, can you, Matteo?' she persisted. 'That you wanted Sophia?'

'What do you want me to say?' he demanded. 'Because by then what I did or didn't do was irrelevant! We were no longer a real couple. We were so far apart from each other that we might as well have been existing on different planets.' He looked at her across the confined space and his dark eyes were sombre. 'You know we were.'

Jennifer bit her lip so that he wouldn't see it trembling, because now there was pain in *his* eyes, too, and somehow that made it worse. It was far easier to think that Matteo was immune to the hurt of their break-up. Because if he shared even a fraction of her heartbreak, then somehow that only emphasised the precious thing they had shared and now lost.

'Oh, what's the point in discussing it? There's nothing left to be said.'

Matteo stilled. 'Well, for the first time in a long time we are of one accord, *cara*,' he said softly.

Another barb. Yet more pain. But Jennifer silently thanked her ability to act as she kept her face from reacting and flicked him an impatient look instead. 'Look, just concentrate on getting us out of this mess, will you, Matt—since you're the one who got us into it.'

'Are you implying that I've trapped you?' he laughed softly.

'No implication,' she answered. 'You have.'

He narrowed his eyes and listened. 'Can you hear anything?'

'Unfortunately, no.'

'Got a phone?'

'No.'

'Me neither. The truly successful never carry phones to events like this, do they?' he mused. 'That would make us far too accessible to the big wide world—and there's always someone to take our messages for us.'

For a moment Jennifer was surprised by the unfamiliar note of cynicism which had crept into his voice. 'Surely Matteo d' Arezzo hasn't become disenchanted with the jetset world which brought him riches and fame?'

'Isn't that inevitable?' he questioned drily. 'Doesn't it happen to everyone?'

'Not to you.' She shrugged. 'I thought that success was your very lifeblood.'

'Success on its own isn't enough,' he said tightly. 'I don't want to stay on this merry-go-round of a life until it chews me up and spits me out.'

Jennifer blinked. 'I can't believe you just said that.'

He looked at her and his eyes were like chips of jet. 'Was I really so ruthless, Jenny?'

She thought about the way they'd pored over their working schedules like two prospectors who'd just struck gold and now she recognised her own ruthlessness, too. Oh, how stupidly short-sighted you could be when fame came tapping at your door. She shrugged her shoulders. 'Maybe we both were.'

She felt the hot pricking of sweat on her forehead and ran her tongue over parched lips, noticing that his black gaze was trying not to be drawn to them. She hoped to God that he didn't think she was giving him the come-on. Fractionally, she moved away from him. 'What are we going to do?'

'We don't have a lot of choice. We wait.'

'For how long?'

'How the hell should I know?' Did she think this was easy for *him*? Her standing so close and off-limits—her luscious body barely covered in some flimsy gown which made her look like…

'Do you want to sit down?' he suggested carefully. Because surely that way he wouldn't have to be confronted by the tantalising thrust of her breasts?

Jennifer didn't know if she dared move. She was aware that her panties were growing damp and that if she wasn't careful Matteo would guess. He had always been so perfectly attuned to her body and its needs that his senses would be instantly alerted to the physical manifestations of desire. Briefly, she shut her eyes, summoning thoughts which would kill that desire stone-dead. But it wasn't easy.

'You're okay?' he asked softly.

She opened them. *Think of his betrayal. Of his doing with another woman what he had stood up in church and declared was for her and her alone.* 'Oh, yes—I'm absolutely fine! Just wonderful! I'm trapped in a service lift in a foreign country with my cheating ex-husband. *Exactly* the way I would choose to spend my Saturday night!' She rubbed her fingertips against the necklace which was digging into her throat.

'Why don't you take that off?' he suggested, as he saw the red mark she'd left there. Her skin was moist and a damp tendril of hair was clinging to her neck.

She met his eyes. 'I beg your pardon?'

He gave a snort of savage laughter. '*Madre de Dio*—don't look at me like that!'

'I wasn't looking like anything!'

'Oh, yes, you were,' he contradicted softly. 'With shock and horror written all over your face. As if I were suggesting some kind of striptease when all I meant was that your necklace doesn't look very *comfortable*.' He ran a disparaging glance over the heavy, wide choker which gleamed around her slender neck. 'Studio told you to wear it, did they?'

'Yes.' But he was right. She was aware of the costly gems digging into her flesh, making her feel as if she was wearing some upmarket dog-collar. Blindly, her hand reached up behind her, tried to reach the clasp, but failed—and there was no mirror...

'You want me to do it for you?' he questioned.

Jennifer hesitated, because it seemed almost too intimate a thing to do. The putting on and the taking off of a necklace was the kind of thing a husband did for his wife in the seclusion of their bedroom when they were properly married—not about to enter one of the biggest divorce battles of the year. Yet what choice did she have?

'I guess so. Never has the word "choker" seemed so appropriate,' she added sardonically.

He gave a wry smile. 'Turn around, then.'

But, confronted with the sight of her bare back, Matteo found his mind slipping into forbidden places. He silently cursed as he felt his erection grow even harder, thankful that she couldn't see his face—for he was certain that it had contorted into a pained expression of exquisite sexual frustration.

'You see…ex-husbands do have *some* uses,' he observed evenly, and lifted his fingers to unclasp the necklace, letting it slide into the palm of his hand like a heavy and glittering snake. 'There. Better?'

'Much…thank you.' Jennifer composed her face and turned—noting the dull flush of colour which was accentuating his high cheekbones. She knew what it meant when he looked like that—or at least she thought she did. Was he just getting overheated, or…?

Did he still want her? Was he imagining what they would have been doing in here if they were still married? Him rucking up her dress and pushing at her panties, unzipping himself and thrusting deep inside her, with her back pushed against the steel wall?

Oh, Lord—what was the matter with her? How could the thought of sex with him be so unbearably exciting despite everything that had happened between them? Everything they'd said and thought and done and accused each other of.

'Do you want me to put it in my pocket?' he asked.

'What?' asked Jennifer blankly.

He held the gems up. 'This.'

'Sure.' She nodded her head and turned away, unwilling to watch him slide them into his trousers, some sixth sense telling her what her eyes did not want to see—that he was hard and aroused.

So why did that thought give her some kind of primitive satisfaction instead of shocking her to the core?

As the minutes ticked by she could feel beads of sweat trickling down her back and a faint dampness gathering beneath the heaviness of her breasts. Shifting her position in her high-heeled shoes, she could see the faint sheen on Matteo's olive skin, and she swallowed as their eyes met in an uncomfortable moment of awareness.

'It's hot,' he said huskily.

'Yes.' She looked into his face because there was nowhere else to look. Nowhere to run. The bare steel walls seemed to be shrinking in on them, and suddenly Jennifer was terrified of this false intimacy—frightened of the sensations which were beginning to creep over her skin and the thoughts which were flooding into her head.

She turned away from him and lifted up her fist, pounding it hard on the metal surface of the wall and wincing as she struck.

'Help! Let us *out*!' she called. But the silence was deafening. She raised her voice. 'Let us *out*!'

'Why do you shout when no one will hear us, Jenny?'

'Somebody's *got* to hear us! Because being in here with you is driving me mad!'

'I thought you liked that aspect of our relationship.'

'I wasn't talking sexual!'

His eyes drifted over the hard points of her nipples. 'Weren't you?'

'Oh, can't you keep your mind on something other than your bloody libido?'

Matteo almost smiled. She *was* angry. And she was aroused, too. He knew that with a certainty which only increased his own desire to an almost unbearable pitch. Would he ever again know a woman as intimately as he did this one?

She wished he would stop looking at her. She wished he was anywhere other than here. Because just his presence was making her have the kind of thoughts which were forbidden. Longing thoughts. Wishful thoughts.

'Help!' she screamed again, and this time she began to drum both fists against the wall. 'Please, somebody—*help* us!'

'Jenny, don't—'

But his words inflamed her even more—or maybe she was just in the mood to be inflamed. And seeing his insufferably enigmatic face as he calmly watched her losing it was like pouring paraffin on an already blazing fire. 'I'll do as I damn well please!' she retorted furiously. 'And you can't stop me!'

He wanted to marvel, because this raging woman was utterly magnificent, but he could see from the rapid movement of her breathing that she was in danger of hyperventilating. 'That's enough! Now, stop it,' he said flatly.

'No!' she yelled, and hot, angry tears began to spill from beneath her eyelids. 'No, I won't stop it!'

Swiftly he moved towards her, wrenching her away

from the wall, and she whirled round, imprisoned in his arms, and began to beat against his chest instead.

'*Si*,' he urged her softly. 'Hit me. Hit me if it makes you feel better, cara!'

'Bastard!' She slapped him. 'You bloody, bloody cheating bastard!'

'*Si*. That, too.'

'*That's* for that bitch you slept with!'

He took her furious punch without flinching.

'And so is that!'

She made a little roar of rage as she drummed against his chest until her hands ached. And then suddenly her rage became frustration, and all the fight went out of her, to be replaced by a different kind of emotion. She shook her head, trying to deny it, her hands falling as she looked up and saw something change in his eyes, too.

The look of understanding, of empathy, and the fleeting look of sorrow had been replaced by something else. Something she knew all too well and had never thought to see again—even though she had longed for it in the sleepless nights which had followed his departure. And it was wrong. *Wrong*. Oh, so wrong. He had been to bed with another woman!

'Was she better than me?' she demanded.

'Jenny, stop it.'

'No, seriously—I want to know. Did you do it to her lots of times? Like you did to me when we first met?'

He winced as if she'd hit him, and then the need to

destroy her foolish fantasy simply overwhelmed him. 'You want to know the truth?' he exploded. 'I did it to her *once*—just once—and it was the biggest non-event of my life. Do you know why that was? Because all I could see was *your* face, Jenny. All I could feel was *your* body.'

'Don't,' she croaked.

'But it's the truth,' he said bitterly. 'It's flawed, and it's not pretty—but it's the way it was.' His black eyes glittered at her bleakly. 'There—doesn't that make you feel better now?'

'Are you kidding?' she demanded. 'It still makes me wretched to think of you with another woman, no matter how much you hated it!'

But that was not the whole truth, for the stark admission had made her tremble with an unwelcome new emotion and her heart began to ache with sadness and regret. How the hell had it all come to this? How could love be so quickly transformed into all these other hateful negative emotions?

His eyes blazed black fire as they roved over her trembling lips. 'You want me,' he declared unsteadily.

'No.' Could he see the terrible need in her? 'No, I don't!'

'Yes. Yes, you do.' He reached out for her and pulled her into his arms in a movement which felt as natural as breathing.

'Stop it, Matteo,' she whispered.

'You want me to do this.' He began to massage the

little hollow at the base of her spine, the way he'd always done when he wanted her to relax, and as if she was acting on auto-pilot she shut her eyes.

'Even if I do—we mustn't. We mustn't do this,' she whispered, half to herself. But, oh, the touch of his body made her feel as though great warm waves had washed over her.

'Why not?' he whispered.

'You know why.'

'No, I don't.'

'You do. We're separated.'

'What's that got to do with anything?'

Her eyes fluttered open. 'That…that…woman.'

'I just told you. It is over. Believe me, Jenny—it never even began.'

And Jennifer was so lost in the thrall of the soft black look in his eyes that his betrayal of the other woman thrilled her. Later she would be appalled at how easily she could be seduced. But not now.

Now her lips were parting with a greedy anticipation she could not seem to deny herself as he slowly lowered his head towards hers.

CHAPTER FOUR

IT FELT LIKE a lifetime since Matteo had last kissed her, and Jennifer's arms reached up to clutch onto his broad shoulders as if she was afraid that her knees might give way. But only her lips did that—parting in a soft sigh as he began to kiss her.

Because to her horror—but not to her surprise—Matt's touch was like lighting a touchpaper. Jennifer's skin was on fire, and her heart was skittering away with excitement and almost a touch of desperation—like a drowning woman who had kicked up to the surface of the water for one last gulp of sweet air.

I just want one last kiss, she told herself. One last kiss from the man I loved enough to marry. The man I thought I would have children with and grow old with. One kiss—is that so very wrong?

But adults didn't just 'kiss' and nothing more—particularly those who had been married and who were still in the throes of a powerful sexual attraction.

Jennifer tore her mouth away from his as he began to rove the flat of his hand over one swollen breast, circling it over and over again until the nipple felt so exquisitely hardened that she sobbed aloud with frustrated pleasure. 'Matteo!' she gasped.

'*Si.*' He ground the word out in between hot and shallow breaths, scarcely able to believe that this was happening. That he was doing this to her and that she was letting him—and, oh, it was good. Too good. *Madre de Dio*—it had been so long. And it was never as good with anyone as it was with Jenny. He teased her lips with his in a soft and provocative kiss.

With a disbelieving sob she moved her mouth fractionally from his, knowing that this was wrong—worse than wrong—it was a kind of *madness*!

'Matteo, we…we…*mustn't.* You know we mustn't!'

God forgive him, but he used his hands as ruthlessly then as he had ever done in his life. He had never wanted a woman more than he wanted Jenny at that moment. Not even on that first night when he had taken her to his bed. Nor the time when he had been a teenage virgin and the older woman who had seduced him had made him wait. *Because a woman likes a man to wait,* she had purred. Well, there was to be no waiting now—he didn't want it and, to judge by the frantic grinding of her hips, neither did Jenny.

For the first and only time in his life he wanted her so badly that he thought he was about to come in his trousers. But he reined his desire in with a rigid self-control not betrayed in his sensual movements. He drifted his fingers beneath the thin bodice of her dress and took her bare breast in his hand, cupping it experimentally and feeling her knees buckle as she relaxed against him.

'Oh!' she squealed.

All she knew was sensation. She felt the rush of pleasure overwhelm her—and somehow all thoughts of this being wrong just melted away. A hunger both sharp and irresistible bubbled inside her like darkest, sweetest honey, and carried her along in its heavy flow as he touched her nipple.

'Matteo!' she gasped again, only this time the word was spoken in wonder and not in half-hearted protest.

Desire was jack-knifing through him in a way that was barely tolerable. He felt the hot pumping of his blood, the frantic pounding of his heart. Could see the gleam of her eyes and the soft moistness of her lips. It was like entering another world—of love and intrigue and lust and betrayal. One where his powers were weakened. And she weakened him. Just as she always had done. Like no one else did.

Stop me, Jennifer, he begged silently as he touched his fingertips to the silken tumble of her hair.

Il Dio lo perdona! He lowered his head, brushing his lips against hers—a fleeting, butterfly graze—giving her time to realise. Time to stop.

But she did no such thing. Her hands moved from his shoulders to his neck, pressing his face closer, so that the kiss deepened almost before he had realised, and she was lacing her tongue with his.

He moved his hand to the fork between her legs and pressed there, hard. She almost jumped out of her skin.

Her words were slurred yet shaky with disbelief. 'Matteo…'

'Si, cara mia?'

'You…you shouldn't be doing that.'

He felt her wetness through the silk of her evening gown and closed his eyes. 'Oh, but I should. You know I should. You were born for just this, Jenny. Oh, God!'

She would stop him in a minute. Just a little more of this sweet pleasure and then she would push him away. Her head fell back against the metal wall of the lift as he began to ruck up her dress, and it was so close to her illicit fantasy of earlier that Jennifer almost fainted with pleasure.

His hand was on her bare thigh now.

Stop him.

And now it was moving up to her damp panties. Maybe she would let him bring her to orgasm first, and then she would call a halt to it.

Matteo felt her thighs parting and he could scarcely believe what was happening. *She wasn't going to stop him!*

He said something soft and very explicit in Italian, and Jennifer knew exactly what it meant for she had heard it many times before. It should have made her put the brakes on, halt this madness once and for all. And every ounce of reason in her body was screaming out at her to do just that. But she was so hot and hungry for him—hotter than she had ever been in her life—that she would have died right there and then sooner than not have him do this to her.

She whimpered as he slid her panties across and she heard the rasp of his zip. He rubbed his thumb across her swollen clitoris and Jennifer gave a tiny scream.

And then, to her utter horror—and his—the lift gave a slight lurch and they heard a distant mechanical thrumming.

They stilled as they listened—every nerve-ending straining for the sound that neither wanted to hear. The lift stayed unmoving.

Oh, thank God, thought Jennifer.

'You want me?' he demanded starkly.

Against his neck she nodded her heavy head mutely.

Matteo acted decisively. Ripping apart her delicate panties so that they fluttered redundantly to the floor, he plunged deep inside her and then effortlessly lifted her up so that she could wrap her legs around his back.

He began to move, slowly at first, wanting to prolong it—to make this heaven last until the end of time and then a little longer still. He made a broken little cry as he thrust in and out of her, knowing that he had never been this hard before, feeling her tremble uncontrollably in his arms. He felt the thrust of her hips towards him in unspoken plea, a gesture he knew of old. And Matteo cupped her buttocks and plunged deeper still, hearing her throaty moan of satisfaction.

And then the lights began to flicker, catching fragments of their movements like an old black and white movie. He moved faster still as the lift began to whirr into life.

Jennifer felt herself beginning to come. 'Matteo, no!' she gasped, but she knew in her heart that it was too late. Sensation caught her up and carried her away and she heard his oh-so-familiar groan as he went with her, felt the helpless shuddering of this big man in her arms.

Mixed in with intense relief and pleasure was confusion and anger as Matteo orgasmed inside her—aware that he had just put both their reputations on the line in a way which was scarcely believable. The flickering lights righted themselves just as he withdrew from her, and all he could see was her horrified face. 'Jenny—'

'What have we *done*?' she whispered.

His mouth twisted. Surely it was a little late in the day for regrets? 'You want a biology lesson?'

Her eyes were huge sapphire saucers. 'You seduced me!' she accused hoarsely.

He almost laughed out loud at her temerity. 'I *seduced* you?' he repeated incredulously. 'You may have always had a problem differentiating between truth and fiction, but that really is taking it a little far, Jenny!'

She wanted to hit him again. And she wanted him to make love to her again. Oh, what was she *thinking*? That hadn't even gone close to 'making love'. What had just happened had been a quick wham-bam-thank-you-ma'am.

All it had been about was swift gratification and intense pleasure. On a physical level it had been wonderful—on an emotional one completely empty. She turned her head away, not wanting him to see the shame and self-contempt in her eyes.

'Now what do we do?' she questioned shakily.

So she couldn't bear to look at him now? Was that it? She hadn't been so damned picky when she was grinding her hips against him! 'There's no time for an in-depth analysis,' he grated, as he heard an echoing shout in French from the bottom of the lift shaft and bent to pick up her discarded panties. 'I think we're about to be rescued.'

The blood was pounding at her temples and in her groin, and she closed her eyes in despair. Rescued? Dear God, no.

Despite his anger and misgivings, Matteo knew that he had to take charge—because otherwise this would develop from a regrettable one-off into a drama which could have lasting repercussions. Quickly he adjusted his clothing and raked his gaze over her, a nerve beginning to work at his temple as he saw that the front of her silk dress was dark with the stain of love-juice.

'Damn!' he exploded softly, as he stuffed her tattered panties into his jacket pocket.

She followed the direction of his gaze and blushed a deep scarlet. Oh, how *could* they have? But she saw the detached look on his face and took her lead from it. She would take it in her stride—as he was so obviously doing. Maybe he does this kind of thing all the time these days? she thought bitterly. 'So, now what do I do?'

'Here. Put my jacket on,' he instructed tersely. He helped her wriggle into it and buttoned it up for her as if she were a child.

Frantically she smoothed down what she could of her hair and wiped a finger under each eye, wondering if her mascara had smudged.

For a moment their eyes met, and Jennifer swallowed, wondering whether she would meet contempt or triumph in his. For what man could not be forgiven for feeling either or both those emotions when a wife who was supposed to hate him had just let him have frantic sex with her?

But there was nothing.

Not a clue, not a glimmer of what might be going on inside his head. He was as enigmatic as she had ever seen him—no, more so—and it was like looking into the eyes of a complete stranger.

Her own senses were clouded and confused, and she was having real problems telling fantasy apart from reality. Sex did funny things to you—it transported you back to another place and another time. It must have done. For why else would she have to stop herself from running her fingertips lovingly over the shadowed rasp of his jaw and following the movement with a series of tender little butterfly kisses? The way she'd used to.

Was that because women were made weak and vulnerable by the act of love in a way men never were?

Women's bodies and minds were conditioned to mate with one partner—while men were programmed to spill their seed all over the place.

And at that thought Jennifer blanched. Had she remembered...?

Matteo's eyes narrowed. 'You aren't going to faint on me?'

'Faint?' She spoke with a brightness she was far from feeling. 'Don't be silly.'

He shook his dark head with dissatisfaction, because even though his jacket covered her to mid-thigh her cheeks were flushed and her eyes were wild. Her appearance gave away *exactly* what they had been doing. And this *was* a service lift, true, but that didn't guarantee that some sharp-eyed employee looking to make a quick buck wasn't waiting at the bottom armed with a camera or a mobile phone which could transmit an offending picture around the world in minutes. Was he prepared to take the risk? Did either of them dare?

No.

Without warning he bent and scooped her up into his arms, cradling her automatically against his chest so that she could feel the muffled thunder of his heart

'What the hell do you think you're doing?' she demanded.

He thought that was maybe a question she should have asked *before* they'd had that highly charged and erotic encounter, but he chose not to say it. Even thinking about it was making him grow hard again.

He shifted position slightly, not wanting her to sense that he had another erection—because having sex with your soon-to-be ex-wife once could be classified as a mistake. But twice? No. That would defy description.

What was done, was done—they just had to deal with the immediate fall-out before they parted again for the last time.

'What do you think is going to happen now?' he demanded. 'That you are just going to stroll out of here with your messed-up hair and your smudged make-up and your rumpled dress? You don't think that will excite some sort of comment?'

She shrugged. 'Well, obviously—but—'

'But what, Jenny? You don't think that anyone with more than one brain cell will put two and two together and come up with exactly the right answer?'

'So what's your solution?'

'That you act! Just act, Jenny,' he urged, as he saw her perplexed frown. 'Act like you've passed out and you're leaning on me—act as if your life depended on it.'

And maybe it did, in a way—when she stopped to think what he'd just said. Certainly her reputation and her dignity demanded that she emerge from that lift not looking as though she had been ravaged by her unfaithful ex-husband.

The lift juddered to a halt, and it was worse than Matteo had anticipated. Outside was an excited crowd of four waiters, a couple of chefs, what looked like a maître d' and a cleaner.

But no one from the studio. Thank God. He knew that their giant protective machinery would have whirred into action to minimise the outcome, but then it would be out of his control. And he would not let that happen. Not in this case.

He saw one of the waiters surreptitiously slide a mobile phone from his jeans and spoke in furious and rapid French to him. The chastened man shrugged and replaced the phone.

Jennifer's ear lay against the strong pounding of his heart and she closed her eyes—Matteo's words seemed to come at her from a great distance. His French was as fluent as his English, and she didn't even attempt to understand what he was saying, only knew that there was an excited and jabbering response from the staff.

He bent his head and whispered in her ear. 'Don't worry,' he said softly in English. 'You're going to be okay.'

She wished he wouldn't talk in that masterful and protective way to her, even though he was being both those things. But it was going to make it harder, she just knew it was—so much harder to say their inevitable goodbyes.

She opened her eyes to find that they were following someone down a long and draughty corridor and then outside, through an ill-lit yard which was lined with bins and a large skip containing hundreds of empty bottles.

We must be at the back of the hotel, Jennifer thought, and pressed her head against him as an overwhelming fatigue began to wash over her. But then sex with Matteo always made her sleepy. What was that she had read once? That some hormone was released when you orgasmed, which made you want to curl up and snooze.

'You okay?' he asked.

'You bring me to the nicest places,' she mumbled, and gave a low laugh.

The sound was so delightfully inappropriate that Matteo couldn't prevent the memory which stole over his skin as he remembered the precious gift of laughter which they had brought to each other in the early days. Ruthlessly, he blocked it.

'It won't be much longer,' he said tightly. 'They're getting hold of a car for us.'

She had to stop herself from snuggling up to him, as if they were real lovers instead of estranged spouses who just happened to know the way to turn each other on.

'I ought to get back to the Hedoniste,' she said unenthusiastically.

'That's where you're staying?'

'Isn't everyone?'

Matteo's mouth twisted with scorn. The marble-built palace of a hotel was situated on the choicest part of the Croisette, and would be full to the brim with other actors, producers, directors, models and wannabes. 'No,' he said shortly. 'It's too much of a goldfish bowl—

you can't risk going back there in that state. I'm taking you to where I'm staying.'

He wasn't asking her whether she'd like him to. He was *telling* her, in that autocratic manner which came naturally after a lifetime of having people run around after him. But Jennifer was too tired and too confused to argue—and, if the truth were known, she was glad that he had taken over.

Somehow he had managed to commandeer the use of a luxury car, and he settled her in the soft leather seat beside him, adjusting his jacket so that it modestly covered her and then barking out a terse instruction in French as the vehicle began to move away.

Dreamily, Jennifer turned her head to watch out of the window as the glittering crescent of coastline sped by in a blur of lights. They passed the cool marble splendour of the Hedoniste—and suddenly Jennifer was relieved that they weren't going near it, with its hordes of paparazzi and heaven only knew who else.

'Where's your hotel?' she questioned.

Matteo stared out of the opposite window—anything to avert his eyes from her, and from the knowledge that she was all rumpled, her dress all stained...by *him*... His fingertips were still sticky and warm from having been inside her, and if he drifted them close to his face her particular feminine scent pervaded his nostrils with a potency which made him hard all over again.

'It's not really a hotel.' He swallowed as the car swept

through wrought-iron gates, past the dark shapes of lemon trees and cypress.

In the bright moonlight she could see that the hedges were fantastically shaped, and there was an odd-looking sculpture which was emphasised by soft lights pinned into a nearby tree. It looked old and very beautiful, and Jennifer blinked at it in astonished surprise.

'What is this place?' she asked quietly.

'It was once a villa belonging to one of Cannes's most famous residents—an English aristocrat who discovered the perfect climate here, and the stunning beaches. Now it is owned by an eccentric Frenchman— who will let rooms out, but only if the mood takes him.'

He turned his head and saw her looking down at her crumpled state of undress. 'He is very particular and very discreet,' he added. 'There will be no need to be seen by him, or by anyone else for that matter. One is able to bring guests to a place like this without the whole world knowing. For people in the public eye it is a godsend.'

She couldn't stop torturing herself with images of him bringing other women here in the future. Perhaps similarly unclad, and also recipients of his remarkable brand of lovemaking.

But Jennifer knew that she couldn't bring the subject up—certainly not now, when she was already feeling so vulnerable. The sex had been a mistake—but there was no need to compound that mistake by starting to quiz him about his future plans. That would only make her self-esteem tumble and put her in an even more vulnerable position.

Matteo had every right to do whatever he wished. Sex gave you no rights—not even if it was with the man to whom you were still legally married.

But then she remembered what he'd said about Sophia—and for the first time she was able to think about the actress without feeling sick. Had it been true what Matteo had said, about it only being the once and thinking about *her* all the while? Should the fine detail actually matter?

Of course it *mattered*. A one-off mistake—if that was really what it was—was completely different from a long-term affair which had been shrouded in secrecy and deceit.

But in a way that was worse—because it gave her a faint flicker of foolish hope that maybe the relationship wasn't doomed after all. But it was. Too much had been said and done to ever go back. A bout of wonderful sex wasn't a cure-all. Their marriage was in its death-throes, and that had just been one final, bewitching puff of life breathed into it.

She had to take responsibility for what had just happened between them back there, and then let it go.

But as he led her up a carved wooden staircase which was scented with sandalwood, Jennifer felt a very real shiver of fear ice her skin. *What if she wasn't able to just let it go?*

Well, you don't have the luxury of choice, she told herself. You'll have to.

At least the room was exquisite enough to distract her from her uncomfortable thoughts—with tall, shuttered windows which led out onto a moon-washed balcony. In the distance she could see the coloured glimmer of the town—like a muted version of the fireworks which would later explode in the night sky as part of the Festival celebrations.

'Oh, it's beautiful,' she said automatically, and turned round to find that he was watching her. She gave a nervous kind of laugh. 'What the hell am I doing talking about the view? Isn't this the kind of situation where you wish you could just wave a magic wand and suddenly it's different?'

'Don't you think I spend most of my life doing that?' he questioned bitterly.

'Matt—'

He shook his head. 'Let's not waste any time with recriminations. There's no point.'

'No. But I have to say this. Thanks for...rescuing me and bringing me back here.'

'A while back you were angry with me for having had my wicked way with you.'

She didn't answer straight away, but she knew that she couldn't continue to act like an innocent little virgin who had been coerced into something against her will.

'Maybe I was angry with myself, for having allowed it to happen.'

'*Si,*' said Matteo slowly, in an odd kind of voice. 'I can understand that.' He gave the ghost of a smile. 'So, let's forget it ever happened, shall we?'

'Yes,' she said slowly, hoping her pain didn't show. 'Let's.'

He stared at her, washed pale by the moonlight. 'You can stay here—there's no way you can appear at the Hedoniste tonight—not looking like that.' His black eyes were hard and glittering as he saw her lips part in protest. 'Oh, don't worry, Jenny,' he drawled. 'We won't have to endure the temptation of sharing. I'll see if there are any more rooms available. Jean-Claude is bound to have something.'

'But I don't want to kick you out of your suite!' she protested.

His lips curved in a smile which was almost cruel. 'Then what else would you suggest?' he taunted softly. 'That I sleep on the sofa? Or perhaps we vow to share opposite sides of that huge bed?' He nodded his black head towards its satin-covered expanse. 'Want to try it, Jenny?'

And show him what a walk-over she was? 'Forgive me if I pass up your delightful offer,' she said tightly, and heard his bitter laugh as the door closed behind him.

But after he'd gone, reaction to all that had happened set in and a wave of lassitude washed over her. Her head was spinning and her limbs were aching, but really she ought to go and 'freshen up'. To remove all traces of

Matteo from her body. If only you could take a bar of soap and scrub your heart clean at the same time.

Outside, she could hear the sound of circadas as she kicked off her shoes and wriggled out of her dress, letting it fall carelessly to the floor. She didn't care. The designer who had loaned it to her for free publicity would let her keep it. And given the state it was in she was going to *have* to keep it—but she knew she would never wear it again. How could she? She would never be able to look at it again without remembering...

Naked and shivering, she washed her hands and face and then poured herself a glass of wine from the heavy decanter which stood on the antique table by the window.

She meant to take only a sip, but the blood-red liquid filled her with a fleeting peace and contentment and she finished the glass and went over to the bed.

It was a typical Matteo bed, with a novel lying half-open on the pillow. She looked at it with interest until she saw that it was Italian and she didn't understand a word. But when was the last time she had read a book? She'd used to devour them in those days before the merry-go-round of publicity had filled her every spare hour.

On the bedside table was his mobile phone, and for a moment she was sorely tempted to flick through it and look at the messages. But she resisted. Dignity, Jennifer, she told herself sleepily. Try to retain just a little bit of dignity.

She sat down on the bed, moved the novel to one side and lay down, putting her head on the soft pillow. In a minute she would go and wipe off her make-up, but for now the room was spinning. She groaned and shut her eyes. Please make everything all right, she prayed. Let this all be over without any more pain—and please don't let me dream of him. Especially not tonight. Just let me have one night off from the tempting beauty of his dark face.

She hadn't been intending to sleep, nor to dream. But she did, and it seemed that her dreams were impervious to her pleas. One came to her which was frighteningly vivid. Through half-slitted eyes she could make out his lean, dark body bending over her. The raw, feral scent of him drifted upwards towards her nostrils.

She writhed against the mattress, holding her arms up, wanting him to stay with her. 'Matt,' she moaned softly. 'Oh, Matteo.'

When she awoke it was morning—with sunlight coming in bright horizontal shafts through the slats of the shutters. Jennifer sat up, blinking as she looked around the room. But the bed was empty, and so was the chaise-longue which lay underneath the window.

Her eyes strayed to the ornate wardrobe door, from which hung a floral sliver of a dress in layers of silk-chiffon in her favourite pink, and a pair of sandals which matched perfectly. Jennifer frowned. Where the hell had that come from? Had the good fairy flown into the room overnight and waved her wand?

Slowly, she got out of bed and went over to investigate. As well as the dress there was a matching bra and pants set, and Jennifer did not have to look at the size to know that they were exactly her measurements. And that somehow Matt had got hold of them at some god-forsaken hour and left them here for her.

And then she found the note.

Jenny. You looked too peaceful to wake and I found myself another room for the night. Don't worry about Hal—I will deal with him. In fact, try not to worry about anything. You should give yourself a break for a while—you look exhausted. Be kind to yourself and let's try to keep the divorce as amicable as possible. Matt.

It was a pleasant note, a reasonable note—the perfect note on which to end a marriage.

So why did she clutch it with white-knuckled fingers, tears beginning to stream down her face as if they were never going to stop?

CHAPTER FIVE

LONDON WAS RAINY and the flat felt cold and unwelcoming. Jennifer had been living there since the marriage split—she and Matteo had agreed that the luxury apartment would be 'hers', just as the ancient stone house on the island of Pantelleria would become 'his'.

The accountants had suggested that they sell their home in the Hollywood Hills, because apparently prices there had rocketed since they'd first bought it. Jennifer wasn't going to break her heart about *that*. It had never felt like a real home to her anyway. But then, where did?

Their schedules had been so frantic that they'd never seemed to have the time to do the things which other newly-weds revelled in. There had been no careful choosing of furniture or browsing over curtain material. Nor had there been any of the usual concerns about what they could or couldn't afford.

They'd been able to afford almost anything!

Matteo had made an almost obscene amount of money since leaving drama school, and his asking price now ran into millions of dollars.

That was one of the reasons why Jennifer had allowed herself to be tempted away from the stage and gone into films herself. Matteo had made hundreds of opportunities possible, and she had seized them with eager hands—for surely it would have been crazy to turn down such chances?

She'd wanted to be his equal in all ways—and yet when her own asking price had rocketed she had felt none of the expected joy or satisfaction. Just a kind of nagging feeling that somehow she'd sold out. And the price she'd paid for her glittering career had been frequent separations from her husband which had fed all her insecurities and doubts.

Sometimes she had found herself wondering what it would have been like if they had created a proper place together. Spent ages lovingly choosing items together, instead of suffering the incessant march of an army of interior designers who had transformed each one of their homes into dazzling displays which celebrity magazines had fallen over themselves to feature. Matteo had drawn the line at that. 'We have little enough privacy as it is,' he had told them angrily.

Maybe she should have done something to try and claw some of that privacy back—but Jennifer had been a brand-new player in the celebrity game, and she'd been too busy enjoying it to want to pull the plug on it. How easy it was, with the benefit of hindsight, to recognise the mistakes she'd made.

She glanced uninterestedly at the unopened post and

the pile of film scripts waiting to be read. Then her mobile rang, and in spite of everything her heart leapt. Because she'd be lying if she denied fantasising about Matteo on her flight back from Cannes. She felt as if he had poured all her emotions into a mixing bowl and stirred them up. Maybe he was ringing her to ask if she'd got back safely? Or maybe just to say hello—because if the divorce truly *was* going to amicable then why *shouldn't* he say hello?

She picked up her phone and made her voice sound as cool as possible.

'Hello?'

'Jennifer?'

Jennifer's heart sank, and she immediately felt guilty that it had. 'Hello, Mum.'

'Where *are* you?'

Jennifer held the telephone away from her ear as the loud voice came booming down the line. Her mother always described herself as an actress too—though she had never progressed beyond the strictly amateur productions at their local village hall. The rest of the time she had spent living out her fantasies through her only child.

Quashing the terrible temptation to say that she was anywhere but England, Jennifer murmured, 'I'm at the London flat.'

'Why?'

'Well, why not?' questioned Jennifer. 'I *live* here.'

'No, I mean why aren't you doing the round of parties

and interviews in Cannes? There's hardly been a *thing* about you in any of the papers!'

'That's because…because—'

'Because that bastard of an ex of yours was there, I suppose?' interrupted her mother viciously.

Jennifer bit her lip. 'Mum, I won't have you talking about Matteo that way.'

'Then you're an idiot, darling. He's made a complete and utter fool of you!'

'Look, I've just flown in—was there anything in particular you wanted?'

'Well, actually, yes! I was hoping to run an idea of mine past your agent! Or that rather nice publicist I met…what was his name? Hal? Yes, that was it! Hal! I think he took a slight shine to me!'

'Mum—'

'There are such *rubbishy* screenplays around at the moment that I thought to myself—well, why *shouldn't* I have a go?'

Jennifer counted to ten. And then on to twenty. Now was not the time to tell her mother that she'd sacked Hal. Or why.

Promising to visit very soon to talk about it, she managed to finish the call and went through to the kitchen while she listened to all the messages that had arrived while she'd been in France.

There were four calls from her agent. Two magazines wanted her on their cover, and a very famous photographer wanted to include her in his coffee-table book of the world's most beautiful women.

But Jennifer didn't feel in the least bit beautiful—she felt empty and aching, almost worse than she had when she and Matt had first split. At least then there had been endless, explosive rows, and she had felt that breaking up was the best thing to do. She had been carried along by the powerful storm of her anger and hurt.

But the episode in Cannes had been poignant and bittersweet. It had emphasised her vulnerability around him and reminded her of what they had once shared—but a pale imitation of the real thing. It had taunted her with what she was missing…that feeling of being properly alive. Because Matt was like the blazing sun in a summer sky, and when he wasn't around the world seemed dark and cold.

She spent the next few weeks lying low. She wore nondescript clothes and no make-up and kept her eyes down when she went out. As she had intended—no one recognised her. If you were a good actress, then no one should. It was more than just appearance. You could slope your shoulders and make your body language as low-key as possible.

She knew she ought to start trying to rebuild her life as a single woman, but her high-profile marriage had affected the way people saw her. She was famous now—and that had a knock-on effect on everything she did. She could no longer have normal friendships, because people wanted to know her for all kinds of different reasons. These days their motives had to be scrutinised, and Jennifer hated that. Fame separated you—left you lonely and isolated.

And going back wasn't easy. There were people she had been at drama school with, but she hadn't seen them for years. She'd just been so busy, with film after film, and she'd been living on the other side of the world. Fame and money changed your life—no matter how much you swore they weren't going to.

And then, before she could relaunch herself on the world, she began to feel peculiar. From being full of energy, she found that she could hardly drag herself out of bed in the mornings.

And her appetite increased. When she'd first met Matt she'd had the normal rounded body of a healthy young woman, but he'd taken her to Hollywood and she had realised that wasn't good enough. It was stick-thin or nothing. She had trained her appetite to be satisfied with sparrow-like portions, but suddenly they were no longer enough.

Now she found that she simply *couldn't* control her hunger, and it was scary to find herself wolfing down a bowl of porridge for breakfast every morning—and covering it with golden syrup!

She blamed the syrup for the nagging tightness of her jeans. But even when she cut out the syrup and dragged herself down to the exclusive gym in the basement of the apartment complex there was no marked improvement. In fact, quite the contrary.

When it hit her, she realized she'd been very stupid.

She wasn't comfort-eating at all. But of course she had denied it—as she expected women who'd taken risks had done ever since the beginning of time.

Except she hadn't taken any risks!

Telling herself it was hysteria, she upped her sessions at the gym and began to wear more forgiving trousers.

But there came a day when her warped kind of logic refused to be heard any more. And that was the day she sent her cleaning lady out to buy a pregnancy testing kit.

She didn't really need to sit and wait to see whether a blue line would develop. She had known for weeks and weeks what the result would be.

Jennifer sat down on one of the sofas and buried her head in her hands. In that moment she had never felt more lost or more alone. But it wasn't as though she was going to waste time worrying about what she was going to do.

There was only one thing she *could* do.

She kept putting it off. And meanwhile time was ticking away. Her shape was changing and the appetite which had consumed her had now deserted her. Maybe that was a blessing in disguise—because she didn't *dare* venture out to the local stores. Thank God for online shopping.

But she couldn't put off telling Matt for ever—and one morning, when the bright blue of the early-autumn sky seemed unbearably poignant, she hunted down her phone and found Matteo's programmed-in number. It rang for a while before he picked up, and his voice was wary in a way she had never heard it sound before. That in itself was a shock—the thought that Matteo was moving on, changing and growing and leaving her behind, while she remained stuck firmly in the groove of the past.

'Jennifer?' he said slowly. 'This is very unexpected.'

Was it really? Didn't it occur to him that she might want to discuss what had happened between them in France? Unless the caution in his voice was there for a more pragmatic reason—because she was disturbing him in the middle of...

Her words came out as if someone was strangling her. 'Can you...?' She swallowed. 'Is it all right for you to talk?'

He frowned. 'Sure.'

He wasn't giving her any kind of help—but then, why should he? *She* was the one who had instigated this conversation, and soon all his ties with her would be severed completely. She bit her lip. Except that they wouldn't. Not now.

'Matteo, I have to see you.'

His voice hardened. 'No, Jenny.'

The room swayed. *'No?'*

'There isn't any point.'

Jennifer felt the blood drain from her face as she realised that she had put herself in a position to be rejected. And that only increased her pain. 'Matt, you don't understand—'

'Oh, but I do—believe me, I do. I've been thinking

about it a lot.' More than he'd wanted to. More than he could bear to. Matteo closed his eyes, wishing that he could blot out the memory of her legs laced tightly around his waist while he thrust deep inside her. Or—even more poignant—the memory of her blonde hair spread all over his pillow in Cannes. But their frantic coupling had been nothing but a mockery of a simple and tender intimacy which was gone for ever. Well, he would tolerate it—but he would *not* be used as some kind of stud to satisfy his ex-wife's sexual needs!

He kept his voice terse. 'What happened between us proved that we're still sexually compatible. That's all. Nothing more. That's not enough basis for a relationship—and it would destroy even the memory of what we once had.'

In her outrage and her shame Jennifer nearly dropped the phone. He thought she was ringing him in order to get him back! He thought she was begging him to come back into her life! Trying to resurrect a relationship that was dead!

She wanted to hurl the phone hard against the wall—to finish this conversation and all future conversations with the arrogant and egotistical *bastard* in the most satisfyingly violent way possible.

But not yet.

'Oh, don't worry,' she said coldly. 'Such an agenda couldn't be further from my mind.'

He felt a nerve flickering in his cheek. 'I'm glad we understand each other.'

'Perfectly.'

'So. Why are you ringing?'

She couldn't say it over the phone. She couldn't. It was the coward's way out and she wanted to see his face. *Needed* to see his face.

'There's some paperwork I need you to look at.' And what? Look into those big sapphire eyes again and start seeing what he wanted to see instead of what was real? Letting himself confide in her and share his thoughts with her? Start wanting to tear her clothing off, with her letting him? Or would she? Maybe this time she would torment him by saying no, by flaunting her magnificent body and torturing him because it was hands-off.

'Can't you get someone else to deal with it?' he questioned impatiently.

'That's your answer to everything, isn't it, Matt? Why bother doing something when you can pay someone else to do it for you? No wonder you're becoming increasingly remote from reality!'

There was a short, angry pause. 'Do you really think I *want* to see you?' he demanded hotly. 'That I would voluntarily put myself in a position where I lay myself open to being insulted by you?'

'Matt, you *have* to see me.'

'*Have* to?' he repeated dangerously. '*Cara*, nobody, but nobody, tells me that I *have* to do something.'

She realised then that there was no way out of telling him over the phone. And maybe this way was best. At least it would be short—if not sweet. She would provide the information in the starkest way possible and leave him with the options. Maybe the best one was for him to leave her completely alone.

'I just thought you'd better know that I'm pregnant,' she said, and then she hung up.

For a moment Matteo listened blankly to the burr of the dial tone, his eyes staring unseeingly at the wall in front of him. And then her words slammed into the forefront of his mind with the impact of a sledgehammer.

'Jenny!' As if saying that would suddenly put her back on the line! He dialled her number, but predictably she let it go through to voicemail.

He shook his head as a floodgate of feelings swamped him. Disbelief and anger and frustration made his heart-rate soar, but the tiniest flicker of hope and joy dazed him.

A baby?

He didn't even know where she was!

Strega!

His mind worked around all the possibilities. She could be anywhere…but it was most likely that she was in their London flat. *Her* London flat, he reminded himself. He knew she wasn't crazy about staying in hotels—not if she was on her own. And then he remembered the night in Cannes, and his heart contracted.

He frowned as he rang the service number of the exclusive apartment block and spoke to the concierge, using blatant influence, charm and a hefty bribe to en-

sure that his enquiry was not passed on to Signora d'
Arezzo. But, yes, she was there.

He allowed himself a brief, hard smile of satisfaction and then set about flying to England. Normally
he might have cursed at a back-to-back flight from the
States, but this wasn't normal. He didn't get told he was
going to be a father every day of the week.

Beneath the knitted black brows his ebony eyes glittered with a hundred questions. But the one uppermost
in his mind was the most important.

Was she telling him the truth?

CHAPTER SIX

THE KNOCKING ON the door wouldn't stop, and Jennifer knew that she could not lie there for ever, pretending that the outside world did not exist.

Slowly she made her way to the hallway and began to unslide the great bolts which had made their flat into a fortress. When she finally opened the door she was not surprised to see Matteo standing there, but it was a Matteo she scarcely recognised.

Uncharacteristically, he had not shaved. His dark hair was unruly—and his black eyes wild and angry. He walked straight in and shut the door behind him, and when he turned to face her his breathing was unsteady—as if he had been running in a long, long race.

'Now I see that your words are true,' he breathed, because for the first time in his life he felt out of his depth as he raked his eyes over her body.

She *was* pregnant! Rosily and unashamedly pregnant! Oh, the curve of her belly was not huge, but on a woman of Jennifer's slenderness it *looked* huge. Her breasts were swollen, and she had a look about her which made her appear quite different—but he couldn't pinpoint what it was. An experience which had changed her? The most profound experience a woman could have? Or just a kind of luminous fragility which almost took his breath away?

'You thought I would lie about something like this?' she questioned wearily.

He lifted his dazed eyes to her face to study that, slowly and properly, and there he could see changes, too. For her skin was whiter than milk and there were dark shadows beneath her eyes. He knew that pregnant women were supposed to glow from within, yet her eyes were dull, with none of their customary inner fire.

'*Dio!* What have you been doing to yourself, Jenny?' His eyes narrowed. 'Come through and sit down!' he commanded. 'At once.'

Jennifer laughed. After doing his utmost to wriggle out of coming to see her—how *dared* he? 'It's *my* home and I won't stand for being bossed around by you!'

He sucked in a low breath. 'I will forgive you your stubbornness because of your hormones. But I am telling you this—if you do not do as I say and go and lie down on the sofa, then I shall pick you up and carry you there myself!'

'Isn't that how we got ourselves into this whole mess to begin with?' she questioned bitterly.

Matteo opened his mouth to ask the question which was uppermost in his mind, but something told him to wait until she was comfortable.

He went through to the kitchen to make coffee while she settled herself, clicking his lips with disapproval as he looked inside the fridge. He carried the tray through and poured her a cup—just the way she liked it—and watched with approval as she slowly sipped it. His own lay cooling. Suddenly he could wait no longer.

'It is mine?'

She put the cup down quickly, before she dropped it. She had been expecting this, and had tried to tell herself that it was not an unreasonable question under the circumstances. But knowing something and feeling something were two entirely different things, and Jennifer felt as if he had driven a knife of accusation through her heart.

'Yes.'

'You are certain? There is no other candidate?'

Her mouth crumpled with hurt and scorn. *'Candidate?'* she echoed. 'You make it sound like a presidential election! No, there isn't another "candidate". I haven't slept with anyone else since the day I first set eyes on you.'

He looked up. 'You haven't?'

She heard the macho pleasure in his voice and felt as if she'd been scalded. 'No. Unlike you.'

His eyes narrowed. 'But...how can this be, Jenny? How can it?'

She looked at him. 'You're thirty-three years old, Matteo—do you really need me to tell you?'

'You took a chance like that when we were separated?' he demanded incredulously. 'You risked getting pregnant?'

Something inside her snapped. The weeks of waiting and wondering and worrying all came to a head. 'How dare you make it sound as if it was something I *planned*?' she exploded. 'It happened in a *lift*, for God's sake! A lift which *you* found! If anyone planned it, it must have been you!'

'Oh, don't be so ridiculous!' he countered, and he saw her eyes darken in response. With a giant effort of will he drew a deep breath, trying to contain his emotions. But it wasn't easy. Yet he knew that he had to make allowances for her condition. He had to. For Jenny held all the cards, and if he was not careful...

'If you were unprotected then you should have told me, Jenny. And, yes, we were hot for each other—but there are other ways we could have pleasured each other without risking this type of consequence.'

Jennifer clapped her hand over her mouth as if she was going to be sick. 'I'm having a baby!' she choked. 'And all you can think about is mutual masturbation!'

'Jenny!' he protested. 'How can you say that? This is not like you!'

'What isn't? I don't know what *is* like me any more! And what do you expect me to say in the face of your monstrous accusation? If you must know—I *was* still on the Pill—'

'And why was that?' he shot back immediately. 'If,

as you say, there was nobody else but me and we were divorcing?'

Jennifer's hand fell from her mouth to lie protectively on her belly as his suspicions reinforced how hopeless it all was. 'Because my periods are heavy—*remember*? My doctor thought it advisable. But it must have let me down.' She gave him a crooked kind of smile. 'Don't they say that the only surefire form of contraception is abstinence?'

'But you never got pregnant when we were married—when we were having sex every second of the day!'

'Maybe I wasn't taking it as fastidiously as I used to.' Jennifer shrugged listlessly. 'Blame it on me, if it makes you feel better.'

'I don't want to *blame* anyone!' he grated. 'Recriminations aren't going to help us.'

Matteo was silent for a moment as for the first time in his life he felt authority slip from his fingers. He could not get his way here by coercion or charm. Jennifer was in the process of divorcing him. She no longer loved him. What happened now was *her* decision. She was in the driver's seat, and suddenly he felt out of his depth. 'What do you want to do?' he questioned quietly.

'I'm having the baby,' she said flatly.

'Of course you are!' But a great warm wave of relief rolled over him and for the first time he smiled—a smile so wide that he felt it might split his face in two. 'And look at you, Jenny—you are so big…it must be…'

She could see him doing mental arithmetic and the expression on his face was almost comical. Jennifer smiled too—realising how long it had been since she'd done *that*. 'Nearly sixteen weeks.'

'That long?' he breathed. 'My God. Jenny…this is a miracle.'

'Yes,' she said simply. And in that moment the divorce and the anger and the bitterness and the tearing apart of a shared life all seemed inconsequential when compared to the beginning of a brand-new life.

But her emotions were volatile, and hot on the heels of her heady exhilaration came the despair of the situation into which their baby would be born.

A shuddering sob was torn from her throat and Matteo sprang to his feet, going over to her side and taking her hand between his. 'You are in pain?' he demanded.

She shook her head. 'No, I'm not in pain,' she sobbed. 'I'm just thinking how hopeless this all is.'

'Shh.' Now he lifted his hand to her wet cheeks and began to smooth the tears away, his heart contracting in genuine remorse as he saw the expression in her blurry eyes. 'It is not hopeless,' he said softly.

'Yes, it is! We're getting a divorce and you don't love me!'

'But, Jenny, I will always—'

'No!' She sat up, her face serious, the tears stopping as if by magic. 'Never say it, Matteo,' she urged. 'Don't say something to try and make it better, because if it isn't true then it will only make it worse. I'm not a little girl who needs to be given a lolly because she's hurt her knee. This isn't about me, or the way I feel, or the mess we've made of our relationship. This is about someone far more important than both of us now…our baby.'

Matteo stared at her, his fingertips lingering for one last moment on her face. 'You sound so strong,' he breathed, in open admiration.

'I have to be,' she said simply. 'I'm going to be a mother—maybe it comes with the job description.'

And he needed to be strong, too.

He needed to take control. But he must not do it in a high-handed way or she would rebel; he knew that. He must allow Jennifer to think that *she* was making all the decisions.

'Have you thought about what you want to do?'

'I've tried.' There had been a fantasy version, about taking a time machine and fast-rewinding so that the episode in the lift had never happened. Or back further still, to a time when they'd still been in love and they could have conceived their baby out of that love, instead of out of lust and anger and passion.

But she was dealing with reality, not fantasy—and that posed all kinds of problems.

'Oh, Matt—I just don't know *what* to do for the best. If I stay around here—or even if I go back to the States—it'll soon become obvious that I'm pregnant.' She glanced down at the swell of her belly. 'Though you can tell that even now, can't you?'

'Yes. Any eagle-eyed observer would spot it—and there are hundreds of those out there.'

'I know. And once word gets out everyone will want to know who the father is—and I won't know what to say.'

'But you *do* know who the father is!'

'And think of the questions if we tell them! Are we getting back together? And if we aren't then *why* am I pregnant by you? Or what about the worst-case scenario? Some sleazy journalist bribing someone at the hospital to get my due-date! Then they could work it back to the Cannes Festival—and I'll bet that at least *one* of the staff at the hotel could be bribed into giving them a story that we came out of the lift in a state of partial undress! Can you imagine the scoop *that* would provide?'

'Jenny—'

She shook her head. 'Or, if we *don't* tell them, then the questions and conjecture will be even worse! Every single man I've so much as said good morning to will come under intense scrutiny! There will be all kinds of tasteless headlines—*Who Is The Father Of Jennifer's Love-Child?*'

'Jenny, Jenny, aren't you getting a little carried away?'

'Am I?' Her blue eyes were clear and defiant. 'Think about it, Matt—is it really such an incredible idea?'

And that was the worst of it—he *could* see it, quite plainly, as if someone was playing a film inside his head. In a way, fame robbed you of simple humanity. They had become *things*—to be dissected and picked over. He shook his head and his eyes were clouded with a bleak kind of sadness. 'And I brought you into this crazy world of showbiz,' he said huskily. 'What kind of a lover would do that?'

A few months ago she might have agreed with him, but so much had changed—and not just the baby. Though maybe *because* of the baby. And it was all to do with responsibility—acknowledging it and accepting it. It took two to do everything in a relationship—to fall in love and then to wreck it. You couldn't place the blame on one person's shoulders.

She shook her head. 'Oh, Matt—that's not what I'm saying! You didn't frogmarch me into the studios with a gun at my head, did you? I wanted fame, too. I saw what you had and I wanted it with a hunger which sometimes frightened me—but not enough to stop me! But none of that's important. Not now—we can't change the past. But I don't want any more pressure—because that will put pressure on the baby.' She looked at him with an appeal in her eyes. 'Just what kind of story *are* we going to give the press?'

He swore in Italian, getting up to pace up and down the polished oak floors of a flat in which he had slept for barely more than a dozen nights in the two years he'd owned it—he, a man who'd grown up in a cramped tenement building in New York? How crazy was that?

'Why should the press be our first consideration?' he exploded.

And, in spite of everything, Jennifer's lips curved into a rueful smile. 'That's like asking why the grass is green!'

He let out a pent-up sigh and went to look out of the window. Below lay Hyde Park in all its glory. Joggers moved along the paths and mothers and nannies strolled with pushchairs beneath trees which were beginning to be touched with autumn gold. Soon winter would arrive. The London streets would be washed with rain or dusted with frost or even—if they were very lucky—heaped with snow.

And Jennifer might trip and fall!

He turned round. 'Have you told your mother?'

'Are you kidding?'

'Don't you think you should?'

'Why? The first thing she'll do is think that being a grandmother is going to make her sound old. And the second will be to give me a hard time over the damage this is going to do to my career.'

'She hates me,' he observed.

'She hates all men, Matt, not just you. Ever since my father walked out her view of the world has been distorted.'

It occurred to him that Mrs Warren had influenced her daughter more than Jennifer had perhaps ever acknowledged. Had she learned at her mother's knee that all men were inherently unfaithful? Was that why she had always been so suspicious of him? Only now could he see—too late—that maybe he should have sat down and talked about it with her instead of becoming increasingly frustrated at her lack of trust and her willingness to believe the rumours instead of listening to *him*.

'You're going to have to tell her some time.'

Jennifer briefly closed her eyes. 'I know I am. Just not yet. If we think outside interest would be intrusive, then just imagine…'

Matt shuddered. 'I would rather not.'

It occurred to him that the two of them had not spoken with such ease for a long time. And that was good, he told himself. Jenny was right—they could not change what had happened, and in the conventional sense their relationship was over. But civility between them must be maintained. He had wanted that before, but in view of the baby it had now became imperative.

'Shall we go to Pantelleria?' he asked softly. 'To the *dammuso*? We could both do with a little rest and recuperation.' His eyes narrowed as they took in her pinched face and pale skin. 'Particularly you,' he added.

Her mouth suddenly dried, but only her attitude of mind could save her from plunging into regret. For surely Matteo's suggestion made sense? A place which she knew offered refuge and peace. Possibly the only such place in the world—at least for them.

Pantelleria—the black pearl of the Mediterranean. The beautiful island where they had spent their honeymoon. Where wild flowers bloomed and rare birds visited.

There, Matteo owned a simple square white house built of volcanic stone, with shallow domes and thick white walls which stayed deliciously cool in summer. She remembered them lying together in bed on the last morning of their honeymoon and vowing to return as often as they could. But of course that had been one of many promises broken by a lack of that most precious commodity…time.

And nothing had changed there.

She stared at him blankly. 'How can we? I've got two films lined up.'

Matteo shrugged. 'Cancel them.'

'I can't do that!'

His black eyes glinted. 'Can't? Or won't?' he challenged softly. 'What's more important to you—your work or your marriage?'

'I notice you're not offering to do the same!'

'Oh, but that's where you're wrong, Jenny.' He gave a brief, hard smile and his eyes were as brittle as jet. 'If I have to cancel a couple of films to take this course of action, then so be it.'

It was like seeing a side of Matteo she'd never seen before—it was certainly the first time she'd ever seen a chink in the tough armour of his ambition, and Jennifer was momentarily taken aback. 'You'd risk your career?' she whispered. She nearly added *for me*, until she reminded herself that it wasn't for *her*—but for their baby. And what was wrong with that?

'My career will always pick up,' he said arrogantly. 'But films can wait. This can't,' he finished, with another shrug of his broad shoulders.

Jennifer knew that despite his almost careless air this was a supreme sacrifice for Matteo. He had made films almost back to back ever since she'd known him—and way before that. As if he was frightened of stepping off the merry-go-round of successful work which bred still more work.

And now that it had become a real possibility—instead of a throwaway remark—Jennifer could see the sense in Matteo's suggestion that they escape together, to a place which she could see might act like a balm on their troubled spirits.

The island lay halfway between Africa and Sicily—where Matteo's ancestors had come from and where secret-keeping was legendary, taught from the cradle. On Pantelleria Matteo wielded the influence of his birthright, not that of the fickle fame brought about by celluloid.

They had been happy there—and part of her wanted to hang on to those precious memories and leave them intact.

He saw her hesitation and suspected he knew its cause—for did he not have misgivings about returning there himself? Would it not unsettle him—reminding him of the dreams they had shared and never realised?

'You know you would be safe there.'

Safe? Alone with Matteo? That was a definition of *safe* she wasn't sure existed. Jennifer felt as if her life were a pack of cards which someone had thrown into the air to see where they would land. 'But how long would we stay there, Matt? I mean—I don't want to have the baby there.'

The brittleness had gone and now his eyes gleamed. 'You think that no child has ever been born on Pantelleria?'

'How long?' she persisted quietly.

'Long enough to bring the colour back to your cheeks and for you to rest and eat good food.' There was a pause. 'And long enough to decide what we are going to tell the world. To decide what our strategy will be.'

From a supposedly hot-headed and passionate Italian it was possibly the coldest and most matter-of-fact declaration Jennifer had ever heard.

CHAPTER SEVEN

MATTEO ORGANISED THEIR trip to Pantelleria with a degree
of organisation to rival a military campaign. Despite the
loyalty of his staff—who these days had to sign a water-
tight confidentiality agreement—he entrusted relatively
few of them with the knowledge of their whereabouts.

As he said to Jennifer—this was just too big a story
to risk.

And that was all this was, she reminded herself. A
damage limitation exercise over a story which had the
potential to explode in their faces.

Jennifer had forgotten how extraordinarily protected
you could feel in the exclusive coterie of Matt's inner
circle—but this time there was a subtle difference.

'Your staff are being unbelievably nice to me,' she
said, as they waited for their baggage to be loaded onto
the private jet which would fly them to the island.

Matteo snapped shut his briefcase and frowned as
he looked up at her. 'Aren't they always?'

Jennifer switched her phone off. 'Oh, forget I said

anything,' she said airily. She certainly wasn't going to blow the whistle on anyone.

But Matteo laid his hand on her arm, and the unexpected contact caught her by enough surprise to lower her defences. 'Jenny? Tell me. Because if you don't then how the hell will I know?'

And maybe it was her duty to tell him. Nobody dared tell Matteo anything. And even when they did they told him what they thought he wanted to hear. 'They normally put a barrier between you and the rest of the world.'

He narrowed his eyes. 'Well, yes, I suppose they do—but surely you can understand why?'

'From the world, yes—from your family, no.' She hesitated. 'Once, I remember trying to get through to you on the phone, and being completely stonewalled and unable to reach you. They dismissed me as if I was some kind of disgruntled ex-employee! It made me feel so...'

'So what?' he prompted.

Jennifer hesitated—but what did she have to lose by telling him? 'So isolated, I guess.' Jennifer shrugged. 'Mind you, that was after we had separated. Maybe they were acting on your instructions.'

His face darkened. 'I gave no such instructions.'

In fact he remembered feeling pretty isolated himself. The rupture of their relationship had given him a sense of being cut adrift from all that was familiar. Because even when their marriage had been in an appalling state they had still been in contact. She had still been his anchor, the person he turned to to confide in. He'd telephoned her from locations around the world, or she him. But once she had left—that had been it. Nothing. As though he had never even occupied a tiny part of her life. She had cut contact completely—or so he had thought.

Now it seemed that his staff had been instrumental in that sudden severing of all ties, and his eyes narrowed thoughtfully as he stared at her. He employed people to act on his decisions, not to make them for him.

'So, how many of the famous d' Arezzo workforce will be accompanying us to Pantelleria?' asked Jennifer.

'None.' He savoured the moment. '*Nessuno*. Just us.' Jennifer blinked in surprise. 'No chef?' she echoed. 'But you always take Gerard with you!'

A sense of regret washed over him. Was this what he'd intended when he had started chasing his dreams? To employ so many staff that he seemed to have lost control of his own life? 'I'll do the cooking,' he drawled.

Jennifer's surprise increased. '*You?*'

'Do you really consider me incapable of living my life without any staff to help me, Jenny?' he demanded exasperatedly. 'That I never knew what it was to be cold or go hungry? Or to take jobs that I hated in order to survive before I got my big break?'

'Well, in theory, no—of course I don't. But when I met you you were so successful that it was hard to imagine you being anything else. Like a slim person telling you they once had a weight problem. You can't quite believe it.'

'Well, believe it,' he said quietly, and smiled. 'And come and meet our pilot.'

He had given her a lot to think about on the flight, but the reality of what they were doing hit her when the luxury private jet touched down, and she turned to him with wide eyes. 'Are we completely mad, do you think?'

He gave a lazy smile. 'Very probably.'

And the easy intimacy of that smile spelt danger, reminding Jennifer to be on her guard. To be careful to protect her feelings. Because nothing had changed between them. This trip didn't mean that they were compatible, or that they weren't in the process of getting a divorce. She was having a baby. That was all.

Pantelleria's October air was still deliciously warm, and coastal flora bloomed in a profusion of pinks and reds and yellows. The crystal blue waters which surrounded it were rich in lobsters, and in the fertile valleys of the interior grapes grew as large as plums. It was like paradise.

Matteo felt the weight of expectation lift from his shoulders as he drove along the familiar unchanged roads to the Valle della Ghirlanda and his *dammuso*.

These days, superstars visited the island, but Matteo had fallen in love with Pantelleria as a child—when his parents had saved up enough money to send him to stay with one of his aunts during one long, dry summer. His family had laughed when he said he'd own a house there one day, but sure enough he'd done it—buying the *dammuso* with his very first film cheque. He had set about completely modernising the old building, whilst making sure it retained its natural charm.

It offered two terraces—one by a vast swimming pool which had a backdrop of the distant sea. The high walls hid a secret pleasure garden, with an irrigation system which had been built by the Arabs during their four-hundred-year occupation.

But it was the cool, domed main bedroom which Jennifer longed and yet dreaded to see—with its huge bed and restful simplicity. If only she could close her eyes and take herself back to the person she'd been then... would she have done anything differently? Would he?

'I guess you'd better sleep in here,' said Matteo, as they both stood in silence looking into the room.

'And you?'

He shrugged. 'The guest room is prepared.' He wondered if she would heed the unspoken question in his voice. Was she thinking of inviting him into her bed—to maybe build some kind of way back through the physical intimacy of being close once more?

But Jennifer didn't hear; she was struck dumb by the chain reaction of feelings which had been sparked by being in this room, this house. Delight, sadness, regret and sorrow—all those emotions and a hundred more besides flowed over her in a bittersweet tide.

She stared at the bed as if it was a ghost—and in a way it was. And imagine if the ghost of her honeymoon

self were to look up and see what had become of her
and Matteo. Separated—with only an unplanned baby
holding them together. How heartbroken that madly-
in-love Jennifer would have been.

'Our baby should have been conceived in a bed like
this,' she whispered—as much to that ghost of her former self as to the man by her side. 'Not in some seedy
lift.'

'So many *should haves*, Jenny,' he said, and his deep
voice was etched with pain, too. 'We should have listened more. Trusted more. Talked more. We should not
have been too proud to say what was on our minds.'

'We should not have been parted so much,' she ventured—because this was a game it was frighteningly
easy to play. There was a whole list of things they had
done wrong without meaning to. Had she and Matteo
just got unlucky? Or had they simply been too bound up
in selfish interests to cherish their marriage properly?

'Do you think those problems happen with all couples—only some work out how to deal with them?' she
questioned.

'I think we both struggled so hard to make it in our
own careers that we forgot to put any work into the relationship,' he said slowly. 'And I think that once success arrived we felt that our lives were charmed and
nothing bad could touch us.'

'But we were wrong,' she breathed.

'Oh, yes.'

'Oh, Matt,' she said brokenly.

He wanted to take her in his arms and hold her tight against him, kiss away her cares, but she looked so tense—as if one touch would shatter her into a thousand pieces. In the dim light of the shuttered room he thought how pale her face looked.

'And now?' he questioned. 'What must I do to ensure that there will be no regrets in the future?'

Be in love with me again, she thought. But you couldn't ask for that. A precious gift like love could only be given, never demanded. 'You think I have a magic formula?'

Now he noticed the shadows which darkened her eyes and he wanted to kiss them away—but he had forfeited the right to tenderness a long time ago. 'I am burdening you with too many questions. So sleep,' he instructed grittily. 'I will leave you in the peace and the silence and you will sleep.'

And, miraculously, she did. For the first time since she had left Cannes—and maybe even before that—Jennifer slept as if someone had drugged her.

Sliding on a filmy white kaftan over her swimsuit, she left her hair loose beneath a wide-brimmed hat and went out into the bright sunshine to find Matteo.

He was lying on a lounger by the pool, wearing wraparound shades and reading a film script. He had on nothing but a pair of swim-shorts, and Jennifer's feet faltered as she grew closer, for the sight of his near-bare body was utterly spectacular. And, let's face it, she thought, you haven't seen it for a long time.

His skin gleamed like olive satin, each muscle so carefully defined that he could quite easily have featured as an illustration in a medical student's anatomy book. Dark hair curled crisply over his chest and arrowed down to a V over his hard, flat belly, darkening over the powerful shafts of his legs.

She blamed the heat for the sudden drying of her mouth as Matteo slowly lifted his head. His eyes were unseen behind the shades, but Jennifer knew that he'd been aware of her watching him.

'Enjoying the view?' he questioned softly.

She jerked her head to stare out at the sapphire stripe of distant sea. 'It's…exquisite.'

He smiled. 'Come and sit down over here. I'll fetch you something to drink.'

Her legs felt like cotton-wool, and inwardly she despaired. Wasn't the whole point of being here to get herself fit and rested? If she started living on her nerves and constructing fantasies about her ex then she might as well have stayed in England and faced the press.

He brought her something cool and fizzing which tasted of lemons, and she gulped it down.

'Hungry?'

'Not really.'

'Am I going to have to force-feed you, Jenny?'

'No. Just give me a little time to acclimatise. Anyway, I ate on the plane—and I'm not stupid.' She sank into a lounger. 'Ooh, that's nice!'

'Isn't it?' He gave her a hard smile as his eyes flickered over her kaftan. 'Aren't you going to get a little sun on your body?'

What could she say? An excuse would sound feeble but the truth would sound far worse. That she felt suddenly and inexplicably shy about disrobing in front of him.

But you're having his baby, for God's sake! And you were married to him!

'Of course,' she said lightly, and turned her back.

Behind his dark glasses, a thoughtful look came into Matteo's eyes. Shyness indicated that she was uncomfortable. Or was it something else? He leaned back against his lounger, affecting rest—but his body was tense as she turned around again and a sigh of something approaching wonder escaped from his lips.

In the bikini, her pregnant shape was like a visual feast—with its brand-new curves and soft shadows. He saw the swell of her belly properly for the first time and was filled with a fierce and primitive pride. For—no matter what the circumstances of the conception—nothing changed the fact that beneath her heart, his child grew.

His own heart pounded, and he swallowed down the sudden lump in his throat. His child.

And Jenny was still his wife. By law they remained married, with all the rights that gave an individual—

even in these days when marriages could be dissolved so easily. Was he really going to let that go so easily now, when there was a baby on the way?

True, she might grow strong and well here on Pantelleria, and true, they might fabricate such a wonderful explanation about why she was pregnant with his baby that no one would ever bother them again. But even if this latter and extremely unlikely scenario occurred—where did that leave him?

On the sidelines, that was where. While Jenny would go on to give birth and, sooner or later, another man would fall for her pale blonde beauty and her quirky character and her particular talents—and then what?

He would be relegated to weekends, and then to less and less contact with the child. And why not? He would never have lived properly with its mother—so why should he expect the child to love him?

An unbearable pain caught him unawares. It churned in his guts and twisted in his heart.

At that moment he saw Jenny slide her leg up to bend her knee, and he knew that he still held a powerful weapon. Could he not work on her desire for him and tie her to him with *that*, even if that was as far as it went?

He lifted the sunglasses from his eyes and put them on the ground as the sun glinted off the pale flesh of her thigh.

'You'll burn,' he said thickly.

She heard the note in his voice and knew what it meant. She knew that she had a choice. She could either thank him for his concern and go up to her room and cover herself from head to toe in Factor 20, or...

She shut her eyes. 'Do you want to cream me up?' she murmured.

Her words made him so aroused that for a moment he wondered if he had dreamt them. But the languid pose she was holding told him that she had said them and meant them.

He noticed that she had her eyes closed, and that amused him as he moved slowly towards her. Was she trying to block out the sight of an erection which felt as hard as a rock against his belly?

He kneeled down beside her and squeezed a dollop of cream into the palm of his hand.

'Turn over,' he commanded.

She wriggled onto her stomach and, starting with her back, he loosened her inhibitions, unclipping her top and massaging the cool cream into her baking skin.

'Now lie on your back,' he instructed huskily.

Jennifer tensed as he peeled down her bikini top, and she nearly passed out with pleasure as he began to circle the palm of his hand over one hard globe, marvelling at the new and intricate tracing of blue veins there.

The cream felt deliciously cold, and Jennifer squirmed as her nipple peaked against his hand. 'Oh!'

But Matteo said nothing, for he sensed that words might shatter the highly charged atmosphere of erotic desire. He began to work on the other breast instead, hearing her gasp and seeing her squirm as he let his fingertips slowly glide down over the swell of her belly.

It was like being on familiar territory but discovering a whole new landscape. Like finding that a lush orchard had grown on a piece of previously barren land.

Wonder made him momentarily break his vow of silence. *'Madre de Dio!'* he whispered, and pulled down her bikini bottoms, sliding his finger to her wet, warm heat and hearing her gasp again, only sharper this time.

He began to kiss her until she moaned in an unspoken plea and he kicked off his shorts, carefully lowering himself on top of her so that they were properly naked at last. Her arms encircled his neck and Matteo buried his face in her soft neck and sighed. like a man who had come home.

They stayed like that until he lifted his head at last, tracing her mouth with his fingertip. 'I don't how I'm supposed to do it with a pregnant woman,' he murmured.

'You?' Her voice was slumberous as she smiled. 'Just do what you normally do.'

'But I don't want to hurt you. Or the baby.'

Matt could hurt her in a million different ways, but never like this. 'Just do it,' she urged. 'Let go.'

He reached down to find that she was soaking wet, and with a sigh of exquisite relief he thrust inside her. He began to move, slowly at first, teasing her and teasing her and teasing her. Enjoying the luxury of a long coupling—but it was never going to be long enough.

He could barely wait for her to orgasm, but somehow he managed it—and then he let his own happen, in glorious golden waves which just kept on rocking him.

It seemed to take for ever to come back to earth, and when he did he lifted his head to look down at her, inordinately pleased at the dreamy smile of pleasure which curved her mouth.

'Jenny?' he whispered.

Her eyelids fluttered open and she looked up at him. *I love you,* she thought. *Is there any chance that one day you could love me, too?* 'What?' she mumbled drowsily.

'Can I sleep with you tonight?'

The wind made music out of the chimes which hung in the trees, and the world seemed suspended as it waited for her answer.

Jennifer closed her eyes and touched her lips to his neck. It was not what she had wanted to hear, but it would do. 'Yes,' she breathed. 'Yes, you can.'

The days drifted into one another, like a river running into the sea, and Jennifer grew brown and slow and contented. She slept and ate good food and swam like a fish—sometimes in the pool and sometimes Matteo took her out in his boat to splash in the clear waters—and her hair grew pale and he told her she looked like a mermaid.

And every night he slept with her, and made love to her in a hundred different ways, both in and out of bed.

In fact, it was almost like a second honeymoon—

except that honeymoons were held together with the glue of shared love, not the unreliable adhesive of an unplanned pregnancy.

'What is it?' he questioned softly one afternoon, when they had gone upstairs to lie beneath the cool, curved dome of the bedroom ceiling for their customary siesta.

'I didn't say anything.'

'You didn't have to. You were frowning.' His fingers traced an imaginary line just above her nose.

Jennifer closed her eyes, because the subject playing on her mind was one that she would rather keep hidden away. It was so like paradise here that she didn't want to introduce the serpent of reality.

And yet hadn't their inability to communicate been one of the primary causes of their break-up? Geographical distance had been the reason for that—but you didn't need to be thousands of miles apart from someone to fail to interact with them on an adult level. And they couldn't keep pretending that there weren't a million unresolved issues simmering beneath the surface of this extended holiday.

'Well, we haven't discussed how long we're staying here, or what we're going to do when we get back—in fact, we haven't made any real plans at all. We've been burying our heads in the sand, and—whilst it has been lovely—I feel a bit as if I'm in limbo. As if the real world were a million miles away.'

'Well, that *was* the intention in coming here.'

'But it can't continue indefinitely,' observed Jennifer, smoothing her hand over her belly and watching as his black eyes followed the movement with fascination.

She remembered the very first time she had slept with him. In the morning she had woken first and lain there feeling slightly dazed, thinking, *I'm in bed with Matteo d' Arezzo!* 'Can it?'

'No.' The rumpled sheet lay tangled around his naked thighs as he moved over her, the powerful shafts straddling her, and for a moment Jennifer thought that he was going to drive his erection into her aching body. But his face was dark and full of tension. 'Tell me what it is you want, Jenny.'

She shook her head. 'That isn't fair. Are you too frightened to say what it is that *you* want?'

And at that moment he *did* know fear—he who had been fearless for most of his life. But it was time to take a gamble. To lay down the guidelines for the only situation he could see working for the two of them. He just hoped that he had softened his prickly ex-wife enough for her to be agreeable.

'I'm Italian—' he began.

'You were brought up in America,' she pointed out. 'And what's that got to do with it?'

'I *believe* in marriage,' he breathed. 'But especially a marriage which involves a family. I want us to try again, Jenny' he said, and Jennifer heard the unmistakable ring of determination in his voice. 'To be man and wife. To bring our baby up within a secure family unit. Don't you want that, too?'

She nodded, too choked for a moment to speak. Had she thought that he might threaten her with a legal battle if she did not accede to his will? Possibly. The very last thing she had expected was that heartfelt appeal, and it affected her more than was probably necessary. Or wise.

'Of course I do,' she said eventually. 'It's what every mother wants for her baby.'

Not for herself, Matteo noted coldly, but he nodded and kept his face impassive.

She wanted to say, *And if there were no baby, would you still want me, even then?* But she wasn't strong enough for that. Because she might still be in love with Matteo but not so much that she would let it blind her. Because if there was no baby, then there wouldn't be a relationship.

'We need to do it properly this time around.' He tilted her chin up and his black eyes were hard and glittering. 'We will not lead separate lives again, *cara*. I don't know how we'll work it out, but we will.'

'And I won't listen to rumours…won't allow jealousy to flourish.'

'I won't give you cause to feel jealous ever again,' he grated.

'You're going to give up being a film star?' she said, half joking.

He smiled, his mind already working out their schedule. 'Shall we fly to England and tell your mother together? And I'll tell my office to answer any enquires with a short statement announcing that the divorce is off.'

Jennifer recognised the light of triumph which burned at the back of his eyes as she nodded her head in agreement. This might be as good as it got, but she wasn't going to knock it. She had tried living without him, and that was much, much worse.

CHAPTER EIGHT

'I CAN'T BELIEVE IT!'

'Just say you're happy for us, Mum!' pleaded Jennifer.

She and Matteo had driven straight from the airfield to her mother's elegant cottage near Bath, knowing that as soon as they were back in England word would get out about the pregnancy, and wanting her to hear it from them first. But now, looking at her mother's expression, she began to wonder why they'd bothered.

Mrs Warren's heavily made-up eyes flicked over her daughter and came to rest on Matteo again. She shook her head in disbelief. 'But I'm too young to be a grandmother,' she declared.

Matteo's expression didn't flicker, and he did not risk glancing over at Jennifer. He squeezed her hand instead. 'Of course you are,' he said smoothly. 'Everyone will believe that you are the baby's aunt!'

'Do you really think so?' Mrs Warren looked slightly mollified as she automatically patted her faded blonde hair. 'Does this mean the marriage is back on?'

This time he *did* risk it, and he read the understanding in Jenny's eyes. *'Si,'* he said slowly. 'It is. We have settled our...*differences*.'

Mrs Warren nodded. 'Well, I suppose I'd better look on the bright side—I always got much better service on airlines when I mentioned that Matteo was my son-in-law!'

Matteo's mouth twitched. 'Then that is a good enough reason for the marriage to continue, surely?' he said gravely.

'Mum, Matteo's going up to London on business, and I thought that I might stay here with you for a day or two. We could have lunch, if you like.'

Mrs Warren brightened. 'In a restaurant, you mean?'

Jennifer nodded. Her mother loved eating out with her famous daughter, and all the attendant fuss. 'If you like.'

Matteo's eyes narrowed. 'You're sure?'

She shrugged. 'Why not? No good hiding away—we were spotted and snapped at the airport, after all.'

'I'm sending two minders with you,' he said grimly.

'Ooh, goody!' squealed Mrs Warren.

In a pale restaurant overlooking the beautiful old city of Bath, they ate exotic seafood and salad, and Mrs Warren drank copious amounts of champagne 'to celebrate, darling!' while the minders sat a not-so-discreet distance away. Jennifer even posed for a photo with a little girl who was waiting outside the restaurant with her mother.

Maybe I'll have a little girl too, she thought as she crouched down and smiled. And she'll have dark eyes, just like Matt's, and gorgeous curly hair.

But when they got back to her mother's house there was a crowd of pressmen milling outside, and the minders had to barge their way through.

'What the hell is going on?' asked Jennifer, frowning. 'How ridiculous! Surely one pregnant actress doesn't merit *this* kind of interest?'

The phone was ringing when they got inside, and Mrs Warren took the call, her face growing white as she listened. 'Yes, she's here—I'll see if she'll speak to you.' She held the phone towards Jennifer. 'It's a reporter. Wants to speak to you.'

Jennifer pulled a face and took the phone. 'Hello? Jennifer Warren speaking.'

'Jennifer—were you aware that Sophia Perotta has given an interview to a London evening paper about her affair with your husband?'

'I wasn't,' she said calmly.

'Did you know that he was cheating on you with her throughout your marriage?'

There was a pause. 'I'm not going to comment on that,' she said, still in that strange, small voice of calm. 'And now I'm really going to have to go. Goodbye.'

She put the phone down and ignored all her mother's questions, but inside she felt queasy, and the feeling of nausea just grew and grew inside her. She only just

made it to the bathroom before she started vomiting—
and the frightening thing was that she couldn't stop.

'I'm calling an ambulance!' her mother exclaimed
dramatically. 'I knew you should never have got back
with that cheating bastard!'

Feeling as if she was taking part in one of her own
films, Jennifer was rushed to hospital with sirens and
lights blazing, wishing that her mother would just go
away. She rolled around in agony, clutching her abdo-
men—her stomach was empty but she was unable to
stop the dry retching which was making her throat burn.
'Am I going to lose my baby?' she cried.

'Shh! Try to calm down,' soothed the nurse in the
emergency room. 'The doctor is on his way down now
to see you.'

Which did not answer her question at all. And Jennifer closed her eyes as tears began to creep from behind her tightly shut lids.

All this for nothing. Now she would lose the child
she had longed for, and along with that terrible heartache would come her final separation from Matt—for
he would not want her without the baby. Why would he?

Around a large table, Matteo sat with his lawyers—his
face chalk-white beneath the tanned skin. On the front
page of London's biggest-selling evening newspaper
was a huge photo of a pouting Sophia Perotta—her
brown eyes as widely innocent as a baby deer's. And
there was the splash:

Cheating Matteo Was A Stallion In The Bedroom!

'Can she say this?' he demanded hotly.

'She already has.'

Matteo's fists clenched and he banged one down hard onto the table, so that the lawyers jumped. 'Let's sue her. Let's take the bitch for every penny she's got!'

'Are you certain you want to, Matteo?'

'It's a pack of lies!'

The lawyer coughed delicately. 'Did you or did you not have sex with her?'

Matteo flinched. 'Once!' he gritted, a feeling of disgust creeping over his skin. 'And only when my wife was divorcing me.'

'That's your story,' said the lawyer stolidly.

Matt turned on him, his black eyes flashing with anger, and suddenly he understood. 'Oh, I see,' he said slowly, and nodded his dark head. 'It's her word against mine.'

'Precisely. She's deliberately vague about dates and times, but explicit enough about your er…skills…in the bedroom department to make it clear that you *did* have sex with her. The dispute is when. She says it was during your marriage. You say it was not. We can try fighting it, if you want, but the publicity…'

He let his voice tail off, and Matteo knew what he was saying. 'I've only just got back with my wife,' he said urgently.

And she's pregnant.

Oh, Jenny.

Jenny.

It was at precisely that moment that one of his aides came grim-faced into the room, with a message from the hospital.

The journey back to Bath was a like a trip to hell. The worst thing was the not knowing—but no one would tell him anything and he couldn't get hold of Jenny's mother. It was an exercise in powerlessness, and Matteo had never felt so frighteningly out of control.

He made silent pleas to God. He prayed for their baby, and he prayed for much more than that, too. But Jenny would never forgive him for this. How could she?

'I want to see my wife!' he said to the overwhelmed receptionist at the desk.

'Mr d' Arezzo?' she verified breathlessly.

'Let me see her,' he pleaded.

'The doctor wants to see you first, sir.'

'Jenny!' he cried.

'He looked like a broken man,' the receptionist was to tell her colleagues in the canteen later.

Fearing the worst, Matteo paced the room they'd placed him in, and his eyes were bleak when the doctor walked into the room.

'My wife? How is she?'

'Your wife is fine, sir—'

'And the baby.' Matteo swallowed. 'She has lost the baby?'

The doctor shook his head and smiled. 'No, the baby is fine.'

'It is?'

'Absolutely. The heartbeat is perfect—the scan is normal. We've put a drip up, of course, because your wife was dehydrated, and we'd like to keep her in for—'

'But why has this happened?' breathed Matteo, and dug his nails so hard into his clenched palms that he did not notice he had drawn blood. 'It is shock which has caused this?'

'Shock? Oh, no. Your wife has food-poisoning, Mr. d' Arezzo. You should tell her to keep clear of prawns in future—particularly during pregnancy.'

Hot on the heels of exquisite relief that his wife and his baby were going to be all right came the bleak re-alisation that Jenny would never want him now. How would he feel if the situation were reversed? Could he bear to think of her in the arms of another man? And then to read about it in graphic detail in a newspaper, even if the facts *had* been twisted?

He walked along the corridor, and when they showed him into her room she was asleep against a great bank of pillows. She looked so small and so fragile that his heart turned over, and seeing the curve of her belly made an indescribable pain hit him.

Feast your eyes on her now, he told himself. For this will be the last time you shall see her so defenceless and vulnerable. Your access to her and to the baby will be barred from now on, and she will look at you in the wary and watchful way in which divorced wives do. From now on your relationship with Jenny will consist of brief meetings and visitation rights—and a whole legal framework.

'Aren't you coming in?' she said softly, without opening her eyes.

He stilled. 'Jenny?' he whispered hoarsely, as if a ghost had spoken to him.

She opened her eyes. 'Hello.'

He started. 'Did you hear me come in?'

'Yes.' And she had felt his presence, too—her senses were so alerted to him.

He rubbed his hands over his face, suddenly weary. 'I'm sorry.'

'So am I.' She managed a smile, wanting to banish some of the bleakness in his black eyes. 'But that's what comes of eating seafood! I shall have to be more careful in future.' She gave him a wobbly smile. 'But the baby is safe, thank God.'

He felt as if she had driven a stake through his heart. 'Jenny, don't!' he said savagely. 'Rail at me and tell me you hate me, send me away, but don't do this to me! For when you are kind it makes it so much harder, and I cannot bear to see it crumble—not what I thought we were on the way to regaining—' He shrugged his big shoulders. 'I just don't think I can bear it,' he repeated brokenly.

Jennifer stared at him. 'Matt—you're not making any sense. Didn't you hear me properly? Don't torment yourself. Please. Your baby is safe. Isn't it wonderful?'

'Yes, it's wonderful,' he said heavily. 'But I deserve all the torment in the world.'

'Would you mind telling me what the hell is going on?'

He blanched, praying for the courage to give his wife the facts which would finally put closure on their marriage. 'You haven't been shown a newspaper?'

Jennifer stilled. 'No. They've been keeping me quiet.'

He nodded. 'Well, you're going to find out sooner or later.'

'Matt, just *tell* me!'

'Sophia Perotta has given an interview claiming that I cheated on you with her throughout our marriage.'

Jennifer stared at him, searching his black eyes, the sombre slash of his mouth. 'You told me that it was just once. Afterwards.'

He nodded.

'So she's lying.'

Matteo stared at her. 'Jenny?'

'You told me you did not stray in our marriage. I believe you.' She had to believe him, or else there was no future for them.

She had done a lot of thinking in that quiet white hospital room, and had come to the conclusion that she couldn't spend the rest of her life reacting like a spoiled teenager. She was a woman with a baby on the way— who needed to look at a bigger picture than pride and hurt feelings.

'I know what happened between you, and I have to

learn to live with that—but that doesn't mean I need to torture myself with badly written detail. We've both made mistakes, Matt, and one of those was my lack of trust, I don't intend repeating it. It's the way things were—but I'm more interested in the way things are *now*. And I'm going to work at our marriage—because I want it to survive.'

'Survival?' he asked, and his heart sank. 'That is all you hope for?'

'Isn't that enough? Trust and respect make a pretty good substitute for love. When we were apart I missed you more than words can say, and I want to be married to you. Just as you want to be married to me. B-because we're having a baby.'

'No!' he denied furiously. 'No!'

She started. 'You don't want to be married to me?'

He could have kicked himself. She was ill, and yet managing to be so understanding that she'd taken his breath away—while he was behaving with all the finesse of a bull. 'I don't want to be married to you *just* because of the baby,' he corrected. 'I want to be married to you because I love you.'

'Don't say that,' she said shakily. 'Please.'

And then he saw his own fears and uncertainties reflected in her sapphire eyes. 'Even if it's true?' he whispered. 'And you the great champion of the truth? Do you know something else, Jenny—I will carry on telling you that I love you even if it takes for ever for you to believe me and to learn to love me back again.'

Joy licked over her skin with warm fingers, and tears began to well up in her eyes and spill down her cheeks. 'I'm a quick learner,' she wept. 'I already do. I've never stopped—and if you don't come over here and hold me properly then I shall create a scene as only an actress can!'

He was smiling as he took her in his arms—as if she were a delicate parcel and any pressure might make her snap.

'Hold me tighter,' she protested.

'Later,' he promised, as he eyed the needle in her arm. 'I'm not risking the wrath of the doctors.'

And Jennifer laughed, because she had never seen her husband look intimidated over *anything*. 'Won't you at least kiss me?'

'Mmm.' His mouth curved. *'Posso controllare quello,'* he murmured, and touched his lips to hers. He kissed her until he felt her heart hammering like a little bird, and he rested his palm over it and sighed softly. 'Now you must rest,' he said firmly. 'And listen to what I have to tell you about our future.'

She leaned back against the pillows.

'After my next two films I'm taking a break from acting—because there are a thousand possibilities out there and I don't want to be at the opposite end of the world from you any more. Especially if you're on location with the baby.'

'But I won't be on location with the baby,' she said softly. 'Because I don't want to live that kind of life any more, Matt.' She edged her way a little farther up the bed. 'Acting works well for lots of people, but I want to look after my baby myself, and concentrate on you and me. At least for a while. After that we can reconsider— maybe take it in turns to film. Or maybe I'll just retire and have a big, old-fashioned, Italian-sized family!'

Matteo stared at her, his black eyes full of gratitude and wonder. And excitement. Because for the first time in his life he could understand what it was all about. The houses didn't matter, nor did the awards and the fame and the riches. Jenny and the baby they would have— *they* were what mattered. His family. *Their* family.

They were still blinking at each other like two people who had emerged into the sunlight after a long time in the dark when there was a brisk rap on the door. In walked a nurse, with two minders close behind.

One of them came up to Matteo and spoke rapidly in his ear. When he'd finished, Matteo looked over at Jenny.

'Much as I'm grateful for your mother's spirited defence of my morals—I think I'd better go downstairs, *cara mia*,' he said, a smile playing around the corners of his mouth. 'I'm afraid that your mother has just started to hold a press conference!'

* * * * *

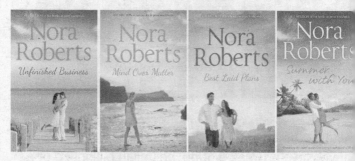

MILLS & BOON®

The Thirty List

* cover in development

At thirty, Rachel has slid down every ladder she has ever climbed. Jobless, broke and ditched by her husband, she has to move in with grumpy Patrick and his four-year-old son.

Patrick is also getting divorced, so to cheer themselves up the two decide to draw up bucket lists. Soon they are learning to tango, abseiling, trying stand-up comedy and more. But, as she gets closer to Patrick, Rachel wonders if their relationship is too good to be true...

Order yours today at
www.millsandboon.co.uk/Thethirtylist

MILLS & BOON®

Want to get more from Mills & Boon?

Here's what's available to you if you join the exclusive **Mills & Boon eBook Club** today:

✦ *Convenience – choose your books each month*
✦ *Exclusive – receive your books a month before anywhere else*
✦ *Flexibility – change your subscription at any time*
✦ *Variety – gain access to eBook-only series*
✦ *Value – subscriptions from just £3.99 a month*

So visit **www.millsandboon.co.uk/esubs** today to be a part of this exclusive eBook Club!

The World of
MILLS & BOON®

With eight paperback series to choose from, there's a Mills & Boon series perfect for you. So whether you're looking for glamorous seduction, Regency rakes or homespun heroes, we'll give you plenty of inspiration for your next read.

Cherish™

Experience the ultimate rush of falling in love.
12 new stories every month

Romantic Suspense INTRIGUE

A seductive combination of danger and desire
8 new stories every month

Desire™

Passionate and dramatic love stories
6 new stories every month

n o c t u r n e™

An exhilarating underworld of dark desires
2 new stories every month

For exclusive member offers go to
millsandboon.co.uk/subscribe

WORLD_ M&B2a

The World of
MILLS & BOON®